The Orphans from Liverpool Lane

Eliza Morton was born in Liverpool and worked as an actress. She is known for playing Madeline Bassett in *Jeeves and Wooster* and Lucinda in the Liverpool sitcom, *Watching*. As well as TV, she has also worked in theatre and film. She trained at Guildhall School of Drama and with The Royal Court Young Writers' Group. She is an award-winning short story writer and has also written drama for TV, film and theatre. In her formative years at convent school, she spent her weekends playing the piano accordion in northern working men's clubs. She lives with her husband – the actor Peter Davison – in Middlesex and is the author of *A Last Dance in Liverpool, Angel of Liverpool* and *The Girl From Liverpool*.

Eliza Morton

The Orphans from Liverpool Lane

PAN BOOKS

First published 2023 by Macmillan

This paperback edition first published 2023 by Pan Books
an imprint of Pan Macmillan
The Smithson, 6 Briset Street, London EC1M 5NR
EU representative: Macmillan Publishers Ireland Ltd, 1st Floor,
The Liffey Trust Centre, 117–126 Sheriff Street Upper,
Dublin 1, D01 YC43
Associated companies throughout the world
www.panmacmillan.com

ISBN 978-1-0350-1520-7

3 5 7 9 8 6 4 2

A CIP catalogue record for this book is available from the British Library.

Typeset in Sabon by Palimpsest Book Production Limited, Falkirk, Stirlingshire
Printed and bound by CPI Group (UK) Ltd, Croydon, CR0 4YY

Visit **www.panmacmillan.com** to read more about all our books
and to buy them. You will also find features, author interviews and
news of any author events, and you can sign up for e-newsletters
so that you're always first to hear about our new releases.

For Joel

Prologue

When the child was born the sky split into bands of colour as a wintry sun set over the River Mersey and the dust of the city glittered in the golden hue. The young woman, ten days short of her twenty-third birthday, was astonished at how this perfect thing had slithered from her as she bit into her pillow and stifled a cry of – what? Pain? Sorrow? Intense joy?

It seemed miraculous that her baby, so tiny and curled, was alive. Miraculous that all this time she had kept her secret from everyone, bound by the rags tied around her body and the lies clasped tightly as iron bands around her heart. The strange, sudden love she felt for this child squirming on the peg rug had pulled her up short and terrified her. Nine months had passed since, under a pale moon on the stone floor of her mother's kitchen, feeling numb and cold under her bare back, with the light bulb swaying in and out of focus, she had weakened. *Don't, don't . . . Don't stop!* she had said to the man who had promised her the world. And it was done. And now here she was, allowing herself for a moment to stare in awe at the tiny, velvety miracle, before the dock bell

1

rang in the distance and shocked her into doing what she knew she must.

The park gates were shut. Snow clouds were bulking the horizon, but she would wait here on a bench with her bundle until it grew dark. St Mary of the Blessed Angels, which she had passed so many times on her way to church, had a particular step worn smooth by time, and she knew she was one of many who had gone before her.

Half an hour later, as snowflakes began to fall steadily, she kissed her baby girl's soft head for the last time and tucked the blanket around her tiny body. Each stitch of the blanket that she had crocheted herself, each coloured thread, blue, green, yellow and red, had been a stitch of love. Her heart was breaking, and it was more than flesh and blood could stand, but it was time.

'Another one,' said Sister Cyril, after she had answered the doorbell. 'That's the third this month.' She bent and picked up the baby from the step as the little hands seemed to instinctively reach out for her with tiny grasping fingers and nails like butter.

'She hasn't made a noise. Strange,' she said to one of the sisters in the nursery. She pulled back the coverlet. 'Oh, and aren't you the bonniest,' she murmured. After she had left the child to be dealt with by Sister Hilda, she walked down the dimly lit corridor, heels clacking on the polished floor, and picked up the telephone in her office.

'Mrs Worboys? I have news. A girl. And she's beautiful.'

*

Marcia and Cynthia, standing in the cold and unfamiliar dormitory room upstairs clutching suitcases and gas masks, had heard the doorbell too. They had gone to the small attic window hoping someone had come to collect them, that it had all been a mistake – after all, they were still dressed in their coats and hats – but all they had seen was a huddled, blurred figure scurrying away from the building, leaving footprints in the snow.

'You're the new girls?'

They turned and saw a slim, dark-haired girl standing in the doorway wearing a brown pinafore dress and battered plimsolls; she looked about eleven or twelve, like Marcia. Her bowl haircut was, Cynthia thought, about the worst thing that could have happened to a girl her age. No one wore their hair like that nowadays. Apart from girls who lived in orphanages.

The girl plonked herself down on the end of one of the iron beds, her dress making a hammock between her wide-apart knees, and produced a pack of cigarettes from under the cuff of her sleeve. She lit one and offered up the pack. Marcia looked shocked, Cynthia less so, but both shook their heads politely. The slim girl shrugged.

'I'm Ellie,' she smiled. 'The nuns said you were sisters. You don't look like sisters. You can be my friends if you want. I'm dead famous, you know.'

'Famous?' Cynthia's eyes lit up.

'Sort of. Me grandma were standing right underneath the first bomb the Germans dropped on Liverpool. Or nearly the first. Gram were the only person I had in the world. I had me picture in the *Echo*, though.' She took a puff of her cigarette and blew a plume of smoke from the side of her mouth. 'You'll hate it here, but we can still have larks, doing over the nuns, that kind of malarkey.'

Marcia was unsure what that meant, but she didn't like the sound of it.

'We won't be here long, will we, Cyn? Our parents are alive. It's just . . .' Marcia searched for words to explain the unexplainable.

'Father Donnelly made us come. The nuns said it would be like a holiday,' Cynthia said.

Ellie took another casual puff and leaned back on her hands, a knowing look on her face.

'You're orphans of the living, then. That's what they call you.'

Marcia and Cynthia's arms and legs felt leaden. Ellie got up and stood in front of them, a wistful look on her face. She sucked coolly on the cigarette and flicked ash onto the floor, then rubbed at it with the toe of her plimsoll.

'No, we're not orphans of any sort. It's just a holiday,' said Marcia, firmly.

'A holiday? You wish. It's not like any holiday I remember.'

Chapter 1

Four years earlier: May 1940

'Keep up, Nissy! Full steam ahead, kids!' John Rogan held the wicker basket precariously above his head, jostling Marcia and Cynthia, who were both trying to keep hold of their mother's hand in case they got lost in the crowd. As they came down into the lower deck, the two sisters with their distinctly different eyes – Marcia's big, blue and worried-looking, and Cynthia's brown and knowing – searched the crush of people on the gangway ahead of them.

There was the usual scrum to get off the ferry as it bumped and bounced against the tyres on the quayside and the metal gangway crashed down, all clanking and shivering chains, with more pushing and barging accompanied by wolf-whistling, jeering and laughter.

They had spent the past three evenings getting ready for their annual May trip to New Brighton. Their mother, Eunice – or Nissy, as her husband affectionately called her – had busied around their small two-up, two-down in Liverpool Lane, preparing. She had carefully wrapped the four china teacups and then the teapot in newspaper and put them at the bottom of the wicker basket, where they nestled among Bovril caramels and fig rolls – *Fresh fruit in a biscuit for hungry men at work!* they had all chorused, quoting the tin giddily as they packed. She had walked over a mile from the sooty terrace where they lived down at the docks, to the grander houses and St Mary's orphanage at the other end of Liverpool Lane, where the road divided at Scottie Road, searching for shops that sold these treats that were lately so hard to get hold of. With a bit of luck, they wouldn't have to waste their pennies on food and could instead save them for the Helter Skelter and the arcades.

Cynthia hooked her string bag over one arm and shouted over her shoulder as she ran off towards the promenade, 'I'll find a spot on the beach!' She tried not to get distracted by the stalls, though it was hard not to, her head twisting this way and that. She didn't know where or what to look at first: the boxing cats, Madame Julie the fortune teller, or the wooden dolls that a man was dancing up and down on a plank.

'I'll go too,' said Marcia.

'No, you won't,' said John, hooking a finger under her cardi and pulling her back. 'You're too young.'

He gazed out towards the beach and promenade. On the breeze he could hear the laughter, a hurdy-gurdy and the moaning of seagulls. In little more than a month the beach would be closed. Who knew for how long? He had heard there were rolls of barbed wire waiting within the walls of Fort Perch Rock. He wondered if these people with their buckets and spades would be the last 'friendly' invasion of this place. Would their lives ever be the same again? He swallowed hard as he looked down at Marcia.

'There's a woman over there wobbling on a unicycle, Da!' she cried.

'Everything about that woman is wobbling,' he laughed.

They wandered down the ham and egg parade, being hurried on by Eunice, who was worried these stalls would gobble up their sixpences before the day had even begun.

'Is the diving man here?' Marcia said. 'Can I give him a penny?'

Their mother smiled at John. 'Surely not after last year. He nearly drowned.' But then she gasped. 'Oh, heavens to Betsy. I don't believe it. Look, he is! Sir Gordy's here!'

There was a crowd of people jostling to get a closer view of the tanned, wrinkly one-legged man in his red swimming trunks as he hopped forward along the diving board that stuck out from the pier. As he bowed with a flourish, his gold-embroidered cape flashed in the sun. Someone started chanting, 'Gordy! Gordy! Gor-deee!' The man raised his arms to the sky, stretched into a side bend and then tugged at the waistband of his red swimming shorts, as if letting in air would make the difference between success and failure.

'Da, can you lift me onto your shoulders so I can see?'

'Come on, then. Up you go!'

'Can you lift me, Da?' said Cynthia, appearing at his side.

'Not likely. You're too big,' he laughed.

'Do it! Do it!' everyone was chanting. Had the diving man got his leg blown off in the last war?

Eunice wondered. The war to end all wars, that one was supposed to be. And now here they were with another started. Please God it stayed overseas. Poland, now; Belgium, the Netherlands, Luxembourg. And rumours that France was about to go the same way. What if . . . ? But she put the thought aside.

Raising his hand, Sir Gordy patted the air and, as if he were part man, part fish and part bird, dove into the water, splitting open the silver sea like a knife passing through butter. He had gone. Had he gone forever? Eyes scoured one way and the other. The sea was like a mill pond. It was taking too long . . . no one could survive under water for that long . . .

But no! There was his head popping up, gasping, the swimming cap bobbing about like a blue egg, and one arm waving triumphantly.

'More!' they all shouted.

'The poor man,' said Eunice.

'Why?'

'They should leave him alone.'

John laughed.

'Put me down, Da!' said Marcia.

He lifted her off his shoulders and slid his arm around his wife's waist, kissing her tenderly on the top of her head.

'Girls, go and get the hot water for the tea. Nice cuppa and we'll be in heaven,' he said.

People were already crowding around the bandstand. On their way to fill the teapot, Cynthia and Marcia pushed forward to see what everyone was looking at. There was a round-faced man on the stage. 'Rays and shine! Rays and shine! How does Mr Sunshine like his breakfast? Sunny side up! I thank you! What do pigs say in the sunshine? I'm bacon hot! What's hairy and wears sunglasses? A coconut on holiday!' There were titters from the people sunning themselves in deck chairs.

Marcia left Cynthia watching the show and went back down the ham and egg parade to the stall where, for a penny, you could fill up your teapot with boiling water. After she took it back to her mother, taking care not to spill a single precious drop, she set it down on the tartan rug laid out on the sand.

'Do the honours, love,' said her father. Marcia scooped tea leaves from the tin and mixed them into the hot water, swirled the pot around and poured the tea into the pretty cups. Her mother, who had already changed into her bathing costume, took a sip, said 'Ahh, that's nice,' and then lay back on the sand, crossed her feet at the ankles and propped herself up on her elbows.

Cynthia suddenly appeared and sat beside her and rolled up her skirt, bunching it around her thighs and tucking it into her knickers. Seagulls swooped overhead. The sun was shining and the sea and sky shimmered into a blur on the horizon. Marcia buried her bare feet in the sand and wiggled her toes.

'This is the flippin' life, Niss,' murmured John, closing his eyes lazily. 'Just me and my girls.' He grinned. 'Three of you, though. I don't stand a ruddy chance, do I?'

Eunice thumped his arm affectionately but couldn't quite bring herself to smile as much as he was. She recalled the note she had seen on the fortune teller's tent: *A shilling to say what's going to happen to your soldier boys.*

They got back to Liverpool Lane after it was dark and emptied shoes, turned out socks, discovered they had left the lid of the teapot behind, then flopped exhausted into chairs and onto the battered sofa. Their noses were stippled with freckles and Marcia had a red stripe around her neck where the sun had burnt her. Unlike Cynthia with her olive complexion, Marcia was pale with skin that never tanned, just freckled and bubbled up into blisters at the tiniest hint of sunshine. She could feel heat rising from her shoulders.

'When can we go again, Ma? I don't half love the beach,' asked Cynthia.

'Let's enjoy what we just had and be grateful for what we've got.'

'Besides, we've got our own beach right here,' said John, tipping more sand out of his boots.

Their mother crossed the room to hand Marcia a mug of Ovaltine.

'The man. The diving man. Da said he had his leg blowed off when he was shot down in his plane by the Germans.'

'Did he now? But he's alive, isn't he? He survived. That's the wonder of it.' Eunice shivered, and John glanced at her. His expression was grave and Marcia sensed worry in the room.

That night, in the hollow of their bed, John put his arm around his wife, pulled her to him and kissed her with a strange compulsion. She opened herself to him, allowing him to explore her body with tongue and fingers, arching her back and moaning with pleasure as he touched the parts of her that after twelve years of marriage had become so sweetly familiar, he could have drawn a map of her. He paused, lifted his head from the mess of her curls. 'You'll always love me, Nissy? Whatever happens?'

'Of course. What an odd thing to say,' she replied. A tugboat sounded its horn on the Mersey, and she let his hands begin their roaming again.

Chapter 2

'Saucepans!' cried Eunice, urgently.

The sickening sound of the air-raid siren rose in pitch; the horrible, eerie wailing that they had all grown used to still had them clamping their hands over their ears and wincing.

'I can't be bothered,' said Cynthia, leaning against the sink. 'I'll take my chances. It's too hot in here.'

The sun had been out all day. It had been so warm it had made the squat Liverpool terraced houses wobble and the air was heavy with the smell of bitumen and melting tarmac. No one wanted to be in the Corpy shelter.

'Get under the table with me and Marcia, you silly girl. And put that saucepan on your head.'

'Please, Cyn,' said Marcia, sweating, sitting cross-legged, peeping out from under a galvanized bucket.

Cynthia sighed. 'I look daft.'

'Who's looking!?' said her mother. 'Apart from Hitler, rubbing his hands with glee seeing a stupid girl in Liverpool is happy to get her head blown off because she's too much of a dozy mare to keep herself safe. Bad enough we've stopped going to the shelter.

If your father knew, he'd be furious. I'm only glad he's not here so he doesn't have to see this.'

'It stinks in the Corpy shelter. Doesn't it, Marce?'

Marcia nodded. 'Aye, Ma. It does. And there were rats the other day.'

Cynthia sighed. 'Do we have to keep the lights off? Can't we at least light a candle?'

'Of course not. Whose side are you on? Hitler's?'

'I'm bored.'

'I wish Da was here,' Marcia said in a small voice.

'Yes, so do I. But he's not, he's in Burma, so the least we can do is make sure we're alive when he comes back home.'

When the bombing began in Liverpool, it had been a horror Eunice had only imagined in nightmares. There had been over a year of relentless shelling. On every corner there was a soldier, or a spade and a bucket of sand, or the Emergency Water Supply water tanks, or a mobile hut. The Christmas Blitz had been the worst, but it had started all over again in May and by now they had seen whole streets disappear, buildings turned to dust and rubble. The city was unrecognizable. Familiar cut-throughs had gone overnight. Familiar faces also. Mr Tattersall, the fishmonger who lived opposite, had lost his wife in a tragic incident when she had stepped on an incendiary bomb while delivering fresh cod to the fire station. Nearly four thousand people dead; ten thousand homes destroyed. It seemed unbelievable – as unbelievable as how very quickly the extraordinary had become ordinary.

John had been called up in September of 1940. Two weeks later he had found himself on a military bus to

Catterick, where he had stayed for two months while the army tried to decide how he might usefully contribute to the war effort. After six weeks he had been pegged to join the Royal Signals. He had claimed that he could fix radios, although this was only based on having once thumped Auntie Norma's Bush radio with a kitchen broom, after which it had miraculously spluttered back to life. Then one Friday night, as he was entertaining lads in the mess hut with his bad jokes and bird impressions, an officer had burst into the hut and stopped him in his tracks. The next day, in a shroud of mystery, John had left Catterick for Ipswich. For a time, with all the chaos, there had been only infrequent letters like the one Marcia carried around with her between the folds of a handkerchief in her pocket.

December 1940

Darling Marcie,

I'm afraid I can't say much, but I'm doing my top-secret bit here in Suffolk. There are some fellows from Liverpool who bring news regularly and keep me updated about what's happening. They have a map on the wall and stick little pins in it to say which parts have been bombed. It's fairly covered and soon we will run out of pins. So I advise you to stay close to your mother, she's always been hard to pin down! Ha ha!

You'll be fine. I miss you all. I say a prayer each night and hope you do the same for me.

I had something called scrag pigeon pie the other day. It was delicious. Scrags are the

*stray birds who come back with the carriers
and get shot to make stew or pie. Not half
bad. Get your ma to see if she can find one of
the birds pecking about by the lions at St
George's Hall and bring it home and cook it.*
   Your loving Pa

   *PS I am so happy to receive your letters.
Keep them coming, dear. Be good for Ma.
Look after her for me. And don't be afraid to
ask for help from your auntie if you need it.
Or anyone else who's offering.*
   *PPS I heard some evacuees are having a grand
time. Tell your mother that, in case she might
change her mind about you going to Wales.*

Then, one warm March morning in 1941, he had
just appeared again unannounced, smiling, at the front
door, with his kit bag slung over his shoulder and a
cigarette drooping from his lip.

'Da!' Marcia had cried, jumping into his arms as
he spun her until they were both dizzy. That night
there was a small get-together at Auntie Norma's
house in Vauxhall.

'Do your birds, John!' her aunt said, in that shrill
voice of hers.

Without much persuasion he stood in the middle
of the living room, wobbling on the leather pouffe.
'Shush, then. I give you . . . a nightingale!' He closed
his eyes and trilled like a nightingale.

There was applause and calls from Marcia and
Cynthia for more. Norma wiped away a tear as the

room hushed and John moved effortlessly from one birdsong to another, cupping his mouth with his hand and gently blowing into it. She clapped vigorously and said, 'Such a talent!'

'Enough now,' Eunice said. 'That's enough.'

'Hey, John, what's this top-secret stuff you're up to down in Ipswich then?' said Jimmy Snaith, Norma's neighbour, with a smirk. John had never liked him.

Marcia, standing beside them both, looked up at her father with round eyes, waiting to see what he would say.

'I can't talk about that,' he replied.

'Only I heard a fellow in the mess at Catterick told an officer about your bird impressions, and that's how you got to work with the pigeon carriers.'

'It's not as simple as that,' muttered John.

'They say they're dropping the birds off behind enemy lines in Europe with messages, hoping that someone will read the notes and send back another message telling us what Hitler is up to over there. Pigeons fighting the war for us? Thrilling stuff.'

John bristled. He wanted to stare this man down, maybe even punch him on the nose; but Eunice gently moved Marcia out of the way, stepped between them, came close to her husband, pulled his lapels towards her and kissed him on the lips. 'Who would have thought that a party trick would get you to your top-secret pigeons in Ipswich, love?'

He put his arms around her waist and drew her close.

'I'm sorry, Niss,' he replied. 'He's right. It was a waste of time. The only top-secret part of the whole affair was that I was the bugger who cleaned up the pigeon doings all day. So . . .' He faltered. 'I applied for a new posting.'

She looked at him quizzically. 'What do you mean, a new posting?'

He knew this was the worst time he could have chosen. He should have told her the moment she opened the door to him that morning. Nothing for it now; full steam ahead.

'They're sending me to Burma.' He smiled hopelessly.

Eunice pulled away. 'Burma? Where the blazes is that?'

The room went quiet. Marcia grasped Cynthia's hand. All eyes were on John now.

'That'll be South-East Asia, dear,' said Auntie Norma, helpfully.

'I know where bloody Burma is,' Eunice yelled, spinning around and almost blasting Norma out of her chair. She took a deep breath, gathered up what was left of her dignity and left the room.

A few hours later, as they lay in bed together, Eunice, softened by the miracle that is love, sighed worriedly.

'South-East Asia. What if this war goes on and on for years? You can hardly nip back from Burma to see us. Why couldn't you stay with the pigeons? How will me and the girls cope? We need you, John.'

'Don't fret,' he said, placing a calming hand on her shoulder. 'Everything will turn out fine. I'll be back in no time. And if I say it once, I'll say it a hundred times: never be afraid to ask for help.'

Chapter 3

It was hard to believe the war had just 'gone on and on', as Eunice had feared. Eventually the bombing had stopped in Liverpool but there were very few letters from John once he was overseas, and there was nowhere near enough money or even enough food to put on the table. Peace in Eunice's frazzled head still seemed as unlikely and as unreachable as when Chamberlain had hoped for it some years earlier. The war was showing no signs of ending. Were things about to get even worse, now the dreadful silent flying bombs with wings had arrived in London? Everyone was fearful about what horror might be next.

Marcia was constantly pestering: *when's Da back?* Not long now, was always the answer. Meanwhile, as months passed by and then, somehow, years, John became even more of a vague, shadowy figure. And at the same time Eunice, to use Auntie Norma's words, 'began to slip'.

'Damn it,' her mother mumbled when Marcia arrived back home from the washhouse. She was slumped in a chair in front of the range. 'Damn and blast it. My eyes. I can't see a thing. Hopeless.' She threw down the needle that she was trying to thread in order to sew the gloves she was supposed to mend.

The woman from Jones's was arriving to collect them in half an hour and she had only done three out of five pairs.

'I can thread it for you, Ma. Don't be sad.'

Eunice looked up and smiled weakly. 'I had one of the sisters from St Mary's orphanage here earlier, what about that?' she remarked. 'She was nice. There are kind nuns, don't you think?'

Marcia frowned. Why was Ma asking her that?

The next morning, Marcia put on her uniform for school: the hated scratchy pinafore dress and shoes with the seams that were split; the pullover that had been unravelled and re-knitted with mismatched balls of wool, so that it now looked like it was striped. Cynthia was late again. She was always late these days and she had told Marcia she didn't want to walk with her.

'Is it my fault?' Marcia had asked.

Cynthia had given her a withering look as she clipped up her hair.

'No. The whole world doesn't revolve around you, Marcia.'

Marcia left the house with a brown paper bag containing a bundle of material that her mother had given her the night before, for the skirt she was supposed to be making in Sister Bernard's needlework class. Peeling off the side street into the main road, she was joined by a gaggle of boys and girls. Ahead of her she saw Cynthia's friend Denise, swinging her satchel confidently.

'Move, squit,' said Cynthia, galloping past her

down the hill to catch up with Denise. Marcia watched them link arms.

When they reached the gate everyone filed into the playground and lined up in their class groups. Sister, clanging the handbell, demanded silence. The twitching and shuffling abated and she finally decided that they were behaving well enough to go inside. They all feared the scissors hanging off her belt with her keys and rosary beads and the small magnifying glass.

After changing from outdoor to indoor shoes and locking their outdoor ones in cages in the cloakroom, they trooped through into the gymnasium that smelled of Vim and socks. They filed in, smaller in number now that so many had left the city. The nun in her flat, lace-up men's shoes clomped up the steps at the front and onto the raised stage, joined her hands and closed her eyes.

'I'm waiting, girls . . .' she said, squinting at them all. Each interminable second passed more slowly than the last. A cough or a sneeze, a murmur, was enough for her to start tutting and rolling her eyes. 'I'm happy to stand here all day if I have to.'

Silence settled and the nun made the sign of the cross. 'Dear Lord, we've all suffered so much because of this war already. The poor in particular have suffered. But remember, girls, the poorest people are not those who are without hot water and an inside lavatory, or, dear God, a Sunbeam Mixmaster – can you believe these gadgets they come up with? Not that any of you will be lucky enough to have one of those – no, the poor are the ones without Jesus in their hearts. Let's pray for those wretched sinners.'

'She's talking about you again, Cyn,' giggled Denise.

'Ma's put down her name to start a job at the munitions factory in Kirkby,' Cynthia whispered. 'There are those a lot worse off than us.'

'I didn't mean the poor. I meant the sinners. I heard you kissed Alfie Maloney down the back jiggert.'

'Who told you?'

'Alfie Maloney.'

'Quiet! Cynthia Rogan! Denise Dwyer!' snapped the nun. Her beady eyes bore into the second row where they stood. 'Someone has lost a pencil case. Fortunately, they have written their name on the front. A boy. Perhaps one of St Paul's. If anyone knows a Frank Sinatra, tell him to come to my office.' A giggle rippled around the room. 'Quiet!' she shouted. 'I don't know what you're all laughing at, but you've just earned yourself another rosary. Well done, girls. Very well done indeed.' She steepled her fingers. 'Now I am very happy to stand here all day and praise Him with the Glorious, Luminous and Joyful mysteries, but I suspect some of you might find it a little tiresome. It's in your hands, girls. In the name of the Father, and of the Son, and of the Holy Spirit . . .'

The morning passed for Marcia like most other mornings, overseen by a variety of nuns – earnest, bad-tempered, jolly, bored – who, with different degrees of enthusiasm, either dictated from a book at a rate of knots or silently click-clacked away on the blackboard. This morning Marcia felt worry rising like a heatwave from her toes to her fingers. There

21

were always prayers before and after lessons; there was the Angelus at midday for good measure, followed by a canter around the playground, even though they weren't allowed to run unless it was a hockey lesson.

At half past one, she sat at her desk with her chin propped up on her palm.

'Lay out your material,' said the nun with the moon-shaped face who had just swept into the room. Marcia hesitated. She wondered if she could pretend she had forgotten.

But as the nun walked around the room, every so often pausing to feel a piece of fabric between thumb and forefinger or to lovingly smooth out a crease, she knew it would only prolong the agony. Her cheeks flamed as she rummaged in her bag for the bundle of scraps. She could feel her heart thumping.

'What's this you've brought me?'

Marcia felt her lips quivering.

'Is this from George Henry Lee's, like I told you?'

'No, Sister,' she said in a small voice.

'Where is it from?'

'I don't know.'

'I think you do.'

'Greatie Market,' she mumbled, head dropped, fixing her gaze on her fingers, picking worriedly at the skin around the base of her nails.

'I thought so.' Frayed around the edges, this was not the smooth, silky fabric that unfurled from thick rolls in ripples and was cut with a large pair of gleaming scissors sliding through the material like a knife through butter. It would bunch up when you tried to put a needle through it and pucker in the middle. Any fool could see that. 'You were told to go to George Henry Lee's. Why didn't you?'

Marcia wanted to tell her that George Henry Lee's wasn't for the Rogans. Her mother could barely afford to clothe them or pay the rent man. You stopped and pressed your fingers against the plate-glass window at Lee's, gazing longingly; rarely did you go inside.

Marcia blushed to the tips of her ears. How many times had she been told that this school would be the making of her – that an education would be what would lift them out of Paddy's Market, and the tick-man, and the washhouse? But they were still firmly on the Corpy's list, with people coming around at strange times of the night to check their heads for nits and measuring them around their waists and making them stick their tongues out and say *aah* . . . and trying to persuade Eunice to have the girls evacuated.

'What's your name?'

'Marcia Rogan.'

'Ah, Marcia, of course.' The nun stared at her as though seeing her for the first time. She hadn't paid much attention to this girl with the red hair and pale face. She was a quiet one. She knew her older sister, all right. Everyone knew Cynthia. And the mother was on their list.

'Thirty Hail Marys and the rosary. In my office, Marcia Rogan.'

An hour later, after Marcia had prayed to Our Lady on the sister's prickly mat while everyone else got to work on their A-line skirts, she rubbed at the red rash on her knees.

'Go on home,' said Sister Bernard. 'But before you do . . . Here. For next week. You've done your penance.' She opened a drawer. 'Remnants. But good enough.' She handed Marcia a bundle of silky tomato-red fabric.

Marcia's eyes widened. 'Thank you.'

'Marcia, wait. I heard your mother is not well. How are you all coping?'

'Fine,' she mumbled.

'It doesn't hurt to say if it's not fine, Marcia. And, dear, if it gets . . . difficult . . . your ma knows we're here to help families like yours. Just remember, whatever happens will be for the best.'

We're here? Whatever happens? What did she mean? thought Marcia.

Chapter 4

'It will be just like a holiday,' her mother said the following week, her fingers closing anxiously around a glass of sherry which she then raised to her lips. She was sitting on the battered sofa with Cynthia. Marcia stood beside them, looking fearful.

'A holiday! At the orphanage? What are you talking about?' said Marcia. 'I thought you were going to tell us Da was coming home.' When Ma had summoned them into the parlour she had known it must be serious, but neither of the sisters could have imagined this.

'Sister Bernard said you'll like Sister Cyril from the orphanage. I can't put it off any longer, girls. I'm at breaking point here.' She gestured around the room at the piles of washing on chairs, the dirty mugs and plates on the sideboard and the dust-covered surfaces. 'This job at the factory . . . Travelling back and forth to Kirkby each day. It's killing me.'

Had sending them to the orphanage been her mother's idea? Marcia thought darkly.

'She wants to meet you. She sent me a note and I've invited her for tea. Sister Bernard says she's a kind person,' Eunice said with a quivering smile. 'I'm not going to force you. But why don't we give it a try, eh?'

*

The following day, Marcia and Cynthia sat on the sofa. The room had been hastily tidied, the piles of washing stacked and the surfaces dusted. Both girls flinched when they heard the knock on the door.

'It's a pleasure to meet you, girls,' Sister Cyril said when they were introduced. She was solidly built and seemed mostly made of bosom. If Eunice had known that she was here because Father Donnelly had set things in motion after hearing the gossip flying around Liverpool Lane, she might have bolted the door. *She leaves them alone, you know, when she goes off to Kirkby. Those kids have starvation in their eyes, mark my words. And have you even seen her lately? When she comes back she's never out of Fred Tattersall's house – he offered to feed those girls of hers in return for Eunice doing his washing. At least, that's the story. And still no sign of John Rogan since he went to Burma. Three years ago now and she's not seen hide nor hair of him.*

But unfortunately for Eunice, she had no idea about the rumours. Eunice, who held only three things sacred in life: her family, a sly Woodbine, and a cup of tea with a priest. Whenever Father Donnelly came to Liverpool Lane there was always a commotion as she scrabbled together pennies from tins, coat pockets and the red mission box on the mantelpiece. Before he arrived there would be a frenzy of spitting on surfaces and on the teapot and rubbing furiously with her pinny to make everything shine. She would fling open the curtains and take him into the front room, making her feel better than her feckless neighbours, better even than the Maloneys across the road – Tom Maloney might have a car, but she would be the one flying straight to heaven. It was about the only time anyone was ever allowed in the front room, and she would fuss around like a flapping bird. Today was no different.

We are here to help families like yours, the note had said, and Eunice had announced to her daughters that it wasn't every day girls received such kind words from someone as virtuous as Sister Cyril from St Mary of the Blessed Angels orphanage.

'You might be wondering what kind of things we do at St Mary's. Pruning the roses in the nuns' garden is always a favourite at this time of the year.'

Cynthia narrowed her eyes. Pruning roses? From what she had heard it was more like floor-polishing and laundry, every time of the flaming year.

'Normally one of the boys helps me, but you know boys – largely more trouble than they're worth. And so I was thinking you might like to help instead, dears? Henry Cherry was going to do it but I've asked him to see to my turnips. You know Henry, Eunice? One of the altar boys at church.'

There was a silence. Eunice and the nun exchanged a polite smile. But then Eunice noticed Cynthia was stifling a giggle.

'Cynthia, what's funny?' she hissed, narrowing her grey eyes.

It was hardly the time for laughter, thought Marcia. But she knew Cynthia often did this when she was nervous.

'Nothing. Except . . . Henry Cherry.'

'What about Henry Cherry?'

Cynthia started to giggle again. 'It's a funny name. Henry Cherry.'

'Girls, get Sister Cyril a cup of tea. Pot's on the range. Move your bottoms. Grass grows quicker than these two getting out of a chair. Tch. You'd think I'd dragged them up.'

'Not at all, they're lovely,' said the nun, without conviction.

Marcia rose to get the tea but Cynthia remained on the sofa. Her lips were faintly stained with pink lipstick and she had one leg wrapped skilfully around the other, with a slipper hanging off the end of her foot. She examined her nails and sighed.

'It's turning colder, Sister. They say there might even be snow,' Eunice said, trying to distract the nun from Cynthia.

It was a relief when, after a few minutes of stilted conversation, Marcia returned with the pot of tea, a pretty flowered milk jug and cups and saucers on a tray. She placed it on the small table and sat down again beside her sister. Eunice, noticing Marcia chewing worriedly at her stubby nails, thought it was hard to decide which of her two daughters was making the worst impression.

'Well, isn't this grand, Marcia and Cynthia,' said the nun.

There was a pause; no one could think what to say next.

'I'm going to be a Tiller Girl one day. Or a movie star. Has Ma told you?' said Cynthia, suddenly.

'Oh? A Tiller Girl?' smiled the nun.

'You know, tap and kick. Fancy dancing. Moonlight in June. *Moonlight in Joo-hoon*,' she trilled.

'Oh my,' Sister Cyril said.

Eunice bristled. She would have to have words with Cynthia later on. Such a mistake, calling her Cynthia! What came first – the name or the girl? she wondered. Eunice had wanted to call her Pamela; she should never have listened to her husband.

'Can you believe the nonsense this girl comes out with!' she said. 'She'll be the death of me. Begged me for lessons at the Laffertys' dance school, didn't you, Cyn? We can't afford it. Especially since I'm trying to manage on John's army wage. The time she wastes jiggling her hips. I've prayed to Saint Rita for my daughter to spend even an hour on her homework, you can't imagine. When Mr Rogan comes back he'll have a thing or two to say about that, Cynthia.'

'Lovely Rita. The patron saint of impossible tasks.'

'I'll help with the pruning,' said Marcia.

Her mother turned to the nun. 'Marcia's a good girl. She's given me no trouble. Apart from the time she glued her hair to the steam iron.'

All eyes were on Marcia now; Cynthia was clearly a lost cause, after laughing at Henry Cherry and the nun's turnips. Not to mention mooning over any boy that crossed her path. It had been that way ever since she'd started her dancing lessons, with Mr Tattersall quietly settling the bill each week for Eunice. Now she spent all her time shuffle-toe-shuffling and rolling up her waistband to hitch up her skirt, obsessed with her gramophone records and hit parade and dreams of being a Tiller Girl.

'And tell me, is there any news of Mr Rogan?' asked Sister Cyril as she sipped her tea.

'He's in Burma. He had enough of the pigeons,' Marcia blurted.

'Pigeons?'

'Aye. The pigeons was all top secret, so we can't say any more.'

'Oh my. Yes. Careless talk does cost lives. And how have you been yourself, Mrs Rogan?'

Marcia frowned. Surely her mother wouldn't tell the nun about the headaches? Or the forgetting things – Eunice had even forgotten the washing on the bus the other day. And there always seemed to be problems about money lately. *Three pounds a week isn't enough! Why on earth did he agree to overseas? How am I expected to manage?* Their Auntie Norma had swirled her glass of sherry and gently pointed out that fellas didn't tend to have much say in the matter; they went where they were told. Her mother had said Da should have stayed with the pigeons, and her aunt had sighed and suggested she should have signed the girls up to be evacuated if she wasn't coping – but Eunice wouldn't hear of it.

Marcia especially didn't want her mother to tell the nun about the debacle with all the jobs Eunice had started and left within a month – the Meccano factory, Bryant and May, Lewis's – and each time another excuse, her nerves or her swollen ankles or her dizzy spells, or someone had 'taken agin her'.

'I'll be fine when Mr Rogan gets back. But we've heard nothing lately,' said Eunice. Cynthia and Marcia stared at her, waiting to hear what she would say next. 'Nothing new,' Eunice went on. 'We're hoping he'll be back soon. That would be the answer to all our problems.' She faltered. This wasn't a conversation she wanted to have in front of her girls.

'Soon when, Ma?' asked Marcia suddenly.

'Soon. Soon, please God, this war will be over soon,' Eunice said, and made a quick, glancing sign of the cross with a forefinger touching forehead, shoulders and heart.

'We pray for him every night,' said Marcia in a small voice. 'Don't we, Cyn?'

Cynthia shrugged.

'And let's hope your prayers will be answered,' replied Sister Cyril brightly. 'I'm sure they will. God will be looking down on a good girl like you, Marcia, dear. I have no doubt your da'll be walking through that door right as rain any day now.'

Cynthia pursed her lips. The slight of being so casually passed over hadn't gone unnoticed.

'More tea?' asked Eunice, scooping up the pot and holding it wavering in the air.

Cynthia got up and wandered to the window, positioning herself behind the nun and her mother, then stuck her thumbs into her ears and wiggled her fingers at her sister. Marcia glanced away, maintaining her serious expression with merely the flicker of a frown playing across her forehead, but it was enough to prompt her mother to look round.

'Cynthia, what are you doing? Playing silly beggars again?'

'Nothing,' Cynthia replied.

'Go and do the coal,' said her mother crossly.

'Not likely. Not in this dress.'

*

'I'm not letting them cut my hair!' said Cynthia when the nun had left.

'Of course they won't cut your hair. Don't be daft.'

'A holiday is Blackpool. Butlins! Margate! Not the nuns!'

'Margate? We can't even afford Ourgate,' Eunice said, trying to raise a smile. The girls remained expressionless. 'Remember, your da's joke whenever we were making plans for a holiday? Let's all go to Ourgate? That always used to make you laugh.'

'Not funny any more, Ma. And we don't even have a gate. We've gorra front step,' said Cynthia. 'And who cares about pruning!'

'Lovies, what am I supposed to do? They've offered me a room at Kirkby. The munitions factory has a hostel on site. It would be so much easier than traipsing back and forth each day. It makes sense for you to go to the nuns. I'm no good to you, girls. I'm exhausted. They expect us to work no matter what. Even when the buses and trains were cancelled after the raids, they expected everyone to walk all the way from Liverpool. Can you imagine?'

'We can stay here at Liverpool Lane on our own,' Cynthia said. 'I can look after Marcia.'

'No.' Eunice shook her head and half laughed.

'Why not?'

'Because.'

'Please, Ma,' said Marcia, falling to her knees. 'I don't care much about pruning either.'

Eunice wavered. 'What about school? How could I trust you?'

'Mr Tattersall can look after us.'

She sighed again. 'Out of the question. What would people around here say?'

'Ma. Please,' said Marcia.

Eunice paused. She pursed her lips and frowned. Then she let out a long breath and pressed her fists against her eyes. 'If I agree . . . and I mean *if* . . . I'm not telling anyone, d'you hear? If I let you stay on your own, no one knows about it. I mean it. No telling Denise or Alfie. Not even Mr Tattersall.'

Chapter 5

The house felt empty without their mother. But with strict instructions not to open the door to anyone without peeping from behind the frayed curtain, for nearly a week the girls had managed to get to school on time, cook up the blind scouse – stew without meat – that she had left in bowls in the larder, keep the fire on the range and fill the coal scuttle. Eunice had promised them she would come home on Friday evening and leave on Monday morning, and that would be enough to keep the nosey parkers at bay. The arrangement lasted barely a week.

Mr Tattersall was waiting for Marcia at his fishmonger's. The smell of fish seemed to follow him everywhere, no matter how hard he scrubbed himself down, but the shop was clean – you could eat your dinner off Fred Tattersall's counter, Eunice would often say. Underneath the counter were trays of fish in ice; above it, on a shelf, were huge jars of pickled onions, pickled eggs and pickled cabbage. Anything Fred could pickle, he would.

'Hello, Marcia,' he said, looking up when he heard the bell tinkle. He was smiling, chopping onions on the counter. 'Tell your ma I'm doing fried brains and spinach tonight.'

'Aye,' replied Marcia. She said nothing else. She didn't quite have the words.

'You all right, love? You seem a bit quiet.'

Marcia nodded. 'Here's your washing, Mr Tattersall.'

'Thank you, dear,' he said. When he smiled his eyes disappeared into the pillows of flesh that were his rosy cheeks. He gratefully took the bundle of washing she had just collected from the washhouse, as she did every second Thursday. 'Here, I've got something for you to try before you go . . . Scouse caviar . . .' he said.

He reached under the counter and brought out a saucer of mushy peas, slid it towards her and took a scoop of it with a teaspoon. 'Have some.' Before she knew it he was pushing the spoon forward, and feeding the peas into her mouth. 'You like it?'

'Grand,' she replied, to be polite.

'My special recipe. Splash of vinegar's the magic ingredient. So, when will I be seeing your lovely ma? Tell her I'm doing scallops wrapped in bacon this weekend if she fancies.' He smiled generously and ruffled the top of her head. He had a soft spot for Marcia, just like he had a soft spot for her mother.

Marcia fiddled with a piece of her hair. 'Oh. She asked me to tell you she's busy.'

He raised an eyebrow. 'Too busy for me scouse caviar? Busy? What with?'

'New job,' she said, staring at her feet.

The knife slid off the side of the onion he was slicing. 'Blinking thing,' he said, sucking the flesh of his hand where he'd nicked it and then examining it to see if he had drawn blood.

*

The munitions factory had changed Kirkby from a country village to a small, dusty bomb-manufacturing town of intersecting streets and huts and vans trundling to and from Liverpool carrying workers, mostly women. The noise inside, at the production lines, was deafening. The ear defenders hardly helped.

The explosion this morning had only been a small one, but since Eunice had moved here they seemed to happen every other day. They had all been evacuated from the building and forced to stand on the forecourt for two hours in the cold winter air. The bitter east wind blew into her face, and the combination of the hard ground and her flimsy shoes turned her feet to blocks of ice.

Finally, the foreman told them to go back inside. Eunice took her place in a line of workers in front of what looked like a cement mixer. Each woman would take a small watering-can-shaped container and fill it with the fierce-looking TNT liquid, which they would then pour into the shells. In front of her there were two girls in their twenties.

'I had to walk home to the hostel barefoot last night,' the one wearing a paisley-patterned turban was saying. 'Some bugger nicked my shoes! My gold slingbacks!'

'I told you, you shouldn't have worn new shoes to work. Surely you know that. No one nicks scuffed ones with worn-down heels. You leave your best things, or anything smart for that matter, in the cloakroom and they're gone. I wish they'd give us lockers.'

Another woman behind her whistled as her friend joined her with her can. 'Oh, look at you in your fancy overalls!'

'A few stitches here and, look, here. And a little pleat at the waist. And here at the hip.' The young woman did a twirl and patted her hair, and the other girls nodded admiringly. 'Took them home last night. Sewing until my eyes hurt.'

'Who are you doing that for?' said her friend.

'Not my fella, that's for sure. He's with the RAF. God knows when he's coming back.'

'In the meantime, hope you get lucky.'

Eunice looked at them. Should she be sewing pleats into her baggy overalls to make herself look more attractive, like they were all doing? Of course not; she had a husband. Even if she hadn't seen him for years.

'Hey, Stu, lover boy. June's been sewing pleats into her overalls so she doesn't look like a sack of potatoes like us lot. Did you notice? I reckon it's you she's done it for.'

The foreman laughed.

'Daisy!' the woman cried. 'What did you say that for?'

"Cos you said he had lovely eyes. She did, Stuart.'

The girl didn't seem embarrassed. Throwing her head back, she guffawed. Stuart was the one who flushed pink to his ears.

Eunice filled her can. She walked over to the table and poured the yellow contents into a tray.

'Mind out!' a voice said. She twisted around to see a woman propelling a trolley, somehow losing control of it and barging into the line.

'No!' cried Eunice, as the tray upended itself and wobbled off the bench, tipping its contents all over her.

'Someone get the doctor!' the girl yelled. 'Someone ring the bell!'

The man in the jacket came running over. Stuart barked at Eunice to take off her blouse.

'It's on my face. It's burning!' she cried.

'That stuff sets. You have to wait for it to set. That's how you get it off. Try not to touch it or rub at it.'

'It's up my nose!' cried Eunice. She was spitting and coughing now. Her instinct was to press her hands to her eyes, even though she knew that would make it worse. Someone was telling her that, and slapping her hands away. There was the sound of more men running. It was a drill that was sadly familiar. 'I can't see!' she spluttered.

'Calm down! Where's that trolley?'

She had a vague notion of the trolley arriving. Someone picked her up and put her on it – Stuart, she guessed – as she was covered with a blanket. The lights swung in and out of focus. Voices came and went but she could make no sense of them. They were indistinct and unrecognizable. 'Try not to move your face,' someone said. 'Once it sets, we'll peel it off. But washing it off with water's no good. So, try not to move your face and stay calm. Just stay calm.'

'Marcia Rogan? Where's your grandmother? Or your aunt? Whoever looks after you,' said the woman standing on the step with a clipboard at Liverpool Lane.

'Out,' Marcia stuttered.

'Dear. I'm from Kirkby munitions. There was an accident at the factory this morning.' Marcia's heart leapt to her mouth. 'Don't worry, we're here to tell you that your mother is fine. Who's looking after you, dear?' She stared at Marcia over her gold-rimmed spectacles.

Marcia's lip trembled. 'Accident?'

'It happens all the time. One of the hazards of the job. Your mother was filling the shells with TNT. Can I come in?'

Marcia put her foot in the door and shook her head. The woman cocked her head suspiciously.

'You do have someone looking after you? Your mother wouldn't have left you kiddies on your own, would she? I know some don't like the journey to Kirkby. Especially if they cancel the trams and buses. Too long, I know. But it's not allowed.' Marcia gulped down the lump that had lodged like a plum stone in her throat. 'So, if you could just give me the name of your guardian?'

'Cynthia Rogan,' she stuttered.

'And who's she?'

'My big sister.'

There was a pause. 'How old?'

'Thirteen,' Marcia muttered.

The woman screwed up her very pink face as if she was eating a sour lemon, and shook her head. Marcia felt her heart kick at her chest and her stomach tie into a knot.

'Oh no, dear. That won't do. But that won't do at all.'

'It's your fault!' cried Cynthia to Marcia as their mother packed a small case for each of them, stuffing in knickers and mismatched socks and reminding them to take their gas masks. It had all been settled within days. Sister Cyril was coming round to Liverpool Lane and Eunice was planning to sign the forms that afternoon.

'If it's anyone's fault, it's mine,' said Eunice, wiping her sweating forehead with her forearm, still bandaged where the tender skin had not yet properly healed from the accident. 'I should have known it was a silly idea. Should never have let you persuade me that you should stay here on your own. Why your aunt still refuses to have you, I don't know,' she said through clenched teeth.

'Her fellas,' said Cynthia, darkly. 'Comings and goings.'

The journey they made to St Mary of the Blessed Angels was silent and brooding. They managed to find a seat upstairs, away from the other passengers, but as they made their way in the dark on a bus, through the battle-scarred city, past the 'hollas' and the 'tinnies' – bomb-sites and corrugated-iron fences – and towards the leafy end of Liverpool Lane, they barely uttered a word. They just sat and stared out the window, wondering what awaited them. Marcia rested her head on the glass and fought back tears.

'Please come and get us before Christmas, please, Ma,' she begged when they reached the gates. There was a chill in the air and she shivered.

Her mother reached out and, for a brief moment, touched her cheek with gentle fingertips. 'I'll try my best. I love you both. As soon as I've saved enough, or Da comes back. I promise. You believe me, don't you?'

Chapter 6

They said goodbye to Eunice and waved sombrely to her until her tiny, stooped, sad figure had disappeared. Sister Cyril, who had met them, beaming, at the orphanage gates, said it was too cold to be getting tearful and they should get inside immediately. As they turned and started crunching their way up the gravel path carrying their small cases, it began to snow.

The large Gothic red-brick building, with its gables topped with crucifixes and studded with stone gargoyles, looked from the street like any other grim Liverpool religious institution. But once you were inside the gates, in its gardens ringed by high stone walls lined with tall conifer trees, it was as if you were in the countryside. It was hard to believe that outside was a war-ravaged, bombed-out city. There was ivy covering a high brick wall; in the alcoves there were statues of the saints. The place felt ancient. The snow drifted gently, and it was utterly quiet.

'Where are the children?' asked Cynthia, puzzled.

'Over that wall. This part here is the convent, where the sisters live. This is the abbesses' cemetery and those are their graves,' replied Sister Cyril.

Everything was covered in velvety layers of moss. Marcia and Cynthia could hardly believe they were barely a mile from the docks and the court houses and tenements, and that their shabby terrace was on this same road. The graceful red-brick arches created an elegant courtyard, and in the middle of the lawn there was a statue of the Virgin Mary with yellow primroses growing at her feet. The double gate had pillars either side topped by stone urns; the words ST MARY OF THE BLESSED ANGELS ORPHANAGE were displayed across it in graceful wrought-iron letters, painted gold. The gravel path was circular and swept round from the entrance hall, leading to a smaller gate that looked as though it opened onto another enclosed garden.

Everything felt designed, everything felt ordered. There was no sign of the usual chaos that inhabited the girls' home life – which, since their father had left and their mother had struggled to hold down a job, had seemed to get worse and worse.

'That building is where you'll both be sleeping with some of the older girls. Follow me, dears, it's freezing out here.' Sister Cyril led them through a garden of neatly tended flower beds – presumably the ones they were going to be pruning – and a puzzle of paths, towards the house. The snow was heavier now and Marcia could feel it on her cheeks. 'You'll have your meals in the refectory. You'll come to chapel every morning, and over there is the schoolhouse.' They could hear sweet singing floating from an upstairs garret window. Notes piled upon notes, crushing against one another and making a strange and beautiful sound.

'Are they the orphans?' asked Marcia.

'No, dear, that's the sisters,' replied the nun,

stamping the snow off her feet after they had gone inside through the front door.

The entrance hall was airy and the drifting snow threw shadows that moved slowly across the white-washed walls. Sister Cyril led them into a room with long tables running down the middle.

'This is the refectory,' she said, her voice echoing. 'And through here is where we have evening prayer. After evening prayer there is time for reflection. Do you sing?'

'Yes, Sister. *Moonlight in Joo-hoon . . .*' Cynthia trilled.

The nun's eyes widened. 'Very good,' she said, a little shocked by Cynthia's sudden and energetic rendition of another verse and a chorus. 'The Lord has praised us with the sisters' voices.' She placed her hand gently on Marcia's shoulder, tipping her head to one side. The sound of singing seemed to float down through the smooth plaster ceiling.

'Now then, let's get you to your room. You'll share it with one other girl.'

They went up a small, narrow staircase and down the echoey corridor. The zig-zag parquet floor was so well polished, it felt slippy and smooth under their feet.

'Down there is the room where our children come in the mornings for religious instruction. There are more dormitories on the floor above. The day children come from all over the place. Some of them are from the blind school. Children just like you, and others that have no fathers or mothers. The war has this place bursting at the seams.'

'Children like us?' asked Cynthia.

'Some of these children, they're wild, unruly things with good-for-nothing parents. You're different. You can tell you have a good mother and father.'

Marcia thought of Eunice struggling to get up some mornings. But then she thought of her father. He was the loveliest person in the world, she wanted to say to the nun. He did bird impressions and knew all the names, and he could make lemon meringue, and he helped her with her arithmetic and made her laugh when he twisted his tongue into a clover and wiggled his ears.

'Our mother says she will be coming to take us home soon,' said Cynthia.

'Yes, and don't we all hope for that.'

'I might go to my auntie's,' Cynthia added.

The nun nodded her head again. 'Auntie Norma?'

Marcia flinched. How did Sister Cyril know Norma's name?

'We tried her, but she refused to take you in. I'm sorry, dear. But you knew that, didn't you?' As she spoke, the nun had been leading them up another staircase to the attic, where she opened a door and took them inside.

Marcia blinked away more confusion as she looked around the bare room with its small iron beds, wooden crucifix and chest of drawers. The clock on the wall ticked softly. Sister Cyril explained that these hours were usually filled with silent contemplation, so perhaps they should rest. Without another word, she left and shut the door with a soft click. Marcia and Cynthia walked over to the attic window. They looked down into the darkened garden, where everything was covered in a white blanket of snow. There was a muffled quiet.

Then Marcia took in a sharp breath. 'Look, Cyn. Someone out there in the snow. Carrying something.' Her breath blotted the glass and she pulled her coat sleeve over her hand and rubbed at it.

'This place gives me the creeps,' said Cynthia. 'What on earth are we doing here, Marce?'

The two sisters looked at each other dolefully. Neither had an answer. How they had found themselves here was too big, too complicated for mere words, and when they heard footsteps in the corridor it was a welcome distraction.

'You're the new girls?' said a voice at the door.

Chapter 7

'Everyone says we should think of it as a holiday,' Marcia repeated to Ellie.

Ellie laughed and swung her legs, which dangled over the bed and didn't quite reach the ground.

'But now the nuns have told us we've got to go to church every flipping day and say the rosary. And do arithmetic and Latin on a Saturday. It's not my idea of a holiday either,' said Cynthia. 'Blackpool is my idea of a holiday. Or New Brighton. That was grand. Remember, Marce?'

Marcia nodded.

'Like I said, we make our own kind of larks. We get up to all kinds of things,' said Ellie.

'What like?' asked Marcia.

'Sliding down the banisters is a good one. Though one girl got her plait cut off for that. They left her all lopsided for a whole year, as a warning to the rest of us. But the funniest one was Our Lord in the semolina.'

Cynthia was beginning to warm to Ellie but Marcia worried that she could get them into trouble, sitting there smoking her cigarette, bold as brass.

'I did it with the rice pudding an' all,' Ellie went on. 'And the porridge. I made Jesus's face.'

'Did anyone believe it?' asked Cynthia.

'No, of course not, but that didn't stop us from having the craic. I swore the face appeared to me as a vision from God.' She laughed. 'I've been warned about it loads of times but I can't help meself, and I'll keep it up for as long as it takes. So maybe someone will eventually believe me and I'll be made a saint and that's how I'll get out of here. Then the nuns will be serving *me* apple cake, not the other way round. Do you go to school?' she asked suddenly. 'Some of the others who are out of control, or if their nits are bad, stay here, and some go to school . . . and some . . .' She trailed off and paused, then said: 'So, do you two want to be my friends?'

'Yes,' said Cynthia.

Marcia didn't reply.

'You as well?' Ellie said.

Marcia shrugged a yes.

'Good. I don't have many friends. In fact, I don't have any friends. Except you're not going to get adopted, are you?'

They looked alarmed. 'No, of course not,' replied Marcia.

Ellie nodded. 'That's good. They don't normally adopt the older ones. No one wants us. They don't usually want the orphans of the living, either.'

'We're not orphans of the living.'

'So what are you, then?'

The question remained unanswered, hanging in the air, as the shadows of drifting snow glided across the walls.

*

The first week wound on. Guided by the slightly odd but entertaining Ellie, who had been assigned to settle them in, Marcia and Cynthia barely had a moment to spare. They had already learned how to thread rosary beads and how to stitch the borders of devotion cards – though when the nun explained that the cards and rosary beads would be delivered to various homes and parishes, that it was a joy to do God's work and people were very generous with their donations, they could only think of their mother scrabbling around in the coffee tin for pennies. They also were shown how to help the smaller raggle-taggle children, in their brown shorts and pinafores, find their way into the classrooms; and how to collect and stack the dishes on large wooden trays in the refectory. They had even pruned a rose bush or two as promised, but it wasn't exactly the highlight of the week and the thorns had pricked and scratched their hands.

It had all been made bearable by the knowledge that when Saturday arrived, Eunice would come to visit. As promised, she appeared and took them out to Cooper's cafe as a treat.

'Ma, you've overdone it with the blush. Hasn't she, Marce?' said Cynthia as they climbed onto the tram.

'That's from the accident,' their mother replied. 'It's not getting much better.'

Half an hour later, they were sitting drinking milk-shakes through straws at Cooper's. It was crowded, but Eunice had managed to get the last free table. Despite wearing her best blouse with the Peter Pan collar and pinning her straggly hair up in a chignon, she looked worn out.

'How much longer do we have to stay there?' asked Marcia.

Eunice rubbed her temples and smiled a brief, tight smile. 'Just a few more weeks. Just need to save a bit more. Give me a breather. It's not too awful, is it?'

'I'm not doing the flaming rose pruning again. Look at my hands. Cut to ribbons. And my nails.' Cynthia humphed.

'Cut to ribbons? Don't exaggerate,' said her mother.

'Ellie is nice, isn't she, Cyn?' said Marcia. 'Ellie smokes like a chimney and she gives the nuns the slip,' she explained to Eunice. 'She's crafty, and she's good at climbing the walls.'

'Where does she get money for cigarettes?' their mother said, shocked.

Cynthia grinned. 'She shows her drawers to the boys for a penny.' Her mother's eyes widened. 'And she pretends that she sees visions of Jesus. In the rice pudding and semolina.'

'And porridge,' said Marcia.

Cynthia slurped the remains of her milkshake. 'She thinks one day she'll be made a saint, like Saint Christina the Astonishing, she's her favourite – she says Christina thought sinners were smelly and flew up to the ceiling like a bird because she couldn't stand the pong of their sins. Ellie is as bonkers as Saint Christina.'

'Ellie thinks if she carries on with her visions the nuns will eventually have to beatify her and that's how she'll get out of that place.'

'Well, that's a bit silly. Don't you go getting any ideas.'

'I've had enough of it there, Ma,' said Cynthia, the smile sliding from her face.

'I don't like it there either. Can't you take us home?' said Marcia.

Eunice lowered her glass, placed it carefully on the saucer and ran her finger round the rim. 'Dear. It's not practical. You saw how the journey from Liverpool Lane, each day back and forth – it nearly finished me off. I'd take you to Kirkby with me but the rooms at the hostel are only for munitions workers, not their families. It's nice for me to be able to bring you to this kind of place, though, isn't it?'

She gestured around them at the people sipping tea amongst the aspidistras in their brass pots. In a corner, a man was playing 'Night And Day' at the piano.

'Flaming Father Donnelly,' sighed Cynthia. 'I'm sure he was the one who snitched. Saying we were neglected.'

'No one snitched. We were just found out when that woman came round to tell us about ma's accident. Ma . . . Ellie asked us if we are orphans of the living. Are we?'

'What a horrible way to put it. No, dear. Of course not. You're on holiday. And when I get another job nearer to Liverpool – one where I'm not turning yellow, and knee-deep in that dreadful TNT stuff – I'm coming straight back here to get you. Who knows, they're saying the war might be over soon. And when Da gets home from doing his bit, everything will be back to how it was. Chin up, girls. Flipping Hitler, eh?'

When they got back, Ellie was lingering in the entrance hall. Sister Cyril, passing through, stopped when she saw them.

'Tch. Ellie! What are you doing here?' she said.

'Waiting for Marcia and Cynthia.'

Sister Cyril nodded. 'I see. I hope you've not been telling them about your antics with Jesus in the semolina?' She turned to Cynthia and Marcia and smiled. 'Do I look like I was born yesterday? Ellie's never been the same since she had scarlet fever, have you, Ellie? She tells all sorts of stories. About visions and other nonsense. Don't you take any notice of that. No one's falling for it, Ellie, no matter how long you keep it up with the porridge. Now, polishing candlesticks, girls. Is that all right? You could do it together. I'll see you all downstairs.'

'She likes you,' said Ellie, after the nun had gone.

'Does she?'

'She wouldn't ask me if it was "all right" to do the polishing. She would just tell me to get on with it, or give me a good crack on me arse. Still, when this war is over, I'm leaving. I'll be glad to see the back of this place.'

'Are you going back to your ma and da?'

'Don't be daft,' she laughed. 'They're both dead.' She beamed. 'I'm going on an adventure. Sister said there are exciting plans for orphans like me. I'm going to Australia.'

'Ellie – I need you,' called a voice from somewhere

51

down the corridor. 'I would like you in the refectory. Now.'

Ellie raised her eyes. 'No rest for the wicked when Sid is around,' she said.

'Who's Sid?'

'Sister Cyril. That's what we call her.' Ellie winked at them, then turned away with a cheerful wave.

Chapter 8

Another week crawled by, but Marcia and Cynthia slowly settled into a routine. In the mornings a gaggle of children arrived at the chapel. It was Marcia and Cynthia's job to sit at the back shushing them, tying shoelaces and wiping noses, while Sister Cyril read them Bible stories. The children made Christmas decorations for the tree that the nuns had brought into the hall, and they would sit at Marcia and Cynthia's feet adoringly, ask them to plait their hair, pester them to read to them. Even Cynthia melted. When a little boy with a flat head and callouses on his fingers mastered his six times table with her help, she felt a sense of achievement. The babies, though, were their favourites. They had to wheel them in big Silver Cross prams around the garden whatever the weather – and it was a November colder than they had ever remembered.

Ellie had quickly become a firm friend. She showed them how, when you were threading rosary beads, you could cut corners by throwing four into a bag and making it look as if you had done five. She also told them a little more about herself. Her mother had divorced her father and they had all thought he was dead, been shot down in the war – but in fact he was living with her mother's sister in Morecambe, and they had twin boys. After that, Ellie's mother had just stopped doing anything and never managed to get out of bed. Ellie had a brother and he had been evacuated for a while, but when he came back home, he didn't settle. Now he lived in Wales with a farmer and she would probably never see him again.

One afternoon, when she came home from school, she had found her mother with her head in the oven. Although her mother survived, Ellie was moved from house to house before ending up with her grandmother; but when her grandmother died in the Blitz there had been nowhere left for her to go. Eventually the nuns had arrived, put her in a car and brought her to St Mary's.

'. . . And here I am,' she said. Astonishingly, she was smiling.

'And you can bear it?'

Ellie shrugged. 'Not much choice, have I? Ma and Da are both both dead now. Da of drink and Ma of . . . who knows. She always had the bronchitis, just like me . . . Iffy pipes.'

'I don't mind it so much now. I like the children, even if the nuns don't let us mix with them that much. Maybe because we're not here for long,' said Marcia.

'It always smells of cabbage when you walk in. And Jeyes Fluid,' said Cynthia.

'Aye,' Ellie nodded. 'And nothing is what it seems. You see some of the kiddies in the garden, all chubby and smiley in pretty frocks and shiny shoes. But then you find out it's only 'cos there are people coming from the outside to pick a little 'un, or Father's coming to say Mass, and then it's back in the old dungies and plimmys. Like you two dopey Doras have been told you're on holiday. Which is unpaid help, I reckon. Your ma know that?'

'She misses us. She didn't even want us to be evacuated, did she, Cyn?'

'Her problem is that she loves priests and nuns and can't imagine them doing any harm. She thought this would be the best for us.'

'Mmm,' Ellie said.

'She does love us, doesn't she, Cyn? And Da.'

Ellie paused and cocked her head, then she yawned and switched her smile back on, raking her hands through her bowl-cut hair. Her eyes flashed mischievously.

'So what do you think that is?' she asked as she lay on her back and pointed up at the ceiling. They both looked up. 'See? That handprint up there? It's the Hand of God.'

Cynthia laughed.

'Well, how do you think it got there?'

'Someone could've brought a ladder.'

'No one brought a ladder. It's a child's hand, it's a tiny, teeny, small hand. It's the Hand of God, I'm telling you.'

Marcia and Cynthia looked at each other and laughed.

'At least, that's what I told the nuns. But can I trust you and let you into a secret?' She leaned in and whispered to them, putting her arms around their shoulders. 'I climbed up onto that wardrobe. It was a bit wobbly, but I'll show you. Watch me.'

She scrambled up the side of it, heaved herself up and crouched like a leprechaun on top of it, then spat on her hands. Then she propelled herself forward with such force, shrieking as she leapt up and off the wardrobe and slammed her hand flat on the ceiling before landing on the empty iron bed with a cry and a thump and a great creaking and rattling and shaking of bed springs. The girls gasped, then exploded with laughter. Ellie folded her arms and beamed.

'The Hand of God. That's how I did it. I won't stop, I tell you. Sid is falling for it, I swear.'

'What's that noise?' said Sister Cyril, slamming open the dormitory door as if on cue.

'We don't know, Sister. The door shut and the bed shook all by itself. I was just telling these two about the Hand of God. Look, there's another one appeared.'

'Drop this nonsense, Ellie.'

'But it's a beautiful mystery. How do you think it got there, Sister?' she asked.

'Get downstairs, immediately,' the nun snapped. 'You'll be the death of me, Ellie Kinsella.'

That night, Eunice Rogan looked around her at the meagre furnishings in her little hostel room. The air felt chilly. Opening her pay packet, she tipped out six shillings onto the small bed.

Was it really worth it? Not only was she suffering, but she also worried about the effect it might have on the girls, being left with the nuns. She was unsure about this Ellie character they had mentioned. And Marcia had seemed so small. Yes, it was good pay; but she had been here a month now. What difference was it actually making? They could perhaps afford nicer clothes – they wouldn't have to rely on Mr Tattersall for food, and maybe they could manage a few days out when summer came. Perhaps even a holiday in a boarding house. But where would they go – back to New Brighton? It wouldn't be the same without John. And the Ministry of Defence might be urging people to pack their buckets and spades and go to the seaside again, but the war was still going on. Not much fun with rolled-up barbed wire on the beaches.

There was a knock on the door. Go away, she wanted to say. But then a voice said brightly, 'Letter for you, Eunice. It's been sitting on the table downstairs for two days now.'

A letter? Her heart leapt to her throat. She got up from the bed and opened the door to Daisy, who smiled at her. 'You must have missed it in the commotion.' Eunice took it, trying not to snatch.

Dear Eunice,

I can't write too much. But would you believe it, I'm on another boat. The Japanese have been causing more merry hell down in —. We were heading to — and we saw fish leaping out of the sea. At first we thought they were birds skimming the surface. But they were flying fish. It reminded me of Sir Gordy. There's something peculiar about a fish behaving like a bird, or a man behaving like a fish. But good news. I think I might be coming home. We have two more weeks here and then go to —

Eunice held the letter to the light, squinting in frustration. She couldn't make out the words that had been redacted, struck through with a thick black line.

I hope to see you soon, all being well.
Your loving husband, John

But it was enough. And her decision was made.

A week later, Eunice sat in Sister Cyril's small office.

'It was my eyelashes that were the worst, Sister. It took ages to get it off.'

'Gosh, we have been in the wars. But you're sure you're ready to have the girls back so soon? It must have been quite a palaver. Have you really recovered?'

'Mr Rogan is coming home, so I'll be fine. We'll all be fine. I'm never setting foot in that factory again, and it's being with my girls that will help me get back on my feet. Though I'm grateful to you for taking them.'

'When will your husband be back?'

'They tell us nothing. Soon.'

'Let's hope so. I'm pleased for you, Mrs Rogan. But I'll miss your girls. They're good girls, especially Marcia – not like some of the guttersnipes we have here. And if you need us again, if Mr Rogan – if he – I'm sorry, I mean, *when* he comes home . . . you know where we are.' She smiled. 'We'd be happy to have them back. God's work is never done.'

Ten minutes later, Cynthia and Marcia stood in the doorway with their suitcases.

'Are you ready, girls?'

They nodded.

Eunice smiled and took her daughters' arms, leading them down the gravel path and out through the wrought-iron gates. 'It's so good to have my girls with me again. I'll bet you're glad to get out of that place.'

'I'll miss Ellie, though. We never said goodbye, and she's going to Australia,' said Marcia.

'Australia? Are you sure?' said their mother, then shrugged the question away.

'Will Da be there when we get back?' said Cynthia. 'Sister said that's why we're going home.'

'Not yet. Soon, though. He'll be back soon. And isn't that the best news we've all had in months!'

Chapter 9

Eighteen months later: June 1946

'Do I have to go to Cyn's competition?' said Marcia.

'Of course, Marcia,' replied her mother through a mouthful of pins as she put up her hair, winding it into a tight, neat bun. She had never quite recovered from the accident at the munitions factory. She could feel her eyes itching and the palms of her hands looked swollen. These hives would never go; they flared up with worry, or a change in the weather, or when she got the Curse. It made the simplest of tasks difficult, like pinning up her hair.

'Why?'

'She's your sister,' Eunice replied, as if that was enough and always would be.

An hour later, Marcia, wishing she could still be outside in the sunshine playing in the hollas, found herself perched on a bench at the parish hall with her bottom going numb, waiting for Cynthia to come on the stage. There were about twenty other hopefuls, too, all trying for the 'Miss Lafferty's Song and Dance' cup, all in mismatched homemade dancing outfits varying from elaborate pink tulle affairs to rehashed communion dresses, all wearing battered pink satin ballet shoes with ribbons criss-crossing their shins and tied in plump bows in their hair. Cynthia was getting ready to perform her 'Moonlight in June' with Mrs Caddle from down their street bashing out the tune on the piano. The blackout curtains made the place dark and they had put a spotlight on the floor which pointed at the stage.

'Stop fidgeting, Marcia,' hissed her mother, fanning herself.

'I can't help it. It's like a blooming oven in here.'

The tatty fringed velvet curtain began to jerk open, but stuck halfway. A skinny boy in shorts and tap shoes shot out and yanked it with his hand. Then the first girl, with shivering sausages of curls, wearing a brighter version of Cynthia's off-white party frock and a better version of Cynthia's old ballet shoes and saggy socks, took her place and shuffled and squinted in the spotlight. '*Moonlight in Joo-hoon . . .*' she warbled, as Mrs Caddle's foot tapped wildly.

'That's what our Cynthia's singing.'

'Yes. That's what they're all singing. It's a song and dance competition.'

The realization hit Marcia that she was going to have to sit through 'Moonlight in June' from all the other caterwauling, simpering hopefuls as well. She did a quick calculation. This could go on for hours. After the fourth girl came out and started up with 'Moonlight in Joo-hoon', she thought she was going to explode.

'When's our Cyn on?'

'Soon, be quiet.'

'I need the lavvy,' said Marcia. Her mother humphed. 'I'm going to burst.' She squeezed out, past tutting mothers and fidgeting, squirming children.

Ten minutes later, she returned.

'You missed her,' said her mother. 'You're for it now,' she said with a sigh.

Cynthia sulked all the way home.

'Chin up. It doesn't matter that you didn't win. It's the taking part that counts, Cyn,' said her mother.

'No, it's not.'

'Yes, it is,' said Marcia.

'Shurrup. You didn't even see it. Mam told me.'

'They were all a year older than you, Cyn, love. In a year's time, you'll be just as good as them.'

'That's a daft flipping thing to say. When I'm a year older, they'll all be a year older too, so they'll still be better than me,' she wailed. 'Anyway, that girl who won, sneaking in those splits at the end. It's not fair. I practised and practised.'

'Life's not fair, love,' muttered her mother, half to herself. 'If it was, your da wouldn't still be halfway across the world when he promised he was coming home. And we wouldn't be drowning in unpaid leccy bills and IOUs to the tick-man, would we?'

Marcia dragged the coal bag down to the coal hole. She heaved it along the passage and filled the scuttle, like her mother had asked. When she was done, head down, she set off in the sunshine to the hollas at the end of their street, where a whole row of houses had been bombed; the site was now a wasteland. Flopping down on the tiny patch of grass, an oasis that had miraculously appeared amongst the rubble, she focused on a patch of daisies and began pulling them up, one by one, from the earth.

She saw Alfie Maloney, Cynthia's sweetheart, on the other side of the hollas. He was looping a rope over a lamp post so that three mucky children could leap on and hang off it. When he pushed it, it gathered momentum and swung in a wide arc.

'Oi! Over here! Hop on!' he cried to Marcia. She shook her head shyly. Alfie was a few years older than the rest of the kids they played with in the street; he was handsome with long, lithe legs. Like his dad, who was always offering everyone cigarettes or rides in his new car, he always seemed to have a few bob in his pocket – or a paper bag of flying saucers and liquorice shoelaces that he would dole out whenever the mood took him.

'Come on!' he encouraged.

It did look like fun. She stood, brushed herself down and went over, gingerly walking across the plank that had been laid on top of larger pieces of rubble, then stumbling over potholes before joining him on the other side of the wasteland. As the rope swooped around the lamp post, he hooked his arm around her waist. 'Hold on to me!'

She yelped as he scooped her up. Pressed against his chest, her legs tightly wrapped around his hips as she clung onto the tangle of bodies, she felt his heart beating. 'It's the craic, isn't it?' he laughed.

'Aye.'

'Want to come with me to Otterspool?' he said, when they all eventually slid down the rope and he and Marcia separated from the group. 'I'm on me way to catch smooth-hound fishes. Your Cyn doesn't want to get her feet wet.' Marcia paused and cocked her head to one side. 'You can help me with my rods,' he added.

'All right,' she replied, happy at the thought of an excuse to get out of the house for a few hours. He picked up his fishing rod, a small bucket and a bag that he looped over his arm.

'I caught a sole last week. Will you carry me worms? You're not frightened, are you?' She shrugged, took the small bucket and trotted behind him as, with his head down and hands thrust deep into his pockets, the rod wedged under his arm, they set off in the direction of the docks.

When they reached the main road, Alfie jumped onto the platform of a tram that was hurtling towards them, pulling her up with him. They sat with the sound of the light bulbs rattling in their cases and when they arrived at the dock road, they managed to jump off while the tram was still moving – and all without paying for a ticket.

They walked down the promenade to the place where it dwindled into a stony path. Alfie took her hand and they went down the slippery, moss-covered slope to the estuary, where the shore stretched out in ripples like dried-out washing. Marcia felt herself sink into the silt with the sludge coming over the top of her shoes. Each step made a squelching sound as the mud sucked her feet. 'My shoes,' she said.

'I'll give yer a piggyback. It's best out towards the channel. Other side of the mud. It's sandy there. I saw a conger eel the other day. And a smooth-hound.' She stood behind him and jumped up onto his back, her legs neatly wrapped around his hips and his arms supporting her under her thighs, her arms around his neck. It felt intimate to have her cheek pressed against the side of his head, her mouth speaking into his ear as the wind buffeted and roared around them. Their clothes clinging to them, they reached a shrimping cart and Alfie scrambled up, held out a hand and pulled her up the side of it. The cramped terraces, the hustle and bustle of the city, seemed a world away when facing out to the estuary and looking across the Irish Sea.

'I'm going to go to America one day.'

'Are yer? With our Cyn?'

He laughed. 'Mebbe. What about you?'

This vast steel-grey sky always made Marcia feel the world was full of possibilities, but unlike Alfie, she just didn't know what they were yet.

'Mebbe,' she echoed. She paused. 'Alfie, you know me da,' she said suddenly.

'Aye.'

'Our ma won't tell us much about why he's not come home. The war finished ages ago and he wrote a letter saying he was coming back, but he's still stuck in Burma. In one of them camps. Or somewhere.'

'So what do you know?' he asked, as he pushed a hook through a wriggling worm he took from a small pot. 'I know about what they did over there. They made them work all day and all night. Build bridges, chop down trees in the jungle. Bamboo is like knives. And they got sick. They didn't look after them and they would just drop dead, sometimes in front of their pals. Some of them just starved to death. Fellow my dad knows says things were so terrible lots of them topped themselves. Your da is one of the lucky ones if he's alive.'

Marcia nodded seriously. But then she frowned. The conversation was too troubling to carry on with. 'Alfie, d'you love our Cynthia?' she asked.

He laughed. 'A bit. She's pretty. And she's gobby. I like that.'

Alfie hoicked the fishing rod over his shoulder. As they made their way back over the sand, the mud made squelching noises.

'Billy Brennan says stuff about Ma and Da all the time. Says that's why he's not come back to me ma. It's not true, is it?'

'Not likely. Mr Tattersall wouldn't do anything with your ma. Sexy stuff. They're just friends.'

'Mr Tattersall? Sexy stuff?' Her cheeks pinked. She sounded shocked. 'I meant Da having a fancy woman, not Ma.'

'Oh. Yes. I thought . . . Never mind.'

The tide was coming in and heavy black clouds were forming on the horizon. Alfie stood with his rod firmly planted in the sand and the line stretching out before him into the calmer water, beyond the breaking waves. 'Got a bite!' he cried eventually. Something was tugging the line and as he pulled at the rod a silver fish came shimmering, flipping and curling, out of the water. He unhooked it, caressed it, and dropped it with a plop into the bucket. He smiled at Marcia. 'What a beauty. You brought me good luck, Marce.'

*

The next day, Marcia set off to do the messages. Ahead she saw one of the Liverpool Lane gang, Billy Brennan, dangling upside down with both of his legs hooked over one of the handrails that ran down the hill. He twisted his neck when he caught sight of her. With his palms placed flat on the floor, he did a flip and stood to his feet, then cocked his head and gave her a quizzical stare.

'Hey, Marcia, your da back yet?'

She blinked away the question. Three boys were crouched on the pavement playing a game of jacks. One of them, sucking on a liquorice twig, regarded her with a quizzical stare.

'Is he?' Billy pestered. Marcia shook her head and hurried past with small, rapid steps, but the boy ran after her, reached out and grabbed the strap of her bag, yanking her back to him. 'Eh, la. Stay here and talk to us,' he said.

'No. Can you let me past?' she mumbled.

'Your da back yet?'

Marcia froze.

'He's never coming back to your ma. Not now,' said another boy, casually flicking a jack onto the pavement slab.

Marcia bristled. 'Yes, he is.'

When he laughed, they all glanced at each other slyly and grinned.

'When?'

'Coming home soon,' she replied. She felt herself sweating.

'Coming home, like Carol's dad? Back in Liverpool but not come back to her mam? Not when he found out she was up the duff with the coal man. I heard your ma's the same as Carol's ma?'

She tried putting her hands on her hips defiantly. It wasn't the first time Billy had teased her about her ma and da, but she found the gesture hard to commit to and she felt herself fast losing confidence. 'My da was in the jungle, he's a hero.'

'The war was over ages ago.'

'Stop it, Billy, you're behaving like an idiot again,' said a calm and assured voice. It came from a tall, fair-haired boy standing by the railings.

Billy laughed. 'Keep out of it, Cherry.'

'Yeah, sod off, Henry,' said another.

The boy pushed his spectacles up his nose. 'No, I won't be doing that.'

Marcia cocked her head. He looked a gentler, kinder, wiser boy than the others, older than his fifteen years.

'Marcia Rogan, your ma's coming round to the charity all the time. Them clothes you wear.' Marcia felt tears spring to her eyes. 'Some bloody hero.'

Henry walked over and placed his shoulder between Marcia and Billy. 'That's enough, Billy.' His calmness was compelling.

Something about his quiet persistence gave Marcia confidence to speak. 'Yes, that's enough. Or me and Henry will show you what's what. State of you in those baggy shorts with a string for a belt,' she retorted.

Henry turned and looked at her, fighting a smile.

'That's your game, Cherry? You going to stick up for her? Let's fight, then,' said Billy, raising his fists.

'Oi! No-marks!' cried a voice. Cynthia had appeared from nowhere, nostrils flaring, striding up the hill. 'You pestering my sister again? You saying things about our ma and da?' she said, jabbing her finger at Billy.

'It's all right, Cyn,' Marcia said. 'Me and Henry have told them what's what.'

'Who's Henry?' she asked, puzzled.

'This one here,' said Billy, indicating Henry, who'd politely stepped to one side to allow Cynthia's frontal assault. 'Sticking his nose in where it's not wanted.'

'Aye, well. It's none of your business either, Billy! Shut your cakehole and leave my sister alone. You don't know sod all about our da.'

The other boys laughed.

Perhaps it was because Cynthia felt that her family seemed to be the only ones in their street for whom the war had gone on so long. Perhaps it was just that she was so fed up with being poor; with this place, and these people who felt so narrow and limiting. Whatever the reason, her response took the form of a swift thump with her fist that landed squarely in the middle of Billy's chest.

He staggered backwards, stunned and grinning stupidly. Cynthia took aim and came at him again, this time with her feet and roaring like a tiger. Gasping, he fell to the ground, struggled, then drew himself up. As he was getting to his feet, Cynthia took her chance and ran at him head down like a bull, grabbing him around the waist and pushing him flat to the ground. Quick as a flash she straddled him and pressed her palms down on his forearms. As he squirmed like a fish underneath her, she spoke nose to nose directly into his face.

'Leave! My! Sister! Alone! You're a bully. You should be ashamed, especially as she's younger than you lot. And if you start on at her again about our da, you'll have me to answer to.' She jumped up, leaving him helpless and winded.

Henry stepped forward calmly and bent over Billy. 'Oh, and that goes for me too, by the way.'

Marcia, astonished, just stared at her sister in shock and admiration. She could barely believe what had just happened. Pride swelled in her chest. She had never known her sister do something so brave and heroic – and she had done it for Marcia.

She was also thinking about Henry Cherry. What was so familiar about him? Of course! Henry Cherry, seeing to Sister Cyril's turnips; Cynthia giggling at his name and having to explain herself.

'He does that again, I'll give him a Kirkby kiss, I will,' said Cynthia.

They walked together the rest of the way home, Cynthia stomping on resolutely and Marcia trotting beside her, wide-eyed with disbelief and gratitude that her sister genuinely cared about her after all. It made her feel warm and glowing inside.

'Thanks, Cyn,' she said, with a worshipping smile on her face.

'He's a pillock. They're all pillocks. Fellas.'

Marcia wanted to ask her sister why, if they were all pillocks, she ever had anything to do with them. Why bother with all that bum-wiggling and lippy? And Alfie. Instead, she said, 'Why did they say that thing about Da not coming home to Ma?'

Cynthia stopped and faced her, smoothing down

her hair. Tenderly, she took the end of her plait and stroked it. 'Oh, love. Wait until we get home.'

The sunshine had turned to grey, then to soft rain, and now to a heavy pestering drizzle. The rooftops sloping towards the river made Marcia think of wet boots.

Cynthia sighed, sat on the edge of the bed. 'Marcia, haven't you noticed how Ma seems bad with her nerves sometimes? I know why Da has taken so long. It's not because he has a fancy woman, like Billy says. It's because he's been too sick to come home.'

'Why hasn't she told us?'

'It might shock us. Apparently.'

'What?'

'Him. How he is. He was one of the unlucky ones that was sent halfway across the world. He was coming home on leave and then he got captured. He was in that camp for nearly two years. D'you even remember him? Five years is a long time not to see someone.'

Marcia frowned. 'Of course I remember. He used to do those tricks with cigarettes. Pull them out from up his nose and behind our ears. And I remember his bird impressions and the boiled eggs.'

Cynthia gave a half smile, thinking back to when they would squeal with delight when Da would smash the upside-down empty shells with a spoon and they would roar with laughter as he played along with the charade. She saw Marcia instinctively turn her head towards the creased, grainy picture propped up against the oil lamp. It showed her father in a uniform

71

in the desert, smiling in the fierce sun, leaning on a spade in front of a tent.

She hesitated, then said: 'D'you want to see the letter? Are you old enough?'

Marcia's eyes widened.

Cynthia reached under the bed, found a yellowing envelope and flung it over to her. 'Don't tell Ma I've shown you. She's had it for nearly four months.'

Marcia took out the letter from the slim envelope and, in the half light, began to read the spidery words that sloped across the page.

> *St Anne's Sanatorium, Singapore*
> *February 1946*

Dear Eunice,

I expect after all this time, you never thought you would hear from me again. How many letters did I write that never arrived, I wonder? And you to me? None, I expect. When the American troops finally got here last September, they found a warehouse in Singapore full of Red Cross parcels and letters that had never been delivered. Well, I'm in a military hospital in a small town three miles outside of Singy. I've been in a kind of coma for months. They gave me injections twice a day. Beriberi, they say. That's what caused the paralysis in my legs, but the old pins seem to be working now. I then had another parasitic illness that they don't have a name for. Eats away at your skin between your toes. And after the blasted Yellow Fever and Eczema.

I'm afraid I still don't know exactly when I'll be back in Liverpool, still too sick to travel, they say, so don't tell the girls yet. I still need a few months to get a little better, but they are at last making arrangements. I even scared myself when I first saw myself in the mirror! I need to put some meat on these bones but even that's tricky. When the nurses brought us cakes, none of us could eat them! Years on boiled rice does things to your insides.

I'm here with a few others from the POW camp and we're treated well now. When the guards heard the Americans were coming to save us they told us to dig our own graves, so we were lucky. Out of our regiment, only five returned. Though I'm a shadow of myself and I've been sedated for God knows how long, I'm alive. Just about. The electric shock treatment has calmed my nerves. I'll fill you in when I'm home. One poor blighter on the ward who tried to jump off the roof of the hospital has just been lobotomized and I don't fancy that, so I guess I got off pretty lightly. The worst of the horrors, at least, are only in my dreams now. But that's still pretty difficult to get on top of.

Hope my babies are happy and well.
Your loving husband,
John

PS They've told us when we get back on civvy street we shouldn't talk about the war,

*seeing as how everyone has moved on. The
government has said that. They gave us a
pamphlet and it was written down, strict
instructions in paragraph after paragraph.
There is nothing people want to hear about
when it comes to what happened in the
camps, they say. Instead talk about rebuilding
Britain and look forward to the future. Has
everyone really moved on? People want to
forget about the war, is that true? Anyway,
there'll certainly be no celebrations for us
poor beggars. No fanfare or bands playing
'Land of Hope and Glory' on the quayside for
us. But that won't stop you and me, I hope.*

Marcia read the letter again. Hands quivering,
breath coming up short, sometimes not coming out
at all unless she took great gulps of air.

'What does he mean? The worst horrors are only
in my dreams?'

'He's been very poorly.'

'What kind of sick?'

'The kind that makes you sick in the head.'

'And – electric shock treatment, what's that?'

'Numbs you in the brain.'

'Oh.'

'Everyone's talking about it round here. The
Maloneys' cousin Davey ended up doing a stint in
the looney bin when he eventually came back from
Egypt. Mr Tattersall keeps Ma updated. Just don't
tell Ma I've shown it to you. Promise?'

'Promise,' replied Marcia.

Chapter 10

The following day Marcia gathered up the washing, loaded it onto the old pram and began pushing it down the hill. The noise of the washhouse when she arrived was deafening: the swish of the new machines and the clatter of irons, the hissing of steam. But it was the chatter of the women's voices, the gossip flying, that made this place strangely comforting despite how she was feeling at the moment. The large room with its vaulted ceiling and condensation wiggling down its huge windows was always filled with laughter, high and tinkling, loud and gusty. You could rely on someone breaking into song now and then.

As usual she was hit by a blast of thick, warm air. One of the women, sipping a cup of tea, saw her struggle with her bundle and came over to help her sling the washing into the machine. Meanwhile Mrs Gibney, wearing a colourful turban, started singing a song Marcia hadn't heard before. 'Who knows this one?' she cried, as she put one hand on her broad hips and thumped the air. '*She had to go and lose it at the Astor!*' The whole place erupted in laughter. Someone shoved two fingers into their mouth and whistled. Marcia untied the second bundle. She ran the taps and hot water gushed into the sink. Mrs Gibney always knew how to get things going.

For half an hour the slapping of wet clothes on washboards, the slop, slop of buckets being emptied, the sound of sinks and coppers being filled and the hissing and whooshing of steam irons lulled Marcia into a kind of trance. She wiped her brow. Sweat had broken out across her forehead and her hairline, and she could feel a tickling sensation as moisture dribbled down the nape of her neck.

'Marcia, how's your ma?' said a woman stirring a copper with wooden tongs. It was Mrs Buckley from the butcher's, sleeves pushed up to her elbows revealing pink, fleshy forearms. 'Your da still away?' she added, as she stopped to wipe her gleaming face with a handkerchief.

Marcia nodded; she didn't want to say anything much to Mrs Buckley, so she began quietly sorting through the wet washing just as she always did. White petticoats separated from navy blue knickers. Lace antimacassars separated from striped pillowcases. And then there were Mr Tattersalls' shirts to put in another pile, his smalls, vests and long johns.

'What's with Marcia washing them long johns?' Mrs Gibney asked Madge Hallett in a low voice while Marcia went to find a pair of tongs. 'Is there a fella in the Rogan house? John Rogan won't take kindly to that when he comes home from wherever in the world he is.'

'All started when Eunice and the girls began sharing his shelter. Those girls were wasting away. Eunice started doing his washing and in return for ironing his shirts and smalls, Fred Tattersall has made sure they never go hungry. They don't have a penny. That woman seems unable to hold down a job.'

'So all perfectly decent and above board? Mind you, I'd let Fred Tattersall have me ha'penny for his salmon fishcakes any day of the week.' They both laughed, throaty and dirtily.

Marcia took the washing out of the machine. There were the copper boilers still, but these new machines did the business in half an hour and today she was in a hurry. She fed the washing through a mangle and then hung it out on the drying cages to be slotted back into the wall. Gladys Gibney began to serenade them all again. '*I've got the deepest shelter in town!*' she sang gustily, to more hoots of laughter.

'Ma? What's the matter?' Marcia asked, when she got home. She had come into the kitchen and found her mother pacing the room. Eunice looked pale and was fanning herself and clutching at her housecoat lapels with one hand, all the time reading something. A letter – no, a telegram, it looked like.

'Oh, goodness,' she murmured, sinking into a chair as though her legs had wobbled from under her.

'What, Ma?' said Marcia, placing the washing on the table.

'What's up, Mam?' said Cynthia, appearing in the doorway.

Their mother seemed jittery, excited but also nervous. She didn't reply; instead she picked up the hand mirror from the dresser and looked at her reflection, put down the mirror, smoothed down her apron, then patted her hair, picked the mirror up again and turned her head to one side and then the other. Cynthia scooped up the telegram and scanned the page as she read it aloud, skimming over words.

FINALLY GOOD TO GO STOP ON BOAT FOR HOME STOP BACK IN THREE WEEKS STOP THINGS MOVED FASTER THAN I THOUGHT STOP ARMY ARRANGING TRANSPORT FOR US STOP PUT KETTLE ON AND WARM BED PAN — JOHN

Eunice looked as if she was finding it hard to breathe. 'Oh dear. Oh goodness me. Oh my. We've work to do around here.' And then she threw her hands up in the air. 'Da's coming home!'

'Are you sure?' said Cynthia. 'You've said that before, but still no sign of Mr Invisible.'

'Of course I am. This is different. He's on his way! Thank God!' Eunice's eyes flitted around the room. 'That grate hasn't been done properly for months. And why don't we make a start on emery boarding the stove this weekend? We need to get this place spick and span.'

'Oh, Ma!' said Marcia.

Her mother skittered around the table, fanning herself more. 'I can hardly believe it.' Her eyes were shining, and she clutched Marcia's hands. 'In three weeks!'

'Why can't he come home sooner?' asked Cynthia, her voice hard with suspicion.

'It's complicated,' replied her mother vaguely. She snatched the telegram from Cynthia and slid it into her pocket.

'Alfie says all the POWs get sick. Will he be OK?' said Marcia.

'Not all of them get sick. He's going to be fine. The nuns have been looking after him. Oh dear, I need to get ready. This place. It's such a mess . . .'

'Nuns! Bloody Nora!' said Cynthia. 'Da's been with the nuns? Why?'

'Lots of nuns are nurses. And don't swear. That's another penny you need to put in the mission box. I'm telling you now, that will have to stop when your father comes back.'

Cynthia rolled her eyes. 'Why has it taken Da so long to come home? How sick is he exactly?'

Eunice made a shape in the air with her hand, as though she was going to say something important, but didn't. Somehow she managed to swing the conversation towards the urgency of beating the rugs and getting a new bit of material from Paddy's Market to cover the threadbare armchair, without telling them a single detail about the worrying words in the letter: *electric shock treatment*.

'Oh dear. Look at me. Have I got fat? I'm as big as a house. I'm a whale. I swear this dress was baggy on my hips when I last wore it. I can barely do up the zip. And these lines . . . I look a hundred years old . . .' Eunice murmured, tracing the contours of her face with her forefinger.

Marcia frowned. Old? Fat? Her mother was as thin as a rake. What on earth was she talking about? 'By the way, Ma, I took Mr Tattersall's washing and he said he's doing liver and onions and mushy peas for you this weekend,' she said brightly.

'I know. Now put the iron on the range,' came the brief reply.

'With your favourite, he said. Scouse caviar.'

'Scouse caviar . . . that's just silly,' murmured her mother.

Cynthia, leaning her bottom on the edge of the table, watched her mother flapping about. Marcia went back to sorting out the bundle of washing and took out the wooden clothes horse on which to hang the damp washing in front of the range to air.

'Oh no – Mr Tattersall's apron, Ma,' she said.

'Take that back as soon as you can, Marcia,' Eunice said flatly.

And then, instead of hanging it out, her mother picked up the apron and whisked it away. Marcia and Cynthia watched her stuff it back into the calico bag. Why? Marcia wondered if she should say something. She wasn't sure. It might be easier to leave it than start a conversation which, by a strange sort of instinct, she worried might end badly.

'Why doesn't Ma want to go and have her tea with Mr Tattersall?' Marcia said after Eunice had left the room.

Cynthia just looked at her witheringly and rolled her eyes.

'Why not?' Marcia said. 'Cyn, why not?'

That evening, Marcia lay on her bed and turned her face to the wall. The plaster was so soft, you could pick away at it and it would crumble off under your fingers. An inch above the headboard there was a bit of wall that she had fiddled with so much there was now a perfectly round little hole that she could spy through to the other side, into her mother's room. Sometimes she would stick her finger all the way in and wiggle it and her mother, whose bed was pushed up against the side of the wall, would grasp it and kiss it. But tonight the hole had been blocked up with an old rag.

Half an hour later, Cynthia sat on a low stool and blotted her red lips on a handkerchief. She snapped the compact shut and put the lid back on the lipstick. 'Right, I'm off. Cover for me, squit.'

'Where are you going? It's nine o'clock at night.'

'Town with Denise. Ma won't know. She's asleep. She's exhausted.'

'That's three times this week you've done a flit. Where d'you keep going?'

'Never you mind.'

'Dancing again? She'll kill you. It's a school night.'

'I don't care. I've decided I'm going to make the best of Liverpool and go full-on floozy before summer ends,' said Cynthia, waving a hairbrush as she sat primping herself in front of the propped-up mirror on the dressing table. She got up and slipped her feet into her Cuban-heeled sandals. 'Flipping 'eck! There's still sand on the floor from your trip to the beach with Alfie. I can feel it.'

'What d'you mean, full-on floozy? What about Alfie?'

Cynthia sighed dramatically. 'This war is over. We've been scared to death of Hitler and his bombs for years but I'm planning to make up for lost time. I'm going to go dancing and flirt with as many boys as I can. I need to find a proper fella.'

'You're only fifteen. And you still haven't answered, what about Alfie? I thought you were going to marry him?'

Cynthia twirled a ringlet of hair around her finger. 'Don't be stupid. The man I'm going to marry is going to have to speak French and drive a car. Alfie's useless.'

'Why did you kiss him, then?' Marcia remembered that she'd once seen Alfie kissing Cynthia in one of the bombed-out houses.

'Dunno.' She sat down at the dressing table again. 'But Alfie's a kid. And if Mr Attlee says I'm old enough to leave school and get a job, I'm old enough to kiss boys. I don't know why Ma is even forcing me to stay at school. I should have left when I was fourteen. I need to get in some practice on that front. Not just Alfie.'

'Alfie says he wants to go to America.'

'Does he now?' replied Cynthia.

'He said he might take me fishing again.'

Cynthia narrowed her eyes. 'You stay away from him. He's mine. You stay away from boys altogether. Besides, he's too old for you.'

'But you just said you were going to go full-on floozy! I don't get it. Are you two-timing Alfie?'

'No. You don't get it, squit, because you're a baby.'

There was a short pause and then Marcia said, 'What's it like? Kissing a boy?'

Cynthia laughed as she fluffed powder over her cheeks. 'Nice. You feel all fluttery in your tummy and your legs go hollow.'

Marcia's eyes widened. She thought about how much Cynthia loved boys: hanging out with them, giggling and whispering behind her hand with her friend Denise and giving them marks out of ten. Boys shoved their fingers in their mouths and whistled at her when she walked past them, and she would turn and wink at them. She didn't even need to stuff her bra any more. Chubby Bunch, her mother used to call her. Not now. She had proper curves and a bottom like a ripe peach, which she liked to show off with wide belts and tight skirts. No wonder, thought Marcia, that she had her sights set higher than Alfie and the pals they kicked about with in Liverpool Lane.

'Ma said we can't leave school until we do our matriculation. She says she has high hopes for us.'

'Pish. If I get a job in show business, I'm off.'

'Show business? What are you on about?' It sounded ridiculous.

'Look, stop worrying. I'm not leaving you yet, squit. I'm just going out dancing. Mr Labone has said if I practise, I can audition for his tour.'

'What you talking about? Who's Mr Labone?'

'Never you mind.' Cynthia hoicked her breasts up. 'I'm getting better. I can almost do the front splits.' She pulled up her skirt and tucked it into her knickers, slid her legs apart, hands supporting herself on the floor, heaving and puffing. Then she collapsed and fell to one side, landing on her bottom with a thump.

'Ma won't let you leave school.'

'The problem with our ma,' mused Cynthia, 'is that she thinks you have to suffer for what you get in life, probably because they've had it so hard in the war. But I've had enough of school. I've got my career to think of.'

Career? thought Marcia. Who had a career round here? People had jobs, not careers.

'Don't be late, Cyn. Ma'll be banging with the brush for you to do the grate early tomorrow and you'll catch it if she finds out you've sneaked off again.'

'I don't care. You do it,' Cynthia said, looking at herself in the mirror. She thrust her hips back and forth, warbling a verse of 'Chattanooga Choo Choo' into the hairbrush, her voice swooping up and down the octave like she was trying to find the right note but couldn't quite decide where to land. Flouncing across the room, coiling her long hair up into a French twist, she added, 'I mean it – this could be my last couple of weeks of freedom if our da puts his foot down . . .'

'Why?'

She sighed. 'You'll find out soon enough. Things will change, squit. And I don't want to be around to see it.'

'Things? Like what?'

'Da's are pretty strong-minded about what they like and what they don't. We've had it easy with Ma. But she'd better watch out as well, with . . . you-know-who . . .'

'No. I don't know.'

Cynthia regarded her with a dead stare. 'You must know by now?'

Marcia shook her head.

'Fred Tattersall?'

'What about Mr Tattersall?'

'Oh, Marcia, you're so annoying,' her sister said wearily.

'Tell me.'

'No.'

'Tell me,' she insisted, getting out of bed and tugging on Cynthia's sleeve as her sister started putting on her gabardine coat. Their mother had once said that if you don't annoy your big sister for no good reason from time to time, she'll think you don't love her any more; so for good measure Marcia asked her again.

'Stop mithering! Some think they're . . . at it.'

'Ma? And Mr Tattersall? But – but . . . Ma's pretty and he's – he's . . .' Marcia, truly shocked, started to cry.

'Oh, stop being such a baby. You're fourteen now but you act like you're three. You forced me to tell you! I don't know. But that's what everyone says. That's what the boys were saying.'

Marcia pressed her fingers to her eye sockets. 'No . . .' she said tearfully, going back to her bed and burrowing under the threadbare eiderdown.

'Marcia, don't hide. Sometimes it's better to face things head on. Work things out for yourself. Now I'm off, so not a flipping word.'

'Tell me where you're going, then,' Marcia said, poking her head out from under the eiderdown.

'I already have! Into town. Stop pestering.' Cynthia started to climb out of the window. 'Cover for me.'

Marcia heard her muttering as she lowered herself onto the privy roof and slid down the drainpipe, falling to earth with a bump. She got up, went over to the window and whispered into the dark: 'You all right?'

Cynthia was brushing herself down. She glanced up and nodded, winked and smiled, giving Marcia the thumbs up. 'Nearly did meself an injury in these heels,' she whispered.

'Cyn! Wait,' Marcia hissed.

'Shush! What?'

'I love you, sis.'

From her small sequinned bag Cynthia took a packet of cigarettes, pulled a bent one out and straightened it, tapped it on the back of her hand and put it in her mouth. Turning away from the wind with a quick smile at Marcia, she struck a match and lit it. Sucking on it, she let the smoke fill her lungs and then expelled it in quivering rings. 'I love you too, squit,' she whispered. 'Now go back to bed!' And she trotted off down the alley in the direction of the tram.

Chapter 11

'Ah, Eunice. I've done liver and onions. Will you come over and have some?'

Eunice paused. It had become a pleasant habit, every Friday night, supper with Fred.

'I'm not sure,' she said quickly. 'I've heard from John. Finally, we have a date for him coming home.'

If Mr Tattersall felt a sadness, he didn't show it. 'That's lovely. I'm pleased for you. Even so, I'll bring you round a shepherd's pie and leave it by the back gate, shall I?'

'Thank you,' she said. All was calm, all was understood.

'Eunice . . . while you're waiting for him to come home – I'll still pay for Cynthia's dancing lessons, shall I?'

She blushed, feeling awkward. She wondered if he believed that John was truly coming back. She wouldn't be surprised if not; after all, it wouldn't be the first time she had got her hopes up. But this time felt different.

'Or I could lend you some money,' he offered.

'No, thank you – you've been so kind already, but John wouldn't hear of it.'

'Very well,' he said, fiddling with his bow tie and rocking back on his heels. 'But a shepherd's pie wouldn't go amiss, Eunice. Please, let me do that for you. Just until he gets back. As I said, I'll leave it at the back gate later, shall I?'

The knock at the front door of the Rogans' house that evening was loud and persistent. Eunice sighed, raised herself out of the chair and went to answer it. Fred obviously hadn't listened. He had said he would leave the pie at the back, so why was he knocking at the front?

When she opened it, she felt her legs begin to collapse underneath her. 'Good God! John! You're two weeks early,' she cried.

The smile puckered around her husband's lips. 'That's a nice greeting. Thought I'd surprise you. Aren't you going to let me in?'

Eunice's heart thumped at her chest. 'Oh my. Come in, of course.'

She wondered if he could tell how horrified she felt at the change in him. The man standing in front of her was a pale shadow of the one she remembered. 'Come in, come in. You'll have the neighbours' curtains twitching.'

His skin was blotchy and yellowing, he looked unsteady on his feet and his shabby uniform was hanging off his stooped, skeletal frame. It looked crumpled, as though he had slept in it. She had imagined this moment so many times – plunging into his arms and feeling him embrace her – but now she felt a strange panic rising in her throat.

He moved towards her, bent forward, looped his arms around her neck, hesitated, then smiled and kissed her on the forehead. His lips felt cracked and sore against hers. She noticed the corners of his mouth were caked in white stuff. She had read about the after-effects of the dysentery, malaria, night terrors . . . but nothing had prepared her for this. Was it the electric shock treatment that had done this to him? The months in hospital had perhaps not been the roaring success he had led her to believe.

He dropped his kit bag and stepped into the narrow hall, then further into the room, looking around.

'I tried to keep it the same,' she said.

He nodded and walked with a limp across the rug. 'Pins still a bit wobbly. Nothing a pan of your scouse won't sort out.'

As she reached out and touched his elbow to guide him over to the chair, she thought ruefully that they were going to need more than a pan of scouse to get him better. He was so different. He seemed so weak. Settling down carefully into the chair with a long exhalation of breath, he ran his fingers along the wooden arms. He had once filled this rocking chair but now there were gaps where his large, granite-hard thighs would previously have bulged out of the sides.

'Come here, queen,' he said urgently. He grasped her arm and pulled her onto his knee, bending to kiss her again, this time diving his tongue between her teeth and twisting around her tongue greedily. He stopped and looked at her face, running a finger under her jawbone, tilting her chin up. 'My lovely wife. You're still so beautiful.'

'Oh, I've aged,' she said, blushing, shifting her weight. He felt bony and sharp and brittle, as though he might crack if she made a sudden movement.

'No, you haven't.' She could feel his ribs through his shirt as he circled her with his arms. 'Kiss me again,' he said.

She raised her face to his. His kisses tasted strange, a little metallic and sour. Tears swelled in her eyes and brimmed over onto her cheeks.

'Hey,' he said tenderly. 'Don't cry.' He kissed her again on her eyelids, his hand squirrelling up her blouse to cup her breast. 'Christ, Eunice. There were times . . . times I thought I'd never hold you again, never see your face.'

Despite the shock of this new version of him, she felt a release in her, she didn't know what – a rush of relief that he was home. So many others from the prisoner of war camps had died.

'Stop,' she said, clutching at the neck of her blouse when he popped the top button out of its hole. Gently, she pressed a flat palm to his chest. 'The girls. They could walk in at any minute. They've only nipped out to do the messages. You haven't forgotten you had two young daughters when you left?'

'Eunice – what a thing to say. I thought of them every moment I was away. But will they remember me? It's been five years.'

'Of course they remember you. I read them all your letters. The ones that arrived. Marcia looks at your picture every night before she goes to bed.'

He nodded. 'Eunice. I need to tell you this now. They say, well, they say . . . The doctors . . . I'm half the man I was. My chest. I nearly died. Yellow fever. And walking. It's difficult. Complete bed rest for now.'

'Nothing a good pan of scouse can't mend,' she

replied, brightly, echoing him. It was a ridiculous thing to say. 'We'll manage.' She slid off his lap, fearful of the weight of her body giving him more pain. Kneeling at his feet, she dropped her head, and to her surprise gave in to another wave of tears and cried silently, clutching his trouser leg and resting her forehead against his knee. 'I'm sorry. I'm not sad. Just overwhelmed. I can't believe you're here. And oh, I do love you. I've missed you like you wouldn't believe.'

He tilted her head up again with a finger under her chin. Leaned down and squirmed his hand inside her blouse and felt the softness of her breast.

'Mam, can I—'

Eunice jerked her head around. 'Marcia!' she cried, flustered.

'Mam?' Marcia asked, confused and shocked, trying to take in the scene playing out in front of her. Her mother was kneeling on the floor with her hair tumbling over her shoulder, when she usually wound it up into a tight bun. And a man was sitting in the rocking chair in their front room. Not a beloved priest. Not her father, surely? He bore no resemblance to the photograph she had kept slipped inside the jacket of her dictionary all these years. None at all. He was angular and thin, and his cheekbones looked as if they would cut you like a knife if you stood too close. The man drew his hand away from behind her mother's neck as quickly as if he had thrust it into the fire. He looked up and smiled.

'Oh, God, love,' said her mother, standing up quickly, smoothing down her skirt, blushing a vivid pink with embarrassment.

The thin man with sallow grey skin, thinning hair, hollowed-out eyes and cheeks, bewilderingly now had a stupid broad smile on his face. Why? It was clear that her mother had been crying. Her eyes were wet and her cheeks were streaked and flushed. Seconds earlier she had been on the floor, kneeling at this man's feet and crying. What had he done to her?

'Mam, are you all right?' she said.

'Of course I am,' replied her mother, wiping her face with her apron and sniffing. 'I'm happy, sweetheart – don't you know who this is?'

The man smiled at Marcia.

'Don't you recognize your daddy from the photographs?'

Marcia rolled her bottom lip between her finger and thumb. She glanced again at the picture on the sideboard of her father sitting on a wall, legs splayed, a white cat in his lap. He had a strong jaw, a magnificent moustache and muscular forearms rippling out from under rolled-up shirtsleeves. She could hardly believe that this man with the black rings under his eyes, skin a strange kind of yellow colour and sharp, angular features was the same broad-shouldered man, with a smile and a shock of black hair, in the photograph that she had so many times fondly kissed goodnight.

'Come here, Cynthia,' he said.

'I'm not Cynthia,' she replied.

'Then you're . . . ?'

'Marcia.'

'My word,' he said, widening his eyes. 'Come here, pet.' He got up out of the chair shakily and stood.

She shrank back, her little shoulders folding in on

themselves, her nose wrinkling. It was instinctive, and she regretted it. But she couldn't help it. He smelled. Actually smelled. Pungent and beery.

'You're a young lady now. When I left, you were still a little girl,' he said. He reached out to touch her but it was as if he was unable to commit to the gesture. Feeling his fingers brush against her arm, she flinched. His hand was clammy. She chewed the plump part of her bottom lip. No matter how hard she looked, this person still bore no resemblance to the photographs. This man was like a ghost. His hands were like a skeleton's hands. Where was her strong, smiling father, with arms like legs of mutton and hands like hams?

'Come here,' he said again. She took a few tentative steps towards him. She didn't know what she should do. She almost felt as if she should curtsy. Her mother pushed her towards him with a firm shove in the small of her back. She could see tufts of hair poking over his collar from his chest. They were grey and wiry, the same colour as his actual hair.

The truth was, she was feeling a little sick, and she could feel her heart pounding and her eyes watering as he kissed her on her cheek. Up close, he smelled even more strongly of tobacco and drink. She felt his bristles scratch and she couldn't help but squirm.

'Don't keep doing that . . .' said her mother.

'You're a slippery thing,' he said. And he guffawed. When he put his hand on her head and ruffled her hair, it felt like a hat of fingers. 'You're not frightened of me, Marcia? Come on, give me a cuddle.'

Roughly, awkwardly, he pulled her to him. What was he doing! She could feel his bones.

'Da?' yelped Cynthia, coming into the room. She squealed and ran over to him, beaming, flinging her arms around him and burying her head in his chest.

'Cyn! Look at you! You're a right bobby dazzler! Marcia doesn't remember me,' he said, laughing and hugging her to him, planting a kiss on her cheek.

'Don't you, Marce?' asked Cynthia, turning to face her, with her arm coiled around her father's waist. 'Maybe she's adopted,' she laughed.

'Of course I remember, I wasn't a baby . . .'

'Look, Marcia . . .' He rolled up his sleeve. 'What does that say?' he asked, pointing at a tattoo on his crepey forearm. 'Eunice, Cynthia . . . and Marcia. Now why would I have these names plastered all over me arm if I wasn't your da? Got you done by a sailor in Cairo, Marcia. Your ma, in France, Cynthia by a snake charmer in Burma. And, wait. Remember?'

He did a strange thing with his tongue. Stuck it out and twisted it into a clover. Cynthia laughed and mimicked him. Marcia had seen Cynthia do this trick before. Her mother laughed and wiped her face again on her apron.

He pinched Marcia's cheek. 'We'll have to teach you, our Marce.'

Marcia stared at her mother. He placed a sweating hand on her shoulder. She worried it would melt through her cotton dress.

'Righty-oh,' he said, releasing her. He winked at Eunice. 'I need to speak to your mother. Can you girls leave us alone? But ladies, it's so good to be home.'

Chapter 12

For a week there was a steady stream of visitors arriving at the house: cousins, pals, John's old workmates from the docks, Eunice's sister Norma in her moth-eaten fur coat puffing on her cigarillos. One former neighbour, who'd lived next door to the Rogans, came all the way from St Helens. Some would stay late, and once or twice men started to arrive at strange times of the night. Eunice was giddy with happiness. 'Come and do your "Moonlight in June" dance for us, Cyn,' she would say when there were people crowding in the parlour. Any excuse. And Cynthia would be climbing on the table, hitching up her skirts. Marcia, he would tell people, was the quiet one. The serious one. Funny little thing, aren't you?

They very soon started to mess the place up, all these people. And Marcia noticed that when they left her father would sink, exhausted, into his chair and press the heels of his hands against his temples and wince.

One Saturday morning he announced he was taking them all to Cooper's in town for tea. Cynthia got dressed up in her flowery tea dress and sandals, Marcia put on her best plaid skirt and blouse, and Eunice wound up her hair into an elegant French coil – but when the time came to leave, they got to the end of the road and John made an excuse about forgetting something; then it was decided it was too late and they would go another day. They never did. The following week he took Cynthia and Marcia to Paddy's Market and they got fish and chips wrapped in newspaper and ate them sitting on a wall outside Sayers', but afterwards he darted into a pub to see a man. There was a lot of 'seeing men', although that too seemed to exhaust him.

'Girls, there's no greater thing than family. Family is what kept me going in Japan, but I have good news,' he announced one evening. He slapped the arm of his chair. 'I've got a job. Start in a month's time, when I've got my strength up and my mind clear. On the guy ropes at Huskisson Dock. Things are looking up. I knew they would.'

Marcia looked at her father stooped over the range. In his singlet, his arms looked sinewy and bony. His ribs were visible over the low curve of the armholes, and they looked like a xylophone set. 'How about I take you out for a treat to celebrate my new job? There's a cafe I know in Bootle. The best apple pie in Liverpool,' he said, banging the table and making Marcia jump.

'I promised Ma I'd do the messages.'

'She's the boss of this place, is she?' He smiled and nudged her. 'Let's take our chance, pet, and nip out and hope she doesn't notice.'

Ten minutes later, they were on the bus. He seemed in a good mood, talking animatedly about how he knew the lady who owned the cafe, how he'd worked there as a lad and she would slip shillings under the table legs for him to find when he was sweeping up.

'There was an opera singer that met our boat in Singapore and she was the double of Kitty, could have been her twin. And I said to myself, first thing I'll do when I get home is have some of Kitty's apple pie.'

'Opera singer? In the jungle?'

'Singapore isn't the jungle. Eh, Marcia, you should have seen this woman,' he said in the next breath, swinging the conversation away. 'She was on the quayside singing "God Save the Queen" and she was wobbling like jelly, every bit of her, she was like a blancmange. Her voice wobbled, her neck, her bosoms, the feather on her turban wobbled.' He grinned. 'All us soldiers were waving and we were trying not to laugh but you couldn't help it. I wish you could have seen her.' He smiled.

She looked at his face. She wanted to ask him about the other things, like the headaches and the chopping down trees and getting sick that Alfie had told her about, even the electric shock treatment, but she didn't dare.

The tram turned off the dock road. She saw her father's smile slide into a troubled frown and his eyes dart from side to side. He no longer recognized these streets. Robinson and Cleaver, with its facade of bombed-out windows and only steel-grey sky behind them, looked less like a building and more like concrete trellising. John clutched the handrail and his knuckles whitened. 'This city has taken some beating,' he said quietly.

'All the kids, we like to play out in the hollas.'

He frowned. 'What's the hollas?'

'The hollows. Where the bombs dropped. Now they've put tinnies up in some parts to keep us out, but kids crawl through the gaps.'

'What's tinnies?'

'The corrugated-iron fences.'

They stared at the bombed-out wastelands as the bus continued its journey past the Victorian memorial and the scaffolded Corn Exchange. 'The lads in Liverpool Lane want it to stay that way. They don't want the hollas boarded up.'

'Is that right?' he said quietly.

They passed the Adelphi and into Mount Pleasant and John announced they had arrived at their stop, so they got off the bus. Standing on the pavement, he looked shocked at the sight of a huge wrecking ball apparatus in front of a whole row of half-demolished houses – too shocked to say anything. It was disconcerting to see just the back walls of the end three-storey building remaining, with something of the inside of the ruined homes visible: fireplaces suspended in mid-air, a clock stopped at twenty past twelve, a crooked painting of a village scene hanging by some miracle on a nail. Remnants of people's lives. As if on cue, the mechanism of the wrecking ball whirred and it pulled back, then smashed against an outhouse. John and Marcia watched as dust rose and they felt their eyes sting.

He took her hand and pulled her away. 'Just around the corner, pet . . . just up here. The best apple pie in the north-west.' But the words withered on his lips. 'Where is it?' he said, looking at the gaping hole in front of him. There was hardly a building standing.

Marcia frowned. He turned to her. 'And you didn't think to tell me this had all gone?'

'I didn't know. I didn't remember.'

They sat silently on the journey back home. 'What a waste of a bloody morning,' he said.

When she arrived back home from school one afternoon her father was sitting in his usual place but somehow there seemed to be even more of his clutter around the room. Overflowing ashtrays; the medicine bottles that he so frequently swigged from when the cough started to strangle him; half-drunk mugs of tea. Soon her mother would be home from another new job at Taveners sweet factory and running around putting things away. Or was he expecting Marcia to do it? There were little papers piled up on the desk. He had the ration book open in front of him on the table and was bent over it, turning the pages and squinting.

'Help me, pet, my eyes are awful,' he said. 'Can you read it?'

She sat down beside him and her eyes flicked through the list: cheese tartlets, silver polish, tea cakes, bananas. He nodded and tapped the pencil against his remaining crooked teeth. 'It doesn't make sense. What about the staples? Why hasn't your ma used these rations?'

She frowned. 'I'm not sure . . .'

She didn't want to be the one to break the news to him that Mr Tattersall provided most of their food. She would leave that to her mother.

He nodded. 'You can call me Da, you know.'

'Yes . . . I . . . mean . . . yes.' She stumbled over her words. She wanted to say 'Da'. She even felt sorry for him that she couldn't. But it felt strange. She just couldn't. Not yet.

'Look, I'm sorry,' he told her. 'I'm neither use nor ornament right now. But when I get better, things will change. I'll take you to New Brighton. And to the circus when it comes to Stanley Park . . . Anyway, your ma tells me you're clever. How about we get you some piano lessons?'

'We haven't got a piano,' she said flatly.

'Oh dear,' he answered, and frowned.

Later, once Eunice had arrived home, she called to them to come to the table where she had laid out haddock pie and pickled eggs. The three of them sat down and twiddled their forks, waiting for Cynthia.

'Is she often late?' asked their father. 'D'you let her come in whenever she pleases?'

'She sometimes stays at the school library to do her homework,' Eunice stuttered.

Library! Marcia could hardly believe what she was hearing. Ten minutes later Cynthia breezed in and, just as she always did, slung her bag on the chair and slipped her shoes off, plonked herself down in the rocking chair and rubbed her feet.

'Where have you been? We're waiting,' their father said. 'Your mother has been slaving away and you can't be bothered to turn up on time?'

'Out,' Cynthia said. 'Not out, out, obviously it's only six o'clock, but me and the girls had a gander and a sticky bun after school at Satterthwaites.'

'Your mother said you were at the library.'

She let out an explosive laugh. 'Me? Library? Why would I go to the library, Da? I was hiding behind the door when God passed out the swot brains,' she said. But he didn't laugh back like she expected him to. Her mother blushed.

He frowned. 'From now on, I want us to eat as a family. Grace before meals. No elbows on the table. When I was in the camp, the thing that kept me going was a routine. I had a routine and it kept us sane, let me tell you. Bless us, O Lord, and these thy gifts which we are about to receive . . .'

They joined hands, bowed their heads and mumbled through the prayer.

'Where'd you get this fish pie from? I didn't see you making it?' he said, as Eunice dished out a large spoonful onto his plate.

'Oh. Fred. Tattersall,' Eunice answered brightly, pushing a forkful of the delicious-smelling pie into her mouth.

'Fred Tattersall?'

'Yes,' she said. It sounded a little forced, thought Marcia. 'You remember Fred? He was kind while you were away.'

John stopped with a forkful of mash midway between plate and mouth and looked at her.

'Fred gives me fish and little cuts of meat and to say thank you I take his bits of washing to the wash-house in return. Do the ironing and whatnot. Stitching and suchlike.' She went on to tell him, in a rush of words, how the war had turned out to be cruel to Mr Tattersall. How his wife had stepped on an incendiary and she was dead three months later. 'Fred didn't even join in with the celebrations on VE Day. He tried his best, hanging out the bunting as the tables had been laid out in the middle of the street, but while the rest of the street ate jelly and jam sarnies and danced, Mr Tattersall sat in a darkened room at the back of the shop and had a good cry. It wasn't much fun for me either. Seeing everyone with their fellows.'

'He did the same on VJ Day,' piped up Cynthia, with her mouth full of potato. 'Said it was the pollen, but everyone knew. He was lonely. Too much for him, wasn't it, Mam?'

John listened to all this with a frown, then grunted. 'So what you're telling me is, you're ironing Fred Tattersall's smalls?'

'Fred Tattersall's smalls are pretty large, aren't they, Ma?' said Cynthia, grinning. But he didn't laugh. 'Come on, Da. That's funny. You have to admit.'

'Marcia, you don't use a spoon for peas,' he said spikily. 'You two girls. Your table manners are a disgrace. Don't talk when you've got food in your mouth. And you put the peas on your fork like this.'

They continued to eat in silence. Marcia wriggled in her chair.

'That's enough for me,' Cynthia said, pushing her plate away. 'And if you think I'm holding my knife and fork like a blooming pen like you're trying to do, I shan't. It's daft.'

He snorted, gestured with the piece of bread he was eating. 'Finish your food. We would have died for just a morsel of this in that blasted camp.'

'I'm not eating those bits of skin. They're revolting.'

'You'll do as you're told, young lady.'

Even her mother looked shocked. Cynthia's eyes widened. Was he joking? She took a mouthful of the remaining food and grimaced. When she stood to leave, he said, 'Wait. What d'you say before you go?'

Cynthia frowned. 'You mean that routine when we were kids? Can I get down from the table?'

'Please may I get down from the table.'

'Yer what?' she said.

'Please *may I* get down from the table. You're perfectly able to get down from the table. Your legs will allow you to do that. But you're not asking me that, are you? You're asking me whether I will allow it, so you say *please may I*, not *can I*. And the answer is no. Not until everyone else has finished. And for pity's sake, knife and fork should go at twenty-five past five, not all over the place like that . . . Anyway, why are you in such a hurry? Where are you going?'

'Oh, Da. Never mind. Shurrup. What a load of piff. Can I, may I. Toodle pip. I'm off.' And she was gone, planting a kiss on her father's head.

He shifted in his seat. 'Eunice. How can you have let her become so bold?'

Eunice lowered her eyes. 'That's just Cynthia, isn't it, Marcia?'

'Never heard of such a thing.' He tutted. 'And Marcia, I nearly tripped over that bundle of washing you left in the hall when I came in last night.'

Don't blame me, she wanted to say, as she stood up to clear the dinner plates. That was because you were squiffy.

But she knew she wasn't as brave as her sister.

103

Chapter 13

The next day started like every other day, with the coughing that Marcia hated so much. It subsided when he reached for the cough medicine but within minutes it rose up again and his eyes bulged and he was off, thumping his chest and stamping his foot.

'What's the matter with him? All this time and that cough is getting worse,' Cynthia hissed to her mother as she bustled around the kitchen.

'He always had a smoker's cough. But he's been ill and it will take time. Terrible things happened to him. Don't worry, it will get better. Don't embarrass him.'

'If he's got smoker's cough, why does he keep smoking?' whispered Marcia. She didn't like it that he would put his cigarette ends down the lav. They would float there, little reminders that there was no corner in this house he hadn't made his own.

'It's his only pleasure,' said her mother.

'That's a lie,' said Cynthia. 'Can't keep his hands off you, Ma.'

'Cynthia Rogan!' said her mother.

'Always grabbing Ma's bum, eh, squit?'

Eunice shushed her. 'For your new job, John. I got it from Paddy's Market. You'll look the business,' she said when he came back in a moment later, bringing all his noise, flinging open the door and stamping on the hearth rug. 'Try it on.'

He put on the shirt over his vest and began to fasten the button collar. Sometimes his fingers were still too weak to do the buttons, but today he moved her hand away and said, 'I can do it, Eunice. I feel good.'

They all hovered, waiting nervously to see what he would do next.

'A man needs to work and thank God, Michaels the foreman has given me a chance. In fact, I feel so good, I got you a present. Come and sit at the table, girls,' he said. He went out to the yard, came back in and placed a large box on the table. 'Open it,' he said, beaming. Marcia, moving around the room clearing up the pots she had used earlier to help her mother make a pea soup, stopped and glanced up at him suspiciously as she approached the table. It was becoming a habit, her father turning up with a present whenever he had been bad-tempered with them. Wilting bunches of flowers, a penny whistle, a box of colouring pencils.

He grinned, eyes shining. 'Go on, open it, pet.'

'What have you got there? Knock-off? You spending your wages before you've even earned them?' said Eunice.

'Pennies it cost,' he said, tapping his nose. Everyone in Liverpool enjoyed the knock-offs – the crates of goodies that would appear out of nowhere to be shared around the pub – Eunice as much as anyone. She was about to say that they still didn't have the money to be splashing out, but the words died on her lips. What was the scratching sound coming from inside the box? Marcia leaned forward and opened the flaps, one and then the other, and gasped. Inside, curled up in the corner, there was a tiny bundle of fur.

'A kitten!' she cried. Her heart melted as she picked it up with care and it mewed. She lifted it to her face and rubbed her cheek against it. 'Is it mine?' she asked, beaming. It was indigo-black, with four white paws and a flash on its head.

'Yours and Cynthia's. A present from me.' She felt its tiny black tail tickle her skin as it wound around her pale wrist.

Eunice started to look at him as if to say he shouldn't have, but a kitten melted all hearts and she found herself smiling as the curious creature crawled inch by inch up Marcia's chest. Marcia could feel its tiny paws prickle against her skin. It nuzzled its nose under her chin as she stroked its fur.

'It's a girl.'

'Thank goodness it's not a tomcat. I'd rather have ten baby kittens than a tomcat prowling around the place and doing its business,' said Eunice.

The kitten mewed softly again. With its little, tiny teeth, it pulled on the collar of Marcia's blouse. They all smiled. Even Cynthia squealed with delight as she came and stood beside Marcia and stroked its button nose.

'What shall we call it?' Marcia asked.

'Hedy,' said Cynthia. 'Like Hedy Lamarr. She has jet-black hair the same colour as this little kitten's fur. I want to be like her, she's beautiful and brainy.'

Her mother tutted. 'Is that so? If you're going to be the next Hedy Lamarr, you'll have to buck up your ideas with the brainy bit, Cyn. That head is full of stuffing.'

Cynthia tutted. 'How about we call her Lucy, then? That's a pretty name. Oh no, wait. Denise's cousin Lucy got knocked up by the leccy man and went into St Jude's mother and baby home and never came out, didn't she? We can't have that. I would feel sad all the time whenever I said the name Lucy.'

'Fluffy,' said Marcia. 'No, I know – let's call her Happy!'

And so that was decided on, and that's how they all felt. All day and all evening, as they rolled cotton reels and dangled bits of string and watched Happy paw and play, as they fussed over and kissed her, it felt like they were beginning to become a family. How long it would last was another thing altogether.

'He got us a kitten,' Marcia said to Alfie later.

'That old trick,' Alfie replied. He was chucking pebbles at an empty house. 'Billy Brennan is still saying your da was in the looney bin.' He dropped the remaining pebbles and sat down beside her on the low wall.

'He's all right.'

'So he's not round the bend?'

Marcia shrugged. She picked up an old tin can, shook it out and began using it to scoop up sand and sort through a nearby pile of rubble. Sometimes she found bits of shrapnel; once she had found a bullet and a piece of metal with German insignia on it.

Sorting calmed her. She ran the palm of her hand over the sand.

'He's fine in the day but he's right gnarly when he comes back from the pub. But it's still me da in there. Somewhere,' she sighed. She craned her neck. 'Alfie. Where does she go all the time? Our Cynthia?'

He sighed. 'Dunno. But some fella takes her and Denise into town in his car.'

She nodded seriously. 'Can you tell her to stop it? It will only wind up me da. His nerves are something shocking. You can't drop a pin without him jumping or getting all worked up. And then he'll just get cross with Ma. Cynthia won't listen to me.'

'She won't listen to anyone, especially not me. Here she comes.'

Cynthia was picking her way over the rubble of the hollas, unsteady in her heels.

'Lemonade!' she cried as she joined them, smiling. They sat with their backs to the wall, taking turns to drink the lemonade through a straw out of a jam jar. 'Delish,' she said. 'Like the nuns made, remember?'

'Aye. It wasn't all bad at the orphanage, was it? Peaceful an' all,' said Marcia. 'Some of the nuns were kind.'

'Really?' said Alfie, slurping the dregs and wiping his mouth on his sleeve.

'Marce, being locked up in the orphanage was bad. Da's temper will pass. You want to watch it, saying you like nuns. Before you know it Ma will send you back to that place for good, and then the nuns will shave all your hair off. And I mean all of it. Down there as well. You thought about that? While I'm being a movie star and Alfie's making his fortune in America, you'll be locked up as a baldy nun praying and eating nettles all day long. Just because Da made you cry a few times.'

'There are some kind ones, Cyn,' said Alfie, as he picked up another stone and randomly threw it at an abandoned mobile tea van without wheels that no one had bothered to move all this time after the war. 'Bullseye,' he cried when the stone hit the middle of a hubcap.

Cynthia snorted. 'What kind of fool wants to be married to Jesus? I want to be married to a real man with a car. You think you'll have a car one day, Alfie?'

'Not 'alf. Rolls-Royce.'

'Mr Labone's got an MG.'

Alfie grinned. 'Has trouble gerrin in an' out of it, though.'

'Who's Mr Labone?' asked Marcia.

Alfie and Cynthia exchanged a glance.

'Mr Labone is going to make me famous.'

Alfie snorted.

'Is it Mr Labone who you go to see at night, Cyn?'

'Might be.'

'Tell her, Cyn. She's your sister.'

'You tell her.'

He sighed. 'Mr Labone plays the trumpet with the Rockets. But he does the bookings for the Alhambra in Birmingham and the Winter Gardens in Blackpool. He's promised to help your Cyn. He was in the army and he had a dance troupe. He's trying to keep it going now he's back in civvy street. Got a finger in every pie, eh, Cyn?'

'He wants me in his troupe. He says I'm *rather lovely*.' Cynthia made a shape in the air with her arms. 'Says I have a great future. Just don't want me da scuppering it. He likes to be in charge, doesn't he, Marce?'

Marcia frowned. It must be nice, she thought, for someone to say you have a great future. She shoved her hands into her skirt pockets.

A hunched figure crossed their line of sight at a distance, scurrying across the hollas. It was unmistakably their father. His lopsided, shuffling gait was more obvious when you saw him from a long way off.

'Uh-oh,' said Cynthia. 'That looks bad. He's been to the pub again when Ma asked him not to. Come on, Marce, let's go. I'll not have him taking it out on Ma and cracking her one.'

'Would he do that?' asked Marcia, shocked.

'Not usually. But if he has a drink inside him, he might. It does that to some fellas.'

The two girls, united in worry, walked along the pavement. Some of the walls they passed were studded with pieces of broken glass that had been cemented along the top edge. They made Marcia think of snarling dogs.

Holding hands, they headed towards the house.

It had probably been a mistake to let the job at the docks grow in importance in the Rogan household with each new day. For weeks there had been discussions about how John should present himself; what he should and shouldn't say about the war and the camps, or his illness; what he should wear. He shouldn't look too smart, as if he couldn't handle the challenges of a dock job – but at the same time he shouldn't look like he hadn't bothered to make an effort. And although Eunice had told him gently over and over again that it might not work out, he was focused on the fact that the fellow had agreed to give him a trial.

He had worried more as each day passed before he was due to start. The missing tooth he now had; the way he found it difficult to move if he got up too quickly from a chair. One morning Marcia had found him practising walking up and down the stairs, then another day hanging from the door jamb trying to do pull-ups; but he was out of breath, and his fingers curled over into a tight fist when he slumped on the chair.

'John?' their mother said nervously, as he returned from the first day. She had made a plum pie to celebrate his return to work. But the delicious smells wafting around the house, and the pretty tablecloth she had laid out with their best glasses and matching cups and saucers, seemed to have been misjudged. The atmosphere when Cynthia and Marcia followed their father in was like a cloud of acrid gas. A shudder ran up Marcia's spine and Cynthia bit the insides of her cheeks. Like their mother, they didn't need a reply; from the way their father was clumping around the kitchen, they all knew straight away something had gone horribly wrong just by the sound of his breathing and furious grunts.

'Stop mithering over me, Eunice,' he snapped, 'and move out the bloody way.'

'But I've made a pie,' she said.

'Leave it,' he said, shoving her aside and elbowing her out of the way sharply so that she winced and clutched her side. 'Stop fussing. Leave me alone. You're as bad as that fool at the docks. Where's me medicine? I've got a thumping headache. I'm going back to the pub.'

He left, glugging from the small brown bottle Eunice handed him.

Cynthia stabbed her fork right into the middle of the pie. 'More for us,' she said. 'Who cares? Miserable sod.'

'Don't start, Cynthia,' hissed their mother. 'This is a disaster. I knew it would be. He shouldn't have tried to go back to work so soon. They'll put a black mark against him for next time. Jobs don't grow on trees, you know. And especially for someone like your dad. He's trying. Makes my heart break. He should at least have the chance of a jacketman job, a decent job where he's respected like the one he had before the blasted war; but they took one look at his file and they won't even let him through the door. It's not his fault he's seen some terrible things. His nerves. You've seen how the slightest thing sets him off.'

'Like when we mention Mr Tattersall,' said Marcia.

'What? Why are you bringing him up? Complete bed rest, that's what Da needs,' Eunice replied tersely.

The next morning, John didn't get up. And it was the same the next morning. And the next. Marcia heard him muttering to Eunice about the foreman, Michaels. *Easy for Michaels to say. How dare he say*

I can't be right in the head, to lose me temper and snap. Just a bit weak in the legs, but a danger to the other dockers! How bloody dare he! After what I've been through!

Her mother seemed to spend the whole time when she wasn't at work running up and down the stairs with a bottle of beer, a cup of milk, a piece of toast or the bottles of cough medicine. She soon began leaving it to Marcia to clear away the ashtrays and beer bottles because she was too exhausted after being up all night. Cynthia, on the other hand, quickly perfected the art of avoiding their father. Every time he walked into a room she left breezily, with an excuse about the messages or the washhouse or school.

Marcia didn't know what to think. She was worried about what had happened to her lovely da, and she wanted the old one back. Mostly she just nuzzled her face into Happy. And the job at the docks was never talked about again.

Chapter 14

Cynthia sat in front of the mirror and blotted her lips. She traced the outline of her brows. How she wished she had high cheekbones instead of her round face with its soft jawline. Anything that would help her escape from this place.

Perhaps she should stop reading her *Picture Post*. Their version of beauty was a girl who should not seem as though she has tried – she should have a flat bridge to her nose and a full mouth. That's what she had read in Audrey Patterson's column. At least she had a full mouth, she thought, pouting at her reflection. But her hair. The untamed curls. She couldn't do anything about the shape of her nose, but her *hair*.

Standing, she started practising her kicks, looking at her reflection. *One, two, three*, and step together *kick, one, two—*

'You woke me up,' said her father, standing in the doorway, smoking, his braces looped around his thighs.

'And you gave me a fright,' Cynthia said, hands on her hips.

'What you doing?'

'Nothing.'

He yawned and rubbed his eyes, then came in and

sat on the end of the bed. 'Now, Cynthia, I've been thinking. The dancing, there's no prospects. But I've got good news. Bleakley's insurance offices are looking for a girl. If you won't do the factory, I thought maybe the insurance office?' She looked horrified. 'Why not? It was good enough for me,' he said sharply.

'I just don't want to. Can't you give me a chance with the dancing?'

'Cynthia, love, are you any good? I mean, it's fine jumping on the tables and singing for my pals . . .'

She screwed up her eyes and pushed her fists against her temples. 'I can be good.'

'I don't know. Some people are built for certain things and some people are not. Sometimes one thing that's easy for some folks is like knitting fog for another. Always remember, I only want the best for you,' he grunted.

The best? She wanted to strangle him. This man, she thought, raging round the kitchen swigging at cough medicine and telling us all what we should do with our lives. But she didn't say it. At least not today.

Meanwhile Marcia, left alone outside, sighed and pulled a handful of the daisies that had struggled up between the paving stones. She pushed her fingernail through the stalks and threaded one flower through the other. After laying the daisy chain on the step she pulled her faded paisley skirt over her knees and picked up a stick, poking it into the jam jar of water sitting at her feet that she had just fetched from the kitchen. The jar was full of pink petals she had just plucked from the wild rose clambering up against the end wall of the terrace. Strange how in this city, so full of grime and still bearing its scars after the war, you could still find beauty in the dankest and sootiest of places.

The sodden petals soon began to fade and lose their colour as they turned into a brown mush. She bent her neck to sniff. Not quite the heady sweet smell of their mother's Coty L'Aimant perfume, which Cynthia would borrow and liberally dab all over herself, but it was pungent and sweet. She stirred it with the twig.

'Cynthia,' she called, craning her neck back towards the inside of the house. 'I'm making perfume. And I've made a crown of daisies. I can make you a necklace if you want!'

Cynthia stomped out and glared at her. She grabbed the jar, raised it to her nose. 'Eugh. Smells horrible.'

'No, it doesn't,' Marcia replied, snatching it back. She dipped her finger in it, dabbed moisture on the inside of her wrist and held it towards her sister's nose. 'It smells lovely.' She stuck her wrist out further and said, 'Sniff.'

Cynthia smelled her arm and grimaced. 'Flamin' 'eck,' she sighed. She picked up the jar and tipped the water and petals out into the gutter.

'What did you do that for?' Marcia cried, watching it trickle down the hill and dribble away down the grate.

'Because it stinks.'

'But I wanted us to play . . .' she said, feeling a lump rise in her throat.

'Forget it. It's babyish.'

Marcia looked crestfallen. There was nothing she liked more than spending an hour with Cynthia weaving flowers in her hair and wrapping herself up in a bit of old net curtain, pretending she was Princess Elizabeth.

'Please . . .'

'Marcia, no.'

'. . . Well, I don't want to play with you either. You've become *obsessed*, Cyn,' Marcia said, rolling the word around in her mouth. 'Obsessed with the hit parade and boys, and I've seen you with Ma's lippy and boot polish on your eyelashes and doing your silly dance. The jitterbug thingy. Parading in front of the parlour window trying to get the boys to notice you when you're wiggling your hips. No wonder Da gets cross with you. Wasting your life.'

'Don't you start. It's not a silly dance. It's going to get me out of here. Da's doing his best to ruin it, but I won't let him.'

'He only wants the best for you. For you not to be a floozy.'

Cynthia humphed. 'God, Marce, only someone with a heart as good as yours could defend him. I do love him, but he's different since he's come back and it's getting worse . . . Still, the old bugger won't get the better of me, squit.'

Chapter 15

Henry Cherry, who was now nearly six feet tall and floppy-haired but with the same earnest look in his blue eyes, had applied for a job he had seen advertised in the *Echo*. He hadn't expected for a moment that he would be successful and assumed that at the interview he would encounter a roomful of better qualified, more confident applicants.

As it turned out, there was only one other: a plump boy wearing trousers at least four inches shy of his worn and unpolished shoes. That boy's interview lasted no more than five minutes and then Henry was ushered in. A man invited him to sit down and while smoking a Woodbine cigarette, scanned his application, occasionally glancing up at Henry in his neat suit and smoothed-down fair hair, with only a passing interest. Eventually he stubbed out his cigarette, wrote something in an elaborate hand at the bottom of the form and, without looking up, said: 'Start Monday, top floor, Cunard Building. Well done.'

The following week, Henry arrived promptly at eight o'clock and took the impressive lift to the top floor. The main building itself seemed more like a grand hotel than somewhere that would host the temporary office of the Liverpool Public Assistance committee. It was almost a relief that most of the top floor was being used for storage, with cardboard boxes and bound bundles of papers lining the narrow, empty corridors.

Henry's office was in a front corner of the building, with a view of the river to the west and another looking across the front of the Royal Liver Building to the north. He was sharing the space with two others: a nervous man who seemed much older but was probably no more than mid-twenties, and a stern, elegantly dressed lady called Betty, who had shown him in and directed him to his small desk.

'Mr Higgins will be up to see you shortly. Make yourself at home,' she said, returning to her larger desk stacked with a mountain of files.

The truth was, Henry had nothing to make himself at home with. He carried a small briefcase that contained his fountain pen and a round of egg sandwiches. He took out the pen but thought better of the sandwiches. Too early for lunch, he decided.

A pile of papers slipped off the nervous man's desk and onto the floor. He slapped his forehead in frustration.

Henry took the opportunity to say something. 'Hello, I'm Henry.'

The man shot him a suspicious glance, as if he thought Henry was there to spy on them. 'I'm Dudley. I'm busy,' he replied.

There was an air of confusion and panic about the whole place, thought Henry. Betty would ask Dudley if he'd seen something or other, and Dudley would reply that he hadn't and then enquire whether Betty had seen a bundle he urgently needed. At one point another man quickly looked in to ask if either of them had found his box of files, to which Betty and Dudley replied in unison with an emphatic, 'No.' Henry heard the man swearing loudly as he marched off down the corridor. He looked at his watch. It was only twenty past eight.

Five minutes later, a small man arrived. He wore half-moon spectacles and his bald head was beaded with sweat. He threw a file of papers down on Henry's desk.

'Go through those, sort by order of need, then bring them down to me. I'm Mr Higgins, by the way. I'm your boss.' Henry, who had risen from his chair to greet him, offered his hand, a gesture which Mr Higgins clearly thought ridiculous and so ignored. 'How neat is your handwriting?' he asked, looking Henry up and down.

'Not bad, sir.' In fact, Henry was rather proud of his longhand skills.

Mr Higgins made a grunt of approval, then turned to Dudley.

'I need those informal reports processed by lunch-time, Mr Fortune, and Betty, bring me down a cup of tea when you've a moment.' He turned to go.

'I don't have a moment, Mr Higgins,' Betty protested.

Mr Higgins stopped in the doorway. 'No?' He thought for a moment. 'Bring me one anyway.' He looked at Henry. 'And you – when you bring those files down, grab a writing pad. We have work to do.'

It felt to Henry as if he'd already had a promotion. He smiled sheepishly at Dudley and Betty, who both looked back at him with undisguised loathing.

It was the second report he looked at that bore the name Marcia Rogan. He felt a tingle on the back of his neck. He was looking at the file of a girl he had known for half his life. He felt guilty, but at the same time irresistibly drawn to reading it.

Names and phrases swirled in front of his eyes: *child neglect, Father Donnelly, Burma, prisoner of war camp, electric shock treatment, possible Bromoform addiction. Orphan of the living.*

Chapter 16

March 1947

'It seems things haven't turned out so badly after all,' said Eunice, smiling, sleeves up, kneading dough and sprinkling flour on the kitchen table.

Autumn had unfolded into Christmas, and Christmas had unfurled into New Year. After a cold winter, colder than anyone could remember, they had needed some joy in their lives; there hadn't been much of it in the Rogan household recently. The girls had spent a lot of time tiptoeing around their father – and now tiptoeing around their mother, too – but at Christmas there had been a kind of truce. There had been a turkey and a Christmas pudding with a sixpence, stockings with oranges and a hairband each, and a party at Auntie Norma's, where John had been persuaded to do his bird impressions again and they had all done the hokey-cokey and the conga up and down the stairs and through the house.

Lately, though, there hadn't been much money for anything. It felt as if Cynthia had been out of the house every evening, and the fact that her father couldn't seem to stop her was driving him nearly demented. But spring had arrived, and the warmer weather brought hope and news about work for John.

Cynthia, pulling out a drawer searching for a rolling pin for her mother, stopped and turned around, folding her arms to await whatever Eunice was going to say next. Eunice, for the first time in weeks, had been humming that morning as she went about her chores. Marcia, rinsing the pots, dropped the rag with a splash into the sink.

'Da's finally got a job.'

Marcia clapped her hands together and kissed Happy.

'What job?' said Cynthia suspiciously.

'Cocky watchman. At Stanley Park. Mr Naylor is retiring.'

Cynthia spluttered. 'Cocky watchman? They're usually old fellas!'

'It's a job.'

'And him with all his airs and graces? Always going on about the army, like he's something special? And now he's going to be chasing kiddies stealing apples at the park! It's embarrassing. Everyone will think we're poor.'

'We are poor.'

'I know, but I don't like it. He'll only get worse.'

Marcia stayed silent. It was embarrassing for all of them; their father huddled around a brazier in winter, sweeping up leaves, and shouting at kids in summer for scrumping and throwing stones at the ducks.

And yet, despite this, after John had spent a few weeks in the job, even Cynthia had got used to the idea. And contrary to expectations, their father seemed more content and the house a good deal calmer.

A month passed, and then another, and a routine set in for the Rogan family. Each morning after John left for the park, they tidied around after him, and each evening a plate of bread and margarine was waiting for him on the table. It was decided that Marcia should be the one to take him a bowl of stew or sandwiches to the park at lunchtime. She hated doing it, though, and having to leave school with everyone pestering to know where she was going every day. Especially when they all knew.

Meanwhile, Cynthia managed to slip out of the house unnoticed to her new job at the pie factory now that she had given up on school. No one had been able to stop her the day she had waltzed out, skirts hitched up to just below her knees and socks rolled down, and chucked her books into the canal, declaring, 'Good riddance to bad rubbish.' Marcia continued studying, chores were done, and all the time they were getting used to their new way of life with their unpredictable father. Sometimes it still went to pot, like when he banged a shoe on the table for them to stop talking, or made Cynthia wash her red lipstick off, or told his wife that she must stop going to Fred Tattersall's. Usually, though, once he had a drink inside him, his bitterness drained away. Marcia did worry that it was a slippery slope, and wondered why her mother never questioned the appearance of empty bottles in surprising places overnight. Sometimes John became maudlin, and then he would ask Cynthia to dance her 'Moonlight on Joo-hoon' and Marcia to recite lines from the 'Rime of the Ancient Mariner'. And he would kiss Eunice on the mouth in front of them and start calling her Nissy again, which they thought was always a step too far.

They muddled along for a while in this way – but they should have known it wouldn't last.

'Good grief, your father will have a heart attack if he sees you like that. You're riding bareback on a kitchen knife going outside dressed like that, young lady!' said a horrified Eunice as Cynthia stood chewing gum in the doorway.

For months, Cynthia had carried on slipping out unnoticed, but Marcia had known it would only be a matter of time before that ended. Now Eunice's face was etched with lines of anxiety. Cynthia was wearing a pair of silver high heels and had pin-curled her hair. She wore a dress that outlined her pillowy breasts, with a pinched waist and a hemline that revealed more than a glimpse of knee. The result was just as she intended: the hourglass figure she had seen in Hollywood films.

'Keep your barnet on, Ma. I'll be back later.' Cynthia turned and headed out the door.

'My God, are you wearing stockings?' her mother called after her.

'That's right, Ma. Stockings. I didn't have time to draw a line up the back of me leg.'

'What will I say to your da if he asks where you are?'

'Tell him I've gone to Girl Guides if you want.'

'Girl Guides!' Eunice spluttered.

But Cynthia was gone. Eunice began furiously straightening the table settings, lining up knives and forks and stepping back to squint at them, and then straightening them up again before banging a fork down in a frustration.

'That girl will be the death of me,' she muttered. 'Every woman has one challenge in life. She's either married to it or gives birth to it, and I'm the poor wretch with both. It'll set your da off again if he knows she's out gallivanting. Do you know where she goes, Marcia?'

Marcia just shrugged.

'Where's our Cyn?' John said when he arrived back from the pub. 'Good news! I've got a new job for her if she wants it. Met a fellow in the Boot who needs a girl at his shipping office doing the filing. There's a future in it. Not like the pie factory. Might stop her ideas with this dancing nonsense.' He seemed in a good mood.

'She's out,' faltered Eunice.

'Out? Where?'

'Girl Guides,' said her mother quickly. Marcia's eyes widened. This was even more stupid than the library excuse. Her mother looked as if she regretted it as soon as the words left her mouth. It was a ridiculous thing to say. 'Don't wait up. You'll see her in the morning. You look exhausted.'

He grunted. 'Aye. Stevie O'Shea turned up at the Boot. Flashing his cash. Whisky chasers all round. Me head hurts. Where's me medicine?' He was slurring his words as he slumped into the chair. He never made it up the stairs and soon he was snoring loudly, mouth open and head lolling to one side, interrupted only by occasional stirring and belching.

At first, John thought he was dreaming when he woke up two hours later and saw Lana Turner standing in the doorway. He rubbed his eyes. 'Eh?' he asked, confused.

Cynthia, sequinned purse in one hand and shoes in the other, was moving gingerly on tiptoe, wincing with each step, trying to avoid the floorboards creaking.

'Who's that? Cynthia? I thought it was . . . am I dreaming? Is that you? Good God!' he said.

Cynthia had left for Girl Guides a brunette and – if his eyes were not playing tricks on him and it wasn't Lana Turner after all – his bold-as-brass daughter had returned a peroxide platinum blonde.

'D'you like it, Pa?' she asked, one hand on her hip, the other patting her head.

'What in God's name possessed you to do that to your hair? You look like a flaming hussy!'

Her nostrils flared angrily. 'I don't care what you think I look like. It's my life and I love it.'

His eyeballs were shot red with rage.

'What's happened? When I left, you were the sweetest little thing. Used to sit in my lap and play steeples and cats' cradles with me.'

'When you left? That was years ago, and you never came back for a good long time.'

'And how could I help that? If you knew what I'd seen . . . what I'd—'

127

'Oh, stop going on about the flaming camp. Blah blah, I had it so hard, nearly starved, wonder I didn't die, I'm sick of it!'

He slammed his hand on the table and stood up, knocking the chair across the room. 'No daughter of mine speaks to me like that,' he snarled.

'What? You just moan all the flippin' time. You've never even told us anything about what happened in your precious jungle. And guess what – I don't care. It's old news, fella. Anyway, I'm not one of your kids at the park. You can't shove me around like you do wi' Ma. I can please myself how I do me hair. Especially now I've left school,' she said, clenching her jaw.

'How dare you!' he cried, leaning forward, chin thrust out in fury. 'How bloody dare you? You're not too old for me to—'

'You wouldn't dare,' Cynthia said.

His eyes bulged from their sockets. His hands clenched the arms of the chair, as if doing so was the only way he could hold himself back from leaping up and striking her. 'Show me some respect, lass!'

'Respect! Why don't you show some respect to me ma? Drunk all the time!'

'You! I've seen you, young lady. I've seen you, you and your ways,' he spluttered. 'It's going to stop. No more dancing. No more Rialto. No more Grafton. I'm putting a lock on your door and you're staying in your room from now on. Tiller Girl! Movie star. My bloody eye! You can forget gallivanting around Liverpool from now on! You're ruining your life before it's even started.'

'You can't stop me!' she said, grabbing the poker from the range and stabbing it in the air.

'I can and I will. No more running around town like a harlot. You'll do as you're told from now on! These people you're mixing with, up to all sorts of filth, I bet. Put that thing down!'

She placed her hand on a jutting hip and stabbed the air again with the poker. 'Filth? Well, you might think sex is a disgusting thing. But I think it's God's greatest design.'

'Cynthia Rogan!' he spluttered. 'You wash your mouth out with soap! And put those ridiculous ideas out of your head. You! Go on the stage! What's wrong with office work?'

'Stuck behind a desk! No thanks. I would hate it! Sod you. Stop worrying about the colour of me hair and have another bloody drink!'

He plunged forward to grasp her by the arm and pull her back, furious at her sneering tone, but his legs weren't strong enough. As he was staggering and wobbling towards the door with no objective there was an awful sound from under his feet, a hideous squeal.

'What have you done?' Cynthia cried. She dropped the poker and it slid across the kitchen floor. 'You trod on Happy! She's not moving!'

He looked down in horror, moved away quickly. Cynthia gawped at the limp bundle of fur and then turned away with a piercing cry.

'I can't look at her. You're a bloody brute. You've killed her, you drunken sod! Why don't you leave us alone? I wish you'd never come back,' she wailed.

'Can't bloody see anything with my eyes. It's too dark in here. It's useless,' he muttered, staggering again and thrusting out an arm to steady himself. As he fell against the dresser, the oil lamp tumbled and smashed to the floor. 'Now look what you've made me do!' he moaned. 'Everything is useless. I'm useless . . .'

'You've killed Happy?' a small voice said. Marcia had appeared, eyes round with fright, in the doorway. 'Why did you kill Happy?'

'I didn't do it deliberately! You idiot girl!' he snapped.

'I wish you were dead,' Cynthia spat at him, running to Marcia and hugging her.

'That makes two of us,' he shouted, sweeping everything off the table in a wild temper.

Both girls watched him in horror. They didn't know what to think. Was it his brain? Was it the 'red mist' they had heard him taking about to Eunice through the bedroom wall? Would they ever come back from this?

He lurched at Cynthia again, grappling with her for no obvious reason, tussling on the rug which slipped from under them. It was only when Eunice appeared at the door, flew at them and tried to separate them that they both paused for breath. Panting, they struggled to their feet, glaring at each other with the same wild, staring eyes.

'What's happened?' Eunice cried. She turned her head at the sound of a small mewing and gently picked up Happy from the hearth, stroking her little nose.

John's face crumpled into sadness. 'Happy's alive! I thought I'd killed her . . . Cynthia, Cynthia, I didn't mean . . . I didn't . . . Cynthia, dear? I'm sorry,' he whined. 'Can we forget what just happened? I . . . I . . . I'm sorry . . . I thought I'd . . .' This mawkish descent into self-pity and regret was somehow more awful to see than him raging around the kitchen, bumping into things and yelling.

Eunice bent to pick up pieces of glass from the broken oil lamp. 'You must have just stepped on her tail. Young cats do that sometimes. Play dead. Now, everyone, calm down. We're all here, aren't we? All together. The Rogans. We love each other. So can we stop fighting? Can we?'

Later, John sat sobbing on the end of the bed, plucking at the eiderdown. It was the drink that did it, he told Eunice. He didn't know what came over him. Would she hate him forever? Drinking always seemed to set off the terrible visions that still flashed in his head every waking moment: visions of the flies and the huts crawling with insects, the heat and stench of the jungle. The desperation, the broken men, the endless hacking away at the earth and the sharp bamboo that could cut you in two; a situation in which the only real hope was for death.

'It's the din, Eunice,' he said. 'In me head.'

But it was Cynthia who finished him off.

Chapter 17

Alfie was dragging an old tyre across the hollas. His face was screwed up with concentration and the effort of pulling the rope. As he stopped to wipe his brow he saw Marcia scurrying along the pavement, head down.

'Oi, Marce, grab this rope,' he called. 'Come and help. Come on.'

Marcia stopped, tipped her head to one side and then walked over and took the other end. They pulled at it together, dragging it over the rubble. It wasn't easy negotiating the potholes and clumps of bricks, and she was soon out of breath.

'What we doing with it?' she asked, panting.

'Taking it over there.'

'Why?'

'Fancied a change. I like sitting on it and this way I'll have a better view of the tram.'

She nodded seriously. It seemed a huge effort for not much reason, but when they both collapsed, exhausted, and sat with their bottoms in the hole and their legs dangling over the side, it felt like some kind of achievement.

'What now?' she asked.

'Dunno,' he replied. 'How's your da?'

'I don't want to talk about it.'

'Why?'

She paused and bit her lip. 'His temper, Alfie. Sometimes he's kind enough, but then other times . . . A terrible thing happened.'

'What?'

'I said I can't talk about it.'

'He wallop you?' She shook her head. 'He wallop your ma?'

'No, Alfie. He didn't wallop anyone. He's not like that. He's kind.'

'What, then?'

She sighed. 'He nearly killed Happy.'

'Who's Happy?'

'Our kitten. Remember I told you he got us a kitten? We thought he'd killed it.'

Alfie's eyes were like saucers. 'How? He strangle it or summat?'

'No.'

'Drowned it? Mrs Hallett's cat had six kittens and she drowned the lot of them in a bucket. Every one.'

Marcia fiddled with her bootlace. 'Trod on her tail. By mistake.'

'So not deliberate?'

'No, but . . .'

'And just trod on her tail? That's all?'

'The noise. She squealed.'

Alfie began to laugh. 'That isn't so bad.' She looked at him and frowned. 'Especially with all his troubles. Me da says he can't work at anything except cocky watchman and that's not someone like your da. He had a decent job before the war. Says he was a good fella. Kind. Used to give everyone tips, always saw his round at the pub, and took the young 'uns out and organize the charabanc to Southport.'

'Did he?' she said, surprised.

'Aye.'

'I remember he always used to do all these tricks. Bounce a penny into a glass, list all the kings and queens . . . and he had a grand voice. He could sing. Oh, and light a match with his thumb, and do the sand dance. I remember his bird calls. Sparrow, finch, macaw. He could do an impression of our pigeon, Lawson the Great, and you'd think it were real.'

Alfie leapt to his feet, stood on one leg and hopped backward and forward. 'I can do the sand dance,' he said.

Marcia smiled. He grinned back.

'I could take you fishing if it'd make you feel better.'

'What about our Cyn?' she said, shocked.

'What about her?' He shrugged. 'Or you can sit on me tyre? Sit on it any day of the week. You don't even need to ask me.'

'It's just a stupid tyre. You're acting like that tyre makes you king of the world.'

'Aye. And you'll be the queen of the world if you want, eh, Marce?'

His eyes twinkled. And despite everything, she smiled.

Chapter 18

Marcia came into the passage from the back yard. The small cellar door would be open. She was supposed to be doing the coal but instead she went through the little hatch in the passage and down the steps. The terrace was built on a hill, and you could just about move around in the empty space under these houses if you crouched.

The cellar was a fairly useless space and they didn't have anything much to put in it: just small bits and pieces, an old chair leg, a rotten bit of rug. But it was her secret place. She crawled deeper inside, to the point where there was only a foot above her head. She could feel rubble under her feet and all around her was dank, but there were two bricks with airholes that allowed fingers of bright light to shine in. When she came here, she would listen to the voices of the grown-ups talking in the parlour above and take comfort from them. Muffled, it was difficult to make out what they were saying; just bursts of conversation, laughter, occasionally someone's name. But today, as she strained to hear at first and then acclimatized to the cloaked voices, the conversation was worryingly serious.

'They think I'm a stranger, Eunice.'

'You need to give them time. Kittens won't do it. I told you that was a bad idea. And you're not well. Perhaps we should tell them.'

'Cynthia is the devil but at least she's got spirit. Marcia is so quiet, she's peculiar. She won't talk to me.'

Marcia's palms prickled.

'She's shy. She doesn't know about men. They don't have brothers, they only had girls at school. She was so excited about you coming back. Both of them were. She looked at that photograph every day for years.'

'I'm sorry I'm such a disappointment.'

'No, you're not. You're just not well.'

'But it was a hard thing for me to hear. My own daughter saying she wished I had never come home! Cynthia's wild, Eunice.'

'In that case, she won't feel too badly when we send her away.'

'Aye. She'll be celebrating. What about Marcia, though?'

'Perhaps we should see how Cynthia gets on before we decide what to do about Marcia. The Corpy has said it's for the best. Perhaps they're right.'

Later, Marcia lay in bed, feeling the warmth of her sister beside her. 'Cyn, I heard them talking. About sending you away. And what to do about me. But you won't leave me, will you?'

'Stop worrying about things, Marce. I love you,' she replied, squeezing her hand.

Marcia shut her eyes. Her big sister – who knew when she was fighting tears, even in the dark – who had always been there for her, had not really answered her question.

Burrowing her head under the greying lace curtains the next morning, Marcia pressed her face up against the window. With a hand shading her eyes she squinted into the sunlight and watched the boys kicking a ball across the street. Two women, arms folded over their chests, were talking on their front doorsteps. A postman delivered a parcel.

Normal people, doing normal things. Not always worrying that their families might be torn apart at any moment. Her warm breath misted the pane of glass and she pulled the cuff of her shirt over the heel of her hand and wiped it clean.

'Marcia!' called her mother from downstairs. 'Have you any idea where Cynthia is?'

Marcia stepped out of the bedroom and shrugged. 'She left before I got up.'

Her mother looked a little pale. She was holding a crumpled piece of paper in her hand, which appeared to be trembling. She thrust it towards Marcia. 'Stupid girl,' she said.

Marcia scanned the hastily written note.

Dear Ma – I'm sick of Da moping around the place. I can't take it any more. I'll not let him ruin my life. Don't try and find me.

In the kitchen, Eunice paced anxiously. 'What if something's happened to her? What if she's tied rocks to her feet and jumped into the Mersey?'

John looked up from his *Echo*. 'Don't talk nonsense. She's run off because she wants to please herself and she doesn't like being told what to do. It's your fault. You've only got yourself to blame. Too many years treating them soft.'

Marcia saw her mother's back stiffen. 'I did my best,' she said in a small voice.

'Clearly your best wasn't good enough,' he muttered.

'Shall we call the police?'

'The police! Don't talk daft. Why would you go to the police? She'll be back. Mark my words,' he said, getting up and going into the yard.

'Marcia, go and ask Denise where Cynthia is. Go on, quickly.'

But Marcia stood there, twisting the end of her shawl. 'Ma. She goes places at night,' she said quietly. Her eyes flicked to the floor, then back up to her mother.

'Goes places? Where?'

Marcia shrugged. It felt as if she had lost the power of speech.

'Pretty obvious to me she's up to something. She always seems to have money. Where did she get money to dye her hair from?' said their father, coming back in from coughing his guts up in the lavvy, wiping his red face.

Eunice looked bewildered. Marcia's bottom lip trembled.

'You know where Cynthia is going to end up, don't you?' he said. 'The home. The home for errant girls.'

'It's not called that any more. Stupid, stupid girl.

As if this running away will help matters! Go and ask Denise where she is, Marcia. Now.' Eunice turned to John after Marcia had left. 'Maybe it is my fault? I don't know. I was always tired. I had two jobs,' she said meekly and sadly.

He shrugged, humphed and lit another cigarette.

A bored Denise, with rollers in her hair and cold cream all over her face, answered the door to Marcia.

'Have you seen our Cynthia?' Marcia asked.

Denise shrugged. 'Why?'

'She's upped and left.'

Denise raised a pencilled eyebrow. 'Done a flit? You worried she's dead or something? She's not. She'll be fine. She's with Mr Labone, most probably.'

'Mr Labone?'

'All I know is, she's been spending time with Wally Labone lately. She has ambition that would strip paint, your Cynthia.'

'She won't tell me much about who he is.'

'Everyone knows Mr Labone. Always hanging out at the Rialto, eyeing the girls for his shows. He's an old fella.'

Marcia frowned. Bad enough that Cynthia had been sneaking off out – but sneaking off to see a man three times her age, one who was promising her the world, would only make things worse.

'But I wouldn't worry about your Cyn. Even though he gives her money.'

'Money? What for?'

'She won't tell me. So she's not going to tell you, either. Where d'you think she gets the dosh for those new shoes and lippy from? And the Almay powder. That's expensive, that is.'

Marcia shrugged. She thought of her sister dipping the feathery puff into her pot of loose powder, and the scented cloud that filled the room when she shook it.

'She can look after herself,' added Denise, coolly examining her painted nails.

'Please tell me, Denise. Where does he live?'

Denise sighed. 'I'll tell you where you can find him, but you didn't hear it from me. In town. In a room above the pawn shop next door to Rushworth's. He has an office. He's a theatrical agent. Like I say, he likes girls like your Cyn. But don't go rubbing him up the wrong way or you won't get a thing out of him.'

'Ma's going out of her mind with worry.'

'I don't know why your Cyn can't please herself.'

'It's just me da,' Marcia said dolefully.

She went back to the house. Leaning back against the Belfast sink, she narrowed her eyes, opened her mouth to speak, then turned away. She knew not to say what Denise had told her. That would only cause more fireworks. Instead, she chewed her lip, ran her hands under the gushing tap and announced that Denise had no idea where Cynthia was.

She found Alfie on his way back from fishing, carrying a bucket of wriggling worms. News of Cynthia's disappearance had spread quickly. 'Is she come home yet?' he asked.

'No,' replied Marcia. 'Maybe she's gone off to find her fortune with a show. A dance troupe. Like running away to the circus?'

'What dance troupe? Don't be daft. Cynthia's useless.'

'She can nearly do the splits now. The side ones, not the front ones.'

'Yes, well . . .' Alfie smirked, mischievously.

Marcia glanced nervously over his shoulder. She knew it would be such a betrayal to say anything more, but she was also worried. She imagined her sister dead and dumped into a bin with just her legs and those high heels sticking out. Pushing down the thought, she decided to do something about it.

She took the bus into town. Standing outside Rushworth's, she craned her neck to look up at the windows above the pawn shop next door. Two storeys up, she saw the words WALLY LABONE THEATRICAL AGENCY in a graceful arc of gold letters on the glass of an upstairs window. She pushed the door open and went up a dimly lit, winding staircase that felt spongy beneath her feet. The place smelled of something musky she didn't recognize; something between onions and damp. The air felt heavy. And then, as she went further, a new smell – of dog? Or was it cat? Some kind of animal. At the top of the staircase, three flights up, there was a stippled glass-panelled door. Through the panel, Marcia could see the shape of a figure sitting at a desk.

'Come in, my dear,' said a man's voice. 'Give it a good shove.'

Marcia leaned on the door heavily. It flew open, and a bell tinkled as she stumbled into the tiny smoke-filled room. She was met by a large, dribbling golden retriever jumping up at her, pawing and poking his nose up her skirt. The man, wearing a dogtooth suit and a garishly striped, shiny red and blue tie, was wedged into a high-backed leather chair. He sat behind a desk on which there were three dusty black telephones, piles of photographs and mountains of printed flyers. Lining the windowsill were a few empty bottles and stacks of scripts and playbills.

'Monty is harmless,' he said, stretching out a large, flat liver-spotted hand. 'Pleasure to meet you, sunshine. Sit down.' He winked at her and grabbed her hand, almost crushing her knuckles. She lowered herself into the moth-eaten red velvet chair. Mr Labone took out a frayed and crumpled handkerchief from his breast pocket and blew his florid nose so loudly, it sounded like someone playing a trombone. He crumpled the handkerchief again, energetically wiped his forehead with it, leaned back his chair with his hands behind his head and grinned expansively. 'You're young! Are you my twelve o'clock?'

Marcia waited as he rooted amongst the debris scattered over his desk and produced the stub of a cigar. He examined it and shook his head as if it had let him down badly, then chucked it over his shoulder in the approximate direction of the waste-paper basket. He leaned forward in his chair, gave a dry cough, and cleared his throat.

'No, Mr Labone. My sister, Cynthia Rogan, has run away from home,' she said.

He didn't flinch. Instead, he took out a fresh cigar from a wooden box and rolled it between his fingers, put it under his nose and breathed in the smell of it.

'She's been away for two days,' Marcia went on.

'I thought you might know where she's been. It's just that my mam is going out of her mind. My dad is going to be so angry with her. I'm frightened of what he might do when she comes back.'

Tapping the cigar, Wally Labone put it into his mouth, lit a match and sucked on it.

'Slow down. Slow down. Run away?'

'Yes. We haven't seen her for two days. She left a note, saying she's not coming back.'

'Love, I don't know what this has got to do with me.'

'She said that you were going to change her life – so I thought . . .' Marcia's words tailed off.

'Did she now? If I had a penny for every girl who thought I would change her life . . . well, they all think I'm going to make them a star, so I'd be a rich man, love. I never make promises, but it doesn't stop them dreaming.'

'So you don't know where she is? My da wants her to stop dancing. He doesn't like it. It puts him in a rage.'

'No. I haven't seen Cynthia in a while, sweetheart.' He exhaled a plume of cigar smoke that caused Marcia to cough and brought tears to her eyes. 'If she comes here, I'll let you know.'

'Thank you,' she said.

Monty growled and stiffened his neck as she stepped over him to get to the door.

'He won't hurt you,' said Wally Labone. 'He's a sweetie. Harmless. But best shut the door when you leave.'

Chapter 19

'Cynthia!' exclaimed Marcia when she got home and found Cynthia sitting at the kitchen table as if nothing had happened. Eunice, however, was whirling around the kitchen in a rage. As quickly as she had thrown her arms around Cynthia and hugged her, she was hitting her about the head and telling her never, ever to do such thing to her again.

'Where were you?' asked Marcia, puzzled.

'Auntie Norma's,' Cynthia said.

'Why didn't you tell us?'

'I did, I left a note.'

'Don't lie!' said her mother. 'There was nothing in that note apart from you saying some nonsense that you were leaving home.'

'You could have gone to Norma's and found me.'

'It's miles away.'

'You could have telephoned.'

'Norma hasn't got a phone.'

'Like I said, I can't help it if you didn't think of Norma.'

The question of Norma and the note seemed to evaporate, overtaken by bigger questions about Wally Labone, but Cynthia just insisted that they had been stupid to worry. And anyway, she had exciting news

– news that, apparently, Mr Labone had given her. He was going to put in a good word and arrange an audition for her at the Empire after Christmas, and if that went well, most probably soon she was going to be dancing at The Floral Hall. 'It's in Southport. I'll finally get away from here,' she said.

'And who is going to tell your father that? Will you do it or shall I?'

'I don't care,' Cynthia said. 'But he's not going to stop me.'

Eunice shook her head and left the room. Marcia stood with her back to the kitchen range. She felt a panic rising through her.

'That man Labone lied to me when he said he hadn't seen you. I don't trust him. What's going on, Cyn? One minute you're leaving home, next minute you're back.'

Cynthia sighed. 'I came back home because Wally told me to. He said he couldn't have people gossiping about young girls on put you up beds in his office. But if I get this dancing job, problem solved. I'll be out of this place soon enough. Don't you tell Ma and Da about Wally, though.'

'What about me?' she said in a little voice. 'What about our dad? I can't stay with him on my own.'

'You've got Ma.'

'Ma's at work . . .'

But they all knew that Eunice was not the woman she had once been. As much as she tried to do what John told her, she seemed unable to so much as pick up a sweeping brush before he was shouting at her, telling her she was doing it wrong. Nothing was ever good enough. It was only feeling so sorry for him that helped her get through each day and rise above his quibbles and complaints – and then, worse, his apologies the next day and the inevitable drunken fumblings.

If only she could go and see Mr Tattersall! Things had been so much better when Fred Tattersall was in their lives. Eunice hadn't seen him for months; she hadn't really seen anyone, in fact. Her life, apart from work, was now just an endless round of fetching and carrying up the stairs for her husband – a packet of Woodbine, a glass of Guinness, even spoon-feeding him on occasion now that the shaking was getting worse. And when John came home with bottles of beer bulging in his pockets, she would move around him silently.

Chapter 20

'Norma's new flat is like a palace in the sky,' said Eunice.

Finally, after Christmas and soon after Marcia's fifteenth birthday, it had been decided behind closed doors and in hushed voices what to do about the troubling matter of Cynthia. Auntie Norma had agreed that Cynthia should move in with her. Norma, stuck in a flat, had changed her views about taking the girls in because she was now desperate for company – at least, that was the story told to Marcia – and the flat was near a factory in Bootle that was desperate for machinists. Cynthia would start work there the following week.

Marcia's bottom lip trembled. 'What about me?' she asked.

'What about you?' Eunice had said brightly. 'You're still at school, love.' Her father looked at her. Marcia knew a conversation like this could twist into an argument and tears in minutes, but she wasn't deterred.

'I could leave school. I'm fifteen. Please can I go with her?'

147

'Your father has high hopes for you, Marcia.'

Cynthia nodded seriously. 'It's true. I'm a lost cause, squit.' She winked at Marcia.

On the day Cynthia stuffed her suitcase, Marcia sat on the bed in a candlewick bathrobe, twisting the end of her sleeve and sucking it. The hollowed-out space where she and her sister normally slept felt cavernous.

'You always promised you wouldn't leave me,' she said in her small voice.

Cynthia carried on taking things out of drawers and spoke with her back to Marcia. 'I want to look after you but I also know you can't stay glued to my side forever. You're my sister and I love you, and if there's any trouble, you know where to find me.'

A single tear spilled onto Marcia's cheek.

Eunice appeared in the doorway, pausing as she took in their expressions: Marcia tearful, Cynthia determinedly calm. She came in and rested a hand gently on Marcia's head. It was as if she couldn't find the words either. 'Girls, I promise. We won't be broken apart,' she said. 'Your father will get better soon and we'll all be together again.'

'I don't want you to go, Cyn,' said Marcia wretchedly. Suddenly unable to help herself, she leapt up and threw herself at her sister, clinging to her and burying her head in her chest, still crying. When Cynthia tried to peel her off gently, she sprung back as if she was on a coil. 'Don't go! Don't leave us with Da!'

As soon as the words were out, her hand flew up

to her mouth as if to push them back in. Her mother looked frozen with shock and sadness.

'Marce,' said a sombre Cynthia, 'it's just his head-aches.' She pinched Marcia's forearm hard, in the hope that the pain might shock away her tears.

'Come back for me, promise?' Marcia whispered. 'I think I will die if you go. I might as well just kill myself now.'

'Oh, Marce, don't, your face has gone all squidgy.'

'Or he will kill me. Or kill Ma. The other day when he came in from the pub he got so angry because the tea was cold he threw a kettle at the wall. What if he gets worse? We'll be like those people in the newspapers. One of those terrible stories where everyone regrets it, but it's all too late, and everyone feels desperate and sorry and guilty and—'

'Now you're being stupid,' tutted her mother.

Marcia had hoped Cynthia would throw her arms around her and offer to take her with her, but Cynthia just nodded helplessly and said, 'Oh, squit. I'll be back. Here.'

She rooted in a bag and took out a lipstick. It was ruby red and Marcia knew it was Cynthia's favourite; she just wasn't sure what she expected *her* to do with it. She had never worn lipstick in her life. She wasn't about to start hanging out at dance halls and kissing old men, she thought darkly.

'You be careful. And I promise I'll be back.'

'I'll miss you, Cynthia,' John grunted as they bunched together on the front step half an hour later, ready to wave her off. They were a little huddle of sadness framed in the doorway. Marcia could see her father's bones separating and tensing.

'Say something to Daddy, Cynthia,' said her mother.

Cynthia grimaced. 'Daddy? Since when have we called Da *Daddy*?'

Her mother raised her eyes. 'Stubborn,' she muttered.

They went back inside. 'She can't even be civil when she says goodbye. So that's it – just us three now,' John said, shutting the door. Marcia felt a tear roll down her cheek and splash onto the tablecloth. 'Thank the Lord you're a good girl, Marcia.'

Marcia pushed her fists into her eye sockets. She felt a dull ache in her heart. Why can't I be the bad girl? she thought. She didn't want to be a good girl. Not if good girls got left at home with their mad, unpredictable fathers and hopeless mothers while the bad girls got to drink gin and French and smoke Lucky Strikes in their auntie's palace in the sky.

Her eyes were still brimming with tears as she went outside to find somewhere she could breathe. She made her way to the hollas and sat on an upturned hubcap.

'What's up?' said Alfie, poking his head through a broken window.

She shrugged and continued to scrape a tin can across the ground, filling it with sand and pouring it out.

'Tell me what's up? I want to help you,' he said, coming to sit beside her on an old tyre that was lodged at an angle in the rubble.

She sniffed. 'He's spoiled everything.'

'He's not right in the head, me da said.'

'Aye. And Ma. It's like she's become a different person. His chest rattles and he coughs and if we say anything, she's always telling us to be quiet and not to upset him, but when he doesn't like something, he roars at us anyway.'

'Oh, Marce.'

'Me ma follows him around every minute of the day. And he grabs her whenever he can. He loves grabbing. I can hear noises all the time through the walls. Like animals.'

Alfie took her hand. 'Stuff your hands in your ears.'

'Always spitting on the range. It's disgusting.'

'My da says the prisoner of war camp was brutal.'

'Aye. That's why he's still yellow. That's why he shakes so much. He can't hardly hold a spoon now and when Ma feeds him, he slurps. Like this . . . ' She demonstrated an exaggerated slurping noise.

He laughed. 'That's what fellas do.'

'He scratches his knackers all the time.'

'That's what fellas do an' all,' Alfie grinned. 'He's a hero. War hero.'

'I don't care. I wish he'd never come home. He was supposed to get better but he's getting worse. They let Cynthia go to me Auntie Norma's. I'm all on me own.'

'Hey, Marce. Cyn may be gone, but you've got me.'

She sniffed and wiped her nose with her sleeve. He picked a buttercup that was struggling up between the pavement slabs.

'Let's see. Sunshine means everything will be all

right.' He craned his neck and held it to the underside of Marcia's chin, seeing if the sun would throw a yellow reflection on her alabaster skin. 'Yes. Future happiness for you,' he said, smiling.

Marcia sighed. 'Kids' games,' she said.

He paused. 'I'll always look after yer,' he replied.

For a long, silent moment they just looked at each other. It occurred to her that he had beautiful, soulful brown eyes and long, dark lashes.

'You mean it? That's what Cynthia said.'

'Yes. I promise. Cynthia's grand but she's a flibbertigibbet. I've lost me brother, so I know what it's like.'

She smiled.

'Marcia! Marcia! Get back here! Da needs you to do his eggs!' her mother called.

'See what I mean?' She rolled her eyes as she stood up. 'Alfie, thanks,' she added as she turned to go. 'You're kind.'

'It will be all right,' he said.

And her heart felt a little lighter as she headed for home.

Norma's house, a small top-floor flat in a new block on the outskirts of the city, was like nothing Cynthia could have imagined. Hot water gushed out of the tap, the lavatory was inside. There were no mildew stains, no cracked window panes with tape stuck over the peeling wallpaper, no paintings strategically placed to hide spreading damp. It had a small white cooker, a white fridge and a good-sized bath.

When Cynthia arrived she expelled a long puff

of air and said, 'Coo-ee, this really is a palace in the sky.'

Norma laughed as she showed her around. 'What d'you think about my new bar?' She waved towards it with her cigarette, which was stuffed into a long pink holder. Cynthia's mouth fell open. An actual bar, apparently made of gold, in the corner of the room, with bottles of sherry, Bristol Cream and crème de menthe on mirrored shelves.

'I can't believe it,' replied Cynthia.

Norma gave her a hug and said, 'I'll be glad of the company. Jimmy Snaith has moved in next door but I need female company. Nothing better than a girly chat over a Babycham. How is your mother?'

Cynthia shrugged. She didn't want to tell her aunt how things had slid. How her mother, who for years had hardly ever seen a drop of drink pass her lips apart from sweet sherry, was now reaching for the bottle at two o'clock in the afternoon; how she would probably love Norma's bar. How now, every Friday – which had once been the day when the priest came to visit – now meant Eunice getting tipsy and tearful.

'Fancy a ciggie?'

Cynthia's eyes widened and she took one gratefully. They were pink with gold tips.

'I love having a smoke on the balcony.'

From up here you could see all the way across to the river and down to the docks, to the overhead railway and the green fields beyond and even the blue smudge of the Welsh hills. 'Everyone looks so tiny. They seem like ants.'

Norma wrapped her arm around Cynthia and

squeezed her fondly. 'You'll be all right. Your da will get better. I said to your mother Marcia could come here as well.'

Cynthia frowned. 'Oh, no, Marcia will be fine. I'm the problem one,' she said. She did feel a twinge of guilt, but when Norma led her into the bedroom where she would be sleeping – with its big bed and pink satin quilted eiderdown, and the dressing table with its glass surface and pink satin frills around the edge, not to mention the hairbrush and matching hand mirror and mother-of-pearl comb and clothes-brush on a silver tray – she decided she really would rather not share it with her sister.

'You like my walnut veneer?' Norma said, noticing Cynthia looking at the wardrobe made of smooth, satiny wood with stipples and swirls on it that looked a little like frog spawn. The headboard matched, and the drawers matched as well. 'Unpack, and when you're done let's have a girly chat in the lounge.'

Cynthia sat down at the dressing table on a padded white stool with curved legs. The mirror had two winged panels. She twisted her head from side to side, looking at her profile, and touched the end of her nose. Seeing herself from this angle, she realized for the first time how much it sloped upwards.

Norma called the living room the 'lounge'. She had something called elevenses, which she said to Cynthia was an excuse for a fag and a biccy. There was a red velvet sofa and when Cynthia sat on it, she sank down so deeply that she felt as if she was being swallowed up and her feet lifted off the floor. Norma, who hadn't bothered to get dressed yet, teetered around in a pair of slippers with actual heels on them and a floaty dressing gown over a pink negligee, tied with a pink ribbon in a large, floppy bow. Who ever thought of that? Matching nightie and dressing gown. She had sponge curlers with plastic clips in her hair, poking out from under a purple chiffon scarf. Slippers with heels. How sophisticated, Cynthia thought. For the first time in months, she felt happy.

'You've got to make the best of what God gave you. Your mother doesn't hold with that. She would probably take a dim view of me saying this, but you're a lovely-looking girl. You could stop traffic, darling. Reach for the heights and don't let anyone stand in your way. Has anyone ever told you that?'

'Mr Labone says, "Don't let anyone dull your sparkle",' Cynthia told her.

'Ah, does he now?' Norma said mysteriously.

Chapter 21

Marcia had known it was going to be hard living at home without Cynthia. But it turned out to be even harder than she had expected.

How many times had she wished to be able to stretch her legs out in the bed without being shoved by her sister? How many times had she longed to be rid of the clutter of potions and lipsticks and make-up all over their dressing table? How many times had she wished for just a bit of peace and quiet before being woken up by Cynthia chattering and singing and borrowing her clothes and spraying her stinking hairspray everywhere?

But then there was the time when she'd had her first Auntie Mary, and how Cynthia, when she had found her crying, had lent her her sanitary belt and told her how to tie the towel onto the hooks and not to worry. Or the times when she'd let her frozen feet slide between her thighs to warm up, or shared her biscuits in bed. Her sister, who was her opposite but also her mirror and could always be relied on to tell her the truth – no matter how hard the truth was to hear – had been gone for months now.

She soon realized that if she stayed at the library after school and came home late, she could spend less time in the house. But one afternoon when she came in, she found her father sitting at the table with his neck sadly stooped and his head in his hands. Straight away, she could tell that he had been drinking.

'I didn't think this would be so hard. We're piss-poor. I need proper work. But I'm not getting any better.' His gaze was slightly off centre and his speech was slurred.

'Da, I'm sorry,' she said.

'Not your fault. Hitler's bloody fault, love,' he said, sniffing the glass he was holding and then taking a slug. Marcia blinked away the worry. 'Come on, Marce, love,' said her father. 'Where's that sunny smile gone?'

She just glared at the floor.

This place was such a mess. No wonder they never had the priest around any more. A few minutes later, when John had shuffled out of the kitchen, her mother came in and said tetchily, 'You've left the window open. What on earth are you doing? You're going to make Da get a chill. And if it gets to his chest . . .'

'Perhaps if he stopped smoking, Ma, that might help him get better.'

The smell of cigarettes still lingered in the air long after anyone had been smoking. She could feel it in her skin. Seeping through her pores. She had to fling open the windows every morning.

'Don't you think I've told him that?'

Her father wandered back in with a bowl of porridge. His hand shook as he held the spoon between mouth and bowl and it was as if the whole room was shaking with him. Marcia noticed the yellow tobacco stains on his fingers.

'Too salty.' His voice sounded as though there were pieces of glass in his throat, brittle and scratchy.

Eunice took out the tablecloth and spread it over the table. Marcia watched her as she laid out the knives and forks, the cups, the plates.

'What's for tea?' asked their father, scowling.

'Stew. I bought a scrag end from Hegarty's.'

'Not Fred Tattersall's stew?' he said.

'N-no,' she stuttered.

Marcia longed for Mr Tattersall's cooking as she sat at the table half an hour later and ate the cold, flavourless stew with greasy dumplings floating in it. She glanced up and saw her father grimace. 'This is tasteless, Eunice.'

'Oh, don't be such a miseryguts. The stew is grand.'

The room turned as cold as the stew. 'Oh, is it? The stew is grand? Everything is grand? My bloody legs are grand? My Jimmy Riddler is grand, is it?'

'John!' cried Eunice. 'Not in front of Marcia! And I told you, Fred Tattersall has been kind to us.'

He stirred and grunted. 'I will not have that man's name mentioned in this house again.'

'But dear, he's not the kind of person to take advantage.'

'Just because there's them could've been quicker to jump into our bed while it was still warm, doesn't mean he wasn't thinking of it.'

'No,' said Eunice, through gritted teeth and with a pained expression. 'But please, don't take it out on me. Or Marcia.'

'Eunice, oh, Nissy . . .' He slumped, closed his eyes and dropped his head as if all the life was draining out of him. There was a tense silence. 'I'm sorry, but it doesn't do a man good, knowing there are others out there who have been spending time with my woman. No matter how good their pasties are. Where's my medicine?'

The following evening, Marcia sat outside the King's Arms pub with a packet of crisps. She unwrapped the small blue bag of salt inside and shook it over them. People passed by and looked at her, skirt pulled over her knees as though this was the most natural thing in the world, to be sitting on a cold step on a foggy night with a cold bottom and a dripping nose, waiting for her father, who was probably getting drunk inside the pub. He had told her to come with him just in case he felt dizzy and someone had to be called.

Cynthia would not have allowed herself to be dragged around the streets like this, feet aching and hands frozen, she thought ruefully. As she pulled her threadbare coat around her tightly, a voice said, 'How are you, love?'

'Mr Tattersall,' she said, standing up and brushing down her skirt. 'Cynthia's gone,' she added glumly.

'I heard.'

'Just until Da gets better. He just needs a rest.'

He nodded and smiled his kind smile. Why did everyone seem as though they had something to say but couldn't bear saying it? Marcia felt her world was full of people opening and closing their mouths like fish.

'Awful what this war has done to folks,' he said. 'And we're all supposed to just get on. Like life's a picnic.'

'I'm waiting for me da. He's inside the pub.'

'Aye. I best be off, then,' he said quickly. 'But you take care of yourself, love. And you know where I am if you need me. The same goes for your ma.'

A moment later, hands thrust angrily deep in his pockets, her father came bursting out of the carved glass door as if he was ready to do battle.

Marcia had to jog to keep up with him. 'Before you ask, job's down the swanee. Don't speak,' he said.

'Why?' she asked, shocked.

'Never mind. Bloody kids,' he mumbled.

Once home, he sat hunched and spitting, globules of phlegm hissing as they hit the hot metal of the range.

'How am I supposed to drink that?' he moaned, his face knotty and cross, pointing at the cup of tea she handed him ten minutes later. Marcia trembled. She felt tears prick her eyes. 'It's like dishwater. I've told you about drowning the pot.'

'I'll get you another . . .'

'Marcy, Marcy, I know I'm neither use nor ornament. But if folks had seen the things I'd seen. Those kids riling me up. No wonder I snapped,' he said bitterly.

She left him drinking at the table and started up the stairs, carefully avoiding the bottom step, which always gave a creak like the last gasp of a dying man.

'Marcia! Come back! Help me get out of this chair.'

She came back and, with a weak smile, put her arm under his and tried to heave him up. But when he stood, both of his legs wobbled. They were like bits of cotton, crumpling under him.

'Damn, damn,' he said, swaying drunkenly, his cheeks purpling, face screwed up in frustration. 'What's happening?'

160

She winced.

'Too much drink. Like string. Me legs. What am I going to do now? Help me, girl,' he said angrily. 'I don't understand. They've just stopped working. I'm squeezing blood out of a turnip here.'

She squinted away her tears and bent to lift him again. But it was impossible, he was a dead weight. He looked so frail and yet he was so heavy, like ten bags of coal. Was he so drunk it had rendered him paralytic? And then the coughing started. She felt equal parts frightened and worried as he banged the table, lowered his head and took great rattling gasps, waiting for it to stop so he could catch his breath.

'Get me onto the sofa,' he said.

Summoning up all the strength she could manage, she heaved him off the chair. As she tried to drag him, she felt her arms might come out of their sockets. Her heart was beating fast with the effort and strain of it all.

'I'm sorry,' he muttered as he made it to the sofa and heaved himself up onto the cushion with his arms.

'Can I go?'

'Aye, love.'

She nodded but as she left, he called her back yet again. 'You probably think it would be better if I had died, don't you?'

'No . . . Don't say that . . .'

'Before you go, I need you to do my leg,' he grunted. She felt a shudder shiver down her spine. This would normally be her mother's job but she was at Mrs Caddle's delivering the gloves she had mended for a much needed extra few shillings. Lapsing into silence, she filled the bucket.

Her father's eczema was a problem that just wouldn't go away. If anything, it was getting worse. She knew the smell but she still wasn't prepared for it as she knelt and unravelled the bandage and dropped it, sopping and moist, into the bucket at her feet. She thought about how tenderly her mother wiped the rag over his cracked, sore, shins. *This is how you do it*, she had said to Marcia once. *In case I'm not here.* She tried her best, but he winced as the bandage, that had stuck to his flesh, pulled the hairs on his legs and made little pinpricks of blood appear.

'You're doing it wrong,' he muttered.

She mumbled an apology as she wiped him down and put on the new bandage, pinning it with a large pink safety pin. 'My legs,' he said. 'They're not working at all. Help me stand up, Marcia, and see what's what.'

She hooked an arm under each of his armpits, but still he was a dead weight and as much as she tried to help him, he wouldn't move. Then without warning, he just slid off the edge of the sofa and lay there, half on and half off, with his trousers sagging around his hips.

'Can't feel them,' he grunted.

'You're so heavy,' she said, panting as she tried to help heave him back up again. How could someone this thin be so heavy? Why couldn't he move? Suddenly he moaned in pain and clutched his side. Was he about to die? Was he dying?

'I'll see if I can get someone,' she said, panicked. 'What about Alfie's dad?'

'No. I'm not have anyone seeing me like this. Damn and blast. Help me.'

He let out a groan as if all the life was draining out of him. Putting his arms on the chair, he tried to lift himself up, but he was just too weak. He cried out and slumped back down.

'Dammit,' he muttered, thumping the floor in frustration. 'I'm bloody useless.'

'Let me go and get Mr Maloney. He understands about the war and the things in the jungle . . . and . . . and . . . you wouldn't need to be ashamed with him.'

'No,' he said bitterly.

'Then let me go and get Mr Tattersall.'

'Are you out of your mind?' he cried.

She turned her back. 'I need to fetch someone. Need a doctor. I'll be back in a minute.'

She raced off out of the house and down the road. Although it was evening, there was a light on in Mr Tattersall's shop; she could see him inside. She pushed her way through the door, gasping. 'Please – me da, you've got to come and help him.' She explained what had happened. 'He's on the floor. He can't move. His legs won't work. What if he's dying?'

He quickly untied his apron and followed her back down the road and into the house.

'Get out!' John Rogan cried, when Fred Tattersall came into the room.

'I said I'd help Marcia – unless you can get up yourself.' Mr Tattersall, without another word, just went over, heaved her father up and lifted him in his arms as if he was a child. 'Don't fight it, John, don't fight me,' he said calmly.

'Do we need a doctor? What's wrong with him?'

asked Marcia worriedly, seeing her father's head loll to the side.

'Nothing to be scared about. He'll live. Drunk, that's all,' Mr Tattersall said, laying him down on the sofa.

'Go away,' said John. 'Leave me alone. All of you, just leave me alone.'

Marcia went with Fred Tattersall to the front door. She was shaking. 'You'd better go,' she said.

'You shouldn't be doing this,' he replied, resting a hand on her shoulder. 'This isn't a kiddie's job.'

'I'm not a kiddie.'

He squeezed her hand. His was like a bear's paw, padded and fleshy, and it felt warm and safe and comforting.

She went back inside. She was relieved to see her father lying on the sofa, mouth open, snoring gently. Had this been the worst thing that had ever happened to her? Pulling his coat over him, tucking it round his body like she had seen her mam do, she wondered – was this her life from now on? Was there worse to come?

She felt she ought to pull up a chair and sit beside him, but instead she began to gather up the mess around him. But when she picked up his jacket, a small empty bottle fell out of it. This wasn't drink, like Mr Tattersall had said. This was his medicine. *Cough Syrup. Bromoform, Comp. Duncan Flockhart and Co.*, she read on the label.

Her eyes darted around and she saw another one on the table. And, now she thought of it, she had noticed two on the window ledge in the lavvy. She went upstairs and began searching. There were three tucked at the back of the drawer. Another in the pocket of his suit jacket. Shuddering, she knelt down and felt under the bed. There was a whole bag of them, a few more bundled in an old handkerchief, more covered with an old newspaper. Taking one and holding it up to the light, she read the blue label. *Contains codeine and bromoform. One tablespoon a day. Do not use with alcohol.*

She had seen him drinking this tincture straight out of the bottle, gulping it down often and always before he went to the pub, but only now did she realize how much of the medicine he must be taking each day. She had found bottles and bottles of the stuff.

From the doorway, Eunice gasped. 'What did you do?' she said, staring at Marcia, her hands flying up to her face.

'What did I do?' Marcia was astonished.

'What's happened? I've just seen Mr Tattersall! He said you tried to move your father out of his chair and he collapsed.'

'No. It was da who told me to help him up.' Her mother was shaking. That face – it was etched with lines of pain, frustration turning to anger. Her mother who had always been so beautiful, witty, kind, and sharp as a knife, but who had now become another person, someone Marcia barely recognized – just as much of a stranger in the house as their father was.

Chapter 22

Norma was sitting in her lounge, smoking a cigarette. 'Big day?' she said, smiling broadly to Cynthia.

Cynthia nodded. 'I can't believe it's happening. My first proper audition, at the Empire. If it goes well, Mr Labone says I could be at The Floral Hall in Southport this summer, maybe even Blackpool, and it also means I will get a chance to audition for the Tiller Girl school in Manchester. Me! Can you imagine?'

'Good luck, darling. Knock 'em dead. What are you wearing?'

Cynthia clicked open the clasp of the small vanity case at her feet. 'Just this,' she said, producing a plain cotton dress with white piping.

'Wait a minute,' said Norma. She took a couple of puffs from the cigarette and put it out in a chunky pink glass ashtray. Then she rose, went into the back room and reappeared holding up a shimmering voile dress with a full skirt on a padded, ribboned satin coat hanger, with a feather boa curled over it. 'Let's glam you up a bit. This will get you noticed. This and that smile of yours. And remember, it's not about who can kick the highest or who can keep the line going – it's about eyes and teeth. You've got lovely teeth, Cyn, and pretty eyes. I know about these things.'

'How?' asked Cynthia.

'Oh, I had a life once. Hard to believe. Break a leg, darling. Pinch your cheeks for a blush, dear.'

The Empire was where Auntie Norma had taken Cynthia to see her first show when she was six years old. They had come to see the pantomime – it was *Cinderella* – and they were perched on a bench in the very back row of the balcony. It had felt like sitting on top of a mountain, they were so high up; like she might tumble if she were to lean out too far, with possible death only adding to the excitement of the feathers and beautiful sparkling costumes, the clatter of tap-dancers and blousy orchestra and real brushed and beribboned Shetland ponies.

The excitement in the line of girls queueing up at the stage door was palpable. She felt nervous, actually weak with nerves, as if her body had been hollowed out from the inside. It didn't help that these girls all looked like they knew what they were doing, as if they had come straight off the kick line of *Cinderella*. Some were with their mothers. Lucky them, she thought. It was a shame she hadn't had the support of her mother. Eunice had a habit, whenever Cynthia did something she was proud of, of telling her breezily in the same breath how marvellous someone else had been. Cynthia was sure this lot didn't have parents wincing when they sang, or laughing at them when they said they wanted to be famous.

She had arrived with her vanity case and a new lipstick that Norma had bought her from Owen Owens. A thin, birdlike woman, wearing a black polo neck and black slacks with stirrups under flat ballet shoes, was smoking a cigarette while handing out numbers and safety pins.

'Lucky number seven,' she said to Cynthia.

Cynthia cast her eyes around as she pinned the number onto her chest. Some of the girls were stretching and limbering, lifting their legs high and pointing their toes; they looked like proper dancers in their neat buns and hairnets. There were a few putting their feet into a tray of chalk before they all stood in a long line across the stage.

'Teeth,' said the woman. They all bared their teeth and she walked up and down the line making notes on a pad. 'Mrs Bannock!' she shouted to the woman at the piano, wearing a hat with a feather in it. Cynthia tilted her chin and stared into the black of the auditorium. Mr Labone was out there somewhere. 'Follow me, girls! Two, three, four!'

Cynthia copied the thin woman's steps nervously, willing them to lodge in her head. The other girls were older. She felt her confidence drain away, missed beats, found herself kicking with the right leg while everyone was in unison with the left. Feeling flustered, she repeatedly tried to correct herself.

'Again!' cried the woman. 'I'm not looking for clodhoppers! Dancing is a perpendicular expression of horizontal desire . . .' she said, elongating the words and blowing smoke out of the side of her mouth. 'I need to see that . . .' One of the girls giggled. 'I'm serious, dear. It's no laughing matter,' she said sharply.

Cynthia squinted towards the row of red velvet seats at the back as her eyes became accustomed to the low light. She could just about make out the shape of three people in the middle row, watching. One was smoking a cigar. Mr Labone.

'You, you, and you with the big bust, go home. Thank you,' said the woman. 'Now the rest. And one! Two! You know what to do!'

The curvaceous, wide-hipped girl blushed to the tips of her ears, picked up her things and shuffled off the stage.

'Wait! Stop! You at the end as well, thank you, dear . . . And one, two, and three, four . . .' The music continued. 'I said, you, thank you. Off you pop.'

Cynthia stood frozen to the spot. She glanced over each shoulder. Surely she didn't mean her?

'Yes, you. With the lipstick and the hair. Off you go. Thank you for coming.'

Cynthia's eyes filled with tears. She squinted towards where she could now clearly see Mr Labone puffing on a cigar. This was all wrong. This wasn't how it was supposed to go. She shaded her eyes, searching him out again. The piano started.

'Move,' said the girl behind her.

At the stage door, Mr Labone was sucking furiously on the fat cigar. 'Cynthia, love,' he said, touching her elbow. She jerked her arm away. 'It's not that you're no good. I would tell Bonnie to change her mind. Like you say, I'm the boss. I'm not saying no forever. You're a good girl and you kick like an angel. And you're so pretty. But I'm afraid you're just not ready.'

He touched her elbow again, but she shrugged it

away again. 'It's just not worth my while,' he said, a little more tetchily. 'I just can't take the risk. Anyway, why are you in such a rush? You're still young.'

In that moment, Cynthia felt as if everything was crashing down around her; her dreams and her hopes sliding out of her grasp forever. 'That's rich,' she said. 'You said you love it that I'm young. Pure. *Unspoiled*, you said. *Innocent as the driven snow*, you said. Now you wish I was an old trout.'

'And now you're being daft.'

'Mr Labone! You promised. I'm just as good as the other girls! I've practised so hard!' she said, looking at him, distraught.

He sighed. 'The truth is, you're not that special. Besides, I can't take the risk with your da.'

'My da? What?'

'His temper. Your sister Marcia told me about him. I don't want any trouble,' he replied, brusquely.

'My sister! Marcia? She's been to see you?'

He shrugged and tapped the ash from his cigar onto the floor. 'You're not listening to me, love.'

But Cynthia's eyes popped out as if they were on stalks. She could feel spasms all the way up from her feet to the top of her head and the tip of nose. Her whole body began to tremble. Her sister, her partner in crime – the one person she could always rely on – her best friend whom she could never get rid of and who, whatever she did, was always meant to be there for her – had betrayed her.

Chapter 23

The two men at the head of the table didn't look like drinking pals of her father's. One was wearing a trilby and the other was much younger – no more than a year or two older than Marcia herself, in fact, with a kind, innocent face and solid rimmed glasses, his floppy fair hair occasionally slipping down over his forehead. He was smartly dressed and had a notebook with a pen laid in the spine as if he was ready to write something.

'Sit down, Marcia. Mr Higgins is from the Corpy.'

'Henry Cherry here will be taking notes,' said Mr Higgins.

Henry looked up. Marcia's eyes widened in shock. Henry Cherry! I know you, she wanted to say. He nodded at her, as if to say he remembered her too.

She felt the chair push hard against her leg as her mother pulled it out for her and told her to sit down. Her mother glanced at Higgins and back to Marcia. 'Me and your da . . .' Her words tailed off and she blinked away a tear. Eunice had planned for weeks what she was going to say, practising it while pacing around in the kitchen, but she wondered now how she should break the news to her daughter. 'Marcia, dear. The nuns like you. Which is no surprise. You're such a good girl. You never misbehave. You're so kind and sweet. An angel. Which is more than can be said for your sister . . .'

She faltered. That hadn't come out how she'd planned.

Marcia bit her bottom lip.

Mr Higgins shifted in his seat; Henry blushed and, head down, began scribbling earnestly in the notebook. Mr Higgins cleared his throat. 'Your mother and father have decided they need to take steps. Action.'

'It's no good for any of us,' Eunice blurted. 'All of us trying to live together. We've given it a go. A year and a half longer than Mr Higgins here wanted us to. But now . . . I need to get your da better.'

'Your family is in crisis, Marcia. And now that Cynthia is settled with Norma . . .'

'You'll go to the orphanage to stay with Sister Cyril. For now. Your father and I have decided . . .' Her mother took a deep breath and started again. 'Your father and I . . .'

'The orphanage? Ma, no. Henry?'

Henry bit the inside of his cheek and fiddled with his pencil.

'Give your mother a chance to speak, girl,' Mr Higgins grumbled, lifting his trilby and wiping sweat from his forehead with a handkerchief.

Marcia rolled the plump part of her lip. Her mother took a deep breath and began again. 'Your father and I have decided . . . we think it best . . .'

Higgins attempted a comforting smile, failing miserably. 'The nuns work with us all the time. This city couldn't manage without them. Their orphanages.'

'I'm not an orphan.'

He clenched his mouth and continued. 'And fostering. Finding homes for children like you, from families in need. It's often only temporary. But this new act puts you under our care. Terrible what happened to that boy in Wales, Mrs Rogan.'

'Wales?' she asked vaguely.

'Murdered by his foster parents. Worked to the bone by them and beaten to death. We're all keeping our eye on the ball now. A tighter grip now. That's why I have young Henry here. Everything duly noted. Everything written down and reported back. You've Mr Attlee to thank for that.'

'I don't want to go to any orphanage. I've been before. I don't want to go back.'

'Yes, and you didn't hate it. Remember Ellie? You liked being with her, didn't you? And Sister Cyril?'

Marcia glowered.

'Marcia, we love you. It's just that this – situation . . . We can't afford . . . It's only until Christmas. Until your father gets better. And after what happened with Cynthia, when he nearly killed Happy and all the fuss, the crying and shouting and losing his temper like that . . . the red mist he talks about, we think . . .'

'Your father doesn't trust himself and we have your safety to think of,' said Higgins tetchily.

Marcia felt her whole body wobble and collapse into itself. She imagined her father bristling at Higgins's words, and when she glanced at Henry Cherry he blushed again, bright red, all the way to the tips of his ears.

'I can't do everything, and you're too young to be

looking after Da,' said Eunice. 'It should be my job. Not yours. I can take in gloves and lace threading. There's other things I can do from home where I can keep an eye on him.'

'Why can't I go to Norma's with Cynthia?'

'Norma's changed her mind about having you. She won't hear of it now. Cynthia's enough, driving her demented. Says she knows there's a reason why she didn't have children.'

'Cynthia said it was a palace,' she said.

'Marcia, stop being difficult. You're supposed to be my easy one.'

Marcia was suspicious that she was just an inconvenience to her mother; that Eunice wanted her out of the way, so that she and her father could do all their stupid kissing and crying and throwing plates at walls when things got too much.

Young Henry Cherry closed his notebook and chanced a sympathetic smile at Marcia. If it had been him on his own, Marcia thought, she would have told him her suspicions. He had a kind face and looked like the sort of person who would listen. And she remembered how he had stood up for her all that time ago, with Billy, and hoped he might do the same for her again.

When the two men had left, Marcia sank deep into the rocking chair. Her mother put a blanket round her shoulders and knelt down in front of her, taking her hand and rolling up her sleeve. She kissed her on the inside of her forearm. 'Please, this isn't forever. It's just until your father gets better. But it's not fair on you to stay here. Your dad needs help. His legs don't work and he can't get out. I don't like it that you're around to see it. Sister Cyril will look after you.'

'Sister Cyril has enough trouble keeping all the little ones under control, what with the bedwetting and worm tablets. I remember that. She won't be looking after me. Ma, I'm used to Da's drinking now. It's not all the time. I can go to my room. I don't care.'

Her mother tried to explain in more back to front sentences, with more desperate hand gestures. 'It's not just the drinking, dear. The cough medicine. It has something in it. Highly addictive, the doctors said. One of your da's pals had the same problem, chewed his way through his plaster cast in hospital when he broke his arm, he was that desperate and mad to get at the medicine. The doctors had never seen anything like it. We need to try and stop him relying on the medicine, and maybe the drink will follow. But this is no place for a young girl with all that going on. You do understand, don't you?'

'I don't see why I can't go to Norma's?' Marcia clenched her hand and pulled it from her mother's.

'How many times! Norma doesn't have room and besides, she's said no.'

'I can share a bed with our Cyn.'

'No.' She didn't explain further. 'Sister has said you can go to St Mary's, and from there you can go to a family. The family will be nearby. I'll visit.'

'But I don't want to go to a family. I've got a family. This is my family.'

'Yes, but we're not doing very well at the moment,

are we? The Corpy have known that for ages. Gossips in this street. But there's no shame in asking for help.' She took Marcia's hand again. 'It will be all right. And Sister Cyril is very fond of you.'

'What if they want to shave my head? Cynthia said nuns shave their heads and eat nettles and they make you do the same.'

'Don't be daft,' Eunice said. 'Your father needs to build his strength up and with two lively girls, well . . . we just need a bit of time. Is that too much to ask? It's only until Christmas. Don't look so glum, Marcia. It happens all the time. Families splitting up and coming back together.'

Marcia sat and listened, palms sweating and panic rising. How easily families around here just seemed to fray at the seams and fall apart, and no one seemed to care. And what about Alfie? She would miss Alfie, her only friend apart from Happy, who was now with Mr Tattersall.

Eunice smiled. 'You see if you can keep me away from St Mary's. I'll be there every weekend to see you. It's the bloody war that's to blame. If you want to blame anyone, blame Hitler. Don't be blaming me and don't be blaming your da either. He can't help it.'

Marcia looked dolefully around at the wallpaper that was hanging off the walls, pieces stuck back up with a few carpet tacks and some tape. Her father had nailed wooden panels onto sections of the wall and papered over them, but after three months it had just started peeling off again when the mildew got behind it. It was as though the black fungus had a life of its own and had taken against the Rogans.

'I've tried to . . . But things have changed in the last six months. So much washing. Sheets, and nightshirts . . .' Eunice sighed and stared into the distance.

And Marcia realized it wasn't just her father who was struggling with the fall-out from the war. It was her mother, too, with her strange obsession with keeping quiet all the time, and creeping into the house through the back yard, and knocking on doors before coming into rooms.

Her father loped in, put an arm around her and pulled her to him. Eunice took it as her cue to leave. Marcia could smell the sour smell of beer on his breath. She knew he didn't like it that she was resisting; he could feel her body tense, her arms clamped to her sides. She stayed like that while he awkwardly kissed her on the top of her head.

'Off you pop, love.' It was as though he didn't trust himself not to say something he might regret. As Marcia left the room she exhaled a long breath, so as to feel the air return to her lungs without it stabbing at her throat and choking her.

The following week Marcia was in the kitchen, eating a piece of fried bread. She glanced around the room and noticed a bundle of unfinished knitting lying on a chair. Her mother was always starting on something but never seemed to manage to finish anything these days. There were so many jumpers in the house with only one arm sewn in, half-darned socks, tea cosies with no hole for the spouts.

Her mother scuttled in, removed the knitting and sat down on the chair. 'We just want the best for you.

Cynthia has made such a hash of it.' She sighed and pressed the back of her hand to her forehead. 'It's the fault of the medicine. When you're addicted it's like an unbearable itch, and when Da takes the medicine, it stops. But only for a short time. So he takes it again. D'you understand that?'

Marcia nodded.

'That's why we need you to go to St Mary's. Only for a short time. Only until Christmas. Until Dad gets better. We'll bring Cynthia home and fetch you as well. And we'll have a Christmas like no other. Paper bells, and mistletoe, and a lovely tree.'

Marcia didn't doubt her mother's good intentions. But she knew enough to realize that the little bottles were a powerful force to be reckoned with.

Chapter 24

'Cynthia!' cried Marcia when she opened the front door the following day. A huge smile broke across her face at the sight of her sister. But the realization that this was not going to be a happy reunion followed quickly when she saw Cynthia glaring at her from under the brim of the hat she was wearing, tilted forward and at a fashionable angle.

'You snitch! I was getting away from this hellhole, and you have to go and ruin it!' Cynthia cried. 'You've ruined everything! Why did you have to go and see Mr Labone?'

Marcia looked aghast at her sister, whom she loved and resented in equal measure. 'You just disappeared. I didn't say anything. How did I ruin things?' she said in a small voice.

'You've destroyed my life. You shouldn't have gone to see him, stupid!!'

'Cyn, I . . .' she stuttered.

'You told him about Da's temper? Why?'

'Cyn. Ma was going to call the police. I had to . . .' Marcia said, conscious of the note of panic in her tremulous voice.

'How stupid are you? You should've known it would cause trouble! Now he's told me I've got to wait a year. Marcia, he had it all lined up. And I was going to get out of this place.'

'Why can't you?'

'I told you! Mr Labone says I'm not ready! He started asking about Da after you told him about his temper. What he's like when he's on the warpath. Some fella at the pub shouted his mouth off and put him in the picture. My life is over now. I don't know if I'm ever going to speak to you again.' Cynthia was shaking with anger. She stepped forward and thumped Marcia so hard in the chest that she fell back against the dresser. 'Well done, squit!' she added, scornfully.

'I didn't know . . .' wailed Marcia, cowering. 'You've got to believe me . . .'

'Liar. And by the way, trust is like virginity, you only lose it once. Why did you do it, snitch? Answer me!' Lunging forward, she pinned Marcia's shoulders against the shelves, making the plates on the dresser rattle and a vase wobble precariously.

Marcia wrestled herself away. 'We were worried about you. Don't you see that? You're the one who's ruined everything! You've ruined this family!'

'No, I haven't, you have! Now I can't go on tour. I never want to speak to you again. I hate you! I hate you!'

'And I hate you,' Marcia snarled.

A figure appeared: their father, with his braces looped around his thighs and wearing a stained singlet.

'Well, look who it is. Our Cynthia's back, and with lava flowing out of her tongue as usual.'

Chapter 25

Marcia wrote to her sister in shaky, spidery letters the following evening after she had finished her chores.

Dear Cynthia,
Everything is falling around our ears but please don't abandon me as well. I would have told you yesterday but you were cross with me and I hope you'll forgive me for that. Our father is a drunk, but it turns out he's addicted to the cough medicine. It's clear Ma's not going to stand up for me. That's why I need you, Cyn. She used to fight like a lion for us. Remember when Mrs Caddle said we stole her scanties and she went round to hers with the frying pan? How many times did she used to say we were the thing that got her up in the morning? But it's all changed. Anyway, the other news is they are sending me to the nuns while he gets better.
Please don't stay feeling angry with me. I hope to see you soon. You'll find me at St Mary's. I need to get out of here and I hope it will be calm. The nuns' singing is pretty calm. Ma says there's not enough room at Norma's. Is that true?

I'm sorry a million times over. I love you.
Your sister,
Marcia

She dropped the letter into the post-box and prayed she would receive a reply.

Chapter 26

Marcia looked down at her feet after she'd waved a mournful goodbye to her mother, who had kissed her on both cheeks before leaving her at the orphanage gate. There was a vivid red mark on her heel where it had rubbed against the inside of the shoe. It was painful to walk. Was this why Ma had that stoop – because for years she had suffered in badly fitting shoes? She smoothed down her dress and turned to walk up the path with her small case, taking in her surroundings. The garden looked different to how she remembered: pink and white roses, carpets of busy lizzies and clumps of marigolds, and with a manicured green lawn.

'Hello, dear,' said the young nun waiting on the steps for her. 'I'm Sister Dorothea. I'll be looking after you.'

Marcia was surprised by how young she looked. And so many of the sisters had a mean twist to their mouths, but this one had a lovely face, like a pretty bird.

As they walked in she felt the nun's arm curve around her shoulder, but it lay there stiffly. It was as though she was out of touch with touching, but was trying her best to make Marcia feel at home. 'Marcia, we're delighted to have you here. Don't be worried.

And I'll let you into a secret – I'm new, too. I've been at a different convent for two years. So that makes two of us.'

Marcia felt the nun's hand slip into hers. Her palm felt soft and plump. Why would anyone so pretty want to be a nun? 'Mr Higgins has been through it all with us,' Sister Dorothea continued. 'All the forms. Come through. The sisters are saying a novena. Perhaps you would you like to join them later?'

Marcia nodded.

'Let's show you to your room, then.'

The sheets were clean and smelled fresh as she climbed between them that night. She lay there blinking in the darkness, but finally fell asleep to the sound of wind whispering through the trees outside her window. The next morning, when she awoke, she rubbed sleep out of her eyes and propped herself up on her elbows.

'Ellie!' she cried.

'Holy bejesus! What are you doing back here?'

'Why aren't you in Australia?'

'Flamin' war stopped it all happening. But I live in hope! Any day now, the nuns say. As long as I stay well and don't get me bronchitis. I've iffy pipes, like me ma. Am I glad to see you! This place has got worse since you left. The nuns can't seem to get on top of things, especially as we're now packed full of all the GI babies.'

She bounced on the bed. She looked different, thought Marcia. Her hands had red callouses on the knuckles; her skin was pale and pockmarked. But she seemed as spirited as ever.

'You still trying to convince them you're a saint?'

She laughed. 'Ha! Now they just think I'm the devil.'

Marcia grinned. They exchanged stories of what had happened to them both over the last four years, both skirting around the darker times. Marcia told Ellie that Cynthia was in show business; Ellie giggled and said she was in show business too. She regaled Marcia with tales of more of her 'visions' and how with a wet sponge, a hole in the floorboard and a statue of Our Lady, she had almost convinced everyone that Mary was weeping. That time, she had got as far as Sister Cyril calling in a priest.

'He prayed over the statue as I squeezed the sponge upstairs and the water plopped and dribbled onto Our Lady's head, but then all hell let loose when Sid noticed where the drops was coming from. But it were worth it. Even though I only had bread and nettle soup for a flaming week. What they got you doing today?'

'Blackberries.'

'Not the blackberry picking. They think it's the most fun thing on earth.'

'Sister Dorothea is doing it with me.'

'The new one? You watch out. She seems all Doris Day and lovely, but she's still a nun.' She grasped Marcia's hands and kissed her on the cheek. 'Marcia, I'll make sure you're all right. And Marce, I'm so happy to see you, I could burst.'

'Have you seen our garden of silent prayer?' said Sister Dorothea, pointing to the smaller garden through the gate – a garden within a garden. 'It's a beautiful place. No one has uttered a single word in that garden for over a hundred years. We were an enclosed order until quite recently. Some of the sisters still observe. Have a look.'

Marcia stepped forward to peer through the wrought-iron gate. There were green creepers and ivy twisting around a trellis, wild roses tangled up in treacly vines. Nasturtiums wound up conical metal frames. Sister Dorothea, pausing, joined her hands, closed her eyes and began to pray. Marcia felt she should do the same, so she shut her eyes and prayed for her da to get better, and for Cynthia to be kind to her, and for her mother to find some money from somewhere and stop worrying about how she was going to put food on the table. Then the nun breathed a long, peaceful sigh and opened her eyes.

They went around the side of the house to a kitchen garden, where a ladder was already leaning against the wall. Sister Dorothea gave Marcia a tin bucket and directed her towards the ladder; she climbed up it unsteadily while the sister held it at the bottom. From the top of the ladder she had a good view of the orphanage: the lush lawn, the neatly laid out kitchen garden, the clean leaded windows that flashed when the sun hit them. When her bucket was full she came down, her hands stained blood red, the creases in her palms etched out in vivid purple lines.

'Thank you, dear. These berries will make wonderful jam. You've been very kind. And I'll put a jar aside for you. Follow me.' They walked down the path, under a canopy of clematis.

Inside the orphanage, through a side door off the entrance hall, they entered a large, airy room with high ceilings, Gothic arched windows and long tables running down the walls, interspersed with huge Belfast sinks. An old nun sat in a rocking chair at one end. 'This is Marcia, Sister Hilda. She's helping me with the blackberries.'

The nun nodded. 'I remember you,' she said.

But it was the wireless set beside her that Marcia couldn't help staring at. It was made of beautiful mahogany wood with cream and silver dials and there was a turntable with a gramophone record built into the top of it. The nun saw her looking at it.

'Would you like to listen to my gramophone records with me, dear?' she asked.

Marcia widened her eyes.

'Beautiful, isn't it? Eleanor Roosevelt herself bought this wireless.'

What was she talking about? Eleanor Roosevelt? Who's she? thought Marcia. But never mind that – wait until she told Cynthia about the wireless set.

'Now off you go, Marcia. But wait . . .' said Sister Dorothea. She placed a small prayer card and set of white rosary beads into Marcia's hands. The beads were beautiful, pearlized cream with flashes of lilacs and blues, and the card was a picture of a mournful and rather gory Virgin Mary with her dripping bleeding heart pierced with seven spears. 'If you're feeling sad, pray to her . . . Our Lady, Queen of Sorrows.'

Marcia nodded, not quite sure what to make of the nun's words.

'Off you go, now. Thank you for today. You're a special girl. You really are a tonic.'

*

187

The rest of the morning passed quickly. Sister Cyril took her into the kitchen, where she spent an hour churning milk. She passed another hour threading ribbons into little devotion cards. That evening, she was delighted to see Ellie waiting for her at the dormitory door.

'You do the blackberries?' Ellie asked.

'Yes. Tomorrow, they said I have to sit with Sister Hilda.'

Ellie's eyes widened. 'Lucky you! She's mad as a fish but likes someone to sit with her all day and listen to the wireless.' She tipped her head to one side. 'I did the kiddies' sheets. Washing and starching. Come on, let's go for a walk.'

They went outside and up a narrow path into the garden.

Ellie laughed. She took a brief look over her shoulder. 'Let's go into the garden of rest and have a natter. If there's one thing I still like to do, it's break the rules,' she said, pushing the gate open.

'The garden where no one has talked for a hundred years?' said Marcia, wide-eyed.

'Yes,' Ellie said mischievously.

'But we're not allowed, are we?'

'Who cares? Makes it more fun when you do things you're not supposed to. You know, they had a doctor come and take notes about my *contrariness*. Case study, he called it. Won't miss that when I'm in Australia. The bloody doctors.'

'You really are still going to Australia?'

'Sure am.'

'But that's across the other side of the world.'

'Aye, and isn't it wonderful? It's a land of honey and milk, don't you know? The nuns asked us at St Mary's who wanted to go and I put my hand up straight away. I was chosen first. But everyone wanted to sign up. Nearly everyone.'

'But so far away?'

She laughed again. 'I know. Funny thing, one boy thought she was offering to take us on a day trip. All the way to Australia. Tommy thought he'd be back for tea but he's not the full packet. They say that about me, not the full packet, but you should meet Tommy.'

'When will you go?' said Marcia, curious that Ellie didn't seem to mind about not being the full packet. She had even been smiling when she said it.

'Soon, I hope. It's sunny all the time. And you can just pick oranges off trees. Anyway, what is there for me here? Who wants to stay with the nit-infested bed-wetters at the orphanage? I can't stand the smell of Jeyes Fluid any more. Now the slightest whiff of it makes me sneeze and come out in a rash. I've been here too long. I'm sick of the nuns pushing their keys into our backs, racing after us in the playground trying to hit us with a ruler, the way some of the meaner nuns call us just by numbers. Then of course they have their favourites who cosy up to them, but they just take it all out on the younger ones. I suppose that's all they've seen the nuns doing and can't help copying them, but even so. I'm glad you're back. Hey,' she said, slapping her thigh. 'Why don't you ask them if you can come to Australia with me?'

'Oh. No, my mum and dad are still alive.'

'Is that so?' She jumped up and gave Marcia a hug. 'How about you be my pen pal, then? I've never had a pen pal. Will you write to me when I go?'

Chapter 27

It wasn't that she didn't miss home, but to Marcia's surprise, life was peaceful at St Mary's. Ellie could still make her laugh until it hurt with her antics and escapades, and she also began to look forward to her hour with Sister Hilda each day.

One morning, the nun bent and took her hand. 'It's amazing what God gives us for nothing. So many wonderful things from our orchards. Plum chutney, plum jam, plum syrup . . .' The smells wafted through. 'When sugar was hard to get hold of with rationing, the plum syrup was a marvel. It sweetened everything. We used it to make plum cakes, plum date strips, plum almond rolls . . . the gluey leftovers even blocked up a mouse hole in the skirting boards once. But the boiling. It's hard work.'

'It's hard work, Sister Hilda, but now you have Marcia to help,' said Sister Cyril, moving around them picking up crockery.

Sister Hilda held a spoon of syrup over a boiling pan; before long, beads of sweat were gathered on her brow. 'Oh dear, would you mind?' Marcia took the spoon and held it steady. 'Oh, aren't you wonderful,' said Sister Hilda.

When school started again it was a journey of a

tram and a bus to get there, but then it was back to the lounge to sit with Sister Hilda and turn the wireless volume knobs up and down. *Louder, too loud, can't hear it! Why so noisy? Let's play the Andrew Sisters!* And so another week went by. And then, before she knew it, a month had passed.

She liked the quiet orderliness of the place, such a contrast with the rowdiness at home. But she did miss Cynthia. She still hadn't heard from her, but prayed she would in time – she would go to sleep thinking of her clambering up onto the table and patting the air to make everyone be quiet as she gave them her rendition of 'Moonlight in June'.

From time to time her mother would visit, with pie and unfinished knitting and news of their father. He had taken the Pledge from Father Donnelly apparently. Knelt in front of the statue of the Sacred Heart and the whole congregation and promised never to drink again. But when he had turned up drunk one afternoon, singing 'The Fields of Athenry' at the washhouse with a tea cosy on his head, that was the end of that. Ireland was talked of. The relatives. Uncle Declan had moved over there at the start of the war and offered to take them in. But it was hard for Marcia to imagine that her cousins in Ireland would be the ones who would lead her dad to temperance. 'If we go, it won't be long, love. Stay strong and we'll be back to get you soon,' Eunice had said.

Every evening after school she would sit with Ellie, who would pore over a magazine and talk about sun-tans and handsome Australian men and koala bears.

Then, out of the blue, Cynthia wrote her a note. *Meet me at Lyons' Corner House*, it said.

'Oh, squit! What have they done to you?'

Marcia shrugged and touched her hair. 'I don't mind.'

The coffee house was brightly lit. The windows were steamed up and condensation wiggled down the glass panes. Cynthia's peroxide hair now had an orange tinge and Marcia noticed her dark roots showing. She had developed a blousy look, which she accentuated with heavily pencilled eyes and vivid pink lipstick.

'It's awful! Did they actually put a bowl on your head? That orphanage is no place for a young girl.'

'I haven't stopped going to school. And Ellie is still there.'

Cynthia pressed her lips together. 'Ellie?'

'I like having a friend.'

'You've never really had a friend, have you, squit? Only me.' Was Cynthia jealous? 'You need to be out. Out with boys. Have you seen Alfie?'

Marcia shrugged. The waitress came over with a menu.

'Choose what you want. Knickerbocker Glory?' Marcia's eyes widened. 'Go on, my treat.'

'Aren't you going to have one?' she asked.

'I'm watching my waist,' Cynthia replied. She scrabbled around in a little purse for pennies. Was she really watching her weight, Marcia wondered – or was it that she couldn't afford it?

'Do you really like it? When did Ma last see you?'

'A few weeks ago. How's Norma?'

'Tip top. She lets me get on with things.'

'And what about your dancing? After Mr Labone and . . . Are you still trying?'

'Yes. It's going grand, actually. It's exhausting,' Cynthia said, deflecting the question.

'You're a dancer! It's so glamorous.'

'All these entertainers coming back from the war are a problem. Crowding us out. But yes. It is.'

'So, you're not still mad at me?'

'No, squit. I never was, not really.'

'I thought you were never going to speak to me again,' Marcia said.

'I changed my mind.'

Marcia bit her bottom lip. Why? she wanted to ask. Instead she said, 'You look so pretty.'

'Norma has taught me how to do my eyes.'

'Are you going to be a star? You look it.'

'Don't be daft,' Cynthia said. 'But things are going pretty well. I'm trying out for a show in Blackpool. Mr Labone has organized it. Took a bit of pestering but now he knows Da is going away. Do you really not mind about the haircut, Marce?'

'No. Tell me about your show . . .'

Cynthia took a photograph out of her purse and slid it across the table. She was dressed up in a Pierrot costume with her hands firmly clasped around the waist of another grinning girl. 'That's me. I'll get paid three pounds a week if I get the job.'

'Three pounds a week! I can't believe it. What kind of dancing?'

'Oh, you know. Fancy dancing. I've changed my name to Penelope Pompadour. Do you like it?'

'I do. But . . .' Marcia didn't say what she was thinking. Why on earth Penelope? She thought of Penelope as a name for someone little and pixie-like, but Cynthia was big-boned, as their mother often said. She had bosoms to match and a round face. She was certainly not a Penelope, not by any stretch of the imagination.

'So your dreams are going to come true?'

Cynthia shrugged. And then she reached a hand across the table. 'I missed you,' she said.

'That'll show horrible Mr Labone, when you've got your name in lights.'

She smiled. 'He's not horrible. He's helping me. The truth is, I'm not sure how good I was when I did that audition at the Empire. I'm getting better, though,' she said.

'But you're good enough to be in a show now?'

'Sort of,' she said elusively.

Marcia smiled.

'Do you know what I think we should do?' said Cynthia. 'Go to Liverpool Lane. We can say it's Ma's early birthday surprise.'

'When should we go?' Marcia's eyes widened.

'Now, squit. When did you last visit?'

'Not since we left,' she said.

'Shall we go? We could just surprise Ma. Let's see how the land lies. The truth is, Norma can be pretty unkind. She told me I had fat ankles.'

Marcia gasped.

'I know. Shocking, isn't it?' They stood to leave,

and as they walked out and Cynthia linked arms with her, Marcia felt as if the world had been set to rights again. 'And I have to put up with her fellows. Always coming round and pawing me . . .' The sentence tailed off painfully. 'Anyway, I just thought, what about if we visit Ma and Da?'

Ah, thought Marcia, so that's it; she was here because she needed someone to come with her. Because she didn't want to go on her own. Was she afraid what they might find? But never mind. That's what sisters were for, weren't they?

It was a bus ride to their house at the other end of Liverpool Lane and they shared a packet of lemon bonbons on the way. It was quiet; they could see washing strung out over the cobbles and two women gossiping on a step, who followed them with curious eyes.

'Is this a good idea?' asked Marcia, pausing outside the back door that led from the ginnel into their yard. 'What about Da?'

'Yes,' said Cynthia. 'The bugger would only have said no if we'd asked him.'

When they pushed the back door, at first it didn't open. It was as if something was up against it – a chair, perhaps.

'Ma!' called Cynthia, shading her eyes and squinting through the back window into the kitchen. She rapped on the pane. 'It's me and Marce!'

There was no reply. 'Ma!' she repeated and gave it a good push. The latch fell easily out of its casing and the door flew open.

A woman stood at the sink, soap suds dripping from her arms. She turned and looked at them.

'Who are you?' asked Cynthia, gawping.

'Who are you?' the woman replied flatly.

Marcia felt a stabbing at the bottom of her throat and a stitch in her side. It was hurting her just to breathe. There wasn't a stick of furniture she recognized. A new table – a rocking chair – a painting of a horse and cart, and two Toby jugs on a new dresser.

'Who am *I*?' said Cynthia, aghast.

A girl appeared, about Cynthia's age, nicely dressed in a dogtooth suit and a hat. 'Who's this, Ma?' She blinked rapidly and fumbled with the belt on her jacket.

'This is our house. We live here . . .' said Cynthia.

'Not any more, you don't,' said the woman.

'Let's find Alfie,' said Cynthia, marching on ahead and rapping on the letterbox of the Maloneys' house. To her surprise Alfie answered the door, chewing on a piece of toast, his shirt unbuttoned.

'You look peachy, Cyn,' he said. 'And you, Marce. Except what have they done to your hair?'

'Never mind,' she said, touching her head self-consciously.

'Alfie, what's happened to our ma and da?' said Cynthia urgently.

'They've been gone for weeks. Rented the house out to raise money. They tried to sell it but that was hopeless because of the damp. I thought you'd all gone together.'

Marcia looked startled and turned to her sister. 'They've lied to us, Cyn.'

'Bloody hell. That was me gran's house. She'd be turning in her grave if she knew they tried to sell it.'

Alfie told them what he knew – that the Rogans had rented their house out to a nice family and hadn't been back since. He passed Marcia a handkerchief as she began to cry and asked Cynthia not to kick the door again. He also asked Cynthia if she fancied a night at the Rialto, but she replied haughtily that now she was a professional dancer she didn't go to dance halls much. 'Busman's holiday,' she said, breezily, but neither he nor Marcia were quite sure what that meant. 'Gee whizz. You did it then, Cyn?'

She shrugged and blinked away into the distance. 'What now, though?' she said to Marcia. 'I'll have to go back to Norma's and you to the orphanage. I don't know . . . I just don't know.'

'I'll keep a look out and ask me da,' Alfie offered.

Cynthia nodded, but her eyes were full of rage. Marcia wondered how long she was going to be able to control her temper. Just like their da.

'Let's go, squit. I blame Da. I can't believe I'm stuck at Norma's.'

'Nice to see you again, girls.'

Cynthia waved him away dismissively. Marcia looked at him with round eyes. She had taken something out of her pocket and was absent-mindedly turning it over in her hand.

'What's that?' he asked.

She looked down at the little card that Sister Dorothea had given her, as if noticing it for the first time, and read out the text. '*Accept Jesus into your life and you will find happiness.*'

'And you think that will solve our ma and da sodding off?' said Cynthia, crossly.

'No. But it's on this card Sister Dorothea gave me.'

Cynthia snatched it off her, looked at it and snorted again. 'Revolting. Our Lady with all them daggers sticking into her heart and blood dribbling out.'

'Thanks, Alfie,' said Marcia. 'Let us know if you have news.'

When Cynthia got back to the flat, Norma was sitting waiting with her feet up on the leather pouffe, smoking a cigarette with a plate of biscuits in front of her. Her face was covered in white cold cream that had congealed in ridges over the lines in her forehead.

'Did you know Ma and Da have left Liverpool Lane?'

'Have they?' she said vaguely. 'Any more news on the dancing front, love?'

'Auntie, they've gone. They didn't tell me or Marce.'

'I'm sorry, dear.'

Cynthia shrugged.

'You need to lose a few pounds. Don't want you to turn into a Heffalump. Then you'll find it even more difficult to get to your precious Blackpool.'

Cynthia winced. 'Auntie Norma. Can you stop going on about it?'

Norma shrugged and offered her a biscuit.

Marcia wasn't expected to join them for Mass, Sister Dorothea had said right from the first day: 'No one is forcing you; but Father might need help with the kneelers.' When she got to the room off the chapel, the nun looked surprised to see her.

'Whatever is the matter, child?'

'My ma . . .' sniffed Marcia.

'Oh dear,' she said. 'I see. Now come with me.'

She took her into a small office a little way down the corridor and shut the door. The place smelled musty; the wood panelling was rotten where it met the ceiling in one corner. 'They didn't want to worry you. It's only for a short time.'

'Where are they? I want to see them,' Marcia said more firmly.

'I'm afraid you can't.'

'Why?'

She sighed. 'The letter will explain. Now, where did I put it?'

Marcia fixed her eyes on the view of the garden through the windows while the nun rooted through drawers. Eventually she found an envelope, plump and plain, in the middle drawer of the desk. She opened it and handed Marcia the letter.

Her mother's curved handwriting sloped across the paper.

Dear Marcia,

How are you? Please don't be alarmed. I have some news. I'm afraid your da and I will be going away for a short while. While funds don't allow us to stay at Liverpool Lane, we have made other arrangements. As soon as we are back on our feet, we'll return. The Irish sea air will be good for Da, the doctors say.

In the meantime, Marcia, you should finish school. We wish Cynthia the best of luck with her dancing career. I hear it's going grand. The nuns will take care of you, dear.

I'm sorry, but it's not looking possible for us to be home at Christmas. I'm sorry we didn't tell you and Cynthia before we left but things moved rapidly and we had to do a sort of moonlight flit. These damned tick-men and us living on the never-never with Da not able to work. So, you see. It's difficult. Renting out the house seemed the only way to raise money and it was sensible to get out. The damp. Da's chest. We were looking forward to seeing you at Christmas, but once we get organized, we'll all be back in Liverpool Lane. For now, you are a ward of court and Sister Dorothea will take charge of you. It's less complicated that way, with school and shoes and dinner money. I am hearing only good reports of St Mary's.

Your loving Ma

Her eyes smarted. So there would be no paper bells and mistletoe and a lovely tree after all. She folded the letter and slipped it into her pocket. Shoes? Dinner money? Her head whirled. But there was one phrase that stuck out from all the other odd things she had said – ward of court? What did that mean? It sounded the worst of the lot, but she didn't dare ask.

'Don't cry, Marcia. It's no fun being poor, is it? You have to be strong, though,' said Ellie later.

'Why didn't she say anything the last time I saw her?'

Ellie didn't reply. She was staring at the letter. 'The date, look at the date,' she said. 'This was written three months ago.'

Marcia gasped.

'So why did the nuns wait so long to show you it?'

Marcia's brows knitted together. 'Sister said I was "under care of the authorities". What does that mean, Ellie?'

Ellie paused. 'They ask your ma to sign your care over to the nuns.'

'I don't think Ma will sign.'

'If you're under their care, she already has.'

'But I still don't understand what it means.'

'It means the nuns . . . well, they're your ma and da now.'

Chapter 28

'Orphans of the living,' said Sister Dorothea. 'I've always thought that's an unkind way of putting it.'

'Not really,' said Father Donnelly, sitting in the office at the orphanage. He traced a finger over the grooves on the arm of the ornately carved ecclesiastical chair. 'It makes sense. These poor children that come to us might as well not even have parents. Any living parents they do have are often drunks. Prostitutes, some of the mothers are.'

'Oh dear. Prostitutes.' She raised a hand to her chest and a blush flowered on her cheeks. 'Not all of the mothers, though. Some poor souls give their babies away because of the shame. Just girls in desperate situations.'

He frowned. 'Maybe. But after the recent war, many men have come back to find that Liverpool is not how they left it. And neither are their families. Like Ellie Kinsella.'

'Oh dear. That awful war . . .'

'Still, Australia might be the fresh start the girl needs. We're not making any progress with her here. She's on the list. Every week the sisters in Australia

203

are asking us to send "orphans". She's probably a bed-wetter. The washing is constant, isn't it?'

'I'm afraid so.'

'We had a dog. My father used to put its nose in the puddle. Worked in no time.'

Dorothea bristled. These are children, she wanted to say. Only yesterday she had caught one of the nuns making a poor little girl stand with the sheet over her head in the rain. 'You think that works for children, Father?'

'I don't know. I don't know. These children who stay here – they're feral, most of them. We even have four girls who are in the family way. Three boys who have gone straight from here to Walton jail. The sooner we find homes for them, the better chance they'll have of making something of their lives.'

'There's hope for the babies then,' she said.

'True.' He put his feet on the desk and crossed one leg over the other, sighing as he noticed the fine layer of dust on the surface. 'The cleaning never ends,' he said. 'You must get one of the older girls to see to this room. There's a satisfaction in watching the lost souls stoop over a bucket doing God's work, making all the bad in their hearts good by scrubbing their sins away. It's the only hope for these girls. Penance.'

He stood to leave. Dorothea hesitated. 'Father, one more thing. The Worboys are looking for a live-in help for their child. The mother is something of a do-gooder. She suggested I send her one of our girls, and there is one who would be suitable: Marcia Rogan. She's different. Different to most of the girls who come through these doors. I don't think I've ever seen such a good soul in a girl. Father, might I . . . She could well be the answer.'

He looked at her and raised an eyebrow, then exhaled a long breath. 'By all means, but if she's still at school, she'll have to finish her education. We can't be seen to whip them out to work in the middle of their studies. But Sister, whatever you decide to do, you have my blessing.'

The nun nodded. Her mouth quivered.

'Dorothea,' he said gently. 'What's the matter?'

She gathered herself. 'Nothing. I'm fine. Only the headaches.'

The priest nodded seriously. 'I have to go, Dorothea.'

She listened to his footsteps dying away as he disappeared down the corridor, the gentle swishing of his vestments. He had a manly stride. She thought to herself that although he'd given his life up to God and given up women, there was not a single part of the good-looking, broad-shouldered Father Donnelly that seemed less male than any Liverpool dockworker or navvy she had met. It was as if he was unable to contain his masculinity: large hands poking out from white cuffs, wiry black hairs escaping over the top of his dog collar, bristles bursting along his jawline. It seemed such a waste.

Her thoughts turned to Marcia Rogan again.

How different she was to most. Mrs Worboys would be thrilled.

Chapter 29

'Test me again,' said Ellie, standing on the small iron bed.

Marcia took the Bible. Ellie shook her arms and one leg, then another, as if she was preparing for a race, cracked her knuckles and took a deep breath. '*And lo, the children are a heritage of the Lord . . .*' She rattled through the passage at top speed.

'Yes! You got it right that time!' Marcia cried.

'Are you sure?'

'Perfect!'

'So remember, when I give you the sign, you know what to do? You say you feel faint and then I swap your Bible with this one. I'm going to be creating such a fuss they won't notice. Come on. Chop-chop.'

Marcia nodded. Ellie seemed to have a wild energy about her today. Even more than usual.

Half an hour later, the priest walked solemnly through the gardens with the nuns following, singing 'Ave Maria'. The Monsignor, in his white and gold vestments, led the procession and swung sweet-smelling incense. The children who had been told to stay in their rooms were leaning out of their windows, smiling, waving and pointing. When the little party reached the chapel, they stood under the curved brick arch to the entrance. The chapel was full. The mayor, the local bank manager and doctor, their wives and even their children sat in the front pews, though they were kept apart from the orphan children fidgeting and squirming in the back pews and side altars. Two altar boys with shiny Brylcreemed hair and starched white lace vestments were getting ready to process up the aisle with their polished brass candlesticks.

'Doesn't it look lovely?' whispered Sister Dorothea to Marcia. 'You have your reading?'

Marcia widened her eyes. It did look lovely. Everything was white. Everything was sunny and dazzling. The handsome young priest and three altar boys, carrying a plinth on top of which sat a blue and gold statue of Our Lady smiling serenely and squashing a snake under her foot, began to walk towards the altar singing a sweet-sounding 'Star of the Sea'.

Marcia took her place under the statue and looked back over her shoulder, searching for Ellie. Ellie smiled, winked and gave her the thumbs up.

The priest spoke the gospel and then gave a sermon about the Holy Family and how each one of them here were brothers and sisters in Christ. 'Except the snotty-nosed, nit-infested ones who no one wants,' whispered Ellie to the girl sitting beside her.

'Off you go, Marcia,' said Sister Dorothea. 'Head up. Eyes forward to the Lord. Speak loudly and clearly, and remember what an honour it is to be asked to do a reading.'

'I feel a bit dizzy, Sister,' she said.

'It's just collywobbles. Take a deep breath.'

All eyes were on Marcia as she made her way onto the altar and up to the lectern.

'In the name of the Father . . .' She paused and began to sway unsteadily on her feet, gripping the lectern.

There was a collective intake of breath, and then a voice – Ellie's voice. 'She's going to faint!' she said, leaping out of her pew and running towards the lectern.

Confusion followed: Ellie dashing up the steps, Marcia stumbling into her arms, Ellie leading her to a chair at the side of the lectern. And then when she had done so she turned to face the shocked congregation, eyes wild and staring, as if possessed.

'And lo, the children are a heritage of the LORD!! And the fruit of his womb is his reward!' She held the Bible she had taken from Marcia – or it looked as though she had – above her head, then opened it and began to read.

'It's upside down,' hissed Sister Cyril. 'She's not reading it. But that girl, how would she know any of the Lord's words?' she said, shocked.

'And I am full of the Lord. Jesus is in my body. As arrows are in the hand of a mighty man, so are children of the youth! Happy is the man that hath his quiver full of them!'

She started shaking and rolling her eyes. She dropped the Bible dramatically onto the floor as though it was hot to touch. There it lay open for all to see, and bewilderingly, with the pages burnt out – just a sooty hole running through it. There was a gasp. The priest stared, dumbfounded.

'I'll give you quivers!' spat an incandescent Sister Cyril, dashing out of the pew.

'I am your saviour!' cried Ellie.

Within moments, the nun had yanked her off the altar, pulling her by her ear.

'Ow! Sid!' she objected, stumbling down the steps. 'What are you doing? You nearly made me do meself an injury!'

'You heathen girl,' the nun hissed. 'I thought I'd seen it all, but this one takes the biscuit.'

Ellie turned to Marcia. Marcia was willing her shoulders to stop shaking. She was laughing so much that tears were running down her face.

'Marcia, don't cry. Are you all right?' said Sister Dorothea kindly, going over to comfort her. 'Don't cry, dear. Don't cry.'

That night, Marcia and Ellie laughed so much that they clutched their sides and rolled around the bedroom floor in a kind of delicious pain. 'That was the most fun I've had in ages,' Marcia said. Finally, lying on the little bed and staring up at the skylight, they caught their breath and their laughter subsided into smiles.

'I'm for it now, though,' said Ellie.

The following week, Ellie appeared at the door with a small case. She was wearing a coat with a velvet collar and a pair of white lace cotton gloves. 'You'll write?'

Marcia nodded tearfully. 'You're really going? This is so sudden.'

Ellie kissed her on the cheek. 'They're glad to be

rid of me. Our stunt finally convinced them I'm completely crazy. Don't look so worried – it's what I wanted. To be on that list. The nuns say if I don't like it, I can come back. But it's going to be such an adventure.'

'Are you sure?' asked Marcia. 'I asked Sister Hilda about it when we were listening to the wireless and she wouldn't even talk about it.'

'It's going to be wonderful,' Ellie replied breezily. 'Come to the Pier Head with me and wave me off if you want.'

When they got downstairs, Sister Cyril was waiting. 'Where d'you think you're going, Marcia Rogan?'

'Marcia is coming to see me off.'

'Oh no she's not,' she said brusquely.

The girls knew there was no point arguing.

'Write to me with all your news. Every bit. And good luck in your new home,' whispered Marcia tearfully.

She went back to her room, lay on her small bed and pillowed her head in her hands. Rolling over, she read Ellie's parting note once more.

Dear Marcia

I hope I don't get sick on the journey, but I remember about yer da getting seasick so I'll squeeze the bridge of me nose like he did and put me head between me knees. I nearly fainted when yer said it would take that long. I asked Sister Dorothea and she said aye, it might be longer than we thought but she was a bit useless with the details. Anyways, please send letters for me to stop me from getting homesick.

I hope yer get back to your ma and da's soon. Me auntie signed the paper so I guess she doesn't want me. Sister loves yer, that's for sure, and she probably would like to keep hold of yer forever.

Love, your pal, Ellie

Chapter 30

Henry Cherry was crouching down with his back to Marcia, shuffling papers into uneven piles on the floor. He stood up to see who had politely coughed to announce their arrival and knocked two more files off the desk, scattering their contents across the floor.

'Sorry, that was clever. First impressions are so important, aren't they?' He began gathering up the papers.

'Oh, it said Mr Higgins's office outside.'

'I'm pretty low down the food chain here. When I'm not taking down hours of notes, I do the important filing. There's a lot of it.' He gestured at the messy surfaces and piles of folders on top of filing cabinets.

Marcia nodded, her eyes alighting on the picture of the King on the wall above the desk, the faded map of Liverpool in a frame. Her eyes moved from the view of the river outside, back to Henry Cherry.

'Mr . . . erm . . .'

'Mr Cherry. But you can call me Henry, since we do sort of know each other.'

She paused. 'You ever see Billy and the gang?'

'No. We took different paths.'

'Aye. No surprise. I heard he's working for his da's rag and bone business.'

Henry nodded. 'Is he?'

She paused. 'Henry . . . St Mary's. I don't think my ma has been clear with me. What does it mean? Ward of court?'

He looked at her sadly. Glancing at his watch, he sat down at Mr Higgins's imposing desk and gestured for her to sit opposite.

'Usually it suggests that your parents are in difficult circumstances, so they look to us for help. It means you're being looked after by the council if your family are not able to. That's all. We have a duty. If you don't have a relative, or a guardian.'

'I do, though. My Auntie Norma. Norma Bottomley.'

'Oh, yes. Wait.'

He stood up, opened a drawer in a filing cabinet and began rooting through. 'Rogan, Rogan . . . Liverpool Lane . . . Norma Bottomley. Ah, found it. Norma.' He frowned at the file. 'But she's refused.'

'I know, but can't you force her?'

'Oh, erm. No. I don't think we can.' He brought the file back to the desk, turning the pages slowly.

'Can't I just live on my own? I'm sixteen.'

'Where, though? That's why you're still with the nuns. There's nowhere for you to go. If you don't have money . . . wait . . . I see you'll be going to work as a mother's help when a position is found? Says here you're a suitable candidate, hard-working, clean, neat, literate. That's impressive.'

'Henry – you read a file and think you know everything about me? What else is in your file? About my dad and his brain, and the cough medicine? About the jungle that made him mad? About my mother, who doesn't seem to have the will to stand up for me or my sister because she's so tired and afraid? About the house? Yes, you're right about that. I have nowhere. That hope is gone, by the way.'

'What d'you mean, gone?'

'Gone. There's someone else living there. Mr Cherry – I mean, Henry – I feel pretty desperate. Nothing feels right. And now my best friend is leaving, so I'm all on my own. Why can't any of you help me?' Henry looked shocked at her bluntness, she thought, and she made an effort to calm herself. 'I'm glad it's you I've found in here, not Mr Higgins with his silly hat.'

She took off her gloves and gripped the edge of the table. Her lip quivered.

'Try not to cry. Hey, don't cry,' he said. He took a handkerchief out of his pocket, shook it open and offered it to her. 'It's clean.'

She took it gratefully and dabbed under her eyes.

'Miss Rogan . . . I'm sorry.' She looked so sad, he wanted to reach out and hold her hand across the desk, but he knew that he could lose his job for that. 'It is a silly hat,' he said, trying to raise a smile. 'And the thing is, he thinks he looks wonderful in it. I catch him looking at himself whenever he walks past a shop window, but no one dares tell him.'

A smile tugged at the corners of her lips.

'Don't be upset,' he said. 'I'll do what I can to help. There's an added note here about a possible position with the Worboys family. Is that something you would want to do?'

'It would be better than the orphanage, I suppose.'

'I'll tell Mr Higgins to get cracking on it. In the meantime, if there's a problem at the orphanage, I'm usually two floors up – top floor, tiny office. And at lunchtime you can find me at Acropolis Cafe around the corner. Always sitting at the table in the window. Creature of habit, I'm afraid. Or, if you like, I can come and check up on you from time to time,' he said.

'What the devil did you say that for?' Higgins shouted at him half an hour later, when he told him about Marcia's visit. 'If we tried to help every blighter that comes here with a sob story . . . You're green. Got your head in that Cole Porter music. Makes you soft. But you'll learn soon enough. You'll learn, lad,' he added darkly.

Chapter 31

Now that it had been confirmed she had no one at home in Liverpool Lane and it had somehow got around school, everyone had decided Marcia was even more strange. Spring came, then summer, but Marcia was still the girl who lived at the orphanage. A boy in her class, one day, had said, 'How do you stop a tram, Marcia? Throw an orphan in front of it, no one will care,' and laughed. It was the last day she went to school.

It was calm in her room at the orphanage. She was lucky not to have to sleep in the dormitory; Sister Dorothea had arranged that for her. When she wasn't listening to the radio with Sister Hilda, she spent most of her time in the sewing room repairing the nuns' habits, tunics and wimples. She picked apples and raspberries and made more jam; she went to bed tired and slept well. Her other tasks consisted mostly of polishing candlesticks and wheeling the babies' prams.

One morning, Sister Dorothea asked her to go to George Henry Lee's and collect some shoelaces and pipe cleaners. On her way back she headed along the promenade. Alfie was in his usual place, sitting on the wall, legs crossed at the ankle and swinging back and forth as he dangled his rod over the harbour wall.

'Alfie, you're here,' she said.

'Seems like it,' he laughed. 'I'm here every Saturday.'

There was the sound of the waves slapping against the wall. He took a piece of cheese out of his pocket and rolled it into a ball. After carefully pushing the hook through the cheese, he threw the line out and waited.

The rod jerked. 'A bite!' he cried. The line tugged and he laughed. But when he pulled it in, there was just a bit of seaweed tangled up in the hook. 'What you doing here?'

'Just wondered if you . . .' Her sentence tailed off. A boat slid onto the horizon. 'They sent my pal to Australia on a boat like that . . .'

'Australia!'

'Aye. To a farm. Land of milk and honey, at least that's what she says.'

'Are you going to Australia?' he asked.

He didn't even look at her, just concentrated on keeping a firm grip on the rod.

'No, a house by the sea in Waterloo. I'm going to help look after a baby when the family come back from their summer holiday. I'm still waiting for me ma and da to sort themselves and come and get me. Ellie doesn't have a ma. Alfie . . . there's fishing out there, and you can come. Will you come and see me? It's only half an hour away on the train. Number one, Beach Lawn. You'll remember that?'

'Aye. You worried about your pal?'

'A bit.' She shrugged miserably.

'You worried about going to this house?'

217

'No. Not if you come by. We're all split up. Cynthia. Me. My pal.'

He stopped and turned. 'Well, if there's fish.' He smiled and nudged her. 'I'm joking. I'll come and see yer. But it's not the fish. It's you I'll come for.'

She chewed her lip. What was he saying? What would Cynthia say?

'Do you get bored fishing?' she asked, changing the subject.

'No.' He paused. 'You should write your pal a letter. Check she's happy, if you're worried and it's what the nuns say it is. I wouldn't trust them.'

'Aye. I will.'

The rod jerked and he pulled hard. At the end of the line was a silver fish, curling and flipping, flashing in the sun. 'Marcia!' he cried. He unhooked the wriggling fish, held it in both of his hands and inspected it, parting its mouth, turning it over. 'Good luck you brought me.' He dropped it with a splash into his bucket.

'You still going to America?' she asked him.

'Aye. I'd take you with me if I could.'

'And what about our Cyn?' she laughed.

'She thinks I'm a kid. I am, compared to her fellas. She said so.'

'Did she?'

'Aye.'

He blinked and scanned the horizon. 'See you for the fishing!' he called after her.

Normally the nuns were saying Mass at this time, but Marcia was here early. She clutched a letter to Ellie, which she had spent all morning writing, in her hand.

The voices floated up from the small chapel. She moved aside the musty-smelling velvet curtain that separated one end of the corridor from the other. Everything about this place was designed for people to hide behind: the lids over the baths, the curtains fencing off corners. No mirrors to see yourself in. When there was a death, even the large windows were covered with sheets to avoid anyone catching sight of their own reflection.

She knocked on Sister's door. There was no reply. Deciding she should slip in and leave the letter on the desk, she turned the handle and pushed.

She hadn't been in the office since she arrived, and she was immediately struck by how different it looked. The desk was no longer facing the window but pushed up against the wall. There was a curtain with sun motifs hanging on a wire that closed off half of the room, as in the corridor. Sometimes in the winter curtains like these were used to save on heating and keep out the draughts, but it was strange to see it drawn shut on a day like today. The bookcase was flanked by a pair of brass pots holding aspidistras. But most strange of all, a sweet smell filled the room – the smoke of a cigar, or cigarettes maybe. As she moved quietly forward to place the letter on the desk a voice spoke behind the curtain, instantly recognizable as Sister Dorothea's.

'Night after night. It's not getting any better.'

Marcia stood frozen, rooted to the spot.

'Shall we pray?' a second voice replied. Marcia was startled to hear that it was a man's, but whose, she couldn't be sure. Instinct told her that she should leave immediately.

'How is that going to help?'

'Get a hold of yourself now, Dorothea.'

'Father, I can't sleep.'

There was a long sigh. 'I can arrange a plenary indulgence to calm you. It will take some time.'

Plenary indulgence? What was that? thought Marcia. Some kind of sleeping aid? Hardly daring to breathe, she left and pulled the door quickly shut. But there had been the sound of a chair scraping across the floor as she tiptoed out. Panic took hold of her as she hurried away down the corridor, and after a moment she looked back to see Sister Dorothea following her.

'Marcia.' The nun seemed about to say something, but didn't. She seemed conscious of Marcia's gaze, raising a hand to her lips and running her tongue over her bottom lip, then tucking away a stray piece of hair that was poking out from under her habit. Marcia had thought nuns shaved their heads but clearly, underneath the sister's habit was a full head of hair. Cynthia had been wrong – Cynthia, who knew everything.

'Sister, I wrote a letter. For Ellie. I left it.'

'Very well. Now go and finish the dusting,' Sister Dorothea snapped.

Chapter 32

'Marcia, someone to see you,' Sister Cyril called from the doorway. Marcia was in the room beyond with two other girls, shelling a large bowl of peas. 'He says he's from the Corporation.'

Henry shifted nervously from foot to foot. Sister Cyril made him anxious.

'My boss, Mr Higgins, likes everything in order. I have some more forms for Miss Rogan,' he said.

Sister Cyril cocked her head to one side. 'You really work for the Corporation? You're very young. Shouldn't you be at school?'

'I'm an apprentice. I'm learning. One of the government schemes,' he said.

Sister Cyril sighed. 'I suppose if lads your age were grown up enough to get blown up in the war, you're old enough to fill in a few names on a form.'

Marcia finished wiping her hands on her apron and pushed a strand of her red hair behind her ear.

'I can vouch for Marcia,' said Sister Hilda as she arrived in the room.

Marcia stopped in her tracks. 'Oh – Mr Cherry.'

'You know each other?'

'Yes, from a long time ago,' said Henry.

'Then you'll know she's a treasure. Spends a lot of

time with me. We chat and she does sewing, and she listens to the wireless with me and we dance to my gramophone records. We love the Andrews Sisters, don't we, Marcia?'

Henry tried to picture how a person might dance with a nun to the Andrews Sisters, but his imagination let him down.

'Now I must get to chapel. The sisters will be shouting for me. I'll leave you to it. Let yourself out, Mr Cherry.'

Henry was already shuffling through papers and laying them out on the table. He unscrewed his fountain pen and drew a squiggle on the back of one sheet to make sure the ink was flowing. He closed his briefcase, unbuttoned his jacket and sat down. It seemed to Marcia that he was doing everything he could to avoid looking her in the eye.

'Please, take a seat,' he said without looking up.

She remained standing and waited until he looked at her, then gracefully lowered herself into the chair. He checked his forms again, adjusted his glasses and cleared his throat.

'So. How are you, Miss Rogan?'

'As well as can be expected, Mr Cherry. But isn't it your job to find that out?' she said shyly.

He took a moment to consider this by looking down at the papers again, straightening his tie and then glancing up at her, unabashed. 'I suppose so,' he said with a smile.

Marcia twisted her hands in her lap. He was beginning to annoy her.

'Erm. So. Here we go. These are the forms to be

filled in and then we can come to a conclusion. About leaving here. See if we think you're ready for the Worboys.'

'You mean Mr Higgins can?'

'Yes, of course. Sorry. I can leave the forms with you, but I thought it might be a help if I explained them.'

'I don't need you to do that,' she said, more harshly than she meant to.

He nodded, accepting the rejection, and collected several forms into one neat pile for her, putting the rest back in his briefcase. He tightened his fountain pen carefully and put it away in his inside jacket pocket. Marcia looked at all the papers, avoiding his eyes now, but sensing him watching her. He snapped the briefcase shut and moved towards the door.

'I'm very pleased to have seen you again, Miss Rogan.'

'No, wait . . . Is there any news of my ma and da? My sister?'

He came back and sat down opposite her.

'Your sister secured a job dancing at a theatre in Blackpool.'

'Good for Cyn,' she murmured.

'And your parents. They're in Ireland. Your father is recuperating. But as you are a ward of court . . .' He saw her face harden. 'Don't worry, I'm sure it will be temporary. Marine Villas won't be so bad. They're a good family by all accounts, the Worboys.'

'Aye,' she said.

'And if there's any trouble, any upset, Miss Rogan, you come directly to me.'

'Like when you told Billy Brennan what's what?'

He smiled. 'Yes, just like that. You know where I am. Top floor. Lovely view across the Mersey. I can almost see the Worboys from my little window. I'll keep an eye on you.'

He offered her a formal handshake, but she hesitated.

'Actually, would you mind helping me with the forms after all? If you have time?' she asked.

It was dark by the time Henry left St Mary's. He turned his collar up against the wind and looked back at the building. At least she would be getting out of this place. He had heard stories about what went on here behind closed doors, and she was a sweet girl; he wouldn't want to share them with her.

Chapter 33

Sister Dorothea insisted she should be the one to take Marcia to the house by the sea. Beach Lawn was the name of the road where the Worboys family lived. Across the road from their house was a park, and beyond that the dunes and then the sea. The house itself was more like a hotel: a beautiful three-storied, whitewashed Edwardian villa dripping with wisteria, gabled with rooms in the attic, with a pretty veranda and elaborate ironmongery under the edge of the roof and running along the balconies. The door was painted white and mounted with a brass knocker in the shape of a lion's head. There was a large, neatly kept front lawn edged with rose beds, and a sundial.

Mrs Worboys was friendly if a little skittish, with delicate features and fine blonde flyaway hair that she had pinned up in an elaborate coil. 'Be polite and always say thank you,' Sister Dorothea had whispered to Marcia as they went up the path.

'Come and see Dolly, Sister,' was the first thing Mrs Worboys said when she opened the door. 'You must be Marcia. She's just napping.'

'Thank you,' stuttered Marcia.

The downstairs room where little Dolly was sleeping was painted a sunny yellow, with white ducklings on a frieze under the cornicing and a bobbing mobile of teddy bears over the cot. The little girl – she must have been about four years old – was lying on a pretty daybed, covered with a crocheted blanket. She stirred and pushed a tangle of red hair out of her face, then went back to sleep.

'Shall we run through what you would like Marcia to do before Dolly wakes? I feel it's always better to say at the outset what a girl's duties will be, and then there's no room for confusion,' said Sister Dorothea as they stepped back out into the hall. They settled at the table in the dining room, where a grandfather clock ticked gently in a corner.

'Marcia, I would like you to do the sweeping and dusting, and soaking and washing,' Mrs Worboys began. 'And maybe prepare some of Dolly's food; oh, and read to her, which she loves, and take her to the park.' She turned to Sister Dorothea. 'It's my sleeping, you see – it's such hard work and she's up so early in the morning. And I'm very busy with my soldiers' charities. Those poor men. One of my brave fellows was selling matches from the gutters the other day. He's half blind,' she said, wincing. 'Anyway, I get so awfully tired.'

'You don't need to apologize. Especially not to Marcia. That's what she's here for. To help you. You're doing such good work, Maud.'

'Have you ever looked after a little one before?' Mrs Worboys asked Marcia.

'She's helped with the children at St Mary's, haven't you, Marcia?'

'Oh! And here she is! Hello, Dolly.' The child

wandered in, rubbing her eyes with her fists. She held a rag doll in one chubby hand.

Sister Dorothea looked at her with a faraway expression and held out her arms. 'Hello, my dear.' To Marcia's surprise the child went straight over and clambered onto the nun's knee. 'Dolly, this is Marcia.'

Marcia waved and winked at her. Dolly giggled back at Marcia. 'Dolly's such a pretty name,' said Marcia.

'It's the name that was on the little label when she first came to us,' Mrs Worboys replied in a low voice, so that Dolly couldn't hear. 'Most people who adopt change the name of their baby, but we kept it.'

Marcia nodded. She turned her attention back to Dolly and smiled at her again. 'You're a natural, Marcia,' Mrs Worboys said, as Marcia pulled a funny face and Dolly squirmed into Sister Dorothea's chest, hiding her face and laughing each time as she looked back at her.

'She'll need special love, Marcia,' said Sister Dorothea.

Mrs Worboys smiled. 'We've been lucky enough for Father Donnelly to arrange for Sister to be a regular visitor here to assist us through Dolly's baby years. She's getting older now and will be at school soon, so we don't need Sister now. What we really need is a mother's live-in help, Marcia. Housekeeping, chores, as well as nannying.'

Marcia was surprised, and a little caught off guard, when Dolly scrambled down from Dorothea's lap, ran over to her and gripped her arm tightly with one small hand. Such determination! she thought, as the child remained clamped onto her. It wasn't a feeling she was used to.

'We never imagined Dolly would bring such joy to our lives. She is so beautiful, aren't you, Dolly dewdrop?'

Dolly was now toddling around the room, lunging from one piece of furniture to the next and bumping into things. 'Mama, please may I have a drink?'

'In a moment, dear. Marcia, we are so delighted to have you working for us.'

'Mrs Worboys needs a kind, hard-working girl, Marcia, not some slovenly type. Marcia's mother was a daily communicant, Mrs Worboys. If I could describe Marcia, I'd describe her as a typical girl next door. Not like some of the orphanage girls, who might be more typical if you happened to live next door to a whorehouse.' Mrs Worboys laughed a little uncomfortably, and Marcia thought it a strange thing for a nun to say.

'Before you go, tell me – is Sister Hilda still enjoying Mrs Roosevelt's wireless?' Mrs Worboys asked.

'She thinks it's wonderful,' the nun smiled.

Mrs Worboys turned to Marcia to explain. 'Eleanor Roosevelt visited the American military base at Aintree in 1942 and brought them a gift of a wireless. Then, when the GIs left, the army donated the wireless to the Corporation, and my committee ladies arranged for it to end up at St Mary's.'

Dolly crossed the room and held out her doll for Marcia to examine. She took it and wiggled one of the arms as if to say hello. The two women looked at the girls with something approaching envy.

'I ought to get back,' said Sister Dorothea. 'But I can see we're all going to get on like a house on fire.'

Mrs Worboys saw her out, then walked slowly back into the room where Marcia had started to play peek-a-boo with Dolly.

'I'm sorry about your parents, Marcia,' Mrs Worboys said. 'You keep playing and I'll go and get Dolly's drink.'

What did she mean about her parents? thought Marcia. How much had the nun told her? She picked Dolly up and carried her to the window. There was a path that led to a bulging arch of clematis. There were plump dahlias in beds still bursting with colour even though it was September, and daisies pushed their way up through the grass and freckled the lawn. Beyond the flower beds there was a low privet hedge and every so often a car would roar past. A seagull was picking about on the lawn. It was difficult to see where the sea ended and the sky began but she could just about make out Blackpool Tower. Her thoughts turned to Cynthia.

Mrs Worboys showed her more of the house, including the spotless bedroom next to Dolly's where Marcia would be sleeping. It had flowered curtains, a matching bedspread and a view of the sea with the foothills of Wales in the distance. Marcia decided she was going to like it here. The house had two bathrooms, and on the upstairs landing was a trouser press for Mr Worboys. Downstairs there was a clean white-and-green-tiled kitchen with a fridge and a toaster, things that Marcia had only ever heard about.

'Mr Worboys insists the fridge is scoured and cleaned every two weeks, but the toaster is a dream. Two slices perfectly done in a minute,' Mrs Worboys said. Marcia thought about home and sticking forks into pieces of bread and holding them over the smoky fire, and how long it took. She had never seen so many inventions to make life feel simple. If only her mother had had all these contraptions.

Mrs Worboys showed her a machine for washing clothes – a little like the ones at the washhouse but smaller, with 'Hoover' emblazoned on the front – and their brand new vacuum cleaner, also labelled 'Hoover' but this time in large block capitals running vertically down its canvas dust bag. Marcia would use it to suck the dirt off the floors, Mrs Worboys told her, switching it on to demonstrate the backwards and forwards motion needed for best results. It made a frightening growling noise, its strange pillow-like bag billowing as if it was alive. What on earth did people do all day, Marcia wondered, if they didn't need to scrub clothes, sweep the floor or drag coal inside to heat the house?

To the right of the sink there was a large 'Ascot' gas water heater. Mrs Worboys turned the knob excitedly and after a short *whoosh* of the gas lighting, hot water gushed out. 'You'll find it so much quicker for cleaning the pots and pans,' Mrs Worboys said, wiping her forehead as steam rose from the sink. She could see Marcia's eyes widening. 'It means we don't have to have servants, you see. Mr Worboys doesn't like to have strangers about the house. That won't apply to you, I'm sure. He'll get along just perfectly with you. Any questions?'

'I hope I can remember all the right buttons to push.'

'You'll be fine. You can try the washing machine tomorrow morning,' she smiled.

'I'm used to the washhouse,' she said.

'The washhouse? Oh, is that nice?'

Marcia shrugged. 'We have cups of tea and a natter and everyone sings. And it makes us all feel a little better. Mr Tattersall says that when you share stories it makes everything seem a little brighter.'

'Mr Tattersall? Who's Mr Tattersall?'

Marcia hesitated. 'He's a friend of our family.'

'Mr Tattersall is right. That's what I do with my soldier fellows. They get so much joy from being with one another. Perhaps you would like to come along one day? You could help with the teas.'

When Mr Worboys arrived home that evening from his job at Morley and Worboys Architectural Planners, Marcia was sitting in the bay window, pushing a needle in and out of a table runner Mrs Worboys had asked her to darn. She saw him coming up the road carrying his briefcase and recognized him from the formal wedding photograph on the mantelpiece. He was wearing the same dark suit, carried an umbrella and had a serious-looking newspaper wedged under his arm – and it was all topped off with a fine bowler hat. A bowler hat, in Liverpool? It gave him a peculiar authority and made Marcia feel a little nervous.

As he walked, he swung the umbrella out before him and tapped the ground in front of him every second step. When he got to the gate, she saw him pause and prod the umbrella into a clump of flowers. A frown flitted across his brow and he lifted his head towards the house as if to ask why he was the first to notice something amiss. He put one foot in the flower bed and bent down to look at the flowers, but then stood upright, carefully brushing the knees of his trousers. He looked the kind of man who, when action was required, was quite comfortable with getting someone else to do it for him. She heard the front door open.

'Maud. Maud? The ivy is strangling the honey-suckle. We need that pruning before winter sets in,' he said as he came into the room. When he saw Marcia he stopped, raised an eyebrow and said, 'Oh, you must be the new girl – Marcia, is it?'

She stood and nodded shyly. He handed her his bowler hat and umbrella, assuming she would be grateful for the privilege. At least he was kind and said thank you, she thought.

'The blasted ivy.'

'My ma said once it has taken a grip you can't do a thing about it,' she stuttered.

This time he raised both eyebrows. 'Your mother is right. Now where's my Dolly?'

Maud appeared with the little girl, who came running in to him with her arms outstretched. 'Papa!' she cried. He bent and picked her up and held her in the air. The child smiled and he cuddled her to him, loving and affectionate, kissing her forehead before putting her back down. Maud looked on in admiration.

'Kenneth, darling,' she said. 'Boiled spinach and mutton fritters for supper.'

He kissed her on the cheek but went back to the child, scooping her up tenderly from the rug and burying his face in the curve of her neck as he sat down in an armchair. He seemed fixated on her, examining her hands and her knees as he dandled her on his lap. 'Has she had an afternoon nap today?'

'Yes,' replied Maud.

'Time?'

'Three o'clock.'

'How long for?'

'Twenty minutes.'

'Good. But no longer than twenty minutes. Otherwise you won't sleep, will you, darling?'

Maud smiled gratefully. 'Supper's in the dining room on the table, dear.'

Marcia ate her supper sitting in the kitchen. She didn't mind. The house felt relaxed. The food tasted delicious, and it was served on bone china plates. She didn't mind the dress that Mrs Worboys had decided should be her uniform. It was plain but pretty, pale green with a small lace collar and a white belt that nipped it in at the waist. Earlier she had put Dolly into her cot, happily looking at a picture book, turned away to pick up toys from the floor and hang up a small dressing gown, and when she looked again the child had fallen asleep. Outside the window, the beach stretched away in the fading light. She could see lights twinkling at the docks in Liverpool. Somewhere out there were her ma and da, across the water. And the other way – to the right, around the bend of the coast – was Cynthia

in Blackpool. Even further away was Ellie, on her
way to Australia. And Alfie's America was waiting
for him.

She woke savouring the smell of bacon wafting up
from the kitchen. Dolly had woken in the night but
had gone back down without any trouble, and Marcia
had returned to her room and curled up once more
under the thick eiderdown. What luxury. To live in
a house where there were no sleeves to be re-sewn,
no nails hammered into boots to make them last, no
sharing of bath water in a tub in front of the range.
Mrs Worboys had said the night before that she would
be leaving early to attend a committee meeting for
her soldiers' charity, but before going out she tried
to teach Marcia how to operate the washing machine.
It proved a frustrating few minutes for both of them,
partly because Marcia was required to look and listen
while also scraping a bar of Fairy soap into a bowl
with an old cheese grater, while Mrs Worboys raced
through which button or lever to press and in which
order, all the while chatting breezily about her poor
soldier fellows and their terrible tragedies and all the
work she was doing to help them. Marcia's confusion
was made worse by the frequent interruptions of
Dolly, wandering in and asking if she could please
have her breakfast.

'So that's it,' said Mrs Worboys, finishing the
instructions and the listing of her good works. 'Simple,
really. After that you put the clothes through the
mangle and hang them in the garden. You'll cope
admirably, I'm sure.' Dolly reappeared, arms folded

in frustration. 'Ah, my darling, I must leave now, but Marcia will make your breakfast.' She glided past her daughter, briefly kissing the top of her head on her way out of the kitchen.

Marcia glanced at the washing machine with some apprehension, then began preparing Dolly's breakfast. She heard Mrs Worboys call her name from the front door, stopped what she was doing and went out to see her. At the door Mrs Worboys lowered her voice to a whisper.

'It's Dolly's birthday in a couple of months, so I want to go to George Henry Lee's after my meeting to order her a rocking horse. We got her on the second of November but we were assured she was born the day before, on All Saints' Day. After that I may do a little shopping for myself, so I shall likely be out all day. Not a word to Dolly about the horse, of course,' she said and slipped out the door.

All Saints' Day, thought Marcia. That was the day she and Cynthia had arrived at St Mary's. It was carved into her memory. The cold dormitory room, meeting Ellie for the first time . . . and looking out of the window at the woman scurrying away from the orphanage. She remembered Dolly was in the kitchen waiting for her breakfast. Dolly? I wonder, she thought.

It was an hour before Marcia had a chance to sit down at the small kitchen table. The washing machine was gurgling and thumping in the background and Dolly was deep in conversation with her rag doll.

She wanted to write a letter to Ellie but she had

no idea where to send it. She would ask the nuns at the orphanage – presumably they would know where she had ended up. Meanwhile, she had her list of chores and duties written out by Mr Worboys, who seemed to be in control of the running of the house. Most items on the list were concerned with the safety and wellbeing of Dolly and it ended with the under-lined instruction that once a week, on a Thursday, she should soak rags in paraffin and clean the outside of the windows 'as it keeps the flies away that come in from the sea and which are not good for Dolly'. The list was written on a large sheet of paper that had been slipped under Marcia's door early that morning.

Today was a Thursday, but it was also September, and the flies were fast disappearing; but she would do it anyway. It was her first day and she suspected Mr Worboys would not take kindly to any show of common sense. In the afternoon, with Dolly napping, she stole a few minutes to sit in the bay window and look at *Picture Post* magazine. She heard the click of the gate latch and looked up to see Sister Dorothea walking down the path. What was she doing here again? she wondered.

'Marcia! How are you?' the nun said when Marcia opened the door. 'Mrs Worboys is at her meeting, I believe.'

Marcia nodded. 'And I've just put Dolly down for a nap. Until three o'clock. Mr Worboys has a very strict timetable for her.'

'Oh, I see. Never mind.' Sister Dorothea looked crestfallen.

Marcia showed her into the living room and offered her tea, which Sister Dorothea declined. She seemed rather uncomfortable, and kept glancing at the clock on the mantelpiece. Marcia wondered whether there was bad news coming.

'Sister, what about my ma?' she asked, suddenly anxious. 'Why hasn't she written? Her letters have stopped.' Sister Dorothea pressed her fingers to her temple. It seemed as if there was something she wanted to say but she couldn't find the right words.

'Marcia, you concentrate on Dolly for now. Your mother will write in time. I'll give you news of her when I have some, dear.'

'And could you give me an address in Australia where I can write to Ellie?'

Sister Dorothea looked at her sharply. 'What? Why would you be writing to that awful girl?'

Marcia was surprised by her forceful reaction, but she pressed on. 'Because she's my friend. I only want to give her all my news and make sure she's well and happy. Someone at the orphanage must know. Didn't you tell me she was being settled in a wonderful place?'

The nun looked at her. 'Maybe you should trust that I'm correct about that,' she snapped.

Marcia, confused, began to say something else about her friendship with Ellie, but Sister Dorothea raised her hand. 'I'm sorry. I can't wait for Dolly to wake up, and I'm far too busy for this nonsense. Also, I have something. A gift for the child. Make sure Mrs Worboys gets it.' Her fingers were twitching irritably as she reached in her pocket and put a small box on the table. She stood up. 'I'll see myself out,' she said, and hurried out into the hall.

Marcia followed uncertainly. At the door, the nun halted and spoke with her back turned to Marcia.

'I'm very fond of you, dear. You're not like the other girls. This is a wonderful opportunity for you, working for the Worboys and looking after Dolly. Many girls would be eternally grateful for such a chance. To live in this place, to help mother such a lovely child. Remember that, and forget Ellie; she will be fine. She's in Australia, where she will be happy, and you will likely never see her again. Only look to your future, Marcia. Your future, and the future of the others in this house.'

Marcia said nothing. After a few moments Sister Dorothea slowly went out, closing the front door gently behind her. Marcia stood for a moment, listening to the clock ticking on the mantelpiece, and wondered if the nun had quite lost her senses. She had always seemed a little out of place at the orphanage, as though it hadn't been her chosen path. Maybe she shouldn't have been a nun at all? Perhaps she would have been happier marrying someone like Mr Worboys and living in a house like this, with a small child of her own.

'Sister Dorothea was here again?' Mr Worboys said to his wife when he arrived home.

'Yes, but not for long. Dolly was asleep as she was supposed to be. Sister left this, by the way.'

She handed him the box. He nodded, grunted and opened it. Inside there was a pretty silver bracelet with a heart dangling from it. He snapped it shut. 'Too much,' he murmured. Then he looked up. 'Sister didn't tell us she was coming. Maybe she's checking up on you, Marcia.'

Marcia, moving quietly around them removing the dinner plates, listened to the exchange.

'There was no need. Marcia has done everything you asked.'

Mr Worboys glanced at Marcia. 'I'm sure. Now, bath time,' he said decisively.

He certainly seemed to be concerned with Dolly's routine. Had she slept? Had she been fed? Had Dolly been read to? Had she had enough fresh air today? Had Dolly's supper been prepared? She took the plates into the kitchen and washed them quickly. When she came back into the dining room a few minutes later, only Mrs Worboys was sitting there. Marcia went upstairs and was surprised to see Mr Worboys with his sleeves rolled up, leaning over the bath. Dolly was squirming in the bathtub and he was watching her as she giggled and kicked her legs while they sang a song about a fish.

'Not like that,' he said, when Marcia took over and swished water over her. 'Like this.'

Later, he sat drumming the arm of the chair with his fingers and waiting for Marcia to present Dolly at seven o'clock, as she had been asked, in her nightgown and with neatly brushed hair. Mrs Worboys was sitting with a book open on her lap.

He smiled when Marcia brought her in. His nightly whisky had oiled the wheels of his mood and he had begun to relax.

'Will you play?' he asked his wife. She put down her book while he rocked their daughter and hummed as she sat at the piano and played a few bars of a lullaby.

'Join in. I'm sure you have a pretty voice too, Marcia,' he said. Marcia hesitated. 'Come on. "Rose of England", I'm sure you know it? Dolly, sing it with us.'

He gestured in the air as if were conducting an imaginary orchestra as they sang a halting verse and chorus with Marcia *la la la*-ing. '*Throughout a garden, green and gay . . .*'

Half an hour later, a yawning Dolly soon nodded off once Marcia had put her to bed. The routine that was so important to Mr Worboys really did seem to work.

Chapter 34

Two weeks later, sitting in the bay window bathed in the golden light of the setting sun, Marcia picked up a pencil and rested a writing pad on her knees.

Dear Ellie,

How are you? Guess where I'm writing from? An enormous house by the sea called Marine Villas where I have a new job as a mother's help. I have my own room and a huge bed. The little girl is funny and lovely. She's called Dolly. She has everything you could wish for, including a real silver heart bracelet with tiny spears engraved on it and a silver hairclip and a silver eggcup, but still seems mostly fascinated by the metal crucifix I have around my neck. They have strange marble eggs in bowls all over the place. They're Chinese, Mrs Worboys says. No outside lav here!

My mother finally wrote and told me my father is 'recuperating' somewhere. Bit vague on the details. One day we will get back into our house, Ma has promised. But in the meantime, I'm wallowing in creature comforts, which it turns out I could get used to. I've never seen anything like it. Hot water gushing out of the tap, carpets that go all the way to the edges of the walls. Curtains that go all the way down to the floor. They call tea 'supper' and dinner 'lunch'. Cynthia writes to me from Blackpool. She says I can come and see her dancing soon, so that's very exciting. The other day she sent me a pamphlet from the Winter Gardens. They have shows every day but on her afternoons off, she rides up to the top of the tower. When I'm standing on the beach on a clear day I can even see it from here and I wave, hoping she's looking out from the tower towards Marine Villas.

Mr and Mrs Worboys are pleasant enough. She's kind and pretty with such pale skin you can see her veins. She told me if you put one part vinegar with three parts distilled water it stops you getting freckles, so that's a tip for Australia. He can be a bit stern. He wears a bowler hat and carries an umbrella. But he gives Mrs Worboys nearly all his wages for housekeeping and it's not because she's worried about him spending it at the pub. She seems to do what she wants with it.

Please write to me soon. I wonder, did you get my first letter?

Marcia

With the kind help of Mrs Worboys, surprisingly, she had received a note from St Mary's with an address where Ellie had been sent. It wasn't clear who had sent it, but she doubted it was Sister Dorothea.

The weather was turning colder, and outside the sea breeze was invigorating but calming as well. Marcia decided one afternoon to take Dolly for a walk, hoping the fresh air would help her sleep well later on.

They set off through the gate with Marcia firmly holding Dolly's hand and went into the park across the road; Marcia enjoyed the feeling of the fresh air on her face. Dolly frequently stopped to pull up a weed and ask the name of it, or pick up a pebble and press it against her cheek. She was fascinated by a seagull sitting on the green park railings and laughed when it suddenly flew off.

'Marcia? Marcia!' said a voice – Mrs Worboys, upset and worried as she ran towards them. 'Oh, thank God. Always ask me first! I got home and couldn't find you.'

'What? Did you think . . . ?' Marcia trailed off, puzzled.

'N-no,' Mrs Worboys stuttered, hugging Dolly and kissing her. 'I'm sorry. I'm sorry. It's just that . . . It's silly, I know. When you adopt a baby – you worry. You worry so much more.'

Together they went back to the house. Marcia moved around quietly as she made tea while Mrs Worboys talked in short, stuttering sentences, occasionally stroking Dolly's hair and tracing the delicate lines of her nose, her jaw. 'You must know all about adoption, being an orphan.'

'Oh, my parents are alive,' Marcia replied quickly.

'Are they really?' said Mrs Worboys, with a frown

playing across her smooth, pale forehead. 'I thought because you came from St Mary's . . .'

'My father was in the war and he got sick. And my mother has gone away with him while he gets better.'

Mrs Worboys stood and fetched a piece of cloth that was hanging on the wooden clothes horse. 'Where was he?'

'He was in Burma. He was a prisoner of war.'

'Some of our fellows were there. Of all soldiers, I think they perhaps found it hardest. With the camps. Did your father suffer terribly?'

Marcia nodded silently, and Mrs Worboys asked if perhaps one day she would like to come with her to one of her meetings. Marcia flinched. 'Perhaps you're too young. And Mr Worboys might not approve. One day, though.'

'I'd like that. I'd like that very much,' replied Marcia.

Dolly was now sitting on the first step of the stairs, turning the thick cardboard pages of her book.

Mrs Worboys leaned in and discreetly nudged Marcia as she took a packet from the kitchen cupboard. 'Mr Worboys' supper. Can you believe it, it comes from the Co-op in a packet! Powdered soup. They even do Welsh rarebit in a packet. I just pour in milk and a dollop of cream or butter and shush, don't say anything; Mr Worboys is none the wiser. I hide them at the back of the dresser.' She smiled. 'When I think how much time and effort it took me, mixing and weighing the ingredients, and here, we managed to do it in a second. And then I have time to get on with the serious business of life. My poor fellows.'

Chapter 35

When the letter arrived from Blackpool, carefully laid on her pillow by Mrs Worboys, Marcia could hardly believe it. She felt full of such joy at seeing Cynthia's handwriting sloping over the page, full of exclamation marks and kisses.

Dearest Marcia,

This is very exciting! Last night I was shown into my little flat. They call it theatre digs. There's me and three other girls. They are all very friendly, and they've welcomed me into their little group. I headed straight down to the theatre. You can't believe it when you go inside, it smells of Mam's Parma violets! I'm getting measured for my costume. I have three changes, a pretty dress with sequins spilling from the waist to the hem, a Pierrot costume and a candy-striped skirt and blouse with a scalloped collar. There's so many things I've got to learn and a lot of catching up to do. Don't say good luck, you must always say break a leg. Don't ever whistle as that's bad luck and something might fall on your head. And there's a theatre ghost, they say. Which is all a bit silly but not knowing these traditions sets you apart from the rest.

I'm learning the kick lines. You can't imagine how hard it is in high heels!! But I don't mind because they're smashing. They are gold with ankle straps and little round gold buttons. This morning we rehearsed with a lovely man on the piano. And guess what, he didn't laugh when I sang. He points his finger up if we pitch it too low and tells us to stand on our toes to reach the note. Can you believe it does the trick! There's a comedian who thinks he's Tommy Handley and tells jokes mostly about his mother-in-law being very fat. I'm sure he's one for the boys as he's always hanging out in the girls' dressing room and trying on our feather boas. It makes me smile a lot. Dear Marcia, I'm feeling bad about leaving you. But I promise we'll be reunited soon. Norma is only to be taken in small doses. Please stay safe. I'm sure you'll enjoy your new family. I was relieved to hear that you are out of that place. You're my sister, squit. And I love you with all my heart. Must dash. I need to get ready. Curtain up calling.

Cyn xxx

After slipping the letter into her pocket, Marcia took out the fresh rags that had been left for her and fetched a bucket. It was Thursday, so she filled the bucket with paraffin and water, climbed unsteadily up the stepladder leaning against the window, and started to wipe the glass just as Mr Worboys had instructed.

It was hard work, and she doubted there was a living fly within a mile of the house, and a lively four-year-old following her around didn't help. It took her until the early afternoon to finish, but the glass was gleaming and she felt a delicious sense of achievement as she sipped a glass of Vimto sitting on the garden bench. She'd put Dolly down for her nap without any trouble after the little girl had exhausted herself charging about the garden. The weather was unseasonably mild and she was glad to be outside.

'Marcia!' she heard a voice cry, and the gate clanged. She opened her eyes and jerked her head round.

'Alfie!' she exclaimed.

'All right, our Marce?' He paused just inside the gate, grinning.

'How did you find me?'

'There in't many Beach Lawns in Liverpool.'

She was in such shock that she just gaped at him. Alfie grinned like a mad March Hare and began walking up the path.

'Oh, Alfie, I've missed you. You really came here to find me?'

'Aye. And for a day out. I can taste the sea on me lips. Salty.'

'I can't just go off for a day out, Alfie. I'm working.'

'You've landed on your feet here, Marce.'

'I'm lucky to be away from the nuns. My friend, Ellie, left. Went to Australia.'

'I'm getting away soon,' he said.

'America?' She felt her heart sink at the thought.

'Aye. Can I come in and see the house, then?'

'I'm not sure.'

'Go on.'

'I don't know . . . Mr Worboys – he's strict. He would probably have a fit if he knew I was here with you now.'

'Please, Marcie?' He looked at her with a face that was both lovable and forlorn.

She sighed. 'Oh, Alfie.'

'Has it gorra inside lav?'

'It's got three!' she laughed, unable to resist impressing him.

'Whoa. And a butler?'

'No, silly. It's me who does the housekeeping.'

'It's right posh.'

'This is my uniform. See?' Marcia twirled.

He laughed and pressed his face to the window. 'He has fishes on his wall. Can I see 'em?'

'No,' she said firmly.

'Why not?' He looked like a wounded Labrador.

She sighed. 'Oh, Alfie. Well, as long as you're quick.'

He was hopping from one foot to the other as she opened the front door.

'Two minutes. Then you have to go. I don't know when they'll be back.'

He pushed open the door and stepped into the hall. 'Size of them!' he said, staring open-mouthed at the fish mounted and displayed behind glass. He walked up the stairs, squinting at the pictures. 'That's a ten-pounder!'

'Come down!' hissed Marcia. She stepped into the

nursery to check on Dolly, who lay fast asleep on her daybed. 'Let's go now, Alfie,' she said, reappearing in the hall.

Excited, he galloped up the stairs two at a time.

'Eh, Marce. Look at all these.'

'Alfie, get back down here!'

He reached the hall and walked along the landing, taking in the pictures of boats and men in galoshes holding their huge catches.

But then, worryingly, she saw the door of the Worboys' bedroom was slightly ajar. Alfie went towards it and pushed it open wider. Laid out on the bed were a pair of stockings and a pink satin camisole. 'Nice,' he said.

'Alfie, get out of there!'

He walked over to the bed and lifted up the camisole, running his fingers along it.

'Eh, Marce. You'd look pretty in this.'

'Alfie, we've got to go downstairs.' She crossed over to the bed and tried to take it from him.

'Give us a kiss, Marce.'

'I can't do that.' But even as she said it, she wasn't sure she meant it.

'Yes, you can.'

He pressed his lips to hers. Marcia knew it was unforgivable, but she couldn't bring herself to push him away, and found herself kissing him back. They were in the Worboys' bedroom – what was she doing? She felt ashamed and frightened, but her palms were sweating and her heart was beating harder than it had ever done before.

*

Mr Worboys, coming around the corner of Beach Lawn on the opposite side of the road to the house, was whistling to himself, a mood completely out of step with the next few awful moments of his life. Inside the house, Dolly had woken up, escaped the tangle of blankets on the daybed and wandered from room to room with her thumb in her mouth. Finding no one about, she had decided that what she needed at that moment was to go to the park across the road.

Now she came running through the open garden gate and into the road. Mr Worboys dropped his briefcase, shouting her name, as his world slipped into slow motion. An approaching Austin Ten swerved hard to miss her, its brakes squealing, its horn doing its best to warn her as she toppled in fright, head first onto the gravel.

'Dolly!' he screamed again. *'Dolly!'* as she started to wail.

'What was that?' said Marcia, frozen in fear.

'What?'

She pulled away, stumbling, and ran down the stairs two at a time.

Mr Worboys was coming up the path holding Dolly, who was crying gustily. Mrs Worboys appeared as if from nowhere, running up the path behind him. 'Don't worry, I saw it from the corner – he swerved just in time. He didn't hit her,' she said nervously.

'Don't worry! Her damn head's bleeding!'

'Kenneth, she'll be fine. It's just a scratch. Children bounce,' she said, with a worried laugh.

'She could have been . . .' He looked up to see Marcia rushing out of the house.

'I'm sorry, Mr Worboys . . .'

'Sorry? Where were you! What the hell d'you think you were doing?'

Dolly was still crying loudly. Mrs Worboys tried to examine the wound on her daughter's forehead. 'Hold her still, Kenneth, you're scaring her more than the graze is hurting her.'

'What the hell!' Mr Worboys growled, as movement inside the house caught his eye. Stepping closer to the doorway, he saw Alfie creeping out of the drawing room and heading for the kitchen. 'Who's that? A boy? Is that what you were doing? Fooling about with some boy? While you left Dolly to throw herself in front of a car!'

Alfie, realizing the game was up, loped out. 'She's all right, though, isn't she?'

'Go, Alfie. Please, just go,' Marcia hissed.

'Oh, no you don't,' said Mr Worboys, furious. 'You were both in the house. What the hell were you doing?'

'Just looking at your fishes, sir.' Alfie did his best to sound contrite.

'Who is this?'

Marcia felt herself shaking, her cheeks reddening. 'Nobody.'

'Nobody? My eyes are playing tricks on me, are they? Do you see a boy, Maud? Old clothes, scruffy hair? Or am I having visions?'

'Don't be silly, Kenneth. Take Dolly inside, Marcia. No harm done.'

'What's your name, lad? You from the orphanage? When I tell the sisters about you trespassing and that you were up to no good with Marcia, you'll be for it.'

'My name's Alfie Maloney, and no, I'm not from the orphanage. So sir, whilst I'm fairly sure the sisters would tell me I'd go to hell for coming to see Marcia, I'm *absolutely* sure I don't give a stuff. Right, I'm off,' said Alfie. 'I enjoyed them fishes, though.'

Mr Worboys looked as though he was about to burst with rage. Maud put her hand gently on his arm.

Marcia, tears brimming in her eyes, turned and went into the house.

The next day, Mr Worboys dipped a toasted soldier into his egg and scowled at Marcia as she left the room.

'You really think she should stay?'

'Dorothea said she could be trusted.' Maud took a sip of tea.

'But she brought a man into our house and Dolly was nearly killed. It makes me feel ill just to look at her.'

'She's young, Kenneth. She didn't mean any harm. We're all fine. No one died. We've still got a full set of chairs. I'll go and talk to Sister Dorothea and take her advice.'

Chapter 36

Marcia stood outside the Worboys' gate, holding her battered case and waiting for the car to pick her up. For a moment she thought she should just run. Run breathless towards the sea, shimmering silver in the distance, and drown herself. But now there was no way out; she could see the car turning the corner.

She couldn't understand what had happened. Last night Mrs Worboys had told her not to worry, and even Mr Worboys had seemed less angry with her that morning. Nevertheless, on her return from St Mary's, his wife had tearfully informed her that Sister Dorothea thought it best she be returned to the orphanage. St Mary's would send a car to collect her that afternoon.

When she got back to the orphanage after a silent, miserable journey, Sister Dorothea was waiting on the steps.

'Go inside. I've never been so ashamed,' she said.

Marcia winced and bit her lip to stop the flow of more tears.

'Don't speak. Chapel now. Confession.'

She was speechless. How would saying sorry help? It wasn't going to get her job back.

The priest was waiting for her. He seemed to know

her dreadful sin, she could just tell from the rustle of his cassock, the long disapproving sigh.

'Bless me, Father, for I have sinned. But I would never harm Dolly. I would never—'

'Fifteen Hail Marys,' said the voice, bringing the conversation to an abrupt end.

Downstairs, Sister Dorothea was standing waiting for her with a bundle of washing. When Marcia walked towards her, eyes squinting away tears, the sister shoved the washing into her arms.

Marcia was turning away when she heard a voice behind her. 'Wait!'

She turned back to see Sister Hilda shuffling forward, clapping her hands excitedly. 'Oh, Marcia. You're back! Will you read to me? Sister Dorothea, can I borrow her? I've a new gramophone record. Glen Miller!'

'No, she won't read to you, or listen to your blessed popular music. She's doing her penance.'

'Oh, Sister, spending time with an old nun like me will be her penance enough. She's a good girl.'

Sister Dorothea narrowed her eyes, blinking furiously. 'She's not a good girl. And she'll need an awful lot of Hail Marys for God to forgive her sins, let me tell you, Sister Hilda.'

That evening, when Marcia had finished doing laundry at the sinks and thinking sadly of the Hoover washing machine, there was a soft knock at her door.

'Don't take any notice of her,' said Sister Hilda after Marcia let her in. 'She's a fine one to say who's good and who's not,' she added. Marcia wiped away a tear. The nun leaned in close to her and patted her hand. 'You know, we're all sinners. Dorothea as well. There – I've said it. And I don't care. That wasn't Woolton pie.'

'Woolton pie?' said Marcia, frowning.

'Mr Woolton – he would have been delighted. The only one, that's for sure.'

Marcia frowned. She tried to make sense of what Sister Hilda was saying through the mutterings.

'They'll tell you I'm old and mad. But don't you stay here, dear. You go back home to the people who love you. It'll only end in tears if you remain here. Just like with Dorothea. Our Lady of Sorrows has her work cut out.'

Marcia looked at her. 'What d'you mean?'

'The heart. Pierced with the seven swords. Dorothea is a strange one, for sure.'

Chapter 37

Cynthia would know what to do, Marcia thought the next morning. She didn't have much from Maud Worboys, only a few shillings, but she was sure it was enough to get her to Blackpool. She left the orphanage, walked to Lime Street railway station and took a train to Southport. Later that afternoon, she was walking along the promenade.

A flashing neon light announced that Blackpool Illuminations would return soon. There was a feeling that the ravages of war were firmly in the past now. Groups of young men stood leaning against the railings smoking and drinking beer, showing off to their young women huddled in giggling groups. Smiling families walked up and down the wooden pier, linking arms and carrying rubber buckets and shiny red metal spades. There were queues for ice-cream carts and donkeys on the beach, and people shivering in deckchairs, some with blankets over their knees. Despite the chill in the air, everyone looked happy and determined to enjoy themselves, all going somewhere exciting, ducking into doorways of arcades and dance halls with a smile or falling out, flushed, from pubs onto pavements.

She looked at the posters on walls and billboards,

some pasted over peeling war propaganda – The Squadronaires, George Formby, Jimmy Jewel and Vera Lynn. What a charmed life they seemed to have, these entertainers. For a fleeting moment she wished she had the courage, like her sister, to dare to imagine making something different of her life – that she had a future beyond working as a shopgirl or a factory girl. Mr Worboys had said she had a pretty voice. Perhaps Cynthia could get her a job in the chorus . . . but no, this was all stupid.

And then something caught her eye and she gasped, stopping in her tracks beneath the hoarding. There was Cynthia's stage name in huge letters: PENELOPE POMPADOUR. In twinkling lights three feet high, suspended above the canopy of the Winter Gardens!

The matinee show was about to begin so she bought a ticket and went inside, joining the throng in the foyer and then climbing a hundred stairs to the balcony. Passing through the swing door, she entered a world unlike anything she'd seen before. She felt bathed in gold. There were golden chandeliers, gold tassels looped across gold curtains, gold pelmets, golden friezes of angels blowing horns. The place smelled sweet and heady.

The lights dimmed and the curtains swished open. Marcia sat excitedly on the edge of her frayed velvet seat. A woman with a small boy came out and sang 'Don't Sit Under the Apple Tree' in a jolly operatic voice; after that a man came and told a joke about a pigeon 'staging a coo', then sang a rude song about sausages. The audience laughed and some of them shouted out the words, '*Eh, Missus, where do you get those bangers?*' Everything seemed joyous. And then the dancers came on. Marcia squinted at their faces. It was hard to tell the difference – they all looked so alike with their heavy stage make-up, all the same height, all the same hairdos.

The woman sitting next to her saw her stealing a glance at the programme on her lap. She handed it to her. 'Penelope Pompadour's next. You're in for a treat.'

'She's my sister,' whispered Marcia as they applauded. The woman widened her eyes and said how proud she must be.

The music swelled, the drums rolled and there was a bigger round of applause as Penelope Pompadour came on, balancing on a silver ball with a fluffy white poodle under her arm. She was wearing a strapless swimming costume. She began to sing in a tinkling voice: '*Oh, Billy, won't you walk with me through the bluebells . . .*'

The woman patted Marcia's hand. 'She is so talented,' she whispered. And she was.

This woman who wasn't her sister.

When the show was over she jumped out of her seat and politely ignored the woman tugging at her sleeve and smiling. She didn't really want to get into the whys and wherefores of explaining that this Penelope Pompadour, with her jiggling bosom and front splits, who could balance on a ball and sing at the same time, was not her sister. She headed straight outside and around to the stage door, where a queue of people were waiting with autograph books. She pushed her way to the front.

'I'm Penelope Pompadour's sister. Is she sick today? Was that the understudy?' she babbled to the West Indian stage door man, who was wearing a trilby hat at a jaunty angle and smoking a cigarette.

'What, dear?'

'Cynthia Rogan.'

The man laughed. 'Oh, Cynthia – you mean Wally's girl Cynthia?'

Marcia frowned.

'She's your sister? She's giving us all a headache. She's not on tonight. Mr Labone has let her go.'

'Go where?'

'Fired her two weeks ago. She's not been dancing for weeks. She helped with the costumes for a little while. And she did a little bit of stage management. The trouble started with the name. Penelope Pompadour. What a catfight. Mr Labone gave it to Daphne. Insisted. Cynthia was furious. Said it was her name. Lord, she is trouble with a capital T, your sister. Mr Labone decided who got to keep the name in the end.'

Marcia nodded, still confused.

'She lives in the flat at the end of the prom. Boarding house. Nelly's place. Tell her from me, it's Mr Labone who decides. No point stropping off in a huff. She's still working off her temper.'

'My God! Marcia. What are you doing here?' Cynthia said when she opened the door.

It was hard to say which of them was more shocked.

Marcia's gaze travelled over the flat as she stepped inside; it was dingy and shabby and damp. It had scuffed skirting boards and peeling wallpaper and a bare light bulb hanging from the ceiling. Cynthia, wearing an old housecoat, had got fatter. It was like the light had gone out in her eyes. She moved restlessly around the kitchen, all the time sucking on a cigarette. When she opened drawers and cupboards, Marcia noticed her hands were trembling.

'Fancy a brew?'

'Yes, please. The man said this flat, Mr Labone . . . he owns it . . . is Mr Labone here?'

'Not any more.'

'Why?'

'Never mind. But let's just say, turns out I was one of many who he thought he could make into a star. It's all about the money, squit. Everything is.'

'So you're not famous yet?'

'Oh, squit. Never will be. Come here, sit down and drink your tea. You're making me nervous, shuffling about like that and chewing your cardi. What a pair we are.'

'What about Norma?'

'She kept saying I was fat. And that I cramped her style. She said I was as beautiful as I was talented, and I promise you, it wasn't a compliment. I called her a cow and she said she only took me in because Da paid her. He stopped paying, and she wanted me out.' She paused, as though she had an extra piece of information she was about to share with Marcia, but instead she said, 'Tell me what happened from the beginning.'

She listened seriously, nodding from time to time, as Marcia related the story of Sister Dorothea and the Worboys.

'And I've not heard from Ma and Da for months,' she finished, draining the last of the sugary tea.

'That doesn't sound good,' sighed Cynthia.

That night they slept in the same bed. There wasn't the hollowed-out space that they had been used to at home, but they spooned together and Cynthia let Marcia sleep with her head nestled in the crook of her neck, trying to shut out the sound of the ill-fitting door rattling in the blustery wind. When they got up, after a pot of tea and porridge, they went for a walk along the promenade.

Marcia was glad to get outside. The room smelled of damp and Cynthia was clearly a little embarrassed by the mess, the dirty pots soaking in the sink; so it was a relief to leave the wilting pot plants and the overflowing ashtrays behind for a short while. Linking arms and feeling the sea air pasting her hair to her face, the smell of vinegar and candy floss, the coloured lights bobbing between lamp posts, the sound of the slot machines cascading coins as they walked past the arcades, the tea shops and fish stalls, revived her.

'You like to try some winkles?' Cynthia asked.

Marcia shrugged.

Cynthia bought a wooden pot from a stall and sprinkled them with salt and vinegar. They sat on a bench while she explained to Marcia how to poke the stick into the shell and scoop out the inside.

'Well, we never got back to New Brighton, but

here we are in Blackpool,' said Cynthia with a sigh as they stared out over the steel-grey sea, listening to the gently foaming frills of the waves and the gulls pecking at a discarded chip paper.

'Let's go and have a cuppa at the tea rooms.'

The tea room was airy, with potted aspidistras and light flooding in through large windows. They sat at a table for two in the window. Cynthia was about to ask for a refill when her face fell.

'Cyn!' cried a girl with red lips and blonde hair from outside, knocking on the window and smiling. She was with two other girls and clamped her hat to her head with one gloved hand and waved and pointed with the other, indicating they were coming in. 'Oh no,' said Cynthia to Marcia as the girls burst through the door.

'Hello, sweetie,' said one of her companions, a girl with thickly mascaraed false eyelashes that looked like spiders' legs and heavily kohled eyes.

A third girl, wearing a beret and a scooped neck-line that accentuated her pearls, pulled up a chair.

'Cynthia!' she cried. 'Where've you been? Who's this?' She smiled at Marcia.

'My little sister.'

'She's as pretty as you! We've missed you,' the girl said. She turned to Marcia. 'Mr Labone says me and your sister are like twins. But now I've met your real sister, we're not really. My name is Daphne. Penelope Pompadour is my stage name.'

Her hands fluttered over the china cup that had been put in front of her by the waitress, tracing a finger around the rim, fiddling with the frills and ruffles of her blouse, as she told them the story of a fellow who hung around the stage door every night. 'But really he only wanted to get inside of Cynthia's . . .' She paused for effect. 'Dressing room!' They all honked with laughter. They twirled and twisted when they moved, flicked scarves over shoulders, ran pearls through fingers, patted hair, reapplied lipstick and powdered noses in compact mirrors.

'Filth is what comes out of Daphne's mouth, dear. I'm sorry. She's not always like this, sometimes she's sleeping.'

'Dear, we miss you. Mr Labone's a brute. Untangle yourself from him. You'll soon be back, we hope,' Daphne said.

After they'd gone, it felt like a hurricane had rushed through the tea room and left devastation in its wake.

'Cows,' said Cynthia.

'But they love you, Cynthia. Why do you hate them?' asked Marcia, puzzled.

She snorted. 'They don't love me. They loathe me. And I loathe them. They say one thing to my face and another behind my back. That's just the way things are in the theatre. I tried to get used to it. But seeing you again, Marce – you're so honest and good – I'm not sure I ever will.'

They spent the rest of the day tidying the little flat and avoiding the subject of what they were going to do next.

'Mrs Worboys says if you rub wallpaper with French chalk, you can rub the stains away.'

'French chalk? I've hardly got money to eat. I don't

263

even know what French chalk is.' Cynthia flumped into a chair and kicked off her shoes. 'Go to bed. We'll make a plan in the morning.'

'Perhaps if we go and find Norma. What happened when—'

'I don't want to talk about it. Not tonight. What you can see is, you can't stay here, love. And I'm afraid I have to go to the theatre tonight – to see Mr Labone. I'm going to try and get my job back.'

'How are you going to do that?' Marcia said doubtfully.

'Never you mind. Something Daphne said. Will you be all right here for the night on your own?'

Marcia shrugged, knelt down and began to light a small fire in the grate.

'What are you doing? D'you think I've money to burn? Or coal, for that matter? Here, you can light the oil lamp and I'll get you a blanket to cover your knees. Then you'll feel a lot better.'

Chapter 38

Mr Higgins came into Henry's office, carrying files under his arm.

'We're drowning here. Another one for you, son: Rogan. That girl has gone missing. You remember the family? Parents are in Leeds. Father's at a veterans' sanatorium, mother staying nearby. Father Donnelly wants this Marcia Rogan girl found. She's sixteen but still a ward of court. Which means she's the responsibility of the government. That's us by the way, Henry. Us, and the people we put them with. In this case the sisters. The priest wants her taken to Clare House, you know the place, so that's what we'll do. Thinks she might be more amenable to that. Her older sister is living in Blackpool. You drive, don't you? Learned in the army, you said?'

Henry nodded. 'A van. But yes, I have a licence.'

'Nuns think she's gone to see the sister. How do you fancy a trip to Blackpool to bring her back? You can take the department car. Take in a show. Tommy Handley's on at the Grand. Just remember, the department won't be paying for it. Still, this job's not bad, is it? Despite the sewer rats we have to deal with. These kids, there are just so many. How they expect us to get on top of it . . .'

Sewer rats? Marcia Rogan wasn't a sewer rat, Henry thought. All she needed was a good meal and someone to look after her.

'With Alfie?' Cynthia said, furious and horrified. 'You missed that detail when you told me about the Worboys, Marcia. You were in the house with Alfie?' She dragged hard on her cigarette, blew smoke out of the side of her mouth and jerked her head back angrily as she did so. It made Marcia's eyes water. 'What were you two up to?'

'Nothing, Cyn. Don't be stupid. He just came in to look at Mr Worboys' fishes.'

'So why didn't you tell me?' How could someone go from being so kind to being so cold so quickly? thought Marcia, as Cynthia continued pacing about the kitchen.

'Cyn, who told you Alfie was there?'

'Never mind.'

'Who told you?'

'The fellow called Higgins. There was a message for me to ring him at the stage door. He told me the whole sorry story of exactly *why* you left the Worboys. Up to no good with a boy. He told me the boy's name when I asked. Alfie Maloney! I can't believe you went with Alfie behind my back.'

'He came to look at the fish, that's all. Nothing happened!' But the more Marcia denied it, the clearer the memory of kissing Alfie became. 'Anyway, you always thought you were too good for him! I thought it was Mr Labone who was your sweetheart,' she said darkly.

'Don't be daft. He's ancient. He looks after me, that's all.'

'Looks after you? What does that mean? Mr bloody Labone! This is all his fault! If you had stayed at Liverpool Lane instead of leaving us to go off with your stupid ideas of dancing, I wouldn't have been left on me own with Da while you were fawning all over this man who's horrible to you! So don't get cross with me about spending an afternoon with Alfie!'

Cynthia's eyes narrowed.

'And who d'you think pays the rent here? The money fairy? Thank God for Mr bloody Labone. You think I like him being around me? Breathing his cigar breath into my face? Do you! I shut my eyes when he leers all over me because I have to think of something else. But you know what? If I had any sense, I'd open them up and smile sweetly, and my legs too, because my life would be a whole lot better if I let him have his way with me. But this'll surprise you: I can't bring myself to do it. Not even me.' Cynthia flopped down on a chair next to the unlit fire. 'Welcome to the real world, Marce!'

'Please, can't we both go back to Liverpool?'

'Where to? We have no home. And anyway, even if we had somewhere to stay, I can't face it,' Cynthia said wearily. 'I can't face Alfie and Mr Tattersall. And Norma.'

'Oh, Cyn. They all love you. They're the people we can trust. Anyway, Alfie's off to America. You could go back and get a job, and I could too, and we'd both be back on our feet in no time.'

A tear spilled onto Cynthia's cheek. Marcia realized

that she had hardly ever seen her sister cry. 'No, Marcia. Theatre people, they're my family now.'

'Really? You don't even work there. You said they don't like you and you don't like them. You said they're two-faced.'

'Mr Labone says I can have my job back,' Cynthia said flatly. 'At least, understudy to Daphne.'

'Those people, the ones at the cafe. They were nice, but they didn't tell you the truth. They just . . .'

'You don't get it, squit. This is my new home. And I really don't think you should stay here any more.'

'Please – I don't want to go back St Mary's. Have you forgotten what it's like? And now they're putting girls on boats to Australia. What if they send me there?' she sniffed.

'To Australia? Don't talk stupid.'

That night, Cynthia slept on the sofa and left Marcia to sleep in the bed alone. It felt cold and lonely and Marcia, feeling full of worry over their argument, couldn't settle. In the middle of the night, she got up and padded through to the living room.

'Cyn,' she said, shaking her shoulder. 'Are you awake?'

'I am now. What is it?'

'I'm sorry.'

'Go back to bed,' replied Cynthia and pulled the coverlet over her shoulder and turned her back on her. Marcia, dejected, walked back into the bedroom into darkness.

As dawn broke after a restless night, half in and half out of sleep, Marcia thought she heard the sound of knocking. Maybe it's the milkman, she thought.

'Who's this?' Cynthia said, already up, parting the curtains and peering out into the street.

Henry Cherry was standing on the pavement. He waved at the window, pushing his floppy blonde hair from his eyes.

'Henry? What's he doing here?' But Marcia knew exactly what.

Henry sat at the table drinking the cup of tea Cynthia had made him while Marcia stood by the door, as far away from him as possible.

'I have to take you back, Miss Rogan, but not to the orphanage. They say you can't stay here. Sorry.'

Cynthia stood listening at the sink. Marcia didn't reply, but cradled her tea in her hands and nursed it against her cheek.

Henry looked uncomfortable. 'Believe it or not, there are all sorts of people in Liverpool just like you, Marcia, who need help.'

'Where am I going, then?' asked Marcia. 'I can't go back to the Worboys. They won't have me, and nor will Norma.'

'Don't worry,' he said kindly. 'It's a place called Clare House. They only take teenagers. You'll make more friends there, I imagine. Seeing as there are more girls your age. It has lovely gardens and it's out of town a little. Clean fresh air.'

Cynthia sighed. Fumbling in her pocket, she took out a crushed Woodbine that was nestling amongst the lint and fluff and rolled it between her thumb and forefinger to fatten it up, licked the end of it and popped it in her mouth. 'Maybe it's for the best, Marce, love.'

Henry did his best to reassure them, but he used long words that Marcia could barely make sense of – *guardianship. Welfare Act. Compulsory orders.* Eventually she came and sat down at the table, listening dolefully with her head in her hands. Finally, weary, sad and defeated, she quietly let Henry take her arm. She had thought he might be the kind of man she could trust, but now he just seemed like someone who had been given his orders and was powerless to do anything else. He worked for Corpy, she thought, and was only trying to do his best.

The lights of the promenade and the arcades blinked away in the distance, even in the daylight. Henry had parked the little car in a side street. She slid into the front seat. He started the engine, smiled at her reassuringly, hoping she wasn't going to cry, and they set off along the coast road. Marcia gazed out at the sea extending to a steel sky.

'I need to speak to my ma and da. Will you help me?'

'They're in Leeds, aren't they? I'm sorry about that.'

'No, I was told they've gone to Ireland. That's wrong.'

'I'll try and help you find them. But you need to know, Marcia, you might not be happy with what you find. I learned that quickly enough in this job.'

She looked at him worriedly, sighed and fidgeted. 'I don't trust the sisters.'

'Marcia, try not to be too unhappy. Perhaps when Cynthia finishes this dancing job she'll come and get you and you can live with her. She's eighteen, isn't she?'

'She hates me.'

'Does she? Why?'

'We had a row. About a boy.'

'Oh. I see.'

They drove on in silence, turning off the Blackpool road and crossing over the River Ribble. It was a few minutes more before Marcia spoke.

'Henry, my friend Ellie has gone to Australia. I don't think she had a clue what she was getting into. You know anything about that?'

Was that an accusation? He fixed his eyes onto the road ahead, clutching the wheel, counting the cats' eyes and wishing she hadn't asked him. 'Not much. There's plenty about this job I've avoided looking too closely at. When I finish work, I switch off. Listen to my records. That's probably not what I should do, I know, but it stops me getting wound up about a lot of what I see.'

'Who's your favourite?'

The question surprised him. 'Oh, Louis Armstrong. Count Basie. That's what I turn to when I'm feeling blue. You should try it.'

The light took on a softer hue. The buildings became further apart, and then there were none at all. Just green fields rolling in like the tide, with the tall grasses beyond the hedgerows rippling like waves. At first, Marcia wound down the window and let the cool air rush in to keep her awake; but soon after, travelling through the country lanes, just the thought of sleep made her drift off with her head lolling against the side of the leather strap. When she woke, she rubbed the sleep out of her eyes. There was a familiar smell in the air that told her she was near home: the smell of soot and coal and the River Mersey.

'Soon be there,' he said.

They were travelling towards the docks, where the traffic was heavier and the lorries slowed them down; then they turned off, skirting the city and going up Mount Pleasant and towards the tree-lined roads of Childwall. Without warning, the car swung through an ornate set of iron gates that stood open, into the drive of a red-brick Victorian mansion. Its wheels crunched over the gravel. How many of these homes, orphanages, convents, sat in unassuming streets with no one ever knowing what was happening behind their front doors?

Henry got out and opened the door of the car. 'We're here. Clare House.' Marcia stepped out.

'Hello,' said Sister Dorothea.

Chapter 39

Henry went back to the little flat in Tooley Street where he lived above the haberdasher's, sat down at his desk and thought about Marcia. He felt angry that he'd been duped – that having him take her to Clare House had been a way of getting her back in their clutches. He was frustrated that, despite the Corporation's best efforts to make sure their wards of court were properly looked after, once the children were in the orphanages, they were powerless. The priests and nuns were like gods in this city, he thought ruefully.

After dropping her off he had waited outside the gates for twenty minutes, knowing what would happen, and sure enough a car had driven out. He couldn't be sure Marcia was inside, but his instincts told him so. Now he felt queasy about what would happen next. She had looked at him with those big round eyes and seemed so frightened. And in that moment she was beautiful, too. He shouldn't be thinking that way, he knew – it was not the reason he wanted to help her.

He got up, made himself a cup of tea and put a record on his gramophone player. He thought of his own parents and how they had left for Canada, and how, when he had decided to stay, they had been happy for him to make his own way in the world. If it hadn't been for the nuns, who had sent a priest around to show him how to work the boiler – and then the baskets of food from the new curate – he probably wouldn't be here today. They had even suggested he apply for the job at Cunard House. Doing Higgins's footwork, Henry had come across plenty of nuns, and he knew that there were some whose lips pursed into a hard line when they spoke and who had bitterness running through their veins. Like this Dorothea.

He pulled on his coat and set off to St Mary's. Squinting up at the building from under a skeletal sycamore tree, he shivered. This job. He had seen enough of these places to last a lifetime. St Mary of the Blessed Angels. St Jude's. St Sylvester's.

There was a nun pruning roses in the front garden.

'Sister,' said Henry. 'Child Welfare Officer. I'm looking for Marcia Rogan. I believe she came back here from Clare House this afternoon. May I see her?'

The nun sat back on her heels. 'See her? Why would you need to see her?'

He frowned, trying to think on his feet. 'She left something in the car. This.' He waved his briefcase. 'Can I give it to her? Where is she?' He tried to position himself so that he could move quickly through the front doors.

'Wait, you can't go in there—'

Henry tried to barge past, clutching the bag, but she held out a flattened palm.

'Stop, dear. Mother of God! This is an orphanage.

You're a man. You really can't come in here.' The nun looked down at the bag and frowned, as if she was thinking it was an odd kind of bag for a girl.

He paused. Then he took one step to the side, and the nun did the same. He hesitated again. Suddenly she reached out and grabbed the briefcase, trying to wrench it out of his hand, and they did a tug-of-war for a moment or two until finally, with a sigh, he let go. He could see he was not going to get past this woman, who, though she had smiling eyes, was clearly immovable.

'Thank you, dear. I'll make sure she gets it.'

Padding down the corridor, Sister Mary knocked on Marcia's bedroom door.

'I'm locked in,' came a small voice from the other side.

Frowning, the nun put the key hanging from her belt – the one that opened all the rooms – into the lock and twisted it.

'I brought something for you. Your bag. The one that you left in the car. The driver returned it.'

Marcia looked up, puzzled. 'That's not mine,' she said.

Chapter 40

In a small room in a boarding house in Bramley, Leeds, Eunice Rogan felt as if the walls were closing in on her. She still wasn't quite sure how she had ended up here: a cousin, a well-meaning doctor, an aunt. The house was next door to a washhouse and down the road from St Boniface's Veterans' Asylum, where her husband had been treated for the past few months before being discharged to stay with her here. It was warm, but at night, when the cockroaches came scuttling out, the kitchen floor was a shining, shifting sea of black.

'Nissy, I feel cold,' said John Rogan. His cheeks were sunken and his voice, no more than a whisper, trembled when he spoke. She sat with a cloth on his brow.

'It's only to be expected,' she said. She leaned in to him. 'You're still weak but I am proud of you, dear. We should have a ceremony where we throw all those medicine bottles into the fire. Soon we'll be able to go home.'

The stern-looking doctor, after shaking a thermometer and sticking it into John's mouth, wrote in his notebook. 'I'd say the problem was leaving the sanatorium too early. The electric shock treatment, whilst mild in your case, still takes its toll. You needed the Bromoform to get you through the pain in your lungs and the headaches, but it's toxic stuff when you're drinking alcohol. Evil, I'd say. And they don't tell you. Too many making money off it. And you wanted to get back home, didn't you, John? I don't blame you, stuck in Singapore. I've heard the stories about what happened on the railways and the roads and the camps.'

John nodded.

'He describes it as when you have a head full of awful thoughts, you feel like you're sleeping on a pillow full of ants,' said Eunice and kissed John's hand.

'Still no word from the girls?' John asked, sadly.

'I'm in touch with Norma and she tells me that Cynthia is in Blackpool.'

He nodded. His breathing was uneven and laboured, with long pauses between each breath. 'Am I going to die?' he asked the doctor.

'No. But you need more rest if you're to get stronger. You can't have any disruption. We want to keep you out of the asylum.'

'And Marcia, Eunice?'

'She's fine. The doctor has had word from the nuns, who say she's doing well.'

'I'm glad.'

'The nuns keep Norma up to speed with news. Marcia is working for a family. You would be proud of her.'

'I am. I am proud of them both. It's these blasted headaches. You say she wrote?'

She turned away and winced. It pained her to lie to him. 'Yes.'

'And Fred Tattersall?'

'He was only trying to do good.'

'I know. I'm ashamed.'

'Marcia is happy, and for now she should stay there.'

'Do you think the girls will ever forgive me?'

'I'm sure they will.'

She didn't tell him about the latest letter from the sisters suggesting that Marcia might be suitable for the emigration programme. That she had passed the test with flying colours and, as she was an orphan of the living, there was room for her if they would like her to be added to the lists. Orphan of the living? Such an awful thing to say. It was a horrific thought. Eunice had written back and said no immediately.

John was getting stronger – against all odds he had beaten the medicine bottles, he was out of St Boniface's recuperating here, and they would be able to go home soon. Never mind the words 'palliative care' that she had read on the slip of paper from the doctor when he had first arrived at St Boniface's. What did that mean, she had asked? The nurse and doctor had glanced at each other. Their look said it all. Death, that's what it meant. The next two days would be crucial, they had explained. They would see if John was to take a turn for the worse or for the better.

Chapter 41

Norma opened the door smoking one of her gold-tipped pink cigarettes and dressed in a negligee.

'Fancy, this is a surprise! Come in, pet,' she said to a white-faced Marcia.

Marcia stepped in. She tried not to stare at the plush carpet, the cabinet with glass doors and gold swirls painted on them. The walls covered with garish pink and gold flocked paper. 'Tea, love?'

'No, thanks.'

'Glass of sherry?'

'It's eleven o'clock in the morning, Auntie Norma,' said Marcia.

'That late?' Norma quipped. Her hair, just come out of rollers, was piled up on top of her head with a tortoiseshell comb in trembling curls. She had earrings on, hoops of gold threaded with beads hanging from her elongated earlobes. 'How are you, dear? To what do I owe this unexpected visit?'

'I . . .' Marcia had planned out what she was going to say, but her voice quivered and the words didn't come.

'What is it, love?'

'Ma and Da, mostly. I haven't heard from them for ages. They signed the papers. But the nuns . . .'

'I know, love. They only wanted the best for you. But it must have been a shock.'

'Are they in Ireland?'

'Ireland, love? Why would they go there? Ireland is just potatoes. Bloody potatoes. Why would you want to go back to potatoes? That's why we came here, to get away from the blasted things.'

'So where are they?'

'I have no idea.'

'The nuns tried to say I should think of them as dead. That they don't want us any more. I don't believe that for a second. No one tells me anything. Oh, Auntie Norma.' She flung herself at her aunt, clung on to her and sobbed. Norma didn't know what to do. She waited for a moment, then peeled Marcia's arms off her.

'Stop it now, Marcia, love,' she said. 'I suspect the nuns haven't been passing on the letters.'

'Auntie Norma, can I come and live here with you? Now that Cynthia is in Blackpool.'

'Oh, love. If only it had been a more convenient time. Then . . . well . . . maybe, but . . .'

The door opened. A man came in wearing a vest and slippers. His hair was stuck to his head as if he'd just rolled out of bed and he was puffing on a cigar.

'Mr Labone?' said Marcia, looking at him through a cloud of smoke.

The man's eyes flicked to Norma, then back to Marcia.

'Hello, love. I remember you.'

For a second the words couldn't leave her mouth.

'Have you two met?' said Norma, smoking languorously.

'I never forget a pretty face,' he said.

Marcia hesitated.

'Are you? I thought . . . Cynthia said . . .'

'Don't worry about your sister. She's back in the show if she wants. She's a canny minx, but I like her spirit.'

'Who d'you think got her the job in the first place?' Norma said. 'Wally has been a treasure. And Cynthia – she's not exactly a natural. And she does love her pies, doesn't she?' Marcia's eyes smarted. 'But love, that's what I'm trying to say. Wally lives here now. We're not married, so keep that one under your hat, love.'

In sin! thought Marcia. What would her mother say? Or Sister Dorothea?

'Cynthia, turns out, is a bit of a prude. Didn't like it one bit. But we looked after her. Isn't that right, Wally?'

He shrugged and took his place on the sofa, his body spilling over the sides of it, plonking his legs on the leather pouffe as though he owned the place.

'You do understand, dear? You can't stay here. Would you like a biccy?'

The two of them winced when a tear fell down Marcia's face instead of a reply. Marcia stumbled out after a brief conversation about Penelope Pompadour and Cynthia's hair dye staining Norma's bathroom sink. She came onto the balcony, took great gulps of air. Liverpool stretched before her. So many people out there – all rushing to get away from here. How many of them never came back? Her ma and da. Now Alfie . . . Ellie . . . Cynthia . . .

Marcia discovered Mr Tattersall's little shop locked up, but when she went around the back she found him pickling herrings.

'Marcia!' he said, wiping his oily hands on his apron. 'I've missed you. I've just made a brew.' She tumbled into his arms. 'What on earth is the matter?'

He pulled up a chair for her and she felt the kindness in his familiar sympathetic expression and offering of food to comfort her. He listened, nodding, and poured out a cup, stirring in two spoonfuls of sugar. 'Tea with sugar. I bet you've not had that for a while. And a biscuit. Or one of my little almond cakes?'

She took the tea and the plate gratefully, pecked at the biscuit like a bird. 'Mr Tattersall, can I live here?' she blurted.

He looked shocked. 'Oh, well now, Marcia, I can't just take you in. Don't you see how it would look? You're sixteen, and I'm an old man, and people would talk. Like they did with your mother.'

She crumpled, dropping her head with a devastated moan. 'I'm nearly seventeen now.'

'But you can come here every day after school if you like.'

'I don't go to school any more. I left ages ago. Those nuns won't let me come here. They say I'm free, but if that's true, then why do they have a lock on the gate? I had to climb over the wall to get out today. I can't think what they would do if they knew I was here.'

He sighed.

'Can't you be my guardian? Like Norma was Cynthia's guardian once?'

'I could ask the nuns, but dear . . . It takes time. I would have to apply to the Corporation. If the nuns . . . And what about your father? Your ma? How do you think that would go down?'

She felt her shoulders collapsing in on themselves.

'Hey, love, I'm not saying no. I'm saying I'll think about it. What's happening with your Cynthia?'

'She hates me. I don't know if she will ever speak to me again. She seems like she's . . . I don't know . . . not happy . . .'

'Poor headstrong Cynthia. She'll come round, surely.'

'She's stubborn, Mr Tattersall.' Marcia put her head flat onto the table. 'Anyway, no, you're right. It would be impossible for me to stay here. I'm sorry for asking.'

'Don't be daft, love,' he said gently. 'Listen. I've cooked some potatoes and they're warming on the griddle. I'll fry some spam fritters, shall I? It will be just like old times, hey? You look like you've not had a good meal in ages. I've seen more meat on a butcher's pencil. What would you like to drink with it? I've orange juice, or ginger beer.'

He got up, bustled around and filled a plate for her. She took it gratefully and took a mouthful of the potatoes.

'And why can't you go to Norma?'

'She's living in sin with Wally Labone. There's no room for me. Or Cyn.'

'The fella with the trumpet? Everyone in Liverpool knows him.'

'Don't know why Cyn has anything to do with him.'

'He's a chancer, but I don't think he means any harm. He helps your Aunty Norma. It's him who's bought all her mod cons and fancy furniture, kitted out her new flat, I heard. Cynthia probably saw an opportunity if he promised her that he would get her out of this place. Trust me, she wouldn't be the first lassie to think he was the answer to her dreams. If the chance came along to get away from Liverpool Lane for a more exciting future, we'd all take it. I don't blame her for that. Like Alfie. He's heading off abroad, had you heard? Soon there'll be no one left in Liverpool Lane.'

Marcia pushed her clean plate away.

So that was it: the end of the road. Mr Tattersall. Norma. Cynthia. Her ma and da. What about Henry Cherry? He had seemed so kind and well-meaning, but the last time she had confided in him he had taken her straight back to the nuns. She had never felt as lonely as she did now. What future was there for her here? Return to the orphanage and make the best of it? No – she couldn't stand another day in that place.

At Otterspool Promenade, she saw a figure in the distance sitting looking out across the Mersey estuary. She found Alfie alone, the fishing rod stuck between his legs, line bobbing in the flickering river, bicycle leaning against the railings.

'Marcia! What are you doing here? What's the matter?' he said.

'It's a long story.'

'I'm in no rush. Fishing is slow business. That fella got over finding me in his house? His face,' he laughed.

She pursed her lips. 'Never mind that. I heard you're going to America. Can I come with you?'

He laughed. 'Don't be stupid. Anyway, I'm not going to America. I'm going to Egypt now. National service.'

Her little shoulders slumped. 'Why did you say you were going to take me, then?'

'Oh, chump. Maybe one day.'

Marcia curled her hands into tight fists. She could have kicked herself for asking him; it was a ridiculous idea. How could she ever have thought it might happen? He reached for her hand. 'No,' she said, embarrassed by how desperate she had sounded. 'No, leave me alone, Alfie.'

Wearily she turned towards the tram that would take her back to St Mary's. But when she arrived at the back gate, Sister Dorothea was waiting for her.

'Now, dear. I trusted you. I told you not to go getting any ideas about running away. And you threw that back in my face. Your door will remain locked – no more going out for the messages or visits, and you will have one of the new girls with you at all times. See it as a penance. Offer it up to God. Think of all the poor starving children in the world. Let your sin raise you up to the Lord. Go to your room and I'll come and find you in the morning.'

'How long will you lock me up?'

'For as long as it takes, dear. Now I need to go. We have Father coming to talk about the emigration programme. There's a boat on its way to Liverpool, coming to take some of our special children back on the next trip to Australia.' She paused, tipped her head to one side. 'Actually, Marcia, if you want freedom – if you don't like the sound of being locked up – I can always have a word? You've sat through the talks enough times. What a country Australia is. Vast open spaces and sunshine. What I wouldn't give for a few weeks with the laughing kookaburras.'

Marcia frowned.

'You know, sitting in an old gum tree counting monkeys.' Sister Dorothea grinned, pleased with herself for some reason.

Tears of anger stung Marcia's eyes. Looming defeat overwhelmed her. Perhaps Ellie was right. Perhaps she should go all the way across the world to Australia – it might be better than staying here in this prison.

Chapter 42

Henry found Mr Higgins in the pub, quietly sipping a Guinness.

'Mr Higgins, would you mind if I stayed late tonight and went through the filing again? There's just a few I didn't finish. I need the key for the records office.'

Higgins sighed and gave him the keys. 'Lock up. I can't go back, lad. Missus will be moaning. I'm late as it is.'

Henry turned up his collar and went back into the red-brick building. The tiled corridors were quiet and his footsteps echoed. He unlocked the door of the filing room and began to search, pulling open one drawer and then another, searching and sifting through letters and papers.

After several minutes, he found the group of folders he needed. They were in a cabinet he had always avoided, as if by some instinct he knew it contained information too upsetting to read.

The first folder he opened was fairly innocuous – just a few letters about sending over provisions to Tasmania: gentleman's relish, boot polish, talcum powder. But in the next, which had a rubber band around it and a small label saying *Confidential*, there was a large envelope marked *Correspondence from*

Hope Cottages, Tasmania. Sender to address welfare officers. Including letters from emigrated children intended for St Mary's. Urgent. Please forward to the relevant authorities. File pending.

The envelope bulged with letters, all stamped and dated, and all opened. Henry adjusted the angle of the desk lamp, sat down and began the task of reading them.

Dear Sister,

Please can you tell my mam I made a mistake? I need to come home. It's too hot here, I have no shoes, and when I walk it burns the bottom of my feet. I cry every night and they hit me with a birch branch when I wet the bed. Please, Sister, I can't stay here. Can you tell my auntie if me ma still doesn't want me? Can you ask her to come and get me?

Malcolm

His heart lurched. His hands were shaking so much that the notepaper fluttered as he picked up the next letter. He put it down. What was he doing? He didn't want to read any more, but he knew that if he wanted to help Marcia, he had to.

Dear Auntie,

It didn't turn out how I thought, we have all been sent to a little farm but its miles from anywhere. Today I tried to go into the city to post this letter, but I had to do it secretly and the city was too far away. So I am sending this to the nuns at the orphanage to send to you as they let us write to the orphanage. I

*don't know what to do next. But I hate it
here. Sometimes I wish I was dead.*
  Carol

Some of the letters were incomplete. One of them
even had words redacted.

Dear Sister,
  *Please can you tell my nan, I don't know
where she is, but please can you tell her that I
am very sad? It's not what we thought. I want
to come home.*

Henry opened another file. *Official*, it said on the
front. These letters were written on blue lined paper
and had been stamped *Read and received* in the top
right-hand corner.

Dear Mr Higgins,
  *After a short tour of the cottages in the
south of Tasmania I am writing to tell you
that the children here are being treated very
badly and the authorities need to take steps
urgently. These are some of the letters that I
was asked to forward after interviewing some
of the children. But they have no idea what
addresses they should send them to. Rather
than sending to the sisters, I am forwarding to
the welfare offices in the hope that you might
know what to do with them and what steps
to take. The sisters do not believe that this is
of any concern to them. I have spoken to
them. But they do not wish to comment. This
is only to be expected. I believe that the farms*

*are where they are treated the worst. Enclosed
is correspondence I was given when I left
Australia.*
  Niall Rogers

Dear Ma,
  *I'm having a lovely time. It's just as you
said, the oranges hang from the trees and you
can pick them off the branches and they are
lovely and sweet. Our day starts with lessons
and then in the evening we go back to the
cottage and Father brings Scrabble and new
books from the library. I am enjoying my new
friends. Mother, that's the lady who looks
after us at the cottage, is kind and I have
learned how to sew and make lemonade.*
  May God go with you and bless you,
  Peter

Dear Auntie,
  *I'm having a lovely time. It's just as you
said, the oranges hang from the trees and
you can pick them off the branches and they
are lovely and sweet. Our day starts with
lessons and then in the evening we go back
to the cottage and Father brings Scrabble and
new books from the library. I am enjoying
my new friends. Mother, that's the lady who
looks after us at the cottage, is kind and I
have learned how to sew and make
lemonade.*
  May God go with you and bless you,
  Frank

The same letter – but to different people and from different people. Had they been told what to say? And then as he turned one of the letters over, he read on the back.

As you can see, some of the letters have clearly been dictated, which was confirmed in interviews with the children on 15th May 1947.

Dear Grandma,
   They make us climb up to the top of the buildings, and in our bare feet in the scorching hot sun. We are not being taught, we just have to work. It was all a lie. The nuns make us copy out from the black board letters saying we are happy here.

He leafed through more. They were the same, apart from a few spelling mistakes.

Dear Ma,
   Animals are treated better than us. I hate the cold showers. The cottage is horrid. There is no gold in the street. They said we could go home but how?

The next letter was addressed, *For the attention of the Child Welfare Council.*

   . . . Conclusion: the children were told they were going on an adventure holiday and they could return if they didn't like it. Immoral relations are happening in several homes. The Curtis Report has alerted Her Majesty's

Government but still there appears to be silence. Please respond urgently. Note: Curtis Report (1946), 'A comprehensive report of the care of children "deprived of the normal care of their parents".' I put it to you we are still in the same position nearly three years on.

Henry opened another, wearily.

Dear Sir,
    We have told her mother that she may take her daughter back who is unhappy working as a domestic servant. An agreement has been made for her passage home to London, but the sisters have refused to pay. The sisters have said in light of the prohibitively high cost, their mother is happy for the child to remain.

Underneath, in a hasty scribble, were the words: *Mother refused to pay. Case closed. Child will remain in Australia.*

Attention Ellie Kinsella: we have received a letter from the mother of Ellie Kinsella. See below. The child is listed as an orphan. The whereabouts of the mother were unknown, presumed dead before she left. However, there has been a misunderstanding. The child Ellie was told that the mother was dead, when in fact she was not. Between the ages of nine and eleven she regularly visited her daughter every six months. Contact ended due to mother's distressed circumstances but she wrote regularly. In 1948 mother arrived at the orphanage to find out that daughter had emigrated without her knowledge. The mother reported this to the police but to date there has been no follow-up.

And then his whole body trembled as he read the worst, and perhaps most shocking of all.

Dear Marcia,

I can't begin to say how sorry I am to have come here. I don't know how this has happened and I don't know if this letter will even reach you. This place is a bluddy hell hole. And I feel guilty because I'm leaving the other girls and boys knowing what they're being made to do. Every day. I don't know what's crueller, these men or the nuns. The men take a fancy to me all the time. One fella says he loves God but he wants to love me an all. Please, if yer can do anything, tell the werld what it's like here. And tell them not to believe the lies.

Ellie

Henry found Higgins still sitting nursing a Guinness in the snug bar. He thrust some of the letters towards him. 'You knew about this?'

Higgins looked at them for a moment, then shrugged and raised his palms. 'What can you do? You, lad, are walking out of your job if you don't put those letters back.'

Henry curled his fists in fury. That was the least of his worries now.

Chapter 43

Marcia rose early. She swung her legs over the iron bedstead and rubbed her eyes. Taking down a bag from the top of the wardrobe, she stuffed a pair of shoes into it along with a few belongings. She went downstairs and, after a bowl of porridge, headed to the dining hall. There was the usual smell of cabbage and the floor felt icy.

Standing on the raised platform, beside a nun and a man she didn't recognize, was Sister Cyril, smiling her joyless smile. A group of children in hats and coats were gathered in front of her. All had suitcases and small bags. One or two held teddy bears under their arms.

'I shall give tablets out to you all for the seasickness. Take two of these and you shall be fine.' She started to go down the line of children. Some were fidgeting worriedly, but most, Marcia noted, were wriggling and excited. A few were holding hands. Most looked much younger than her: ten or eleven. And they seemed to be healthy, not sickly like some of the children here. The boys were strong and muscular, not the wiry ones; the girls were the ones who were taller for their age, not the waifs. There were so many at the orphanage who never seemed to get up, or had feet permanently curled under them, or calipers; some who used wheelchairs. They certainly weren't here.

'Not now, David,' said Sister Cyril, seeing one of the children popping a tablet into his mouth. 'They're not sweets. Wait until you're on the boat. Now I shall read the list.'

Marcia quietly stood at the back for a few moments, listening. Then she shuddered, picked up her bag and joined the end of the line.

There was a girl crying, sniffing into the crook of her arm. 'I want my mammy.'

The nun put out a hand and placed it on her shoulder. 'Your mother. She's signed the form. I'm sorry, Sylvie.'

'Sister, can I change my mind?'

'Of course you can't. Now wipe your nose, Sylvie, dear.' The nun turned. 'Marcia, give her your clean handkerchief.'

Marcia readjusted the expression on her face to a dead stare.

'What's the matter? You're making the right decision, Marcia. Your only relative who is in a position to have you, your aunt, isn't a suitable person for you to live with. I believe she has a fellow now, to say nothing of a bar in her living room. People get these silly notions from films. We'll all be dancing on the veranda next. Whoever heard of drinking gin and French on your sofa before Cary Grant came along? I'm glad that we had a space on the boat.'

Marcia looked ahead, cold-eyed. She was frightened by what she was seeing.

Sister Cyril drew herself up, clapping her hands. 'Father Donnelly will be at the Pier Head to do the head count and the blessing. And then you'll be off. You really have made the right decision, all of you. You're Jesus's happy holidaymakers. The lucky ones. See this as the first day of the rest of your life. Let's say a prayer and sing the kookaburra song, shall we?'

Marcia turned to the boy standing next to her. 'What even is a kookaburra? I think they're made up.'

He shrugged, hoicked his bag over his shoulder. 'Gorra be better than this place. When you've got nothing, something is always better than nowt.' He put up his hand. 'Sister, Marcia says the kookaburra isn't a real thing.'

The nun tutted. 'Marcia, you were such a sweet child. You're turning into your sister. Of course kooka-burras are real. And you should be merry like that little bird, not pulling a face. Besides, you said you wanted to go. This is the chance for a new beginning. To wipe the slate clean with God.'

'I haven't done anything wrong.'

'We're all sinners, Marcia.'

The van rocked along the dock road. There were benches running along each side of it. As they pulled up alongside the landing stage, Marcia could see from out of the window a boat waiting, with flags and ribbons tied to the decks fluttering in the sunlight. There was a gaggle of other children – and families, men in suits, all crowding on the landing stage, waiting to go up the gangplank, the wind buffeting their backs. The sea was whipped up by a strong breeze and white foam was flying off the surface.

The small boy on the bench opposite looked at her, round-eyed and worried, while they waited for the door to be unlocked.

Please God, Marcia thought, let no one make them start singing songs. She shuddered. Two girls with sagging socks and wearing brown berets and gabardines, looking as if they were going off to guide camp, sat clutching each other's hands. Another with a long pigtail started winding it around her finger. The mood had changed since they'd gathered on the steps back at the orphanage, posing for a photograph as Sister Cyril told them to 'say cheese and then say oranges', baring their teeth and squinting – about as far away from smiling as Marcia could imagine. A prayer, a quick Hail Mary, and then Sister Cyril sprinkling holy water over them, which had made them flinch. 'Just remember, God has chosen you. Enjoy your new lives, and don't ever let the sun set without kneeling down and saying a prayer of thanksgiving for this opportunity.'

'Sister,' one of the boys had said. 'Will there be swimming if it's awful hot? Or will there be a lido? Like at New Brighton?'

'You can jump off the boat,' said the girl with the plait.

'No, dear, that's a bit stupid – it's a big boat. There will be lots of other people on it. And remember, you're representing St Mary of the Blessed Angels. I don't want any stories coming back to the archdiocese about naughty children. You've been chosen because you're our best. Because you're special. Don't let me down. In the name of the Father and of the Son and of the Holy Spirit, amen.'

Now the van driver turned off his engine. 'Right, in an orderly line,' he shouted over his shoulder. 'Take your suitcases and wait over by the railings while we count you.'

The doors swung open. Everyone stood up and started to gather their bags. Marcia felt her heart racing as she came out into the sunshine.

'Well, hello,' Father Donnelly greeted them. He was directing them to stand in front of the chain between two posts that would soon be removed to allow the children onto the boat. He counted heads as they all piled out.

Marcia gripped her suitcase and looked around. There were officers wearing ship's uniforms, even a couple of policemen. Was it her imagination or were they all watching the children closely? Even if she had a mind to run for it, she thought, she wouldn't get more than a few yards. She heard the nun call them to attention, and in a moment they were moving off towards the gangway. She had never seen a ship so big, and certainly never been on one.

Once on board, they slowly made their way down to the cabins along crowded corridors that smelled of the sea and diesel oil. Marcia was faintly reminded of the ferry to New Brighton all those years ago, and tears welled up in her eyes. How had it ended like this?

It took a while to sort out who was sleeping with whom and where, and for Marcia to unpack her few belongings. She had been told the ship was set to sail at three, but she had lost all sense of time and there was no sign of a clock anywhere. She sat on her small bunk bed and tried to collect her thoughts.

Henry Cherry, on his way back from lunch at the Acropolis, looked over towards the Pier Head and saw HMS *Britannic* gleaming in the afternoon sun. He knew it was one of the ships that transported children to Australia. A majestic-looking vessel, he thought, but he felt a stab of anger at the thought of the disreputable job it was doing. He turned away thoughtfully and went into the Cunard Building.

Chapter 44

Sister Cyril gathered the children in one of the cabins, although a few had to stand in the corridor outside. 'It's time to wish you bon voyage. I am so excited for you and for the wonderful life ahead of you. God bless you all.'

There were murmurs from the children. One of them started to sob quietly.

'So, a final head count to make sure none of you have missed the boat,' she chuckled, trying to lighten the mood. She and another nun carefully counted up the children, stopped and looked at each other, and counted again.

Sister Cyril looked worried. 'There's someone missing. Who's missing? Children, help me, who's missing?'

They started to count again; then Sister Cyril stopped, incredulity on her face. 'Marcia Rogan. Marcia Rogan isn't here!' she said in a panicked voice.

Children and nuns looked about them in dismay, but she was right. Marcia was missing.

The narrow steel corridors were packed with people trying to move in both directions. Marcia had slipped away without anyone noticing and was now keeping her head down, forcing herself not to walk too fast. Keep calm and no one will notice, she thought. Someone stepped out of a cabin without looking, causing a bottleneck jam and forcing her to stop completely. Her heart was thumping in time with the low throb of the engines, which she hadn't noticed before. She wondered fearfully how much time she had before the ship pulled away from the dock and the gangways were pulled up, leaving her no chance of escape. When they had boarded, they had struggled down at least three flights of stairs, maybe more; so she knew she must head to the upper decks. But how? Then, to her left, she saw a larger stairway. She squeezed between two big trunks and a gaggle of passengers, grabbing the handrail and swinging herself round to go upwards.

At the top of the stairs, a man in uniform and peaked cap was stretching a thick coil of rope across the stairway. He shook his head at her. There was no option – she had to go down, away from the upper decks, away from her escape route, and perhaps away from Liverpool. She ran down two flights, looked around, and then ran down another. A mixture of panic and resignation gripped her stomach. The stairway was narrower now and she slowed her pace and went to her left, along a corridor that was narrower still.

It was less busy here and the only people passing were crew men and women who hardly gave her a second look. Even so, she felt the need to hide herself away, thinking her brown pinafore made her too conspicuous – as if simply hiding would make this awful predicament go away. To her right was an open door, and she slipped inside and closed it firmly. She was in some kind of a laundry room. There was a large sink in the corner and canvas laundry bags heaped on the floor. She looked inside one of the bags, finding neatly folded shirts and other items of clothing. She opened a cupboard door: it held only a broom and an apron hanging on a hook. She wondered how long she would be safe in here, how long before someone marched into the room.

Then she heard the deep, vibrating sound of the ship's horn. All hope was lost and with that, resignation came. A grim calm enveloped her. She could only wait an hour or so, make her way back to her cabin and pretend to have lost her way. After that there would be the long and terrifying journey to the other side of the world.

She sank down on her haunches in despair, leaning against the cabin wall as she heard the grinding of the engine surge again.

In his office on the top floor of the Cunard Building, less than five minutes from where Marcia was crouching, Henry sorted the papers on his desk. He had gone about his business all morning as usual, and had even managed to get a smile out of Dudley. But after seeing the HMS *Britannic*, his mood had darkened slightly. He thought of Marcia, trapped in that bloody awful orphanage, and what steps he could take to get her out. He idly scribbled her name on the blotting pad in front of him.

Mr Higgins came into the room, out of breath.

'Damn lifts aren't working, out for the rest of the day.' He handed two sheets of paper to Dudley and wiped the sweat from his forehead. 'Passenger lists just in. Couple of additions, all signed off. Ship's leaving in an hour.' He looked at his watch. 'Is that the time? My goodness. Not an hour then, less than twenty minutes. Good riddance.' And he shuffled out of the office.

Henry sat and watched Dudley check off the names. What kind of job was this? Whose side were they on? Dudley didn't seem to care.

'How many from St Mary's?' asked Henry.

Dudley looked up. 'What?'

'St Mary's, how many?'

Dudley sighed as if he'd been asked to count the number of words in the Bible. He looked down at his sheets of paper. 'Ten.'

Ten children who had no idea where they were going or why, Henry thought.

'No, sorry. Make that eleven. One added.'

Henry nodded. He looked down and saw the name he'd written on the blotter: Marcia. He frowned and, without quite knowing why, asked, 'What's the added name?'

Dudley reluctantly looked at his sheet again and traced his finger slowly down the names in the margins. But it didn't matter, because somehow Henry knew what was coming.

'Marcia Rogan. Hey, isn't that the girl who . . .'

Henry was on his feet, out of the door and down the corridor before Dudley could finish his sentence. He jumped over a stack of files and headed for the staircase. Five flights, two steps at a time, nearly killing Betty, who had just delivered tea to Mr Higgins. Bloody lifts! He reached the second floor without breaking any limbs. Now the staircase was wider and carpeted, so he leaned on the handrail and almost slid down the rest of the way. Then he was out on the pavement and crossing the street, running down to the Pier Head. He could hear the ship's horn blowing repeatedly, but the gangway was still in place. Breathless, he frantically waved his arms at HMS *Britannic* as if it might stop just for him. Exhaustion was overtaking every part of his body, but he had to stop this ship from leaving – he had to get on board. A whistle sounded, someone was shouting, and then a policeman grabbed him by the arm. He tried to pull away.

'No, please. Let go. There's someone on board who shouldn't be there.'

'Nothing we can do about that, son. Gangway's going up, look.'

A sailor on the ship looked down from the top of the gangway. 'Everything all right?'

'No!' cried Henry.

'Yes,' shouted the policeman, still holding his arm tightly. 'All fine. Fella's a bit worked up about something, is all.' The sailor gave a thumbs up and the main gangway started to pull away from the ship. Henry could see there was a second smaller one to the stern with people still getting off, but now a second policeman had turned up and, struggle as he might, he was held fast. They pulled him away, sat him down on a bench just along the quayside and gave him a glass of water.

'What in heaven's name was that about?' Both policemen stood directly in front of him, blocking his view.

'There's a girl. On the boat. From St Mary's orphanage. Shouldn't be.' He was babbling, he knew, but he needed to make them understand.

'Always a girl, isn't it? It's too late, son. The ship's away.' They stepped back, and Henry saw it was true. HMS *Britannic* was moving steadily away from the shoreline. Marcia was gone.

Chapter 45

It was a miracle he hadn't been arrested, and only just short of miraculous that he hadn't been missed at the office. Betty had assumed he was dashing downstairs to see Higgins, who in turn had been unaware of his absence because there was no way he was walking up two flights of stairs for a second time in one afternoon.

Not that it could have made things any worse for Henry. He had let poor Marcia down for a second time and now he felt empty inside, hollowed out. It hadn't even been his fault, so why did he feel so bad? He knew why, of course, but admitting it would only have made his life more unbearable.

Picking up the heavy Bakelite telephone, he asked the operator to put him through to the stage door of the Winter Gardens in Blackpool. There was some confusion, but after he'd explained to the stage door man that it was the Corporation of Liverpool calling, and that the Corporation represented His Majesty's Government, and that if he didn't get Cynthia Rogan on the phone, Henry would come down personally and have the theatre if not the whole of Blackpool closed down, the man agreed to fetch Cynthia.

'Is it Marcia? Has something happened?' Cynthia

said, her blood running cold as she took the telephone. Instinctively, she clutched the lapels of her cardigan together. 'Is she all right?'

He faltered. 'I'm sorry. I . . . well . . . We're given the list of passengers from the orphanage whenever a ship leaves the Pier Head for Australia. And one left today, a few minutes ago, and although she shouldn't have been, Marcia was on it. I am so sorry.'

Cynthia felt sick. 'That doesn't make any sense. Oh, God. She mentioned it. But I didn't listen. I didn't think for a moment she was serious.' She began to ramble. 'We had a row. I knew she was going back to the orphanage, but I regretted it the minute she left. I've been trying to get in touch with her, but it's impossible. The nuns . . .' She was talking to herself as much as to Henry. 'She wouldn't leave me. She can't just leave for another country without telling anyone. Do my mother and father even know? The last we heard from them, they were in Leeds. Or was it Ireland? I don't know . . .'

'The nuns don't need to tell your parents. I told you – they have authority over Marcia.'

'But arrangements couldn't have been made that quickly? What about Norma? She's our aunt.'

'I'm afraid when someone like Marcia . . . well, as long as she's under eighteen, if it's been decided that she's in the care of the local children's office – in this case, St Mary's – they're the ones who make the decisions. It's all written down. I can show you if you want.'

Cynthia was shaking. 'But I'm her sister. They should have told me.'

'Something changed when she lost her job. Someone there took against her, I don't know why. But if they think it's best for Marcia to get on a boat and start a new life in Australia, then there's nothing anyone can do about it. She'll be getting on a boat.'

'Stop,' Cynthia said, pressing her hands over her ears. She felt as if someone had put a belt around her chest and pulled it tight, too tight, and tighter. Each time she took a breath she felt pain. 'What's your address? We have to find a way of getting her back.'

'Surely you have a show?'

'That's what understudies are for, Henry. I need your address. Bloody give it to me! I'm getting on the next train. This is a family emergency.'

'Cynthia, she's on a boat to Australia. It takes five weeks to get there, so getting the next train isn't going to help.'

In the end he realized there was no point in refusing, and he gave her the address. 'Oh, Marcia, you silly squit,' she said under her breath as she replaced the receiver.

And for the first time in years, she prayed, because she could think of nothing else to do.

Chapter 46

Two hours later, Cynthia – wearing a pretty polka-dot tea dress with just a thin cardigan that made her look oddly dressed for the time of the year, like a girl who had chosen her clothes in haste – got off the train at Lime Street. The station clock said half past six. She headed for Tooley Street as fast as she could, hoping against hope that somehow Henry Cherry had got it wrong and Marcia would be sitting there with a cup of tea and a piece of toast.

When he opened the door, his ashen face dashed her hopes.

'Come in,' he said sadly. All the nervous energy seemed to drain away from her as they looked at one another. 'I'm sorry. I was too late,' he added.

'It's not your fault,' she said miserably, following him inside.

They went into the small living room. He flicked on the light switch; Cynthia realized he must have been sitting in the dark. It was clean and tidy but it was missing a woman's touch, she thought. There were piles of books and a gramophone in the corner, and records on the shelf above. Shoving a dressing gown behind a chair, he invited her to sit. He looked anxious, putting his hands in and out of his pockets.

She wondered if she was the first girl who'd ever been inside his flat.

'What now?' she asked.

'I'm not sure.'

Cynthia's lip quivered. 'I didn't do enough to look after her. But how on earth can they send children away to another country?'

He shrugged. 'They can. They've been doing it for years and they'll carry on for a while yet. There's this new National Health Service, and the new Children Act – maybe that will start to change things.'

Cynthia looked at him. 'What's that got to do with Marcia? Why are you telling me this?'

'Sorry, I get quite wrapped up in these things. It's what I believe in.'

All Cynthia could think, over and over, was why had she let Marcia go? She had been so cross about Alfie. What a stupid, unfeeling thing to say, to tell her to go back to the nuns.

'It was my fault,' she blurted. 'I told her to go back.' She rummaged in her handbag for a handkerchief and wiped away her tears.

Henry picked up his briefcase and took a deep breath, then said, 'I need to show you something.' He produced the letters he had found at the office and passed them over, explaining, in hesitant, back-to-front sentences and with small, hopeless gestures, what they were and the sad truth of what they meant. Cynthia read them slowly, her hands shaking.

'And this one. Addressed to Marcia. From someone called Ellie.'

'Ellie. Marcia's friend from St Mary's,' said Cynthia.

'If I hadn't been so caught up in all the show-business nonsense . . . Part of me thought she was better off without me. It's such a mess.'

'Don't say that. I'm sure she didn't plan to leave you in this way. I have a feeling it's Sister Dorothea who is behind all this. Marcia won't have had any freedom to choose. If they've decided that it's in her best interests, they can do what they want.'

'Everyone thinks they're doing a good thing.'

'Maybe it's because of the war. People turn a blind eye because there are still so many people who need helping. Another problem out of the way. One thing's for sure, I'm done with Higgins.'

He stood wearily. There wasn't much more to say. He went to the kitchen and reappeared carrying a little tray. 'I made these apple turnovers earlier. Are you hungry?' She looked at him.

'That's a nice thing to do.'

'I find it calming. Baking. I don't know why. I'm on my own so I've had to learn.'

'Thank you. But I don't think I can face food.'

Later, he changed his sheets and made up his bed for her, putting an old eiderdown on the small sofa for himself.

She lay in the darkness thinking about her sister on that ship. Five weeks? What about seasickness? Marcia used to get queasy on the ferry to New Brighton. Then she thought about Henry giving up his bed. He was a strange one. Obsessed with his job; or was it more than that? With any other boy she might have expected to hear footsteps in an hour or so, and whispers of *I can't sleep, can I just lie down next to you?* Strangely, she had no fear that would happen with Henry. She drew her knees up to her chest under the fresh bedclothes and wondered what she would have done if it had.

At eight o'clock the following morning, Henry walked with steely determination up the steps outside the Cunard Building, striding into the lobby without even nodding to the commissionaire. He turned towards the lift. Thankfully the doors were open; if he'd been delayed, he might have had time to change his mind. He pressed the button for the third floor, not the fifth. Now there was no going back.

Mr Higgins was sitting at his desk, contemplating the wall opposite, when Henry walked in. He glanced up.

Henry stopped in front of his desk. 'Sir, I'm not sure what you know about this, but yesterday Marcia Rogan was put on a boat to Australia. This was done entirely against her will, and to be honest, I'm shocked. She was a late addition to the passenger list and as it's me who's been dealing with her case, I think I should have been kept informed that this was going to happen. Did you know?' He crossed his arms, in an effort to show that he wouldn't take no for an answer.

'Good morning, Henry,' Mr Higgins said, slowly and deliberately.

Henry was momentarily thrown and uncrossed his arms. 'Yes, sorry. Good morning. But I need to know how this happened.'

'How what happened?'

'How did Marcia Rogan end up on a ship to Australia?'

Higgins stood up and went to his window, which overlooked the Pier Head and the Mersey. 'The first question that comes to my mind is this – *is* she on a ship to Australia?'

'I'm not following you.'

'I had a phone call last night from St Mary's. Your girl disappeared before the boat left yesterday afternoon. They counted heads and there was one missing – Marcia Rogan. No one saw her get off at the gangway, and there were ships' officers and even policemen around. So one would have to assume she was hiding somewhere on the boat. Unfortunately, the nuns had to leave before a search could be started. Apparently they didn't fancy a trip down under.'

Henry blinked. 'So she's hiding on the ship?'

'That's what we thought. But his morning, I received a phone call from a man called Tattersall. Rather rude bugger. He said he had Marcia Rogan in his kitchen. She turned up last night and asked if she could stay, before bursting into tears. He started lobbing all sorts of accusations at us. Then he had the bloody nerve to complain that we weren't doing our job.'

Henry was staring at him in disbelief. It felt like the floor was shifting beneath his feet. How on earth could she still be here in Liverpool and not on that boat? And his next thought was: if she was still here, how could he keep her safe?

'Are we going to get her, sir?' He thought this was an innocent enough question, but it seemed to tip Mr Higgins over the edge.

'No, we are not going to get her. *You* are going to get her. And then you're going to deliver her back into the safe hands of St Mary's. Yet again. You can take the department car, and when you've done that, you won't interfere in any matter concerning Marcia Rogan, ever again. Do I make myself clear, Mr Cherry?' He was angrier than Henry had ever seen him. His face was bright red, and the familiar beads of sweat had appeared on his bald head.

By contrast, considering the state he had arrived in, Henry was a picture of calm and confidence as he looked Mr Higgins in the eye. 'Perfectly clear, Mr Higgins. I'll be on my way.'

Cynthia was eating a boiled egg when Henry burst into his flat. She stood up apologetically, almost choking, 'Sorry, I hope you don't mind . . . Henry, why are you smiling?'

'Marcia's not on the ship! I don't know how, but she's in Liverpool Lane.'

'Are you being serious?'

'Yes, I'm being serious. Get your things. I have a car outside – we're going to get her.' Cynthia started squealing uncontrollably and doing what Henry assumed were modern dance steps around in circles on the threadbare carpet.

'For crying out loud, Cynthia, we have to go!'

As they ran to the car, she said, 'She must be a regular Houdini, Henry. I mean, how did she manage it?'

'I have no idea. No idea at all.'

Chapter 47

Marcia had been crouched down in the ship's laundry room, still feeling the throb of the engines somewhere below her, when she had heard voices approaching. She jumped up and put her ear to the door: the voices were getting closer. Turning, she found herself looking into the open cupboard and, seeing the apron on its hook inside, decided anything was worth a try. She heard the voices pass by and gently pulled the cabin door open. It could have been the nuns, for all she knew; but thankfully she saw the backs of four or five people in work clothes walking away down the corridor.

Quickly putting the apron on, she grabbed a laundry bag and moved into the corridor as quietly as she could, trying to catch up with the group. She had no idea who these people were or where they were going, but it was clear they were looking for something. At the end of the corridor, the man at the front stopped.

'This is bloody stupid. We've got five minutes or we're buggered.' He saw Marcia standing at the back. 'You trying to get off this boat too, love?' She hesitated for a fraction of a second and then nodded, feeling the blood thundering around her body.

Then a voice further off called out, 'Way out's down here. Quick!'

They walked in single file into the sunshine and onto a small, low gangway at the stern of the ship. No one paid them the slightest attention. There was an argument going on at the end of the main gangway, where Marcia had boarded the ship only a couple of hours before. She didn't dare look properly, but she noticed two policemen holding on to a young man who was shouting like a madman and gesturing at the ship. No one could have timed a distraction better. She wondered who he was, and wished she could thank him somehow.

A few more yards and she would be on to solid ground. By the time the policemen looked in her direction, she had stepped off the gangway and was disappearing into the bustle of the busy quayside. She stopped for a moment and looked back as the last gangway was pulled away, the ropes untied, and HMS *Britannic* eased from her berth and moved out towards the sea.

She had kept a few pennies in her skirt pocket, enough to get the bus to Scottie Road, from where she wound her way up the hill towards Liverpool Lane. When she arrived she stopped at the end of the road and breathed deeply, filling her lungs with the familiar smells of home. It had not been long since she was last here, but so much had changed.

She walked in the middle of the road, over the cobbles. As she neared their old house she tried not to look but could feel her head twisting round. She gave up the struggle and stopped. Someone had painted the front door red, and there were pretty gingham curtains at the window. It hurt her heart to see it.

It was getting dark as she made her way to Mr Tattersall's house and knocked on his door. She had decided she would ask him if she could stay for just one night. She felt tears welling up; her lips began to tremble and she wondered if she would manage to speak at all. Then she heard the click of the latch, and the door opened.

Chapter 48

The department car was a beige 1938 Ford Prefect that had seen better days. It had been struck on various occasions by falling bricks or tiles, and there were even scattered burnt patches where fiery shards of an incendiary bomb had floated down onto the roof during the Blitz. Henry considered himself a safe and reliable driver; he was quite experienced, despite only having passed his test the year before. Cynthia, sitting in the front seat, wished he would put his foot down.

'Marcia's been at Mr Tattersall's all night, you say? Can't you go any faster?'

Cynthia was filled with an energy, fizzing with nerves, as if somehow Marcia might slip through her fingers again if they didn't get to her as soon as was humanly possible.

'It doesn't go any faster. And I'm not breaking the law.'

She watched as he firmly changed gear, and his jaw clenched. He wasn't bad-looking, if a little pedestrian for her tastes. He was tall, though; tall was good.

'What do you think of our Marce?' she asked.

'What do I think of her? I think she's had a bad time of it. You all have.'

'No, I mean, do you like her?'

'Of course I like her.'

'Don't be silly – you know what I mean.'

Henry glanced at her briefly, then looked back at the road. 'I'm doing my job. I'd do the same for anyone in her predicament. I want to change things, though, the way these children are treated. That's why I'm so worked up about Marcia's case.'

Cynthia nodded and gripped the dashboard. Henry turned the car off Scottie Road into Dryden Street and drove up the hill. The car struggled and he changed down a gear.

'Besides,' he said casually, 'that boy. The one who came to see her at the Worboys. I read about him in my notes, Marcia and him doing things together . . . unmentionables, that's how the nuns described it . . . I remember thinking that was ridiculous, just two young sweethearts, but I suppose that's why there was such a tremendous fuss. I'm assuming Marcia likes him.'

Cynthia turned her head and smiled at him with delight. You so nearly convinced me, Mr Cherry, she thought. So close, and then you gave yourself away.

The car jiggled its way down Liverpool Lane and came to a stop outside Mr Tattersall's house. Cynthia jumped out and ran to knock on the door while Henry watched from the car. Somehow, it didn't feel like it was his business to follow her in. This is about sisters, he thought, as the front door opened and Cynthia went inside.

'Marcia! Squit! Oh, Marce!' cried Cynthia, hardly believing what she was seeing in front of her – her beloved sister, standing on the peg rug in the hall. Kissing her forehead, her cheeks, her hair, her fingers, she said, 'Is it really you?'

'Of course, you noodle. What are you crying for?'

'I'm so sorry – will you ever forgive me?' said Cynthia.

'Sisters don't need to forgive. They just do awful things to one another to make sure they love each other.'

'Oh, Marce, I thought you were on that boat.'

'Not a chance. I just needed a way to get out of the nuns' clutches. I hoped they wouldn't notice I was missing after we boarded and once I had bunked off and was back on the shore I would be free to find you and Ma and Da and put things right without them thinking about looking for me. I was imagining perhaps they might even have thought I had fallen overboard or something. Desperate measures, I know.'

'But what if . . . what if . . . I shudder to think, if you had sailed off, what on earth would have happened to you, Marcia?'

'It's a horrible thought. All so miserable and sad. A couple of the children thought they were going on a day trip just like the ferry across the Mersey.' She paused. 'But tell me your news,' she said, almost as if she wasn't yet ready to talk about being locked up at the orphanage and the grim story that she had found herself part of.

'Well, It's hard to know where to start. I've missed you. Show business, eh? They'd stab you in the back quicker than you can do a step ball change, and I've had no one to spill my gossip to. But never mind me, first I want to hear every single detail about what's happened to you since you left me.'

'Cuppa tea?' said Mr Tattersall.

The next half hour was filled with more tears as Marcia spoke and they listened, shocked and saddened by what they were hearing. There was stronger tea, a pork pie with piccalilli, and, at moments, even laughter. Eventually, Cynthia looked at the clock. 'I need to go back, Marce. But I promise, I'll return as soon as I can. I'll leave you in the safe hands of Henry Cherry.'

'Henry?' Marcia paled.

'Oh, blimey, I did you tell you Henry's here?'

'No, you didn't, Cyn. Here – where? He's been waiting all this time?' There was alarm in her voice.

'Outside, in his rusty motor. He's come to get you.'

Marcia's face became deadly serious, and she went to the front door. Henry was still sitting in the car. He got out as she approached him and smiled.

But Marcia wasn't returning the smile. There was anger flaring in her eyes. 'Have you come here to take me back to the orphanage?'

He looked at her, unable to speak. Behind her, a confused Cynthia stepped out onto the pavement.

'Well?' Marcia demanded again. Her sister was raising her palms as if to ask, what's going on?

'I'll take you wherever you want to go, Miss Rogan,' Henry said simply. 'But I promise I will never take you to that awful place again.'

He watched her anger slowly drain away. She looked away and down at her feet.

'All right, I'll come with you. Cyn needs to go to Lime Street. Then you can drop me off at Norma's.

We need to have a serious talk. And I'll be telling her no telephoning nuns and saying where I am and if she argues, you'll do the same. Agreed?'

Henry nodded.

He parked the car on a levelled-off bomb site behind the Empire. After kissing Cynthia goodbye, Marcia stayed in the car while Henry walked her sister to the station. She looked through the windscreen at the scaffolded buildings. Her eyes rested on the old propaganda posters peeling off the side of one of them. They were curled at the edges, yellowing and torn, but the lettering was still visible: *Careless Talk Costs Lives*, read one. A reminder of the war that had killed so many, and so badly damaged her father. Another caught her eye, for some reason more familiar than the rest: *A healthy, happy mother is best for baby. Mr Woolton's delicious pie. Ask Mr Woolton's preggies.*

She read it again. Where had she heard that before? Mr Woolton's preggies? Her mind turned back to the old nun, Sister Hilda. That rambling conversation they'd had about a Mr Woolton, and about Sister Dorothea. The woman in the poster, wearing an apron, was smiling . . . and nestling a bump. She thought of Dorothea visiting the Worboys, the way she was always looking intently at Dolly. How lucky Marcia was to be looking after Dolly, she'd said . . . And then she thought of the child's birthday being on the same day Marcia and Cynthia had arrived at the orphanage – the day they had seen that shadowy figure scurrying away.

No. Surely not? But then a million pieces of the jigsaw fell into place.

The car rocked slightly as Henry climbed back in, but Marcia didn't look at him.

'So where am I taking you? Are you sure going to Norma's is a good idea? I have a friend who lives in Freshdale – you could rent a room, I'd be happy to help out with, you know . . .'

Marcia was unblinking, still staring ahead. 'I've changed my mind. I need to go back to the orphanage,' she said softly.

'No – you can't seriously mean . . .'

'I am serious, Henry. We have to go back to St Mary's.'

'I don't understand.'

'You will. I know everything, Henry. And to think, all this time, I was running from Sister Dorothea! But it should have been her running from me.'

Chapter 49

Sister Dorothea strode down the corridor. She walked determinedly, her rosary beads bumping against her leg and her habit swishing. Then she paused. A figure blurring around the edges, backlit by the winter sun, stood framed in the doorway of the orphanage.

'Jesus, Mary and Joseph! Marcia Rogan! Why aren't you on the boat?' she gasped.

Marcia shrugged, narrowed her eyes. 'Because I'm not as stupid as you think.'

'What are you talking about?' said the nun, uncharacteristically flustered. 'Get away from me,' she rasped. She pinched her lips and screwed up her face.

'I'm not going anywhere,' said Marcia calmly. 'I have unfinished business here.'

The nun drew herself up and said angrily, 'I want nothing more to do with you, Marcia.'

'I'm sure.'

Sister Dorothea moved past her.

'Wait. I need to speak to you,' Marcia called after her.

The nun wordlessly hurried through the front door and outside. Cynthia was right when she had once said it was as though they moved like they were on wheels. Where was she going? She seemed to have such intent, such purpose.

'Sister!' cried Marcia, jogging after her over the gravel path.

Sister Dorothea, habit billowing, swept through the garden gate, past the wall with the statues in the alcoves. Really? The nun's garden of rest? thought Marcia. Did she think that was going to protect her?

Dorothea, mouthing silently, dropped to her knees in front of the statue of Our Lady, shut her eyes tight and joined her hands. The canopy of a Russian vine framed her hunched figure.

'Sister, I need you to talk to me. I need to talk to you about the Worboys' baby.'

The nun twisted her head around. 'You can't speak in here,' she hissed. 'No one has spoken in here for a hundred years. We have taken a vow! And now look what you've made me do!'

Marcia crouched and spoke directly into her face. 'Talk to me. Or I'll tell them. And I shall tell them everything.'

She saw the nun's face contract with rage. 'I have taken a vow of silence,' she hissed.

'Does Mrs Worboys know?'

Sister Dorothea scowled.

'I didn't think so. You should keep away from your daughter,' said Marcia.

'What do you mean?' the nun replied coldly.

'I didn't realize what Sister Hilda was trying to tell me. Mr Woolton's girls. His "preggies". Why would I? You made me think she was mad, and for a while

I did think that. Who'd take any notice of someone who said she had a wireless that belonged to Eleanor Roosevelt! That made no sense to me. But it was true, of course; just as Mrs Worboys said.'

'You're talking nonsense . . .'

'And of course, Dolly's bracelet. With the heart and the seven spears. Our Lady of Sorrows. I know why you wanted me to work for the Worboys. It was because you were afraid you would see Dolly less as she grew older, so you used me as an excuse. So you could walk in whenever you wanted, pretending it was me you needed to see.'

'Don't be ridiculous!'

'Just admit it. Our Lady of Dolours. Mater Dolorosa. Dolores. Or Dolly. Short for Dolores. You named your child after your beloved Queen of Sorrows, didn't you?'

'You're out of your mind.'

Marcia looked at her, steely and controlled.

The nun's face contorted. 'Even if that were all true, no one would ever believe you.'

'Why not? Because I'm just a child? You think I'm just a girl and no one will take any notice of me? That I don't matter? That I'll quietly slip away into the shadows? Or you can ship me off to Australia? When you've seen as much as I have, your mother despairing and your father drunk, him picking up the medicine bottle time and time again, like he's possessed – when you've been ripped away from family and the sister you love – when you've lived through that, you're not a child any more. I've seen my best friend leave the people and the city she loves and be sent to some version of hell . . . all because she's been lied to by people like you, Sister.'

'Ellie? She was no good. She was loose!' Sister Dorothea spat.

'Ellie is my friend. You tried to crush the life out of us, but what you did made us stronger. And now I will not be silenced.'

Dorothea was shaking now. 'No . . . Please . . . please stop . . .' Her voice cracked and then her body seemed to fold into itself. It was as though she dissolved, with all the hatred and spite draining from her, and became just a sad, broken woman crouching on the ground amongst the stones.

'Do you think I wanted a child?' she mumbled, her face crumpling as she clutched at her skirts. 'I didn't know what to do . . . how could I? I was so young. I had no idea, when she came, that I'd love her . . . and . . . You have no idea how terrible, how hard . . . I had already got to know the nuns. My mother was so desperate for me to join the order. And there I was – pregnant. It would have killed her. The shame, don't you see? If it wasn't for Father Donnelly helping me.'

Father Donnelly? Marcia's thoughts went off in a direction she hadn't previously considered. This broken woman was so much harder to rail at. Was this a confession? Was Dorothea asking forgiveness from her? Atonement. Absolution. Was it all she knew? She was still young, and tragic. Marcia even felt a surge of pity for her.

'I didn't know about Father,' said Marcia, remembering the sound of his voice behind the curtain, the sweet smell, his deep sighs.

The nun's hand flew to her mouth.

Marcia turned her face towards the orphanage. 'Sister, I know you've done some terrible things, but giving your baby away wasn't one of them. But sending children away. That's wrong, Sister.'

'Marcia . . .' But Dorothea had no words; they withered on her lips.

'So there's something I need from you.'

'What? I can't do anything.'

'Yes, you can. You need to find my mother and father. And I also want you to find Ellie and if she wants to come back, you will make that happen too. I need to know she's happy. And you need to tell the welfare officer that for now, I am going to stay with Mr Tattersall. Now, please get up.'

'I won't.' Dorothea's face slipped into fury again. And then, angrily, unthinkingly, she sprang up and lurched towards Marcia. For a moment they struggled, Dorothea snarling and her fists flailing, Marcia doing her best to fend off the blows.

'Stop it!' cried Henry from the gate, not quite believing what he was seeing.

Dorothea twisted her head, dropped her arms and fell to the floor. 'Mr Cherry. I – I don't know what came over me,' she stuttered.

'I'm leaving now, Sister. You know what you must do.'

But Marcia herself had one more thing to see to. On her way out with Henry, she slipped in through the side gate of the kitchen garden and found Sister Hilda at her usual place in the corner of her potting shed.

She was sitting in the winter sun with a trowel and a plant pot.

'Marcia!' The old nun reached out and took her hand when she approached. 'I heard the kerfuffle in the silent garden and thought I'd better leave you to it and hide myself in here. Dorothea wasn't too happy, I gather, but it's about time someone had a few strong words in that place. Tranquillity is so overrated.' Gently the nun turned over Marcia's palm and pressed hers against it. 'You look beautiful.'

Marcia smiled. It was always Cynthia who turned heads, and it felt strange to hear this. 'I'm leaving St Mary's, Sister. Will you be all right?'

The sister's features softened, and she smiled. 'Good. You should be living your life, not stuck in an orphanage. But I know what you're thinking: poor Sister Hilda, left alone with Dorothea. I'll be fine.'

Henry was looking at a photograph on the wall of the potting shed. It showed a smiling nun with her head sticking out of the window of a mud hut; the winged habit was bleached white in the hot African sun. 'That's me,' she said to him. 'A tiger came into our garden once. I shooed it away with a broom. And I nursed. That's what I did. I saw the world. You look at me and you just see an old lady, but I like to think I made a difference in some way. It's just this old body holding me back.'

'Sister, I'll miss you.'

'Most nuns start off kind, wanting to be good. But it can be lonely. I've known plenty of sisters to jump over that garden wall.' She smiled and paused.

'Are you talking about Sister Dorothea?' said Marcia, gently.

'I have a feeling she thought she would have a different, more exciting life as a nun – nursing abroad, converting hearts and minds, maybe. She imagined heroic acts, spiritual awakenings and miracles . . . visions . . . and atonement.'

'Go on,' said Marcia.

'Disappointment stood in the way of Dorothea. I first met her when she was twenty-two. Her mother arranged that she should spend a year here. All went well, she was enthusiastic and kind – but it puzzled me that one day she started covering herself in coats, even though she was sweating and it was the middle of summer. She went back home quite suddenly. But the following year she appeared again, came back to take her vows. She seemed the perfect nun.

'She spent her first two years at a convent in Freshdale. But when she returned to live here, there was something . . . off. With her and Father Donnelly. Whenever she was around him, he seemed distracted. And every time I would go to the chapel, Sister would be there rearranging the hymnals, and he would be there pacing back and forth. It meant I started to watch them. And every time, I would see something that alarmed me. It made me think back to a particular winter night. Saints' Day. Father Donnelly had been there. Someone had left a newborn child on the steps; there was such a commotion. Such excitement over the little girl. She didn't cry at all, just looked up at us, wide-eyed.

'Some of the priests think of abandoned babies as

somehow inferior. But this child – for the night we had her here, Father never left her side. It was he who arranged to take the baby to the Worboys. It was almost as if he knew the baby would be arriving. I forgot all about it until two years later, when Dorothea turned up from Freshdale to work here. And then there was Father Donnelly again, always puffing on those sweet-smelling cigarettes at the back gate, where she would meet him. Always after dark. And I wondered why he wasn't walking through the front gate. Most peculiar, as nuns love a priest. Oh, how we love a priest,' she laughed, and her eyes twinkled. 'So then, when he asked me to arrange a plenary indulgence for Sister Dorothea . . . Do you know what that is?'

Marcia shook her head.

'It's when someone does something they're very much ashamed of, something that keeps them awake at night, worrying they will never get to heaven. So, if they can promise to detach themselves from sin, offer themselves up to God . . . live in a faithful state of grace . . . well. It's a deal with the Lord to get into heaven.' She paused. 'Saying it out loud, it sounds a little odd. But it can be a weight off someone's mind, and sometimes it will be the difference between a life spent in purgatory and a life well lived. Oh, and you get a lovely certificate with the Pope's picture on it.' She sighed. 'Our Lady of Sorrows – certainly apt when it comes to Dorothea. Seven swords piercing her heart, for sure. And there you have it.

'I feel a burden of responsibility for what's happened, Marcia. If I hadn't mentioned anything, you might not have arrived at the truth. I think Dorothea was afraid that your suspicions were aroused and told Father Donnelly. He couldn't risk you finding out. What better way to solve the problem than sending you to the other side of the world? I can't bring myself to believe the child is his, but he was so tangled up in the lie. His mistake was to allow Dorothea to join the order knowing her secret. No doubt he wanted to help her, but she should never have been allowed to get so close to the Worboys. And now her life here is her penance. But I'm sure he regretted it.'

Marcia thought again of Dolly's heart bracelet. If you looked closely at the heart, you could see it was engraved with seven swords. Seven sorrows – seven hundred sorrows and more for Dorothea.

Chapter 50

Henry and Marcia drove away from St Mary's for the most part in silence; not because of any awkwardness, but because they were both distracted by their own thoughts. Occasionally they would exchange a glance and a tentative smile, but nothing more. Marcia had said she couldn't face Norma now – there had already been too much drama for one day without Norma firing a million questions at her, and she wanted to go back to steady Mr Tattersall for the night. Outside his house they made a brief plan for the following day and Henry promised he would take her to Norma's at lunchtime.

When he got back to Tooley Street, he parked the car outside his flat, opened the bonnet and pulled the leads off two of the spark plugs. He needed the car tomorrow. If anyone else wanted it, he would say it had broken down; if someone came out to check, the car would still turn over but not much more.

He decided he would go into the office in the morning as usual although it was doubtful he would have a job by the end of the day. He had defied Mr Higgins's instructions in almost every regard. News of his presence at St Mary's, of Marcia's confrontation with Dorothea – or at least a version of it – and of his failure to leave her in the safe hands of the orphanage would have filtered through by morning.

Before he went to bed, he sifted through the papers he had shown Cynthia and removed a few chosen pages. He folded them and placed them in his overcoat pocket, just in case.

The following day, he was awake by six thirty. He lay there imagining the future ahead of him. So many possibilities and so many pitfalls; could anyone outwit fate? Not him, that was for sure. He thought about yesterday. Maybe Marcia. She was making a good stab at it.

He arrived on the fifth floor, punctual as usual. Dudley nodded casually as he entered. Betty's desk was still empty. Henry sat down and browsed through some papers, then got up and looked out the window at the river. He noticed his own foot tapping nervously.

Betty walked in, wished him good morning and sat at her desk. She seemed unaware of anything unusual. He thought he ought to carry on as normal, but it all seemed pointless; somewhere in the building, a time bomb was ticking.

At nine forty-five he decided to go down and face the music. He was picking up Marcia at twelve thirty. That meant roughly two and a quarter hours in which he would be shouted at, respond accordingly, get shouted at again, and be given his two weeks' notice. Then back up here; possibly clear his desk, depending on the vehemence of his dismissal; say goodbye if necessary, get back to his flat, grab the car and drive to Liverpool Lane. Just about do-able, he thought. And so, steeling himself, he got up and went downstairs.

When he walked into Mr Higgins's office, his heart stopped. Father Donnelly was sitting across the desk from Higgins, the two of them in agitated conversation. They looked around, caught out by his arrival. Mr Higgins got up angrily.

'I warned you, Henry. You took that girl to St Mary's and she said things to Sister Dorothea, made accusations that were despicable and untrue. She demanded certain actions be taken that are outrageous and will not be acted upon. You and the Rogan girl owe Father Donnelly an apology.'

Henry looked at them both. 'Why?' he inquired coolly.

'Why? Because both the Father's reputation and that of this department have been tarnished. That's why,' Higgins barked.

'No. I mean, why can't they be acted upon?'

Mr Higgins walked up to Henry. 'You are finished here, Mr Cherry. I am giving you two weeks' notice but I want you to leave the office today. Am I clear?'

In terms of timing, things were going quite well, thought Henry. Everything else was going to hell in a handcart.

'Another thing,' Mr Higgins continued, still fuming. 'I went to get the orphanage file from my cabinet this morning and it's missing.'

Henry looked at him, a picture of innocence. 'What, you mean you've lost it?'

'I suspect you have taken it, Mr Cherry,' he thundered.

'Sorry, sir, but that's ridiculous. If I had seen it,

there's a good chance I would have known about Marcia being on the ship. And as I pointed out to you yesterday, I knew nothing about that.'

'That's because I . . .' Mr Higgins stopped, looking worried he might give himself away.

'Henry.' The calming Irish burr of Father Donnelly's voice drifted across from his chair. 'I'm not too worried about my reputation. But tell me: how do you think we could best handle this problem of Marcia Rogan?' He smiled expectantly.

Henry looked at Higgins and then at Father Donnelly, taking a moment to consider his reply.

'Well,' he said. 'I was there yesterday, and nothing she said was outrageous or untrue. So, all things considered, I think the best chance of your preventing the whole process from falling apart is to do exactly what she asked.'

He turned and left the room. Only ten thirty, he thought. Way ahead of schedule.

Outside his flat, he reattached the spark plugs, started the car and headed north towards Liverpool Lane. He drove slowly and carefully, unsure whether it was legal for him to be driving without permission from his boss. At the corner of Kirkdale Road a policeman was standing with his hands behind his back. Henry kept his eyes straight ahead and glided by. He arrived outside Mr Tattersall's house a good five minutes early. Marcia was waiting outside, and together they drove towards Norma's flat.

'I should warn you that you're in a stolen car,' he said.

'I don't care. What else can they do to me?'

'Send you to Australia, I suppose.' He glanced at her to see her reaction. There was the hint of a smile on her lips.

On the roadway outside the tenement block where Norma lived, they saw Jimmy Snaith waiting at the bus stop. He was smoking his usual cigarette and clutching a paper bag.

'If you're after Norma, she's not in.'

'Where is she?' Marcia asked.

'Gone to Tattersall's house to find you. Have you not heard the news?'

'What news?'

'Nothing bad, but I can't tell you. Better get down there and find out.'

Marcia got straight back in the car. Jimmy winked slyly at Henry, enough to make him follow her lead. He turned the car around and they headed back to Liverpool Lane.

'What news could he have meant?' she said to Henry. Despite Jimmy's assurances, she looked worried.

'I'm sure it will be fine,' he replied. In fact, Henry already knew. He had been clearing his desk of personal items when Dudley had received a hasty call from Mr Higgins that had set the wheels in motion. Now Henry stopped outside Mr Tattersall's for the second time that day.

'I'm scared to go in,' she whispered.

'I promise you, it won't be anything bad.'

She smiled weakly. 'Thanks, Henry, for dragging me around.'

He thought this would be the time to say something heartfelt, but he hesitated.

Then Marcia's face brightened. 'Oh, my gosh. Look – it's Alfie! It's really Alfie.' And she was out of the car and running towards Alfie, who was jauntily walking down the street with his hands in his pockets. When he saw her, he opened his arms wide and she jumped up, throwing her arms round his neck as he kissed her once, twice, three times on the cheek. Then she was knocking on Mr Tattersall's door with Alfie on her arm, and together they went inside.

Henry sat there for a brief moment before he turned the key and started the car.

When Marcia and Alfie came into Mr Tattersall's parlour, they found Norma waiting for them at the table with a cheese flan, cherryade and Wally Labone. Marcia looked surprised to see him sitting there.

'Hello, lovely,' said Norma, leaping up and kissing her, leaving lipstick marks on her cheek. 'You remember my pal, Wally?'

Wally Labone raised an eyebrow at Norma. *Pal?* he mouthed. 'We met once, didn't we, Marcia?' he said.

'Norma has news,' said Mr Tattersall.

'News?'

'Your ma and da. They're coming home!' said Norma.

Marcia gasped. 'How? When?'

'Father Donnelly has been in touch. Hip hip hooray, darling. Apparently, they were coming back in a few weeks anyway. But hold tight: now they're coming home in two days, dearie.' She laughed. 'Look at you, Marcia, standing there like one of Lewis's shop dummies. It's true. They're coming home. Now, what say we have a sherry to celebrate!'

Chapter 51

'You ready, Marcia?'

'Yes,' Marcia replied, her voice quavering as they stood at the foot of the steps at Lime Street station.

Meanwhile, Eunice Rogan was already waiting nervously at a small table in the saloon bar, newly remodelled with plush velvet banquette seats and polished brass furnishings. She looked tired and drawn and seemed uncomfortable in her slightly crumpled hat and slightly crumpled cotton dress, twisting her gloves.

It had been the veterans' clinician who told John that they should both go back to Liverpool as soon as possible. Ignore anyone telling them they should stay away from their daughters, or long words about 'surrendering parental jurisdiction' and 'wards of court governance'. Someone at Cunard House must have moved mountains, he said, because that morning the clearance had come through. Papers had hastily been drawn up and signed by Father Donnelly returning Marcia to the jurisdiction of her parents. That was unusual in itself and should be taken seriously. Seriously, as the girls are in danger of harm? Eunice had asked, and the clinician had placed a reassuring hand on hers and told her not any more and that her daughters were safe for now but she should go home as soon as she could.

Two days later, Eunice and John had arrived in Liverpool and been met by Norma at the station. The saloon bar would feel neutral, she'd suggested. Less chance of John starting hostilities and Cynthia throwing dishes, or Marcia bursting into tears. John's better now, Eunice had replied to Norma – although she still worried. She had made it sound like a truce at the end of a war.

Lime Street was bustling. Restorations were ongoing after the damage from the bombing, but a good deal of it had already been put back to its former glory, including the beautiful curved ceiling, the iron-mongery and the magnificent clock. Perhaps there was hope for the Rogans, too.

'Deep breath, Marce,' whispered Cynthia. 'There she is.'

Eunice's eyes met theirs. She waved nervously as she watched her daughters weave through the tables towards her.

'It's just me,' was the first thing she said. Her worry was evident as she adjusted and readjusted her collar. She was looking more lined and greying around the temples. The girls slid into the booth and sat down. 'Before you say anything, I'm so sorry, sweethearts,' she said in a rush of words, wiping under each eye with her fingers. 'I had no idea the nuns wouldn't have told you where we were, or what was happening with your da.'

Marcia put out a hand to her. 'The nuns told us nothing, Ma.'

'Rest and recuperation. That's why we left. But it wasn't supposed to be for so many months. Your father . . . It's a long story.' Eunice's bottom lip quivered.

Cynthia sat back and folded her arms. Eunice, with a trembling hand, touched each of their cheeks. 'Girls,' she said, settling herself. 'My girls. Of course, the good news is, he's better already. The medicine – it does things to your brain. But after a little help from the doctors, he's made so much progress.'

'Ma, you thought you were doing what was best. And when the nuns said that you had given us up, we didn't believe them for a second,' said Marcia.

'They said that! But I sent you letters. Do you mean the nuns weren't passing them on to you? That's cruel.'

'They weren't all like that. Some were kind. Sister Hilda. Just Sister Dorothea was . . . And that was only because, like Da, a terrible thing happened to her . . .' Marcia tailed off.

'Don't make excuses for that woman, Marce. You say you sent letters?' said Cynthia.

'Yes, I wrote to you every week. I assumed, Cynthia, that as you were away dancing everything was fine, and Norma would fill me in if there were any problems.' Eunice looked flustered.

Marcia shook her head. 'They don't pass them on.'

'I should have known. I even wrote to Sister Cyril asking to have you write back, but each time they made an excuse – saying that you were busy, you were happy. And that I shouldn't pressure you because it would be upsetting to you. To think I believed them . . .'

'Don't, Ma. There's no point,' said Marcia, seeing the sadness etched in the lines in her mother's face.

'Just a minute. Da?' interrupted Cynthia. 'If he's better, why the hell isn't he here?' she said bluntly. Still the same old Cynthia, thought Marcia.

'He was worried you might still be angry with him. Said I should come along first. Make sure you wanted . . . you know . . . to see him.'

'Don't be silly, Ma,' said Marcia. 'He's done nothing wrong. Has he, Cyn?'

Cynthia remained obstinately silent.

'So, girls, you're both living with Mr Tattersall?'

Cynthia opened her mouth to speak, but Marcia jumped in first. 'Yes, I am. The nuns allowed it. They didn't have a choice.'

'You look happy, dears. Both of you.'

Cynthia ran her finger along the edge of the table-cloth. Marcia, meanwhile, leaned closer and placed a hand on her mother's trembling one. 'Don't cry, Ma.'

'We just want to know what happens now, Ma. To you and Da,' said Cynthia.

'I don't know. I don't know. But I'm hoping, if you'll let us, we can start by being a family again. We lost you. We lost your father. But, please God, only for a short while.'

'He is better, isn't he?' said Marcia, nervously.

'You won't believe it. He's a different person, dears.'

'Aye, I am. Much better, thanks, Marcia.'

She gasped, leapt up and knocked over her glass of water.

His voice had sounded stronger, clearer. And their

father, standing in front of them, did look different to the man Marcia and Cynthia had learned to live with. His complexion was ruddy with health. He was clean shaven, wearing a freshly laundered shirt and a presentable demob suit. Still frail, and a little older, but his once hollow cheeks were fleshed out and he looked taller – more like the man in the little photograph Marcia had carried around for so long.

Her mother mopped up the liquid pooling on the table with her handkerchief, and when Marcia threw her arms around him, John allowed himself for a brief moment to hope that Cynthia might forgive him as well.

He sat down opposite her and said a simple hello. There was a moment when they all wondered how she would react. But she just gave a reassuring smile and said breezily that they should relax; what did they think she was about to do, cosh him on the bonce with her handbag? Then, as her family smiled in relief, Cynthia started chattering away about all sorts of things: the new Lewis's, and plans for the Mersey Tunnel, and had he tasted peanut butter? – in short, energetic bursts punctuated with 'You'll never guess what!' and 'You could have blown me down with a feather,' and eventually, a more gentle 'It's good to see you, Da,' which she topped off by announcing, 'I've changed, too.'

He put up a hand to stay her. 'I don't want you to change. You were young and headstrong. Though I'm glad to see you're no longer a blonde. It didn't suit you. All those lovely brown curls. The way they catch the light. You should grow it longer.'

'Now, now,' said Eunice. 'One minute you're saying don't change, and the next you're telling her how to do her hair again.'

Marcia smiled. People don't change, she thought. Hopefully, they just become better versions of themselves.

Eunice put her hand on John's and squeezed gently. She could see his happiness that they were all here, together again, sitting at the table ordering ice-cream sundaes with little almond biscuits, making small talk so easily and quickly as though all the bad things they'd gone through during the past three years had never happened. They talked about the weather, and Cynthia's dancing, and how Mrs Worboys had taught Marcia to keep stockings fresh by soaking them in buttermilk, and how to empty a Hoover bag. And how Norma was worse than ever with her lah-di-dah airs and graces and sounding her aitches – not to mention her fancy man, said Cynthia.

Words tumbled over each other, one story after another, until Eunice pressed her fingers to her temples as if the information was too much to take in. Marcia decided she would leave aside the most important story for now – the fact that the nuns had attempted to send her to another country without asking their permission or even informing them. A crowded station saloon bar, full of shopgirls meeting their sweethearts on the way home from work, was not the right place for that conversation. She would save it for later.

As they left, her father offered his arm to Marcia, looking a little uncertain whether she would accept and delighted when she did. They set off for the tram.

Cynthia took her mother's hand and held it loosely as they walked on ahead.

'Your ma told me what they called you. Orphans of the living? That's an unkind way of putting it.' She held on to his arm more tightly. 'Marcia . . . I really have changed. If you give me a chance, I'll show you. The medicine, it's not doing the talking for me now.'

'I have so much to tell you . . .'

'Save it till we get home.'

'Home?'

His eyes shone. 'Liverpool Lane. That's where we're going. Oi, Nissy! Cynthia! Tram's coming,' he cried.

'Close your eyes,' he said twenty minutes later as they all stood outside their old front door, now painted red. He twisted the key in the door. Cynthia squealed and Marcia gasped as she looked around the little house with its hallway full of packing boxes. It looked so different.

'Da's pal Mick has painted it. He's been working on it for weeks. He was getting it ready to move into next month when we were due to come back, but if we can step around the paint pots, we could move in tomorrow,' said Eunice.

'And this time he's done it proper. Dug out all that damp between the walls,' said John.

'I want some flower boxes with red pansies to go in the windows. We've still some money for decorating left over from when we rented the place out,' Eunice said. 'And they've painted the skirting boards the same colour as the floor. It makes the room look bigger. I read that in a magazine.' They went upstairs. 'You'll each have your own room. The box room is small, Marce, but now all the junk is out of it, it'll do.'

Marcia looked into the box room. There was a single bed covered with a paisley patchwork quilt and a pretty rose-shaped brass lamp on a bedside table. 'Oh, Ma,' she said with tears in her eyes, as Eunice kissed her hair.

The following day, Marcia set about cleaning the place with dusters and mops. It was only the front room that needed a good going over. Feeling under the sideboard in the gap beside the wall, she touched something small and smooth. It was one of the little brown bottles. She wasn't quite sure what to do with it – it felt like a reminder of everything awful that had happened, a connection to something dark and upsetting.

'That's the enemy,' her father murmured when she brought it downstairs and laid it on the table. He was scooping out the ashes from the range, sitting back on his heels. 'Worse than Hitler. Worse than the camps.'

Outside, they could hear voices. Cynthia burst in. 'Guess who's here,' she said to Marcia.

'Come on inside,' they heard Eunice say to someone at the door.

Fred Tattersall was carrying a large dish covered with a spotted linen cloth. The smell of turkey pie and roasted vegetables filled the air.

'John. It's good to have the Rogans back in Liverpool Lane. Mrs Gibney drove out the last tenants with her chickens and singing her bawdy songs in the back yard. At least you know what you're in for.'

'*Oh, she had to lose it at the Astor!*' sang Cynthia, imitating the old lady and throwing back her head laughing.

'Thank you for this,' said John, taking the pie and offering his hand to Fred. 'Will you join us?'

Chapter 52

The next morning, Mrs Worboys was surprised to answer the door to Marcia. A little flustered, she invited her in. They went through into the drawing room, with its curtains like velvet waterfalls. Maud Worboys' hands fluttered over the mantelpiece as she rearranged the Toby jug and a photograph of her husband, then fiddled with the bow of her tunic dress and wisps of her hair.

'Marcia . . . It was all so silly, but I'm sorry – I can't give you your job back. Sister Dorothea was adamant that—'

'That's not why I'm here,' Marcia blurted. 'I wanted to ask you – I know I'm young, but if I can help in some way with your work, that's what I want to do. I can earn money like my ma, sewing and mending, I can always do that, but I also want to do something where I can make a difference. Like with your groups. With your soldiers. Or . . . I don't know. Do you think that's possible?'

'Oh, my dear, my dear; yes, of course it is. We are in desperate need of girls like you. I can tell you right now.' Sitting down, she reeled off a list of organizations: the Red Cross, the British Legion, the Veterans' Welfare Association. She listed their meeting places and those of various smaller local groups requiring volunteers, all of them needy and desperate. After a while, she glanced over her shoulder and then said, 'Come and see Dolly.'

The child was kneeling at a small table in the back room, drawing a picture. She beamed at Marcia. 'For you,' she said.

'For me? Thank you. You've grown. You're inches taller!'

Dolly hugged her, clasping her around her knees. Marcia couldn't help but breathe in the creamy smell of her as she kissed the top of her head.

'It's a bird,' she said.

'We're so happy to see you,' said Mrs Worboys, smiling.

Marcia pressed her lips together. 'Has Sister Dorothea visited recently?'

'No, dear? Why?'

'Nothing.' She ruffled Dolly's curls. She had a feeling it would stay that way. 'I was also wondering ... would it be all right if I took a pamphlet for one of your soldiers' meetings? The POWs you talked about. The concerts.'

'Of course,' Mrs Worboys said, her face lighting up. 'I'd be delighted. You mean for men like your father?'

'I'd like to bring him. I'm not sure whether he'll come. He might be too far gone.'

'They're never too far gone. Oh, my dear. You can't believe some of these poor souls, the tragedies. But when they find other people just like them, going through the same pain – well, I don't know why, but it seems to help and it might seem odd but it really does. They re-enact at the concerts the terrible things that happened to them. The chaps in uniform call *Tenko!* – and they all jump to attention and shout their names. They even re-enact getting bashed over the head. How, I don't know, but you know, they laugh. They laugh until they can't stop. Until tears stream down their faces. That's all I can say.

'It started quietly. But now they do it every year. This year, can you believe it, they even have a concert at the Albert Hall? They have these get-togethers all over the country. It's such a wonderful thing. To see them. They meet people they knew from the camps. They're survivors. They've survived the most terrible things. And I don't know why or how, I don't think the doctors do either, but slowly, they start to get better.'

Marcia had one more thing to do before leaving. She felt the letter in the buff envelope in her pocket; she would leave it in Mr Worboys' office. It was a quiet, solemn gesture. But it was a start.

That evening, Mr Worboys picked up the letter that Marcia had slipped under his *Times* newspaper. Maud had left to meet some friends, and he sat with his glass of whisky in the half light on the chaise longue and began to read it.

> *Dear Mr and Mrs Worboys,*
>   *I am so sorry to have left so quickly after the incident, I hope you will forgive me. I'll come straight to the point. Sister Dorothea,*

whom I know you are very fond of, is not quite what she seems. I hope this is not hurtful, but if there's one thing I have learned, it is that being truthful in the end is less so.

For years I didn't really understand what was happening with my father. Maybe if I had known? I didn't really understand why my mother sent me away, or why Sister Dorothea was so keen to send me to work for you. But I'm older now. I'm writing this because I can't think of how I would tell you face to face.

Dolly, Dolores, is an angel, and the reason Sister Dorothea is so close to her is that she is her child. She gave her away and then, tortured by the guilt, believed that entering the orphanage was a good way of staying close to Dolly. When I found this out I was angry, but now I think I should be more charitable. I have learned that she chose this religious life to partly somehow atone for her sins. She even has a plenary indulgence signed by the Pope. What you should know is that Dorothea has 'bought' Dolly her way into heaven, so she is well intentioned if a bit foolish. I know it's of a great comfort to some, at least if you believe in all that. I'm not sure I do.

I am sure Sister Dorothea will talk to you and explain further if you choose to speak to her. She only wanted to protect herself and Dolly from shame and guilt. And I wonder if we're all in some way to blame for that.

*You are both good people, and I know
nothing will change that.
Marcia*

Kenneth Worboys' hands were shaking as he
finished the letter. Marcia had been taught well by
the nuns, he thought. She had a graceful turn of
phrase and the letter stated clearly what she wanted
to say.

He got up and moved restlessly to the window.
Standing there, watching it streak with rain, he gazed
out at the sea. Of course, it all made sense now.
Dorothea's peculiar attention. The little devotion
cards that she would sneak under Dolly's pillow. The
rosary beads. The sprinkling of holy water when she
thought no one was looking; the engraved heart
bracelet she had bought for Dolly's birthday. And
now this plenary indulgence. He knew about these
things. She would have had to promise to detach
herself from sin, to be faithful in a state of grace for
as long as she lived. And it would be signed by the
very highest priest – the Pope himself would have
granted it. At least, that's what the certificate would
have said.

But it was unthinkable that he should show
Marcia's letter to his wife, or to Dolly. Unthinkable.

Chapter 53

February 1950

'Pigeons?' Cynthia shivered.

'Two of them.'

The sisters were in the back yard, looking at the small shed standing against the back wall. It was a cold late February day and they were both wearing coats with scarves around their necks.

'Pigeons?' Cynthia repeated. 'How are they going to help?'

'Ma thinks it will help him get back to normal,' Marcia replied.

'If she thinks it will get Da back to normal, she's as mad as he is. What's he going to do? Chat to them in pigeon warbles?'

'He seems quite keen on them.'

'Mmm. We'll see how long that lasts.' Cynthia brought out a packet of cigarettes from her pocket, slipped one out and lit it.

'So, you're done with the dancing, are you?'

Cynthia sucked on her cigarette, hollowing her cheeks, her lips forming a pout around the filter. 'It's done with me, I think. I was never cut out for it, really; everything's darling this, sweetie that. They only do it because no one can remember anyone's name. Then when you get a decent part, the other girls start talking, saying you're at it with the director.'

'That's awful.'

She took another puff. 'It all ended badly, of course, when Wally sent me off to Birmingham for the panto. That was a disaster too. My final hurrah, Marce. I'm back here now. I might even take up that offer of Da's pal and go and work at the shipping office. Ma's factory job at Taveners isn't enough.'

Marcia smiled. 'I'm glad.'

'It's bloody freezing out here, can't we go inside?'

'I don't mind the cold. Show business has made you soft,' Marcia laughed. 'Let's sit down, then.'

They squashed up together on the small bench outside the back door. Cynthia carelessly flicked her cigarette away and looked at her sister. They could hear the pigeons bustling in the shed.

'I'm going out with Alfie tonight,' she said.

'That's good.'

'Did you fall for him, Marce?'

'No, not really. Not like that. But he's the opposite of me in every way, isn't he? And I suppose I found that attractive.'

There was a moment of silence between them.

'Are you happy?' Cynthia asked her.

Marcia thought about it. 'No, not really. I wouldn't say happy, but I'm all right. The excitement of getting out of that place has worn off, and now I just have to get on with it. You make do. It feels a bit empty some-times, but . . .' Her words trailed off into silence. Cynthia waited, and wondered what on earth she could do.

'Have you heard from Henry?'

'He wrote me a letter. The day Ma and Da came back. He'd applied for another job. He wished me well, and that was it.' Marcia looked away.

'He came to see me, you know? In Birmingham. He came to the panto.'

Marcia looked back at her. 'Really?'

'We had a good chat and a laugh. I even managed to stop talking about myself for ten minutes. I think you miss him.'

'No, I don't.' Marcia laughed as if the idea was absurd. 'Henry? He would still sometimes call me Miss Rogan, and whenever I thanked him for something he would say he was just doing his job. He barely looked me in the eye – then he writes me a letter to say goodbye.'

'You're talking about him. I'm talking about you.'

Marcia was stopped in her tracks for a moment, before saying, 'Besides, a part of me still thinks he knew about that stuff going on. That he might have been a part of it.'

She looked at her sister, who sat open-mouthed in astonishment.

'Oh, good grief. You really think that? You really think he was a part of it? I always thought you were the clever one, squit, but you can't see the bleeding obvious.' She swivelled around so that she was facing her sister fully. 'Every step of the way, Henry was there in the background helping you. Trying to find a way around Higgins, trying to change things. He even broke into Higgins's office and nicked the files; he showed me all the letters, from the poor kids in

Australia. It was him that found out you were on the ship. He even ran down there to stop it, shouting and waving like a lunatic. He nearly got arrested by two policemen.'

Marcia was trying to take all of this in, but it was too much. It had been Henry by the gangway, with the perfect timing? The memory flashed before her like a fleeting vision.

'Marcia, I don't care if you love him or not. Those things happen or they don't. But I can't have you thinking he was anything but on your side, watching your every step.' Cynthia leaned back. 'I'll tell you what I think – I think you two are a perfect match. You're a bloody fool, and so is he. For crying out loud, Marce. If your life's empty, fill it!'

That evening, Marcia thought about what Cynthia had said. In her head she went over the events of the past two years, since the day she had seen Henry again. As she did so, she became more and more convinced that her sister had been right: she'd been a fool. She wondered where Henry was now, whether he still thought about her. The next morning, she woke up determined that she would find him.

She took the tram into town and went to the address Cynthia had given her, where she looked up at the window and knocked on the door. Eventually it was opened by an elderly lady, who told her that Henry Cherry no longer lived there and she had no forwarding address. Marcia hurriedly made her way to the Cunard Building and went up to the third floor, where Mr Higgins had once had his office, but he wasn't there either. In his place was a man called Dudley Jarvis, according to the sign on his desk.

'Mr Higgins has left. Under a cloud of some sort, apparently.'

'I'm looking for Henry Cherry.'

'Oh, Henry. I've no idea about him. He was fired three months ago, fortunately for him. Everything's changing now the Children Act is in force. This department is closing, and we'll all be gone by the end of February. I heard Henry applied for a job in the new set-up, but I don't know where. He might have gone to Birmingham, at least until it's all up and running here.'

Marcia thanked him and turned to leave.

'Hang on,' he called after her. 'You're not Marcia Rogan, are you?'

'Yes, I am.'

'How about that. You're a bit of a legend around here. You and Henry really stuffed old Higgins. He'd tremble at the mention of your name.' Dudley chuckled to himself. 'Good luck. I hope you find him.'

Marcia hoped so, too. But she had no idea where to look next.

Chapter 54

The Acropolis cafe was quieter than usual. Marcia sat on her own at the back, with the large arch to her left and an aspidistra on a wooden stand away to her right. She had a perfect view of the entrance. This, as far as she could work out, was where Henry sat when he came here for lunch. It was also where she had placed herself on her numerous visits over the last few weeks. She took the smallest sip of tea; it was tepid now, but the waiter was approaching and she wanted to stay for a few more minutes.

'Anything else, beautiful girl?'

'No, I'm fine. Thanks.'

He hovered, standing over her. Feeling slightly self-conscious, she took an even smaller sip.

'Still waiting, are you? For that tall young man. Glasses. Used to see him in this place all the time? Sitting in the window.'

'What?' She blushed.

'The one you was asking about when you first started coming in here. What was his name again?'

She was amazed that he remembered. She thought of herself as instantly forgettable. Invisible. Anonymous.

'Henry. Henry Cherry,' she stuttered.

He nodded thoughtfully, took the pencil from behind his ear and scribbled on his pad.

'I've not seen him, not for a long time. Could be anywhere, couldn't he? Still, as my good friend Yorgos said when his mother-in-law was struck by lightning, miracles do happen.'

He grinned at her, and she smiled back shyly as she went to take a last sip of tea and decided she should leave.

'That'll be stone cold as Medusa's tears. Why don't I get you another pot? On the house. Don't want you to go away disappointed, do we?'

He called a boy to collect her cup and saucer and little teapot, and then he turned and wandered off. Strange, she thought. He was behaving oddly.

The door opened and closed. It was just someone leaving. She looked around the restaurant, feeling conspicuous, exposed, as though she was being stared at. But no one seemed particularly interested in her. No heads turned in her direction.

This was silly. She sighed. How could she ever come in here again now that she'd been found out by the waiter? It would be too embarrassing to return. Anyway, it had been a ridiculous idea from the start. Perhaps it was best that now it was over before it had begun.

Minutes passed. She traced a finger around a cup mark on the table and the next time she heard the door open, she looked up casually. She froze. There he was! Henry Cherry. Standing in the doorway. No, not standing – he was making his way across the room towards her. She remained motionless, afraid she was just imagining him striding between the tables. Afraid that Henry Cherry might evaporate into thin air. But if anything, he was getting closer, and more real.

He stopped, but only because there was nothing but the table between them.

'Miss Rogan? It's you! I didn't know you knew about this place.'

This was Marcia's cue to speak, but she had lost the ability to form words. Besides, what would she say? She had tracked him down, that much was obvious. She must have remembered him telling her about this place, telling her precisely where he sat – and here she was, waiting. Would he think she was desperate? But what about? How stupid to think he had liked her in that way. He had been her friend, and her salvation, yes. But then he had gone.

'Marcia?'

'Henry. It's nice to see you.'

'Is it?' His words hung in the air. 'Sorry, I should have said it's nice to see you too. How is it that you're here?'

This was a mistake, she thought. She couldn't change the rules of love and friendship just because she wanted to. He had walked out of her life when the file on the Rogans was bound with a rubber band and stamped 'case closed'. And besides, he probably had assumed from what happened at the Worboys that she liked Alfie.

'You talked about this place, and I happened to be passing. How have you been? I like your suit, by the way,' she said. He was smartly dressed, wearing a neat white shirt and blue tie. Indeed, the suit – dogtoothed, single-breasted – was much smarter than she remembered. He was also, she noted, a good deal more handsome. He sat down, taking care to unbutton his jacket first.

'I'm very well. I have a new job. Same line. Social work. Takes me away to Birmingham every couple of weeks. And you? I often wonder how you're getting on. How's your Alfie?' He smiled at her.

Marcia cocked her head to one side and felt herself drowning. Her Alfie? She continued to stare at Henry as the thoughts in her head were slowly reforming themselves into what, up to this moment, she had not been able to see.

Henry walked out of my life – he knew I liked Alfie. He always knew I liked Alfie, then he walked out of my life. He knew I liked Alfie, so he walked out of my life . . .

Driven by her thumping heart, the formation of thoughts into mere words was not enough.

'When you went away, I missed you so much. I thought it was Alfie, but it wasn't,' she blurted, gripping hold of the table, her knuckles as white as the linen cloth. 'It was you I missed, Henry. I went to your house, but you were gone. I went to your office, but they wouldn't tell me anything, so I came here. I've come here every day I possibly could for nearly three weeks. I asked the waiters about you, but no one had seen you. You probably think I'm ridiculous and I can't blame you, but I need to tell you, you were the best friend to me, and you stood up for me, and I like you. I mean, I really like you.'

Henry sat with an almost perfectly blank expression on his face. He took off his glasses, cleaned them with a handkerchief, placed them carefully in his pocket, and cleared his throat. Marcia was unsure whether he was about to walk out, start taking notes, or burst into tears. He did none of those things, just kept looking at her with that clear, blue-eyed gaze.

'Say something, Henry.'

Eventually he sighed and leaned towards her. 'Well,' he said, 'I do like to have a certain symmetry in life and the fact is . . .' He paused. 'If I love you, I'm not sure you "really liking" me quite cuts the mustard.'

He was smiling at her, even though she was sure there was a tear in his eye.

'You love me?' She could feel a lump rising in her throat, as hard to swallow as a plum stone. 'Did you say . . . you loved me?'

'I don't get to come down here so much in the lunch hour any more. There's a lot going on and I mostly work through. I heard there was someone asking about me, but no more than that. Then yesterday Dimitri said this certain person had been in the day before, and the day before that, and twice last week. Always sitting in the same place. Then he described you. A beautiful girl, he said, with wide-apart eyes and pale skin and red hair. And I knew. I said if she comes back, the minute he sees her, he should tell me.'

She could feel her bottom lip quivering.

'I rent an office from Dimitri, you see. Very modest. It's upstairs on the next floor. He sent a boy up to tell me.' He was fidgeting wildly with his hands as if the next few words would be the most difficult. 'The thing is . . . I'm pretty useless at this sort of thing. I'm not very good with girls, fear of rejection, I suppose, but I remember the first time I saw you at the orphanage. And for me, well, that was it.'

'I had no idea.'

'No. But why would you? You had other distractions.'

They both jumped slightly as Dimitri indelicately banged the tea tray on the table and said, 'So, you see, beautiful girl?' as the teacup rattled in the saucer. 'These miracles do happen. What did I tell you? Sorry, I interrupt.' And he was gone as quickly as he'd arrived. Henry carefully poured two cups, pushed one towards Marcia and carried on.

'It's very nice, those things you said. Being a friend and standing up for you and whatnot, but really, I owe you much more. You saved me, not the other way around. I might have sat there for the next thirty years taking notes, but you let me help you, and that's the greatest thing you could ever have done for me. But you can't allow that to make you think you love me, just because—'

'No, you're wrong. I do love you,' she said, clutching the corners of the table again.

He put his cup down on the table. His hand was shaking slightly. 'Really?' he said, as though he didn't quite believe her.

'You know what's in your own mind, even if you can't bring yourself to say it. I can't even understand what's in my heart. What hope is there for me? Even when I do understand, I make a mess of it. Not any more. I love you, Henry. I love you, Henry Cherry.'

The tears were rolling down her cheeks. She would have kept on repeating it, but her emotions had the better of her, and she sipped her tea and breathed deeply to calm herself. He passed her a handkerchief, clean and crisp. She looked at him, embarrassed. 'Not very good with girls?' she laughed. 'You're a regular genius.'

They sat there, knowing nothing would ever be the same again.

'Let's go,' he said. He threw some coins onto the table and got up. 'After you, please.'

She stood up and walked round the table, then stopped, facing him. 'Who would have thought meeting me would mean you'd end up with your very own office?' she said with a smile. A memory from her childhood flooded back to her. Without thinking, and not caring who might be watching, she took him by the lapels, pulled him to her and kissed him on the lips.

'Promise me one thing, Henry. Birmingham is fine, but don't you dare tell me you're going off to South-East Asia,' she said.

'What on earth are you talking about?'

She laughed. 'Because if you do, I'll be coming with you.'

'You are loopy. But I'm not going anywhere. And if I ever do change my mind, South-East Asia or Timbuktu, you'll be with me,' he said, and then kissed her and took her hand.

And, feeling as though she had just tumbled down the stairs, her head hurting with a love that had turned her life upside down, she made her way out with Henry Cherry into the street and the pale afternoon sun.

Chapter 55

Marcia let herself into the hallway of the house in Liverpool Lane. She could hear Cynthia and their mother talking excitedly in the kitchen. She needed to go upstairs to her bedroom and sit quietly for a few minutes, holding on to the events of the afternoon for as long as she could. She had walked up three steps of the stairs before Cynthia's loud chattering sunk in.

'Oh, Ma, we've got so much living to do. When Alfie's done with national service, we want to go to Paris. To Switzerland. Rome. We want to do so many things. Me and him are going to go dancing every night, starting now. The Rialto. The Grafton. We'll be twirling around the dance floor, isn't that right, my lover?'

Marcia heard Alfie laugh, and her mother saying, 'Just like your dad and I used to.'

She had the thought that this was Cynthia's moment too, and she went back downstairs and walked into the kitchen. Alfie was draped on the arm of a chair, in a sharp suit and with Brylcreemed hair. He saw her and sat up slightly; then Cynthia, still chattering away about her plans for this and that, caught Alfie's look and turned around, looking embarrassed at her exuberance.

'Sorry, Marce, didn't know you were back. We were just talking about going dancing and whatnot. Alfie's just back from Southampton on leave, you see . . . so we thought . . . we thought . . .' She stared at her sister. 'Marce? Why are you grinning like the Cheshire cat?'

Marcia took a deep breath. 'I found him. I've found Henry.'

Cynthia's eyes widened. 'Oh, Marce! I knew you would. And?'

'Ma, get over here now!' Cynthia had her head between the net curtain and the window pane. Her mother hurried out of the kitchen and looked over her shoulder.

'She's young for serious romance.'

'You married Da when you were seventeen.'

'I suppose I did. Where is he?'

Cynthia smiled. 'See, the tall gangly fella . . . That's him,' she said, nodding towards Henry coming up the road. He was wearing a neat suit with a red tie and clean white shirt. 'Henry is lovely. And guess what, Ma, he bakes. Alfie makes a nifty haddock and bacon pie, but who ever heard of a young fella who bakes? At first, I thought he was bit of a big girl. He's anything but, despite the baking. And Marcia says together they're going to put things right with the world. He's an honourable type, you know?'

'Oh my,' Eunice said. 'That's high praise from her big sister. Is that really him? He's handsome.' She craned her neck to see him.

'D'you recognize him?' asked Cynthia.

Her mother frowned.

'Henry Cherry. He's the one who came to our house that time. Would you like to meet him?' Cynthia tapped on the window, waved and beckoned him over.

'Marce,' she bellowed up the stairs, 'Henry's here. I'm letting him in.'

Eunice patted her hair nervously. She felt a wave of something whoosh through her: hope. A future for the Rogans? Was that what she was seeing in that young man's smile as he strode towards them?

Chapter 56

It was the first morning of June. Marcia felt the pamphlet going hot in her hand. Her father was sitting in the back yard, bent over, doing close work on a canvas shoe. He smiled, held it up and waggled it.

'At least I learned something in that bloody place,' he said.

He had confided in Eunice that amidst the hell of digging roads and mining tunnels out of hard rock, he had spent some time in the shoe repair shop at the camp. The Japanese had worn canvas shoes with rubber soles and he had become skilled at mending them with a needle and thread. He had also learned how to stitch and soften leather, deftly hammer nails into leather soles, and buttonhole.

When one of his pals had turned up earlier in the year with a sack full of shoes, it had seemed at first as though he was making something up for John to do because he felt sorry for him. But then he'd asked him to set up a counter within the horse-shoeing premises he owned, and it had soon turned into a profitable business in its own right. Even Mr Tattersall had placed an advertisement in his window, and people had seen it and started to call at the Rogans' house with their old shoes. It was useful in Liverpool

Lane, during these hard times, to have someone give your shoes a new lease of life for a quarter of the price of a new pair. This meant that gradually, John began to feel useful too.

He moved the swatches away and dropped the needle.

'Marcia, I'm proud of you. And I'm proud of Cynthia.'

She looked at him and his eyes were clear blue. Somehow, they had arranged for him to find a false tooth and when he smiled, she saw how handsome he was. He had Cynthia's curls and lively eyes. 'What's that noise? Music?' he said, tilting his head. 'Ah – the Corpus Christi procession. I've been rushed off my feet with people wanting their shoes fixed for the hooleys tonight. Will you go?'

She winced. 'No. Sister Dorothea – she's not at the orphanage any more but even so, I wouldn't risk it.' She paused, thrust the pamphlet towards him. 'You know the report, about the POWs, the one I told you about? Well, someone asked a question about it today. In parliament.'

He looked at the pamphlet still in her hand. 'Did they?'

'You've only ever told us about how terrible it was. Not what actually happened.'

He silently examined the shoe he was working on. Marcia could feel his attention slipping away. 'Henry told me a bit about the camps,' she said.

'Is that so?' He pick up his needle and started to work.

'Did you work on the railways? Or the roads?'

He looked surprised. 'How do you know about that?'

'It's easy to find out. Everyone's talking about it. There was an article in *The Times*. How they treated men in the camps.'

There was silence. He stared away from her, and sighed. 'The day we set foot in that place. Marcia, love. The things that happened. You don't want to know.'

'I do.'

'No. You don't.'

'Please. I need to know about the terrible things in life as well as the good things.'

He raised an eyebrow. 'Would you be surprised to know there were good things in the camps? Not just sickness and death.'

'Like what?'

'Well, like my pal Red. Broad Scots. With a smile on his face every day he'd call the guards every name under the sun. Never heard such shocking things come out of a man's mouth. The guards didn't have a clue what he was saying and as long as he had that smile on his face they smiled back, nodding. Never understood why we were laughing so much. Laughing until tears streamed down our faces. I had friends like you'd never believe. I miss those fellas. If you were starving, even if they were too, a pal would still share his last morsel.'

'Like at the washhouse. The songs lift the spirits all right.'

His eyes lowered to his cobbler's anvil. 'Something like that. I can't talk about it, Marcia. I'm sorry.

That's why it was hard when I came home; how can you have feelings, if you've no feelings left to have?'

'I know.'

'After it was over, it was all about getting home. Home became this idyllic place in your head, of kindness and peace. All I wanted was to see your mother standing on the step with a nice cup of tea for me. But even when you leave the camp . . . the camp never leaves you. And then the drink numbed it. But not enough. Oh, Marcia, you're too young to hear all this.'

'No, I'm not. I'm seventeen. I need to know these things.' She took a deep breath, nudged the pamphlet nearer to him. 'Every first Friday of the month. The lady I worked with said you're very welcome. Would you come, Da?'

'I can't, love. It wouldn't help. Just leave me to it.'

Mrs Worboys walked towards her down Huskisson Street. She was wearing a trim skirt and a pretty blouse with a wide yellow belt. She threw her arms around Marcia. 'My dear!'

'Mrs Worboys. How are you? And Dolly?'

'We don't call her that now,' she said with a smile. 'We call her Christina. It was her second name, and really was our first choice. We think she suits it.'

Marcia tried not to look surprised, and kept her expression neutral.

'We never much liked Dolores. And Dolly? It's a sweet nickname. But, well . . . It's just not serious enough. Mr Worboys said, "Maud say this out loud: Could you all be upstanding for honourable Member of the House, Dolly Worboys." Dolly doesn't have the gravitas. We prefer Christina. Christina Worboys. Has a ring to it.'

A memory shimmered up from the recesses of Marcia's mind: how her friend Ellie had once wanted to be Christina the Astonishing, flying up to the ceiling, with a gift for smelling out other people's sins. She thought Mrs Worboys was a little crazy, too.

'How's your father, dear?' said Mrs Worboys.

'Existing,' she replied.

'We have a special event next week – POWs from the north-west and a bus from Scotland. Maybe he'd like to come along. It should be fun.'

Marcia knew there was little chance her father would go to something like that – even less if the idea was that it might be 'fun'.

'Yes, thank you, I'll tell him. He doesn't get out much.' Sometimes things happen that leave a person with sadness running through their veins and there is nothing you can do about it, she thought sadly; but she kept the thought to herself.

'And if you'd come along yourself, I would so appreciate it. There's always help needed.' With that, Mrs Worboys turned and strode purposefully away.

Henry Cherry made his way from the back door of Marcia's parents' house, down the uneven crazy paving to the small shed at the end of the yard. He could see movement through the small, grimy window next to the shed door, but even his deliberate and noisy shuffling failed to get a response. In the end he tapped gently on the door. After a few seconds it was pushed open, the bottom edge scraping loudly on a paving stone. John Rogan stuck his head out.

'Who are you?'

'Mr Rogan, my name is Henry Cherry, I'm a friend of Marcia's.'

'Are you?' John Rogan said, as if that was the end of the conversation. He neither shut the door nor opened it further; just waited, as if he hoped this boy might fade away.

'You have pigeons?'

'Yes, lad, I have pigeons. Thanks for pointing it out, though.'

Henry was not to be discouraged. He was there for a reason.

'May I see?'

John Rogan waited a moment, sighed, then pushed the door fully open, stepping back to allow Henry inside. There was a wooden-framed coop on the work-bench at the far end of the shed. Inside were two birds, apparently identical. John busied himself, leaving just enough room for Henry to peer over his shoulder. He opened the chicken-wire door and removed one of the pigeons, closely examining its claws and beak.

'What breed?' said Henry, trying to impress.

John stroked the bird's head, cupping its body firmly in his hand, then returned it to the cage and slipped a small bolt on the door.

'A Racing Homer, nothing fancy.'

'Sturdy, though,' Henry said hopefully.

John ignored him, carefully pouring water into a small tray and dropping some seeds through the top of the coop. Eventually he turned to face Henry, wiping his hands on an old tea towel.

'Know your pigeons, do you?' he grunted.

Henry knew he couldn't keep this up and decided to come clean.

'Actually, no. I don't know anything about pigeons. Sorry. I don't even like them. I went down to Trafalgar Square once and it was disgusting. They don't even sing, do they? They just kind of warble.'

John's eyes narrowed. Henry wondered if he was about to get punched. One of the pigeons shook his feathers violently as if in protest; a few bits of delicate feather shrapnel wafted into the air.

'I bloody hate them,' said John, darkly and with conviction. 'My first posting in the war, six months in Ipswich cleaning up pigeon shit. It was worse than Burma and that's saying something.'

'So why keep them now?'

'Wife's idea. She thinks it will rehabilitate me. It won't. But at least I can hide in this shed and no one will talk at me, no one will ask me questions. That's until some bugger taps on my door, of course.'

'Sorry. I needed to ask you something.'

John nodded and walked past Henry out of the shed. Henry was pretty sure this was an invitation to follow. They walked up the path and John sat on one of the rickety garden chairs under the back window. Henry carefully placed himself on the other.

'I'm not going, if that's what she sent you to ask me.'

The conversation had taken a turn Henry didn't quite understand.

'Who sent me to ask you what?'

'Marcia. This bloody POW reunion. I can't think of anything worse. Why these women think sitting around talking about bad memories will make us feel better. You're lucky, too young – you won't understand either.'

The sun went behind a cloud and the world seemed a little chillier. Henry shifted in his chair.

'The worse it was, the less you want to talk?'

John looked across at him. So young, so unscarred by life, and yet he almost understood.

'Something like that.'

A thought occurred to Henry. 'On the other hand, it might be just the thing.'

John laughed derisively. No, this one was just the same, he thought. 'A bunch of POWs talking about the war?'

'No. A bunch of POWs not talking about the war,' Henry ventured. 'I mean, if you don't want to talk, why would they? No need for questions because you all know the answers.'

John was still looking at Henry, and yet his eyes seemed to drift off to another place altogether. The sun came out from behind the cloud again and he blinked and recovered his senses.

'You said you needed to ask me something? Fire away.'

Chapter 57

Marcia hurried up the road, holding her hat to her head, weaving her way through the passers-by, breathing in the smells of the city and the river that filled the air. She made her way up the steps of the parish hall three streets away from Liverpool Lane. It was the same hall where Cynthia had wiggled her bottom and sung *'Moonlight in Joo-hoon'* all that time ago. She was wearing a dowdy coat but she had a peacock feather in her hat, and a splash of lipstick and rouged cheeks.

Maud Worboys, wearing a pretty cerise dress with a matching chiffon scarf, came out of the hall and onto the steps. She fluttered over and kissed Marcia on the cheek warmly. 'You came!'

Marcia nodded.

'And your father, too!' Mrs Worboys added.

Marcia gasped. Her legs felt hollow. Her heart leapt to her mouth. Standing in a huddle with a few other men, just inside the door, she saw her father – wearing his uniform, pressed and cleaned, boots polished, and looking smarter than she had ever seen him before.

'It is, yes. That's my da. How on earth . . . ?' She lowered her voice to a whisper. 'Don't tell him I'm here, not yet. I'll sit at the back. Please.'

Mrs Worboys nodded. 'I understand.' She wandered over to John, leaving Marcia to hide herself; she found a discreet spot behind the tea urn. She heard Mrs Worboys saying, 'Your first time? John, isn't it? I think you'll have a lot of fun.'

You could already hear laughter, men's voices rising in energy and pitch. There was a smell of polish and pomade There were freshly cut flowers in vases on the windowsills, and where possible, each of the wooden chairs lined up in rows had a brightly coloured velvet cushion placed on it. Union Jack bunting hung from the beams. On the walls were photographs of men in the camps, smiling as they came off the boats and leaning over balconies. There were also grainy images of men on a stage, dressed strangely: some in khaki uniforms, some wearing just shorts and nothing else, emaciated, no more than skeletons; some holding bamboo sticks and buckets.

John Rogan walked over to the corner where there was a group of men crowding around, pointing and laughing at one of the photographs. These men in the pictures were close to death. Painfully thin, their cheeks hollowed out, dark rings under their eyes, mouths caked in a chalky residue. And yet they were laughing.

In another corner a couple of men were smoking, and from their pockets they were taking small tokens out and showing them to one another – a photograph, a medal. There was someone with a camera and Mrs Worboys bustled over. 'Tell me if you don't want your picture taken, Mr Rogan.' He looked at her and shrugged as the camera flash popped and he blinked against it. The old version of him might have turned on his heel and marched off. But he didn't. He nodded thoughtfully.

Mrs Worboys was flitting around, handing out song sheets, guiding people to their seats. John stood putting his hands in and out of his pockets as though he didn't know what to do with them.

'John! If it isn't John Rogan!' cried a man with a shock of red hair, waving his hand in the air.

And then a second man was striding towards him, arms outstretched. 'John!'

His face changed – it was as if light shone out from behind his eyes for the first time in years. The man, wearing numerous medals, slapped him on the back and then firmly shook his hand. 'John, is it really you? Come and meet some of the other blokes. You remember Paddy?'

'Paddy!' said John, his mouth falling open as another man lurched towards him and clasped him in a bear hug. He was gripping his arm, leaning in and speaking to him. They both threw back their heads and chortled. The group was getting larger, and after more back-slapping and hand-shaking they all took their places on the benches.

The lights dimmed. The man at the piano started playing. Marcia stood to get a better view, her smiling face rising up from behind the tea urn like the sun itself. There was laughter and a rustle of the song sheets, although when they all began to sing, nobody needed them; everyone knew the words. These were the songs they had sung in the camp, in the lines for grub, on the railway tracks and on the roads. The sound was a tunelessly joyous one, a chorus of happiness. And when the curtains jerked open to reveal upturned buckets with men sitting on them, their trousers around their ankles, in front of a painted backdrop of palm trees and jungle, bamboo sticks and sand on the floor, there was an eruption of laughter that ricocheted around the room. A man strode onto the stage wearing full Japanese uniform, and they all laughed more. They rocked with laughter, cheered, wolf-whistled and applauded.

Was this her father coming back from the dead? thought Marcia. They slapped their knees as the men began another song. 'Who remembers this?' he bellowed. 'Bellyache Blues!' One man stood up and threw his hat in the air. 'John Rogan!' He squinted out into the audience. 'Where are you? You'll come up here and start us off!' And to her amazement, her father, encouraged by his friend sitting next to him prodding and nudging, got up out of his chair and marched towards the stage to more clapping and foot-stamping. It was going to be a grand night.

What was happening in that hall was a kind of miracle, Marcia thought, as she quietly left after hearing a few more verses and watching, amazed and proud, as her father conducted them all and led the verses in a strong, clear voice. Wait until she told her mother and Cynthia.

She came out into the cool evening air. Her father might never know she'd been there, but it felt right that she should leave him to his private joy. Whatever it was these men were sharing, in that darkened, dusty room with its musty-smelling curtains and out-of-tune piano, she would never fully understand, but she could tell that it was bringing them some kind of peace.

And the best part? If they could recover, then this city, and Cynthia, and her mother, and Mr Tattersall – and even Ellie, wherever she was – could all recover as well.

Chapter 58

The following day, Cynthia and Alfie were frying sardines in the Rogans' kitchen.

'Turns out I'm not quite ready to leave Blighty. When I've done my national service in Southampton I've got a job waiting. In town. Car showroom. I'll make quite a bit of money,' said Alfie.

'That's good. Because I've decided – I don't want to end up like my Auntie Norma. I want children and a little house. I don't want to end up like Penelope Pompadour. Penny, or rather, Daphne, is a pretty sad case.'

He took a sardine, tossed back his head and ate it whole. 'Mmm. Good scran.' He wiped his hands on his trousers and moved in to kiss her, putting his arms around her waist and pulling her to him. She placed her flat palm on his chest. 'Alfie, no . . .'

'No? Why not? You like a lad with a bit of the untamed in him. I'm the only one that can match your hot stubborn head.' He kissed her hard on the mouth as he squirrelled his hand up her jumper, searching out her breast. 'We could live somewhere by the sea, where I can go fishing,' he murmured.

'And somewhere near Marcia.' She gasped at the thrill of his hands tugging up her skirt, moving up her thighs, over the tops of her stockings. 'I'll not let her slip through my fingers again. I'm only half a person without Marcia. Even though she gets on my nerves. Oh no, who's that?' she said when there was a knock at the door.

'Letter for Marcia Rogan,' said the postman when Cynthia had disentangled herself from Alfie and answered it.

'For me?' said Marcia, coming through the door on his heels. She took off her jacket, opened the letter and began to read.

Dear Marcia,

Have I got a story to tell yer. I have the most incredible news. Me ma. She's not dead. It was all a terrible mistake. A flaming mix-up. Turned out that day I got on the boat, Ma had raced to the Pier Head to find me, only the flipping boat had left. Of course, finding out where I was in Australia had been a nightmare. But someone called Mr Higgins, guess what, he helped her! And before I knew it she had sent me a postal cheque and I'll soon be on the next boat home. I'm still not sure why or how it happened. Shocking to think she has been trying to find me. Clerical error, they said. A terrible misunderstanding. Not only were she alive, but she had been told that I had died of scarlet fever on the journey. Sister Dorothea made all the arrange-ments so I guess she wasn't so unkind, after all. Anyways, I dunno what's made things

*change. But needless to say, yer was right. It
was anything but a land of milk and honey.
Just hard, back-breaking work, the poor lads
used as slaves, and us girls . . . well, I can't
even put it down in a letter. But some of the
girls should never have seen the things that we
did or been asked to do the things we were
by grown men.*

*Anyway ours is a happy ending, and I can't
wait to see yer. I'll be knocking on your door
at Liverpool Lane the minute I'm home.*
Your pal, Ellie

Marcia's hands shook as her eyes passed over the
words again and she tried to make sense of them.
She frowned.

'What is it?' asked Cynthia.

'Bad news?' said Alfie, who had gone back to frying
his sardines.

'I'm not sure.'

For a moment Marcia had been overjoyed at the
thought of her friend coming home. But this letter
had been written five months ago – at least, that's
what the postmark said. Surely Ellie would have found
her by now? Had she ever come home? Had her
mother ever found her? Where was she? She was the
only real friend Marcia had ever had. Her sister didn't
count. Sisters come with the furniture.

She went straight round to Henry's office to show
him the letter, along with another article she had
found in the *Telegraph* about the farm stays in
Australia; people had started to complain about them.

'Thank you,' he said, after reading both. He traced a finger over her eyebrows, down her nose. 'I'll send this to the head of department first thing tomorrow morning. Marcia, I have to go to another meeting now. But afterwards – this is important – will you meet me at the Pier Head, in an hour and a half?'

Chapter 59

They sat on what Henry told her was his favourite
bench, a few steps away from the Pier Head. It was
late afternoon and the smells of the river filled the
air. Seagulls cawed and a ship blasted its horn on the
glittering water. To their left was a lively crowd
waiting to board the four o'clock ferry to New
Brighton. Marcia squinted across the river and let the
sun warm her face. She smiled contentedly.

'Why do you like this spot so much?'

'Life in constant motion, isn't it?' he replied with
his usual earnestness. 'The river, the ferries, folk going
to work, or for the craic. The city boys, the scrappy
workers, and all those seagulls looking down on it
all.' He laughed. 'It's not exactly beautiful, but if you
want another kind of beauty, you can always turn
and look at the Liver Building instead.'

'Mr Cherry, I love you. You're like a proper poet.'
She grinned.

'You think I could make a go of it?'

'No,' she replied impishly, and they both giggled.
They were silent for a few seconds before Henry
spoke. 'When we're married . . .'

'Married? Aren't you forgetting something?'

'Am I?'

'I don't remember you asking me. Maybe you've waited too long. There's a good chance I might turn you down now.'

Henry nodded solemnly and put his hands in his pockets.

'Here's the thing. I'd be scared, you see. That if I asked you, after all this time, you might say no so if I was to propose, I'd have to be sure of your answer. That's why . . .' Suddenly Henry was on his feet and had wheeled round, and with an exaggerated flourish he sank to one knee and opened a small ring box. 'Will you marry me, Marcia?'

Marcia stared at him, then at the ring on its velvet pad. On the landing stage, someone had noticed and a few started clapping encouragement. Another stuffed his fingers in his mouth and whistled, and there was a cry of 'Say yes, queen!' Marcia looked over at their growing audience, then back at Henry.

'See,' he smiled, 'you can't get out of it now.'

'You are such a flippin' fool, Henry Cherry. Yes, of course, I'll marry you. Yes.'

She threw her arms around his neck, and he swept her up and spun her around so energetically that she yelped.

'Watch it, lad. You don't want to let go of her, I'm not jumping into the Mersey to save her!' one of the little band yelled. And they all laughed again.

'I love you, Marcia,' he whispered. 'My forever girl.'

And Marcia wondered how it was she could feel so happy; as though everything she had been through during the past few years had just been the world conspiring to bring her to this river, this bench, this boy. 'I love you too,' she murmured, kissing him. 'I love you . . .'

When she showed Cynthia the ring Henry had bought her from Lewis's and told her she was engaged, Cynthia yelped, jumped out of her chair and kissed her.

'And you and Alfie?' asked Marcia.

Cynthia grinned. 'Me and Alfie. Who knows? We're having a lot of fun. Though he wears me out, I must say. I'm exhausted. Never stops wanting you-know-what. He wouldn't stop kissing me on the back of the tram yesterday. I swear if the conductor hadn't come upstairs to take our fares . . . well . . .'

'Cyn, stop!' Marcia said, putting her hands over her ears.

'I'm joking,' she said, grinning.

'No you're not,' said Marcia, giggling.

'Don't tell me you and Henry aren't, you know?'

Marcia thought of all the times lately they had lain in his little bed, entwined in each other's arms, and once again gone to the brink of a place Henry still dared not go, fearful that she would somehow love him less.

'I was just so hoping you had news about Henry, and you have! Going to be married! My little squit!' said Cynthia, jolting her into the present.

Their mother appeared in the doorway. 'Married?' Tears shone in her eyes. 'And your father, strong enough to walk you up the aisle. Whoever would have thought it?'

'Whoever, indeed,' replied Marcia, feeling so happy

to know that there were people in the world who loved her as much as she loved them. Henry, Cynthia, her mother and her father. All back in Liverpool Lane. With Mr Tattersall coming round every Sunday night for hotpot and delivering his mouthwatering meals; and even Norma in her best Sunday dress finding something pleasant to say, now that she had sent Wally Labone packing – at least until the next time she heard him playing his trumpet, and her legs went to jelly, and she decided to forgive him.

'My little sister. And I'm going to be bridesmaid,' said Cynthia. They stood in her bedroom upstairs, touching fingers. 'I'm so happy for you, Marce, I could burst.'

And it did feel as if this was a beginning, the start of something new.

Marcia tilted her head. '. . . As long as you let me choose your dress.'

Cynthia threw back her head and laughed. 'Why?'

'You'll probably want to wear something that makes you look like a floozy.'

'No, I won't.'

'Cynthia, you will! Probably with an awful plunging neckline.'

'Perhaps I'll get that dress from George Henry Lee's with the little winged sleeves, and jewelled buttons. At least let me decide what songs you should have at the evening party after the wedding. I can write out a list for you both. Everyone knows my taste in music is better than yours,' Cynthia rattled on.

'No! Henry and I are perfectly able to choose! It's my wedding! You don't know anything!'

'All right. Congratulations, you finally beat me at something. You choose the music, I'll choose the cocktails. Why don't you have the reception at the Masonic Hall? I saw a blinking marvellous thought reader there the other day.'

'Thought reader! No! It's my wedding, and we're not having thought readers. You're so bossy!'

'Remember, I paved the way for you, Marcia. Never forget that . . .' Cynthia said, grinning. 'I'll always be your big sister . . .'

Her mother, shelling peas into a bucket downstairs in the kitchen, smiled and looked up at the ceiling as she heard their voices rising.

'No one on earth can argue better than sisters,' she said to John, who was half dozing in the rocking chair.

'Different flowers from the same garden,' he replied, yawning. 'And what a beautiful garden it is, Eunice,' he sighed, as a fiery sunset kissed the River Mersey and restful sleep came upon him.

Acknowledgements

Thanks to Gillian Green for her insightful feedback and experience, and all the brilliant editors at Pan. Thanks also to my agent, Judith Murdoch. Thank you to my husband, Peter, whose logical brain forces me to go the extra mile and for always finding the time when I'm writing to talk through my thoughts and ideas. Thank you to Louis and Joel for supporting me in ways they will never realize. Thank you also to my grandmother, Catherine Heery. A mother of ten, when she was widowed, a number of her children were looked after in an orphanage for a time, which meant my father and his siblings were what would have been known then as orphans of the living. They were lucky enough to be taken back home to Liverpool when she found work but this book is dedicated to all those other children who left the UK from orphanages for Australia, Canada and elsewhere, and never returned.

The People's Friend

If you enjoy quality fiction, you'll love
"The People's Friend" magazine. Every weekly
issue contains seven original short stories and
two exclusively written serial instalments.

On sale every Wednesday, the "Friend" also
includes travel, puzzles, health advice, knitting
and craft projects and recipes.

It's the magazine for women who love reading!